"'Read yourself—this once,' he pleaded, 'and let me listen.'"

See page 435

The Deliverance

ELLEN GLASGOW

A Romance of the Vir-
·ginia Tobacco Fields·
With Illustrations by
Frank E Schoonover

New York
Doubleday Page & Co.
1904

THE LIBRARY
COLBY JUNIOR COLLEGE
NEW LONDON, N. H.

To Dr. H. Holbrook Curtis

CONTENTS

Book I. The Inheritance

Book II. The Temptation

List of Characters

———

CHRISTOPHER BLAKE, a tobacco-grower

MRS. BLAKE, his mother

TUCKER CORBIN, an old soldier

CYNTHIA and LILA BLAKE, sisters of Christopher

CARRAWAY, a lawyer

BILL FLETCHER, a wealthy farmer

MARIA FLETCHER, his granddaughter

WILL FLETCHER, his grandson

"MISS SAIDIE," sister of Fletcher

JACOB WEATHERBY, a tobacco-grower

JIM WEATHERBY, his son

SOL PETERKIN, another tobacco-grower

MOLLY PETERKIN, daughter of Sol

TOM SPADE, a country storekeeper

SUSAN, his wife

UNCLE BOAZ, a Negro

LIST OF ILLUSTRATIONS

Book One
The Inheritance

THE INHERITANCE

CHAPTER I

THE MAN IN THE FIELD

WHEN the Tusquehanna stage came to the daily halt beneath the blasted pine at the cross-roads, an elderly man, wearing a flapping frock coat and a soft slouch hat, stepped gingerly over one of the muddy wheels, and threw a doubtful glance across the level tobacco fields, where the young plants were drooping in the June sunshine.

"So this is my way, is it?" he asked, with a jerk of his thumb toward a cloud of blue-and-yellow butterflies drifting over a shining puddle—"five miles as the crow flies, and through a bog?"

For a moment he hung suspended above the encrusted axle, peering with blinking pale-gray eyes over a pair of gold-rimmed spectacles. In his appearance there was the hint of a scholarly intention unfulfilled, and his dress, despite its general carelessness, bespoke a different standard of taste from that of the isolated dwellers in the surrounding fields. A casual observer might have classified him as one of the Virginian landowners impoverished by the war; in reality, he was a successful lawyer in a neighbouring town, who, amid the overthrow of the slave-holding gentry some twenty years before, had risen into a provincial prominence.

His humour met with a slow response from the driver, who sat playfully flicking at a horsefly on the flank of a tall, raw-boned sorrel. "Wall, thar's been a sight of rain lately," he observed, with good-natured acquiescence, "but I don't reckon the mud's more'n waist deep, an' if you do happen to git clean down, thar's Sol Peterkin along to pull you out. Whar're you hidin', Sol? Why, bless my boots, if he ain't gone fast asleep!"

At this a lean and high-featured matron, encased in the rigidity of her Sunday bombazine, gave a prim poke with her umbrella in the ribs of a sparrow-like little man, with a discoloured, scraggy beard, who nodded in one corner of the long seat.

"I'd wake up if I was you," she remarked in the voice her sex assumes when virtue lapses into severity.

Starting from his doze, the little man straightened his wiry, sunburned neck and mechanically raised his hand to wipe away a thin stream of tobacco juice which trickled from his half-open mouth.

"Hi! we ain't got here a'ready!" he exclaimed, as he spat energetically into the mud. "I d'clar if it don't beat all—one minute we're thar an' the next we're here. It's a movin' world we live in, ain't that so, mum?" Then, as the severe matron still stared unbendingly before her, he descended between the wheels, and stood nervously scraping his feet in the long grass by the roadside.

"This here's Sol Peterkin, Mr. Carraway," said the driver, bowing his introduction as he leaned forward to disentangle the reins from the sorrel's tail, "an' I reckon he kin p'int out Blake Hall to you as well as another, seein' as he was under-overseer thar for eighteen years befo' the war. Now you'd better climb in agin, folks; it's time we were off."

He gave an insinuating cluck to the horses, while several passengers, who had alighted to gather blackberries from the ditch, scrambled hurriedly into their places. With a single clanking wrench the stage rolled on, plodding clumsily over the miry road.

As the spattering mud-drops fell round him, Carraway lifted his head and sniffed the air like a pointer that has been just turned afield. For the moment his professional errand escaped him as his chest expanded in the light wind which blew over the radiant stillness of the Virginian June. From the cloudless sky to its pure reflection in the rain-washed roads there was barely a descending shade, and the tufts of dandelion blooming against the rotting rail fence seemed but patches of the clearer sunshine.

"Bless my soul, it's like a day out of Scripture!" he exclaimed in a tone that was half-apologetic; then raising his walking-stick he leisurely swept it into space. "There's hardly another crop, I reckon, between here and the Hall?"

Sol Peterkin was busily cutting a fresh quid of tobacco from the plug he carried in his pocket, and there was a brief pause before he answered. Then, as he carefully wiped the blade of his knife on the leg of his blue jean overalls, he looked up with a curious facial contortion.

"Oh, you'll find a corn field or two somewhar along," he replied, "but it's a lanky, slipshod kind of crop at best, for tobaccy's king down here, an' no mistake. We've a sayin' that the man that ain't partial to the weed can't sleep sound even in the churchyard, an' thar's some as 'ill swar to this day that Willie Moreen never rested in his grave because he didn't chaw, an' the soil smelt jest like a plug. Oh, it's a great plant, I tell you, suh. Look over thar at them fields; they've all been set out sence the spell o' rain."

The road they followed crawled like a leisurely river between the freshly ploughed ridges, where the earth was slowly settling around the transplanted crop. In the distance, labourers were still at work, passing in dull-blue blotches between the rows of bright-green leaves that hung limply on their slender stalks.

"You've lived at the Hall, I hear," said Carraway, suddenly turning to look at his companion over his lowered glasses.

"When it was the Hall, suh," replied Sol, with a tinge of bitterness in his chuckle. "Why, in my day, an' that was up to the very close of the war, you might stand at the big gate an' look in any direction you pleased till yo' eyes bulged fit to bu'st, but you couldn't look past the Blake land for all yo' tryin'. These same fields here we're passin' through I've seen set out in Blake tobaccy time an' agin, an' the farm I live on three miles beyond the Hall belonged to the old gentleman, God bless him! up to the day he died. Lord save my soul! three hunnard as likely niggers as you ever clap sight on, an' that not countin' a good fifty that was too far gone to work."

"All scattered now, I suppose?"

"See them little cabins over yonder?" With a dirty forefinger he pointed to the tiny trails of smoke hanging low above the distant tree-tops. "The county's right speckled with 'em an' with thar children—all named Blake arter old marster, as they called him, or Corbin arter old miss. When leetle Mr. Christopher got turned out of the Hall jest befo' his pa died, an' was shuffled into the house of the overseer, whar Bill Fletcher used to live himself, the darkies all bought bits o' land here an' thar an' settled down to do some farmin' on a free scale. Stuck up, suh! Why, Zebbadee Blake passed me yestiddy drivin' his own mule-team, an' I heard him swar he wouldn't turn out o' the road for anybody less'n God A'mighty or Marse Christopher!"

"A—ahem!" exclaimed Carraway, with relish; "and in the meantime, the heir to all this high-handed authority is no better than an illiterate day-labourer."

Peterkin snorted. "Who? Mr. Christopher? Well, he warn't more'n ten years old when his pa went doty an' died, an' I don't reckon he's had much larnin' sence. I've leant on the gate myself an' watched the nigger children traipsin' by to the Yankee woman's school, an' he drivin' the plough when he didn't reach much higher than the handle. He used to be the darndest leetle brat, too, till his sperits got all freezed out o' him. Lord! Lord! thar's such a sight of meanness in this here world that it makes a body b'lieve in Providence whether or no."

Carraway meditatively twirled his walking-stick. "Raises tobacco now like the rest, doesn't he?"

"Not like the rest—bless you, no, suh. Why, the weed thrives under his very touch, though he can't abide the smell of it, an' thar's not a farmer in the county that wouldn't ruther have him to plant, cut, or cure than any ten men round about. They do say that his pa went clean crazy about tobaccy jest befo' he died, an' that Mr. Christopher gets dead sick when he smells it smokin' in the barn, but he kin pick up a leaf blindfold an' tell you the quality of it at his first touch."

For a moment the lawyer was silent, pondering a thought he evidently did not care to utter. When at last he spoke it was in the measured tones of one who overcomes an impediment in his speech.

"Do you happen to have heard, I wonder, any-thing of his attitude toward the present owner of the Hall?"

"Happen to have heard!" Peterkin threw back his head and gasped. "Why, the whole county has happened to hear of it, I reckon. It's been common talk sence the day he got his first bird-gun, an' his nigger, Uncle Boaz, found him hidin' in the bushes to shoot old Fletcher when he came in sight. I tell you, if Bill Fletcher lay dyin' in the road, Mr. Christopher would sooner ride right over him than not. You ask some folks, suh, an' they'll tell you a Blake kin hate twice as long as most men kin love."

"Ah, is it so bad as that?" muttered Carraway.

"Well, he ain't much of a Christian, as the lights go," continued Sol, "but I ain't sartain, accordin' to my way of thinkin', that he ain't got a better showin' on his side than a good many of 'em that gits thar befo' the preacher. He's a Blake, skin an' bone, anyhow, an' you ain't goin' to git this here county to go agin him—not if he was to turn an' spit at Satin himself. Old Bill Fletcher stole his house an' his land an' his money, law or no law—that's how I

look at it—but he couldn't steal his name, an' that's
what counts among the niggers, an' the po' whites,
too. Why, I've seen a whole parcel o' darkies stand
stock still when Fletcher drove up to the bars with
his spankin' pair of bays, an' then mos' break thar
necks lettin' 'em down as soon as Mr. Christopher
comes along with his team of oxen. You kin fool the
quality 'bout the quality, but I'll be blamed if you
kin fool the niggers.''

Ahead of them there was a scattered group of log
cabins, surrounded by little whitewashed palings,
and at their approach a decrepit old negro, followed
by a slinking black-and-tan foxhound, came beneath
the straggling hopvine over one of the doors and
through the open gate out into the road. His bent
old figure was huddled within his carefully patched
clothes of coarse brown homespun.

"Howdy, marsters," he muttered, in answer to the
lawyer's greeting, raising a trembling hand to his
wrinkled forehead. "Y'all ain' seen nuttin' er ole
miss's yaller cat, Beulah, I reckon?"

Peterkin, who had eyed him with the peculiar
disfavour felt for the black man by the low-born
white, evinced a sudden interest out of all proportion
to Carraway's conception of the loss.

"Ain't she done come back yet, Uncle Boaz?" he
inquired.

"Naw, suh, dat she aint, en ole miss she ain' gwine
git a wink er sleep dis blessed night. Me en Spy we
is done been traipsin' roun' atter dat ar low-lifeted
Beulah sence befo' de dinner-bell.''

"When did you miss her first?" asked Peterkin,
with concern.

"I dunno, suh, dat I don't, caze she ain' no better'n one er dese yer wish-wishys,* an' I ain' mek out yit ef'n twuz her er her hant. Las' night 'bout sundown dar she wuz a-lappin' her sasser er milk right at ole miss feet, en dis mawnin' at sunup dar she warn't. Dat's all I know, suh, ef'n you lay me out."

"Well, I reckon she'll turn up agin," said Peterkin consolingly. "Cats air jest like gals, anyway—they ain't never happy unless they're eternally gallyvantin'. Why, that big white Tom of mine knows more about this here county than I do myself."

"Dat's so, suh; dat's de gospel trufe; but I'se kinder flustered 'bout dat yaller cat caze ole miss sutney do set a heap er sto' by 'er. She ain' never let de dawgs come in de 'oom, nohow, caze once she done feel Beulah rar 'er back at Spy. She's des stone blin', is ole miss, but I d'clar she kin smell pow'ful keen, an' 'tain' no use tryin' ter fool her wid one houn' er de hull pack. Lawd! Lawd! I wunner ef dat ar cat kin be layin' close over yonder at Sis Daphne's?"

He branched off into a little path which ran like a white thread across the field, grumbling querulously to the black-and-tan foxhound that ambled at his heels.

"Dar's a wallopin' ahaid er you, sho's you bo'n," he muttered, as he limped on toward a small log hut from which floated an inviting fragrance of bacon frying in fat. "I reckon you lay dat you kin cut yo' mulatter capers wid me all you please, but you'd better look out sharp 'fo' you begin foolin' 'long er Marse Christopher. Dar you go agin, now. Ain' dat

*Will-o'-the-wisp.

des like you? Wat you wanter go sickin' atter dat ole hyar fer, anyhow?"

"So that is one of young Blake's hangers-on?" observed Carraway, with a slight inflection of inquiry.

"Uncle Boaz, you mean? Oh, he was the old gentleman's body-servant befo' the war. He used to wear his marster's cast-off ruffles an' high hat. A mighty likely nigger he was, too, till he got all bent up with the rheumatics."

The lawyer had lifted his walking-stick and was pointing straight ahead to a group of old brick chimneys huddled in the sunset above a grove of giant oaks.

"That must be Blake Hall over there," he said; "there's not another house like it in the three counties."

"We'll be at the big gate in a minute, suh," Peterkin returned. "This is the first view of the Hall you git, an' they say the old gentleman used to raise his hat whenever he passed by it." Then as they swung open the great iron gate, with its new coat of red, he touched Carraway's sleeve and spoke in a hoarse whisper. "Thar's Mr. Christopher himself over yonder," he said, "an' Lord bless my soul, if he ain't settin' out old Fletcher's plants. Thar! he's standin' up now—the big young fellow with the basket. The old gentleman was the biggest man twixt here an' Fredericksburg, but I d'clar Mr. Christopher is a good half-head taller!"

At his words Carraway stopped short in the road, raising his useless glasses upon his brow. The sun had just gone down in a blaze of light, and the great bare field was slowly darkening against the west.

Nearer at hand there were the long road, already in twilight, the rail fence wrapped in creepers, and a solitary chestnut tree in full bloom. Farther away swept the freshly ploughed ground over which passed the moving figures of the labourers transplanting the young crop. Of them all, Carraway saw but a single worker—in reality, only one among the daily toilers in the field, moulded physically perhaps in a finer shape than they, and limned in the lawyer's mental vision against a century of the brilliant if tragic history of his race. As he moved slowly along between the even rows, dropping from time to time a plant into one of the small holes dug before him, and pausing with the basket on his arm to settle the earth carefully with his foot, he seemed, indeed, as much the product of the soil upon which he stood as did the great white chestnut growing beside the road. In his pose, in his walk, in the careless carriage of his head, there was something of the large freedom of the elements.

"A dangerous young giant," observed the lawyer slowly, letting his glasses fall before his eyes. "A monumental Blake, as it were. Well, as I have remarked before upon occasions, blood will tell, even at the dregs."

"He's the very spit of his pa, that's so," replied Peterkin, "an' though it's no business of mine, I'm afeared he's got the old gentleman's dry throat along with it. Lord! Lord! I've always stood it out that it's better to water yo' mouth with tobaccy than to burn it up with sperits." He checked himself and fell back hastily, for young Blake, after a single glance at the west, had tossed his basket carelessly aside, and was striding vigorously across the field.

"Not another plant will I set out, and that's an end of it!" he was saying angrily. "I agreed to do a day's work and I've been at it steadily since sunrise. Is it any concern of mine, I'd like to know, if he can't put in his crop to-night? Do you think I care whether his tobacco rots in the ground or out of it?"

As he came on, Carraway measured him coolly, with an appreciation tempered by his native sense of humour. He perceived at once a certain coarseness of finish which, despite the deep-rooted veneration for an idle ancestry, is found most often in the descendants of a long line of generous livers. A moment later he weighed the keen gray flash of the eyes beneath the thick fair hair, the coating of dust and sweat over the high-bred curve from brow to nose, and the fulness of the jaw which bore with a suggestion of sheer brutality upon the general impression of a fine racial type. Taken from the mouth up, the face might have passed as a pure, fleshly copy of the antique ideal; seen downward, it became almost repelling in its massive power.

Stooping beside the fence for a common harvest hat, the young man placed it on his head, and gave a careless nod to Peterkin. He had thrown one leg over the rails, and was about to swing himself into the road, when Sol spoke a little timidly.

"I hear yo' ma's done lost her yaller cat, Mr. Christopher."

For an instant Christopher hung midway of the fence.

"Isn't the beast back yet?" he asked irritably, scraping the mud from his boot upon the rail. "I've had Uncle Boaz scouring the county half the day."

A pack of hounds that had been sleeping under the sassafras bushes across the road came fawning to his feet, and he pushed them impatiently aside.

"I was thinkin'," began Peterkin, with an uncertain cough, "that I might manage to send over my big white Tom, an', bein' blind, maybe she wouldn't know the difference."

Christopher shook his head.

"Oh, it's no use," he replied, speaking with an air of superiority. "She could pick out that cat among a million, I believe, with a single touch. Well, there's no help for it. Down, Spot—down, I say, sir!"

With a leisurely movement he swung himself from the fence, stopping to wipe his brow with his blue cotton sleeve. Then he went whistling defiantly down the way to the Hall, turning at last into a sunken road that trailed by an abandoned ice-pond where bullfrogs were croaking hoarsely in the rushes.

CHAPTER II

The Owner of Blake Hall

As THEY followed the descending road between flowering chestnuts, Blake Hall rose gradually into fuller view, its great oaks browned by the approaching twilight and the fading after-glow reflected in a single visible pane. Seen close at hand, the house presented a cheerful spaciousness of front—a surety of light and air—produced in part by the clean white Doric columns of the portico and in part by the ample slope of shaven lawn studded with beds of brightly blooming flowers. From the smoking chimneys presiding over the ancient roof to the hospitable steps leading from the box-bordered walk below, the outward form of the dwelling spoke to the imaginative mind of that inner spirit which had moulded it into a lasting expression of a racial sentiment, as if the Virginia creeper covering the old brick walls had wreathed them in memories as tenacious as itself.

For more than two hundred years Blake Hall had stood as the one great house in the county—a manifestation in brick and mortar of the hereditary greatness of the Blakes. To Carraway, impersonal as his interest was, the acknowledgment brought a sudden vague resentment, and for an instant he bit his lip and hung irresolute, as if more than half-inclined to retrace his steps. A slight thing decided him—the gaiety of a

boy's laugh that floated from one of the lower rooms
—and swinging his stick briskly to add weight to his
determination, he ascended the broad steps and lifted
the old brass knocker. A moment later the door
was opened by a large mulatto woman, in a soiled
apron, who took his small hand-bag from him and,
when he asked for Mr. Fletcher, led him across the
great hall into the unused drawing-room.

The shutters were closed, and as she flung them
back on their rusty hinges the pale June twilight
entered with the breath of mycrophylla roses. In
the scented dusk Carraway stared about the desolate,
crudely furnished room, which gave back to his
troubled fancy the face of a pitiable, dishonoured
corpse. The soul of it was gone forever—that
peculiar spirit of place which makes every old house
the guardian of an inner life—the keeper of a family's
ghost. What remained was but the outer husk, the
disfigured frame, upon which the newer imprint
seemed only a passing insult.

On the high wainscoted walls he could still trace
the vacant dust-marked squares where the Blake
portraits had once hung—lines that the successive
scrubbings of fifteen years had not utterly effaced.
A massive mahogany sofa, carved to represent a
horn of plenty, had been purchased, perhaps at a
general sale of the old furniture, with several quaint
rosewood chairs and a rare cabinet of inlaid woods.
For the rest, the later additions were uniformly
cheap and ill-chosen—a blue plush "set," bought,
possibly, at a village store, a walnut table with a
sallow marble top, and several hard engravings of
historic subjects.

When the lawyer turned from a curious inspection of these works of art, he saw that only a curtain of flimsy chintz, stretched between a pair of fluted columns, separated him from the adjoining room, where a lamp, with lowered wick, was burning under a bright red shade. After a moment's hesitation he drew the curtain aside and entered what he took at once to be the common living-room of the Fletcher family.

Here the effect was less depressing, though equally uninteresting—a paper novel or two on the big Bible upon the table combined, indeed, with a costly piano in one corner, to strike a note that was entirely modern. The white crocheted tidies on the chair-backs, elaborated with endless patience out of innumerable spools of darning cotton, lent a feminine touch to the furniture, which for an instant distracted Carraway's mental vision from the impending personality of Fletcher himself. He remembered now that there was a sister whom he had heard vaguely described by the women of his family as "quite too hopeless," and a granddaughter of whom he knew merely that she had for years attended an expensive school somewhere in the North. The grandson he recalled, after a moment, more distinctly, as a pretty, undeveloped boy in white pinafores, who had once accompanied Fletcher upon a hurried visit to the town. The gay laugh had awakened the incident in his mind, and he saw again the little cleanly clad figure perched upon his desk, nibbling bakers' buns, while he transacted a tedious piece of business with the vulgar grandfather.

He was toying impatiently with these recollections

when his attention was momentarily attracted by the sound of Fletcher's burly tones on the rear porch just beyond the open window.

"I tell you, you've set all the niggers agin me, and I can't get hands to work the crops."

"That's your lookout, of course," replied a voice, which he associated at once with young Blake. "I told you I'd work three days because I wanted the ready money; I've got it, and my time is my own again."

"But I say my tobacco's got to get into the ground this week—it's too big for the plant-bed a'ready, and with three days of this sun the earth'll be dried as hard as a rock."

"There's no doubt of it, I think."

"And it's all your blamed fault," burst out the other angrily; "you've gone and turned them all agin me—white and black alike. Why, it's as much as I can do to get a stroke of honest labour in this nigger-ridden country."

Christopher laughed shortly.

"There is no use blaming the negroes," he said, and his pronunciation of the single word would have stamped him in Virginia as of a different class from Fletcher; "they're usually ready enough to work if you treat them decently."

"Treat them!" began Fletcher, and Carraway was about to fling open the shutters, when light steps passed quickly along the hall and he heard the rustle of a woman's silk dress against the wainscoting.

"There's a stranger to see you, grandfather," called a girl's even voice from the house; "finish paying off the hands and come in at once."

"Well, of all the impudence!" exclaimed the young man, with a saving dash of humour. Then, without so much as a parting word, he ran quickly down the steps and started rapidly in the direction of the darkening road, while the silk dress rustled upon the porch and at the garden gate as the latch was lifted.

"Go in, grandfather!" called the girl's voice from the garden, to which Fletcher responded as decisively.

"For Heaven's sake, let me manage my own affairs, Maria. You seem to have inherited your poor mother's pesky habit of meddling."

"Well, I told you a gentleman was waiting," returned the girl stubbornly. "You didn't let us know he was coming, either, and Lindy says there isn't a thing fit to eat for supper."

Fletcher snorted, and then, before entering the house, stopped to haggle with an old negro woman for a pair of spring chickens hanging dejectedly from her outstretched hand, their feet tied together with a strip of faded calico.

"How much you gwine gimme fer dese, marster?" she inquired anxiously, deftly twirling them about until they swung with heads aloft.

Rising to the huckster's instinct, Fletcher poked the offerings suspiciously beneath their flapping wings.

"Thirty cents for the pair—not a copper more," he responded promptly; "they're as poor as Job's turkey, both of 'em."

"Lawdy, marster, you know better'n dat."

"They're skin and bones, I tell you; feel 'em yourself. Well, take it or leave it, thirty cents is all I'll give."

"Go 'way f'om yere, suh; dese yer chickings ain' no po' w'ite trash—dey's been riz on de bes' er de lan', dey is—en de aigs dey wuz hatched right dar in de middle er de baid whar me en my ole man en de chillun sleep. De hull time dat black hen wuz a-settin', Cephus he was bleeged ter lay right spang on de bar' flo' caze we'uz afeared de aigs 'ould addle. Lawd! Lawd! dey wuz plum three weeks a-hatchin', en de weather des freeze thoo en thoo. Cephus he's been crippled up wid de rheumatics ever sence. Go 'way f'om yer, marster. I warn't bo'n yestiddy. Thirty cents!"

"Not a copper more, I tell you. Let me go, my good woman; I can't stand here all night."

"Des a minute, marster. Dese yer chickings ain' never sot dey feet on de yearth, caze dey's been riz right in de cabin, en dey's done et dar vittles outer de same plate wid me en Cephus. Ef'n dey spy a chice bit er bacon on de een er de knife hit 'uz moughty likely ter fin' hits way down dir throat instid er down me en Cephus'."

"Let me go, I say—I don't want your blamed chickens; take 'em home again."

"Hi! marster, I'se Mehitable. You ain't fergot how peart I use ter wuk w'en you wuz over me in ole marster's day. You know you ain' fergot Mehitable, suh. Ain't you recollect de time ole marster gimme a dollar wid his own han' caze I foun' de biggest wum in de hull 'baccy patch? Lawd! dey wuz times, sho's you bo'n. I kin see ole marster now es plain es ef twuz yestiddy, so big en shiny like satin, wid his skin des es tight es a watermillion's."

"Shut up, confound you!" cut in Fletcher sharply.

"If you don't stop your chatter I'll set the dogs on you. Shut up, I say!"

He strode into the house, slamming the heavy door behind him, and a moment afterward Carraway heard him scolding brutally at the servants across the hall.

The old negress had gone muttering from the porch with her unsold chickens, when the door softly opened again, and the girl, who had entered through the front with her basket of flowers, came out into the growing moonlight.

"Wait a moment, Aunt Mehitable," she said. "I want to speak to you."

Aunt Mehitable turned slowly, putting a feeble hand to her dazed eyes. "You ain' ole miss come back agin, is you, honey?" she questioned doubtfully.

"I don't know who your old miss was," replied the girl, "but I am not she, whoever she may have been. I am Maria Fletcher. You don't remember me—yet you used to bake me ash-cakes when I was a little girl."

The old woman shook her head. "You ain' Marse Fletcher's chile?"

"His granddaughter—but I must go in to supper. Here is the money for your chickens—grandpa was only joking; you know he loves to joke. Take the chickens to the hen-house and get something hot to eat in the kitchen before you start out again."

She ran hurriedly up the steps and entered the hall just as Fletcher was shaking hands with his guest.

CHAPTER III

Showing That a Little Culture Entails Great Care

Carraway had risen to meet his host in a flutter that was almost one of dread. In the eight years since their last interview it seemed to him that his mental image of his great client had magnified in proportions—that Fletcher had "out-Fletchered" himself, as he felt inclined to put it. The old betrayal of his employer's dependence, which at first had been merely a suspicion in the lawyer's mind, had begun gradually, as time went on, to bristle with the points of significant details. In looking back, half-hinted things became clear to him at last, and he gathered, bit by bit, the whole clever, hopeless villainy of the scheme—the crime hedged about by law with all the prating protection of a virtue. He knew now that Fletcher—the old overseer of the Blake slaves—had defrauded the innocent as surely as if he had plunged his great red fist into the little pocket of a child—had defrauded, indeed, with so strong a blow that the very consciousness of his victim had been stunned. There had been about his act all the damning hypocrisy of a great theft—all the air of stern morality which makes for the popular triumph of the heroic swindler.

23

These things Carraway understood, yet as the man strode into the room with open palm and a general air of bluff hospitality—as if he had just been blown by some fresh strong wind across his tobacco fields— the lawyer experienced a relief so great that the breath he drew seemed a fit measure of his earlier fore- boding. For Fletcher outwardly was but the com- mon type of farmer, after all, with a trifle more intelligence, perhaps, than is met with in the average Southerner of his class. "A plain man but honest, sir," was what one expected him to utter at every turn. It was written in the coarse open lines of his face, half-hidden by a bushy gray beard; in his small sparkling eyes, now blue, now brown; in his loose- limbed, shambling movements as he crossed the room. His very clothes spoke, to an acute observer, of a masculine sincerity naked and unashamed—as if his large coffee-spotted cravat would not alter the smallest fold to conceal the stains it bore. Hale, hairy, vehement, not without a quality of Rabelaisian humour, he appeared the last of all men with whom one would associate the burden of a troubled conscience.

"Sorry to have kept you—on my word I am," he began heartily; "but to tell the truth, I thought thar'd be somebody in the house with sense enough to show you to a bedroom. Like to run up now for a wash before supper?"

It was what one expected of him, such a speech blurted in so offhand a manner, and the lawyer could barely suppress a threatening laugh.

"Oh, it was a short trip," he returned, "and a walk of five miles on a day like this is one of the most delightful things in life. I've been looking out at your garden, by the way, and—I may as well confess it—overhearing a little of your conversation."

"Is that so?" chuckled Fletcher, his great eyebrows overhanging his eyes like a mustache grown out of place. "Well, you didn't hear anything to tickle your ears, I reckon. I've been having a row with that cantankerous fool, Blake. The queer thing about these people is that they seem to think I'm to blame every time they see a spot on their tablecloths. Mark my words, it ain't been two years since I found that nigger Boaz digging in my asparagus bed, and he told me he was looking for some shoots for ole miss's dinner."

"The property idea is very strong in these rural counties, you see," remarked the lawyer gravely. "They feel that every year adds a value to the hereditary possession of land, and that when an estate has borne a single name for a century there has been a veritable impress placed upon it. Your asparagus bed is merely an item; you find, I fancy, other instances."

Fletcher turned in his chair.

"That's the whole blamed rotten truth," he admitted, waving his great red hand toward the door; "but let's have supper first and settle down to talk on a full stomach. Thar's no hurry with all night before us, and that, to come to facts, is why I sent for you. No lawyer's office for me when I want to talk business, but an easy-chair by my own table and a cup of coffee beforehand."

As he finished, a bell jangled in the hall, and the

door opened to admit the girl whom Carraway had
seen a little earlier upon the porch.

"Supper's a good hour late, Maria," grumbled
Fletcher, looking at his heavy silver watch, "and I
smelt the bacon frying at six o'clock."

For an instant the girl looked as if she had more
than half an intention to slap his face; then quickly
recovering her self-possession, she smiled at Carraway
and held out a small white hand with an air of
quiet elegance which was the most noticeable thing
in her appearance.

"I am quite a stranger to you, Mr. Carraway,"
she said, with a laugh, "but if you had only known it,
I had a doll named after you when I was very small.
Guy Carraway!—it seemed to me all that was needed
to make a fairy tale."

The lawyer joined in her laugh, which never rose
above a carefully modulated minor. "I confess that
I once took the same view of it, my dear young
lady," he returned, "so I ended by dropping the name
and keeping only the initial. Your grandfather
will tell you that I am now G. Carraway and nothing
more. I couldn't afford, as things were, to make a
fairy tale of my life, you see."

"Oh, if one only could!" said the girl, lowering her
full dark eyes, which gave a piteous lie to her sullen
mouth.

She was artificial, Carraway told himself with
emphasis, and yet the distinction of manner—the
elegance—was certainly the point at which her training had not failed. He felt it in her tall, straight
figure, absurdly overdressed for a granddaughter of
Fletcher's; in her smooth white hands, with their

finely polished nails; in her pale, repressed face, which
he called plain while admitting that it might become
interesting; in her shapely head even with its heavy
cable of coal-black hair. What she was her education
had made of her—the look of serene distinction, the
repose of her thin-featured, colourless face, refined
beyond the point of prettiness—these things her
training had given her, and these were the things
which Carraway, with his old-fashioned loyalty to a
strong class prejudice, found himself almost resenting.
Bill Fletcher's granddaughter had, he felt, no right
to this rare security of breeding which revealed
itself in every graceful fold of the dress she wore, for
with Fletcher an honest man she would have been,
perhaps, but one of the sallow, over-driven drudges
who stare like helpless effigies from the little tumbled-
down cabins along country roadsides.

Fletcher, meanwhile, had filled in the pause with
one of his sudden burly dashes into speech.

"Maria has been so long at her high-and-mighty
boarding-school," he said, "that I reckon her head's
as full of fancies as a cheese is of maggots. She's
even got a notion that she wants to turn out all
this new stuff—to haul the old rubbish back again—
but I say wait till the boy comes on—then we'll see,
we'll see."

"And in the meantime we'll go in to supper," put
in the girl with a kind of hopeless patience, though
Carraway could see that she smarted as from a blow.
"This is Will, Mr. Carraway," she added almost
gaily, skilfully sweeping her train from about the
feet of a pretty, undersized boy of fourteen years,
who had burst into the room with his mouth full of

bread and jam. "He's quite the pride of the family, you know, because he's just taken all the honours of his school."

"History, 'rithmatic, Latin—all the languages," rolled out Fletcher in a voice that sounded like a tattoo. "I can't keep up with 'em, but they're all thar, ain't they, sonny?"

"Oh, you could never say 'em off straight, grandpa," retorted the boy, with the pertness of a spoiled girl, at which, to Carraway's surprise, Fletcher fairly chuckled with delight.

"That's so; I'm a plain man, the Lord knows," he admitted, his coarse face crinkling like a sun-dried leaf of tobacco.

"We've got chickens for supper—broiled," the boy chattered on, putting out his tongue at his sister; "that's why Lindy's havin' it an hour late—she's been picking 'em, with Aunt Mehitable helping her for the feathers. Now don't shake your head at me, Maria, because it's no use pretending we have 'em every night, like old Mrs. Blake."

"Bless my soul!" gasped Fletcher, nettled by the last remark. "Do you mean to tell me those Blakes are fools enough to eat spring chicken when they could get forty cents apiece for 'em in the open market?"

"The old lady does," corrected the boy glibly. "The one who wears the queer lace cap and sits in the big chair by the hearth all day—and all night, too, Tommy Spade says, 'cause he peeped through once at midnight and she was still there, sitting so stiff that it scared him and he ran away. Well, Aunt Mehitable sold her a dozen, and she got a side of bacon and a bag of meal."

"Grandfather, you've forgotten Aunt Saidie," broke in Maria, as Fletcher was about to begin his grace without waiting for a dumpy little woman, in purple calico, who waddled with an embarrassed air from her hasty preparations in the pantry. At first Carraway had mistaken her for an upper servant, but as she came forward Maria laid her hand playfully upon her arm and introduced her with a sad little gaiety of manner. "I believe she has met one of your sisters in Fredericksburg," she added, after a moment. Clearly she had determined to accept the family in the lump, with a resolution that —had it borne less resemblance to a passive rage— could not have failed to glorify a nobler martyrdom. It was not affection that fortified her—beyond her first gently tolerant glance at the boy there had been only indifference in her pale, composed face—and the lawyer was at last brought to the surprising conclusion that Fletcher's granddaughter was seeking to build herself a fetish of the mere idle bond of blood. The hopeless gallantry of the girl moved him to a vague feeling of pity, and he spoke presently with a chivalrous desire of making her failure easy.

"It was Susan, I think," he said pleasantly, shaking hands with the squat little figure in front of him, "I remember her speaking of it afterward."

"I met her at a church festival one Christmas Eve," responded Aunt Saidie, in a high-pitched, rasping voice. "The same evening that I got this pink crochetted nuby." She touched a small pointed shawl about her shoulders. "Miss Belinda Beale worked it and it was raffled off for ten cents a chance."

Her large, plump face, overflushed about the nose, had a natural kindliness of expression which Carraway found almost appealing; and he concluded that as a girl she might have possessed a common prettiness of feature. Above her clear blue eyes a widening parting divided her tightly crimped bands of hair, which still showed a bright chestnut tint in the gray ripples.

"Thar, thar, Saidie," Fletcher interrupted with a frank brutality, which the laywer found more repelling than the memory of his stolen fortune. "Mr. Carraway doesn't want to hear about your fascinator. He'd a long ways rather have you make his coffee."

The little woman flushed purple and drew back her chair with an ugly noise from the head of the lavishly spread table.

"Set down right thar, suh," she stammered, her poor little pretense of ease gone from her, "right thar between Brother Bill and me."

"You did say it, Aunt Saidie, I told you you would," screamed the pert boy, beginning an assault upon an enormous dish of batterbread.

Maria flinched visibly. "Be silent, Will," she ordered. "Grandfather, you must really make Will learn to be polite."

"Now, now, Maria, you're too hard on us," protested Fletcher, flinging himself bodily into the breach, "boys will be boys, you know—they warn't born gals."

"But she did say it, Maria," insisted the boy, "and she bet me a whole dish of doughnuts she wouldn't. She did say 'set'; I heard her." Maria bit her lip, and her flashing eyes filled with angry tears, while

futile appeared any attempt to soften the effect of Fletcher's grossness. Before the man's colossal vulgarity of soul, mere brutishness of manner seemed but a trifling phase.

CHAPTER IV

Of Human Nature in the Raw State

When at last the pickles and preserved water-melon rind had been presented with a finishing flourish, and Carraway had successfully resisted Miss Saidie's final passionate insistence in the matter of the big blackberry roll before her, Fletcher noisily pushed back his chair, and, with a careless jerk of his thumb in the direction of his guest, stamped across the hall into the family sitting-room.

"Now we'll make ourselves easy and fall to thresh-ing things out," he remarked, filling a blackened brier-root pipe, into the bowl of which he packed the tobacco with his stubby forefinger. "Yes, I'm a lover of the weed, you see—don't you smoke or chaw, suh?"

Carraway shook his head. "When I was young and wanted to I couldn't," he explained, "and now that I am old and can, I have unfortunately ceased to want to. I've passed the time of life when a man begins a habit merely for the sake of its being a habit."

"Well, I reckon you're wise as things go, though for my part I believe I took to the weed before I did to my mother's breast. I cut my first tooth on a plug, she used to say."

He threw himself into a capacious cretonne-covered chair, and, kicking his carpet slippers from him, sat swinging one massive foot in its gray yarn sock. Through the thickening smoke Carraway watched the complacency settle over his great hairy face.

"And now, to begin with the beginning, what do you think of my grandchildren?" he demanded abruptly, taking his pipe from his mouth after a long, sucking breath, and leaning forward with his elbow on the arm of his chair.

The other hesitated. "You've done well by them, I should say."

"A fine pair, eh?"

"The admission is easy."

"Look at the gal, now," burst out Fletcher impulsively. "Would you fancy, to see her stepping by, that her grandfather used to crack the whip over a lot of dirty niggers?" He drove the fact in squarely with big, sure blows of his fist, surveying it with an enthusiasm the other found amazing. "Would you fancy, even," he continued after a moment, "that her father warn't as good as I am—that he left overseeing to jine the army, and came out to turn blacksmith if I hadn't kept him till he drank himself to death? His wife? Why, the woman couldn't read her own name unless you printed it in letters as long as your finger—and now jest turn and look at Maria!" he wound up in a puff of smoke.

"The girl's wonderful," admitted Carraway. "She's like a dressed-up doll-baby, too; all the natural thing has been squeezed out of her, and she's stuffed with sawdust."

"It's a pity she ain't a little better looking in the

face," pursued Fletcher, waving the criticism aside.
"She's a plagued sight too pale and squinched-up for
my taste—for all her fine air. I like 'em red and
juicy, and though you won't believe me, most likely
she can't hold a tallow candle to what Saidie was
when she was young. But then, Saidie never had
her chance, and Maria's had 'em doubled over.
Why, she left home as soon as she'd done sucking, and
she hasn't spent a single summer here since she was
eight years old. Small thanks I'll get for it, I reckon,
but I've done a fair turn by Maria——"

"The boy comes next, I suppose?" Carraway
broke in, watching the other's face broaden into a
big, purple smile.

"Ah, thar you're right—it's the boy I've got my
eye on now. His name's the same as mine, you know,
and I reckon one day William Fletcher 'll make his
mark among the quality. He'll have it all, too—the
house, the land, everything, except a share of the
money which goes to the gal. It'll make her child-
bearing easier, I reckon, and for my part, that's the
only thing a woman's fit for. Don't talk to me about
a childless woman! Why, I'd as soon keep a cow
that wouldn't calve——"

"You were speaking of the boy, I believe," coolly
interrupted Carraway. To a man of his old-fashioned
chivalric ideal the brutal allusion to the girl was like a
deliberate blow in the face.

"So I was—so I was. Well, he's to have it all, I
say—every mite, and welcome. I've had a pretty
tough life in my time—you can tell it from my hands,
suh—but I ain't begrudging it if it leaves the boy a
bit better off. Lord, thar's many and many a night,

when I was little and my stepfather kicked me out of doors without a bite, that I used to steal into somebody or other's cow-shed and snuggle for warmth into the straw—yes, and suck the udders of the cows for food, too. Oh, I've had a hard enough life, for all the way it looks now—and I'm not saying that if the choice was mine I'd go over it agin even as it stands to-day. We're set here for better or for worse, that's my way of thinking, and if thar's any harm comes of it Providence has got to take a share of the blame."

"Hardly the preacher's view of the matter, is it?"

"Maybe not; and I ain't got a quarrel with 'em, the Lord knows. I go to church like clockwork, and pay my pew-rent, too, which is more than some do that gabble the most about salvation. If I pay for the preacher's keep it's only fair that I should get some of the good that comes to him hereafter; that's how it looks to me; so I don't trouble my head much about the ins and the outs of getting saved or damned. I've never puled in this world, thank God, and let come what will, I ain't going to begin puling in the next. But to go back to whar I started from, it all makes in the end for that pretty little chap over yonder in the dining-room. Rather puny for his years now, but as sound as a nut, and he'll grow— he'll grow. When his mother—poor, worthless drab —gave birth to him and died, I told her it was the best day's work she'd ever done."

Carraway's humour rippled over. "It's easy to imagine what her answer must have been to such a pleasantry," he observed.

"Oh, she was a fool, that woman—a born fool!

Her answer was that it would be the best day for her only when I came to call it the worst. She hated me a long sight more than she hated the devil, and if she was to rise out of her grave to-day she'd probably start right in scrubbing for those darned Blakes."

"Ah!" said Carraway.

"It's the plain truth, but I don't visit it on the little lad. Why should I? He's got my name—I saw to that—and mark my word, he'll grow up yet to marry among the quality."

The secret was out at last—Fletcher's purpose was disclosed, and even in the strong light of his past misdeeds it showed not without a hint of pathos. The very renouncement of any personal ambition served to invest the racial one with a kind of grandeur.

"There's evidently an enviable career before him," said the lawyer at the end of a long pause, "and this brings me, by the way, to the question I wish to ask —had your desire to see me any connection with the prospects of your grandson?"

"In a way, yes; though, to tell the truth, it has more to do with that young Blake's. He's been bothering me a good deal of late, and I mean to have it square with him before Bill Fletcher's a year older."

"No difficulty about your title to the estate, I presume?"

"Oh, Lord, no; that's all fair and square, suh. I bought the place, you know, when it went at auction jest a few years after the war. I bought and paid for it right down, and that settled things for good and all."

Carraway considered the fact for a moment. "If I remember correctly—I mean unless gossip went very far afield—the place brought exactly seven thousand dollars." His gaze plunged into the moonlight beyond the open window and followed the clear sweep of the distant fields. "Seven thousand dollars," he added softly; "and there's not a finer in Virginia."

"Thar was nobody to bid agin me, you see," explained Fletcher easily. "The old gentleman was as poor as Job's turkey then, besides going doty mighty fast."

" The common report was, I believe," pursued the lawyer, "that the old man himself did not know of the place being for sale until he heard the auctioneer's hammer on the lawn, and that his mind left him from the moment—this was, of course, mere idle talk."

"Oh, you'll hear anything," snorted Fletcher. "The old gentleman hadn't a red copper to his name, and if he couldn't pay the mortgages, how under heaven could he have bought in the place? As a plain man I put the question."

"But his friends? Where were his friends, I wonder? In his youth he was one of the most popular men in the State—a high liver and good toaster, you remember—and later on he stood well in the Confederate Government. That he should have fallen into abject poverty seems really incomprehensible."

Fletcher twisted in his chair. "Why, that was jest three years after the war, I tell you," he said with irritable emphasis; "he hadn't a friend this side of Jordan, I reckon, who could have raised fifty cents to save his soul. The quality were as bad off as thar own niggers."

"True—true," admitted Carraway; "but the surprising thing is—I don't hesitate to say—that you who had been overseer to the Blakes for twenty years should have been able in those destitute times and on the spot, as it were, to put down seven thousand dollars."

He faced the fact unflinchingly, dragging it from the long obscurity full into the red glare of the lamplight. Here was the main thing, he knew, in Fletcher's history—here was the supreme offense. For twenty years the man had been the trusted servant of his feeble employer, and when the final crash came he had risen with full hands from the wreck. The prodigal Blakes—burning the candle at both ends, people said—had squandered a double fortune before the war, and in an equally stupendous fashion Fletcher had amassed one.

"Oh, thar're ways and ways of putting by a penny," he now protested, "and I turned over a bit during the war, I may as well own up, though folks had only black looks for speculators then."

"We used to call them 'bloodsuckers,' I remember."

"Well, that's neither here nor thar, suh. When the place went for seven thousand I paid it down, and I've managed one way and another—and in spite of the pesky niggers—to make a pretty bit out of the tobacco crop, hard as times have been. The Hall is mine now, thar's no going agin that, and, so help me God, it'll belong to a William Fletcher long after I am dead."

"Ah, that brings us directly to the point."

Fletcher squared himself about in his chair while his pipe went out slowly.

"The point, if you'll have it straight," he said, "is jest this—I want the whole place—every inch of it—and I'll die or git it, as sure's my name's my own. Thar's still that old frame house and the piece of land tacked to it, whar the overseers used to live, cutting straight into the heart of my tobacco fields—in clear view of the Hall, too—right in the middle of my land, I tell you!"

"Oh, I see—I see," muttered Carraway; "that's the little farm in the midst of the estate which the old gentleman—bless his weak head and strong heart— gave his wife's brother, Colonel Corbin, who came back crippled from the war. Yes, I remember now, there was a joke at the time about his saying that land was the cheapest present he could give."

"It was all his besotted foolishness, you know— to think of a sane man deeding away seventy acres right in the heart of his tract of two thousand. He meant it for a joke, of course. Mr. Tucker or Colonel Corbin, if you choose, was like one of the family, but he was as sensitive as a kid about his wounds, and he wanted to live off somewhar, shut up by himself. Well, he's got enough folks about him now, the Lord knows. Thar's the old lady, and the two gals, and Mr. Christopher, to say nothing of Uncle Boaz and a whole troop of worthless niggers that are eating him out of house and home. Tom Spade has a deed of trust on the place for three hundred dollars; he told me so himself."

"So I understand; and all this is a serious inconvenience to you, I may suppose."

"Inconvenience! Blood and thunder! It takes the heart right out of my land, I tell you. Why, the very road I cut to save myself half a mile of mud-holes came to a dead stop because Mr. Christopher wouldn't let it cross his blamed pasture."

Carraway thoughtfully regarded his finger nails. "Then, bless my soul!—seeing it's your private affair—what are you going to do about it?" he inquired.

"Git it. The devil knows how—I don't; but git it I will. I brought you down here to talk those fools over, and I mean you to do it. It's all spite—pure, rotten spite; that's what it is. Look here, I'll gladly give 'em three thousand dollars for that strip of land, and it wouldn't bring nine hundred, on my oath!"

"Have you made the offer?"

"Made it? Why, if I set foot on the tip edge of that land I'd have every lean hound in the pack snapping at my heels. As for that young rascal, he'd knock me down if I so much as scented the matter."

He rapped his pipe sharply on the wood of his chair and a little pile of ashes settled upon the floor. With a laugh, the other waved his hand in protest.

"So you prefer to make the proposition by proxy. My dear sir—I'm not a rubber ball."

"Oh, he won't hurt you. It would spoil the sport to punch anybody's head but mine, you know. Come, now, isn't it a fair offer I'm making?"

"It appears so, certainly—and I really do not see why he should wish to hold the place. It isn't worth much, I fancy, to anybody but the owner of the Hall, and with the three thousand clear he could

probably get a much better one at a little distance
—with the additional value of putting a few square
miles between himself and you—whom, I may presume, he doesn't love."

"Oh, you may presume he hates me if you'll
only work it," snorted Fletcher. "Go over thar
boldly—no slinking, mind you—to-morrow morning,
and talk them into reason. Lord, man, you ought to
be able to do it—don't you know Greek?"

Carraway nodded. "Not that it ever availed me
much in an argument," he confessed frankly.

"It's a good thing to stop a mouth with, anyway. Thar's many and many a time, I tell you,
I've lost a bargain for the lack of a few rags of Latin
or Greek. Drag it in; stuff it down 'em; gag thar
mouths—it's better than all the swearing under
heaven. Why, taking the Lord's name in vain ain't
nothing to a line of poetry spurted of a sudden in one
of them dead-and-gone languages. It's been done at
me, suh, and I know how it works—that's why I've
put the boy upstairs on 'em from the start. 'Tain't
much matter whether he goes far in his own tongue or
not, that's what I said, but dose him well with something his neighbours haven't learnt."

He rose with a lurch, laid his pipe on the mantel,
and drew out his big silver watch.

"Great Jehosaphat! it's eleven and after," he
exclaimed. "Well, it's time for us to turn in, I
reckon, and dream of breakfast. If you'll hold
the lamp while I bolt up, I'll show you to your
room."

Carraway picked up the lamp, and, cautiously
following his host into the darkened hall, waited

until he had fastened the night-chains and shot the heavy bolts.

"If you want a drink of water thar's a bucket in the porch," said Fletcher, as he opened the back door and reached out into the moonlight. "Wait thar a second and I'll hand you the dipper."

He stepped out upon the porch, and a moment later Carraway heard a heavy stumble followed by a muttered oath.

"Why, blast the varmints! I've upset the boy's cage of white mice and they're skedaddling about my legs. Here! hold the lamp, will you—I'm squashing a couple of 'em under each of my hands."

Carraway, leaning out with the lamp, which drew a brilliant circle on the porch, saw Fletcher floundering helplessly upon his hands and knees in the midst of the fleeing family of mice.

"They're a plagued mess of beasts, that's what they are," he exclaimed, "but the little lad sets a heap of store by 'em, and when he comes down tomorrow he'll find that I got some of 'em back, anyway."

He fastened the cage and placed it carefully beneath the bench. Then, closing and bolting the door, he took the lamp from Carraway and motioned him up the dusky staircase to the spare chamber at the top.

CHAPTER V

THE WRECK OF THE BLAKES

WHEN Christopher left Blake Hall, he swung
vigorously in the twilight across the newly ploughed
fields, until, at the end of a few minutes' walk, he
reached the sunken road that branched off by the
abandoned ice-pond. Here the bullfrogs were still
croaking hoarsely, and far away over the gray-green
rushes a dim moon was mounting the steep slope
of bluish sky.

The air was fresh with the scent of the upturned
earth, and the closing day refined into a tranquil
beauty; but the young man, as he passed briskly,
did not so much as draw a lengthened breath, and
when presently the cry of a whip-poor-will floated
from the old rail fence, he fell into a whistling mockery
of the plaintive notes. The dogs at his heels
started a rabbit once from the close cover of the
underbrush, and he called them to order in a sharp,
peremptory tone. Not until he reached the long,
whitewashed gate opening before the frame house
of the former overseers did he break the easy swing
of his accustomed stride.

The house, a common country dwelling of the sort
used by the poorer class of farmers, lost something of
its angularity beneath the moonlight, and even the

half-dried garments, spread after the day's washing on the bent old rose-bushes, shone in soft white patches amid the grass, which looked thick and fine under the heavy dew. In one corner of the yard there was a spreading peach-tree, on which the shrivelled little peaches ripened out of season, and against the narrow porch sprawled a gray and crippled aspen, where a flock of turkeys had settled to roost along its twisted boughs.

In one of the lower rooms a lamp was burning, and as Christopher crunched heavily along the pebbled path, a woman with a piece of sewing in her hand came into the hall and spoke his name.

"Christopher, you are late."

Her voice was deep and musical, with a richness of volume which raised deluding hopes of an impassioned beauty in the speaker—who, as she crossed the illumined square of the window-frame, showed as a tall, thin woman of forty years, with squinting eyes, and a face whose misshapen features stood out like the hasty drawing for a grotesque. When she reached him Christopher turned from the porch, and they walked together slowly out into the moonlight, passing under the aspen where the turkeys stirred and fluttered in their sleep.

"Has her cat come home, Cynthia?" were the young man's first anxious words.

"About sunset. Uncle Boaz found her over at Aunt Daphne's, hunting mice under the joists. Mother had fretted terribly over the loss."

"Is she easier now?"

"Much more so, but she still asks for the port. We pretend that Uncle Boaz has mislaid the key of the wine-cellar. She upbraided him, and he bore it so patiently, poor old soul!"

Christopher quickly reached into the deep pocket of his overalls and drew out the scanty wages of his last three days' labour.

"Send this by somebody down to Tompkins," he said, "and get the wine he ordered. He refuses to sell on credit any longer, so I had to find the money."

She looked up, startled.

"Oh, Christopher, you have worked for Fletcher?"

Tears shone in her eyes and her mouth quivered. "Oh, Christopher!" she repeated, and the emotional quality in her voice rang strong and true. He fell back, angered, while the hand she had stretched out dropped limply to her side.

"For God's sake, don't snivel," he retorted harshly. "Send the money and give her the wine, but dole it out like a miser, for where the next will come from is more than I can tell."

"The pay for my sewing is due in three days," said Cynthia, raising her roughened hand on which the needle-scars showed even in the moonlight. "Mother has worried so to-day that I couldn't work except at odd moments, but I can easily manage to sit up to-night and get it done. She thinks I'm embroidering an ottoman, you see, and this evening she asked to feel the silks."

He uttered a savage exclamation.

"Oh, I gave her some ravellings from an old tidy," she hastened to assure him. "She played with them awhile and knew no better, as I told her the colours one by one. Afterward she planned all kinds of samplers and fire-screens that I might work. Her own knitting has wearied her of late, so we haven't been obliged to buy the yarn."

"She doesn't suspect, you think?"

Cynthia shook her head. "After fifteen years of deception there's no danger of my telling the truth to-day. I only wish I could," she added, with that patient dignity which is the outward expression of complete renouncement. When she lifted her tragic face the tears on her cheeks softened the painful hollows, as the moonbeams, playing over her gown of patched and faded silk, revived for a moment the freshness of its discoloured flowers.

"The truth would be the death of her," said the young man, in a bitter passion of anxiety. "Tell her that Fletcher owns the Hall, and that for fifteen years she has lived, blind and paralysed, in the overseer's house! Why, I'd rather stick a knife into her heart myself!"

"Her terrible pride would kill her—yes, you're right. We'll keep it up to the end at any cost."

He turned to her with a sudden terror in his face. "She isn't worse, is she?"

"Worse? Oh, no; I only meant the cost to us—the cost of never speaking the truth within the house."

"Well, I'm not afraid of lying, God knows," he answered, in the tone of one from whom a burden has been removed. "I'm only wondering how much longer I'll be able to afford the luxury."

"But we're no worse off than usual, that's one comfort. Mother is quite happy now since Beulah has been found, and the only added worry is that Aunt Dinah is laid up in her cabin and we've had to send her soup. Uncle Isam has come to see you, by the way. I believe he wants you to give him some advice about his little hut up in the woods, and to look up his birth in the servants' age-book, too. He lives five miles away, you know, and works across the river at Farrar's Mills."

"Uncle Isam!" exclaimed Christopher, wonderingly; "why, what do I know about the man? I haven't laid eyes on him for the last ten years."

"But he wants help now, so of course he's come to you, and as he's walked all the distance—equally of course—he'll stay to supper. Mother has her young chicken, and there's bacon and cornbread for the rest of us, so I hope the poor man won't go back hungry. Ever since Aunt Polly's chimney blew down she has had to fry the middling in the kitchen, and mother complains so of the smell. She can't understand why we have it three times a day, and when I told her that Uncle Tucker acquired the habit in the army, she remarked that it was very inconsiderate of him to insist upon gratifying so extraordinary a taste."

Christopher laughed shortly.

"Well, it's a muck of a world," he declared cheerfully, taking off his coarse harvest hat and running his hand through his clustering fair hair. In the mellow light the almost brutal strength of his jaw was softened, and his sunburned face paled to the beauty of some ancient ivory carving. Cynthia, gazing up at him, caught her breath with a sob.

"How big you are, and strong! How fit for any life in the world but this!"

"Don't whimper," he responded roughly, adding, after a moment, "Precious fit for anything but the stable or the tobacco field! Why, I couldn't so much as write a decently spelled letter to save my soul. A darky asked me yesterday to read a post-bill for him down at the store, and I had to skip a big word in the first line."

He made his confession defiantly, with a certain boorish pride in his ignorance and his degradation.

"My dear, my dear, I wanted to teach you—I will teach you now. We will read together."

"And let mother and Uncle Tucker plough the field, and plant the crop, and cut the wood. No, it won't answer; your learning would do me no good, and I don't want it—I told you that when you first took me from my study and put me to do all the chores upon the place."

"I take you! Oh, Christopher, what could we do? Uncle Tucker was a hopeless cripple, there wasn't a servant strong enough to spade the garden, and there were only Lila and you and I."

"And I was ten. Well, I'm not blaming you, and I've done what I was forced to—but keep your confounded books out of my sight, that's all I ask. Is that mother calling?"

Cynthia bent her ear. "I thought Lila was with her, but I'll go at once. Be sure to change your clothes, dear, before she touches you."

"Hadn't I better chop a little kindling-wood before supper?"

"No—no, not to-night. Go and dress, while I send Uncle Boaz for the wine."

She entered the house with a hurried step, and Christopher, after an instant's hesitation, passed to the back, and, taking off his clumsy boots, crept

"In a massive Elizabethan chair of blackened oak a stately old lady was sitting straight and stiff."

softly up the creaking staircase to his little garret room in the loft.

Ten minutes later he came down again, wearing a decent suit of country-made clothes, with the dust washed from his face, and his hair smoothly brushed across his forehead. In the front hall he took a white rosebud from a little vase of Bohemian glass and pinned it carefully in the lapel of his coat. Then, before entering, he stood for a moment silent upon the threshold of the lamplighted room.

In a massive Elizabethan chair of blackened oak a stately old lady was sitting straight and stiff, with her useless legs stretched out upon an elaborately embroidered ottoman. She wore a dress of rich black brocade, made very full in the skirt, and sleeves after an earlier fashion, and her beautiful snow-white hair was piled over a high cushion and ornamented by a cap of fine thread lace. In her face, which she turned at the first footstep with a pitiable, blind look, there were the faint traces of a proud, though almost extinguished, beauty—traces which were visible in the impetuous flash of her sightless eyes, in the noble arch of her brows, and in the transparent quality of her now yellowed skin, which still kept the look of rare porcelain held against the sunlight. On a dainty, rose-decked tray beside her chair there were the half of a broiled chicken, a thin glass of port, and a plate of buttered waffles; and near her high footstool a big yellow cat was busily lapping a saucer of new milk.

As Christopher went up to her, she stretched out her hand and touched his face with her sensitive fingers. "Oh, if I could only see you," she said, a little peevishly. "It is twenty years since I looked at you, and now you are taller than your father was, you say. I can feel that your hair is light, like his— and like Lila's, too, since you are twins."

A pretty, fragile woman, who was wrapping a shawl about the old lady's feet, rose to her full height and passed behind the Elizabethan chair. "Just a shade lighter than mine, mother," she responded; "the sun makes a difference, you know; he is in the sun so much without a hat." As she stood with her delicate hands clasped above the fancifully carved grotesques upon the chair-back, her beauty shone like a lamp against the smoke-stained walls.

"Ah, if you could but have seen his father when he was young, Lila," sighed her mother, falling into one of the easy reveries of old age. "I met him at a fancy ball, you know, where he went as Achilles in full Grecian dress. Oh! the sight he was, my dear, one of the few fair men among us, and taller even than old Colonel Fitzhugh, who was considered one of the finest figures of his time. That was a wild night for me, Christopher, as I've told you often before—it was love at first sight on both sides, and so marked were your father's attentions that they were the talk of the ball. Edward Morris—the greatest wit of his day, you know—remarked at supper that the weak point of Achilles was proved at last to be not his heel, but his heart."

She laughed with pleasure at the memory, and returned in a half-hearted fashion to her plate of buttered waffles. "Have you been riding again, Christopher?" she asked after a moment, as if remembering a grievance. "I haven't had so much

as a word from you to-day, but when one is
chained to a chair like this it is useless to ask even
to be thought of amid your pleasures."

"I always think of you, mother."

"Well, I'm glad to hear it, my dear, though I'm
sure I should never imagine that you do. Have you
heard, by the way, that Boaz lost the key of the wine-
cellar, and that I had to go two whole days without
my port? I declare, he is getting so careless that
I'm afraid we'll have to put another butler over
him."

"Lawd, ole miss, you ain' gwine do dat, is you?"
anxiously questioned Uncle Boaz as he filled her
glass.

She lifted the wine to her lips, her stern face softening. Like many a high-spirited woman doomed to
perpetual inaction, her dominion over her servants
had grown to represent the larger share of life.

"Then be more careful in future, Boaz," she cautioned. "Tell me, Lila, what has become of Nathan,
the son of Phyllis? He used to be a very bright little
darkey twenty years ago, and I always intended putting him in the dining-room, but things escape me
so. His mother, Phyllis, I remember, got some
ridiculous idea about freedom in her head, and ran
away with the Yankee soldiers before we whipped
them."

Lila's face flushed, for since the war Nathan had
grown into one of the most respectable of freedmen,
but Uncle Boaz, with a glib tongue, started valiantly
to her support.

"Go 'way, ole miss; dat ar Natan is de mos'
ornery un er de hull bunch," he declared. "Wen

he comes inter my dinin'-'oom, out I'se gwine, an' dat's sho."

The old lady passed a hand slowly across her brow. "I can't remember—I can't remember," she murmured; "but I dare say you're right, Boaz—and that reminds me that this bottle of port is not so good as the last. Have you tried it, Christopher?"

'Not yet, mother. Where did you find it, Uncle Boaz?"

"Hit's des de same, suh," protested Uncle Boaz. "Dey wuz bofe un um layin' right side by side, des like dey 'uz bo'n blood kin, en I done dus' de cobwebs off'n um wid de same duster, dat I is."

"Well, well, that will do. Now go in to supper, children, and send Docia to take my tray. Dear me, I do wish that Tucker could be persuaded to give up that vulgar bacon. I'm not so unreasonable, I hope, as to expect a man to make any sacrifices in this world—that's the woman's part, and I've tried to take my share of it—but to conceive of a passion for a thing like bacon—I declare is quite beyond me."

"Come, now, Lucy, don't begin to meddle with my whims," protested the cheerful tones of Tucker, as he entered on his crutches, one of which was strapped to the stump of his right arm. "Allow me my dissipations, my dear, and I'll not interfere with yours."

"Dissipations!" promptly took up the old lady, from the hearth. "Why, if it were such a gentlemanly thing as a dissipation, Tucker, I shouldn't say a word—not a single word. A taste for wine is entirely proper, I'm sure, and even a little intoxication is permissible on occasions—such as christenings, weddings, and Christmas Eve gather-

ings. Your father used to say, Christopher, that
the proof of a gentleman was in the way he
held his wine. But to fall a deliberate victim
to so low-born a vice as a love of bacon is
something that no member of our family has ever
done before."

"That's true, Lucy," pleasantly assented Tucker;
"but then, you see, no member of our family had ever
fought three years for his State—to say nothing of
losing a leg and an arm in her service."

His fine face was ploughed with the marks of
suffering, but the heartiness had not left his voice,
and his smile still shone bright and strong. From
a proud position as the straightest shot and the
gayest liver of his day, he had been reduced at a single
blow to the couch of a hopeless cripple. Poverty
had come a little later, but the second shock had only
served to steady his nerves from the vibration of the
first, and the courage which had drooped within
him for a time was revived in the form of a rare and
gentle humour. Nothing was so terrible but Tucker
could get a laugh out of it, people said—not knowing
that since he had learned to smile at his own ghastly
failure it was an easy matter to turn the jest on
universal joy or woe.

The old lady's humour melted at his words, and
she hastened to offer proof of her contrition. "You're
perfectly right, brother," she said; "and I know I'm
an ungrateful creature, so you needn't take the
trouble to tell me. As long as you do me the honour
to live beneath my roof, you shall eat the whole hog
or none to your heart's content."

Then, as Docia, a large black woman, with brass

hoops in her ears, appeared to bear away the supper tray, Mrs. Blake folded her hands and settled herself for a nap upon her cushions, while the yellow cat purred blissfully on her knees.

Beyond the adjoining bedroom, through which Christopher passed, a rude plank platform led to a long, unceiled room which served as kitchen and dining-room in one. Here a cheerful blaze made merry about an ancient crane, on which a coffee-boiler swung slowly back and forth with a bubbling noise. In the red firelight a plain pine table was spread with a scant supper of cornbread and bacon and a cracked Wedgewood pitcher filled with butter-milk. There was no silver; the china consisted of some odd, broken pieces of old willow-ware; and beyond a bunch of damask roses stuck in a quaint glass vase, there was no visible attempt to lighten the effect of extreme poverty. An aged negress, in a dress of linsey-woolsey which resembled a patch-work quilt, was pouring hot, thin coffee into a row of cups with chipped or missing saucers.

Cynthia was already at the table, and when Christopher came in she served him with an anxious haste like that of a stricken mother. To Tucker and herself the coarse fare was unbearable even after the custom of fifteen years, and time had not lessened the surprise with which they watched the young man's healthful enjoyment of his food. Even Lila, whose glowing face in its nimbus of curls lent an almost festive air to her end of the white pine board, ate with a heartiness which Cynthia, with her out-grown standard for her sex, could not but find a trifle vulgar. The elder sister had been born to a

different heritage—to one of restricted views and
mincing manners for a woman—and, despite herself,
she could but drift aimlessly on the widening current
of the times.

"Christopher, will you have some coffee—it is
stronger now?" she asked presently, reaching for his
emptied cup.

"Dis yer stuff ain' no cawfy," grumbled Aunt
Polly, taking the boiler from the crane; "hit ain'
nuttin' but dishwater, I don' cyar who done made
hit." Then, as the door opened to admit Uncle
Isam with a bucket from the spring, she divided her
scorn equally between him and the coffee-pot.

"You needn't be a-castin' er you nets into dese yer
pairts," she observed cynically.

Uncle Isam, a dried old negro of seventy years,
shambled in patiently and placed the bucket carefully
upon the stones, to be shrilly scolded by Aunt Polly
for spilling a few drops on the floor. "I reckon you
is steddyin' ter outdo Marse Noah," she remarked
with scorn.

"Howdy, Marse Christopher? Howdy, Marse
Tuck?" Uncle Isam inquired politely, as he seated
himself in a low chair on the hearth and dropped
his clasped hands between his open knees.

Christopher nodded carelessly. "Glad to see you,
Isam," Tucker cordially responded. "Times have
changed since you used to live over here."

"Dat's so, suh, dat's so. Times dey's done change,
but I ain't—I'se des de same. Dat's de tribble wid
dis yer worl'; w'en hit changes yo' fortune hit don'
look ter changin' yo' skin es well."

"That's true; but you're doing all right, I hope?"

"I dunno, Marse Tuck," replied Uncle Isam, coughing as a sudden spurt of smoke issued from the old stone chimney. "I dunno 'bout dat. Times dey's right peart, but I ain't. De vittles dey's ready ter do dar tu'n, but de belly, hit ain't."

"What—are you sick?" asked Cynthia, with interest, rising from the table.

Uncle Isam sighed. "I'se got a tur'able peskey feelin', Miss Cynthy, dat's de gospel trufe," he returned. "I dunno whur hit's de lungs er de liver, but one un um done got moughty sassy ter de yuther 'en he done flung de reins right loose. Hit looks pow'ful like dey wuz gwine ter run twel dey bofe drap down daid, so I done come all dis way atter a dose er dem bitters ole miss use ter gin us befo' de wah."

"Well, I never!" said Cynthia, laughing. "I believe he means the brown bitters mother used to make for chills and fever. I'm very sorry, Uncle Isam, but we haven't any. We don't keep it any longer."

Leaning over his gnarled palms, the old man shook his head is sober reverie.

"Dar ain' nuttin' like dem bitters in dese yer days," he reflected sadly; "'caze de smell er dem use ter mos' knock you flat 'fo' you done taste 'em, en all de way ter de belly dey use ter keep a-wukin' fur dey livin'. Lawd! Lawd! I'se done bought de biggest bottle er sto' stuff in de sto', en hit slid right spang down 'fo' I got a grip er de taste er hit."

"I'll tell you how to mix it," said Cynthia sympathetically. "It's very easy; I know Aunt Eve can brew it."

"Go 'way, Miss Cynthy; huccome you don' know better'n dat? Dar ain' no Eve. She's done gone."

"Gone! Is she dead?"

"Naw'm, she ain' daid dat I knows—she's des gone. Hit all come along er dem highfalutin' notions dat's struttin' roun' dese days 'bout prancin' up de chu'ch aisle en bein' mah'ed by de preacher, stedder des totin' all yo' belongin's f'om one cabin ter anurr, en roas'in' yo' ash-cake in de same pile er ashes. You see, me en Eve we hed done 'sperunce mah'age gwine on fifty years, but we ain' nuver 'sperunce de ceremony twel las' watermillion time."

"Why, Uncle Isam, did she leave you because of that? Here, draw up to the table and eat your supper, while I get down the age-book and find your birth."

She reached for a dusty account book on one of the kitchen shelves, and, bringing it to the table, began slowly turning the yellowed leaves. For more than two hundred years the births of all the Blake slaves had been entered in the big volume.

"You des wait, Miss Cynthy, you des wait twel I git dar," remonstrated Uncle Isam, as he stirred his coffee. "I ain' got no use fur dese yer newfangle fashions, dat's w'at I tell de chillun w'en dey begin a-pesterin' me ter mah'y Eve—I ain' got no use fur dem no way hit's put—I ain' got no use fur dis yer struttin' up de aisle bus'ness, ner fur dis yer w'arin' er sto'-made shoes, ner fur dis yer leavin' er de hyar unwropped, needer. Hit looks pisonous tickly ter me, dat's w'at I sez, but w'en dey keep up dey naggin' day in en day out, en I carn' git shunt er um, I hop right up en put on my Sunday bes' en go 'long wid 'em ter de chu'ch—me en Eve bofe a-mincin' des like peacocks. 'You des pay de preacher,' dat's wat I tell 'em, 'en I'se gwine do all de mah'yin' dat's ter be done'; en w'en de preacher done got thoo wid me en Eve, I stood right up in de chu'ch an axed ef dey wus any udder nigger 'ooman es 'ud like ter do a little mah'yin'? 'Hit's es easy ter mah'y a dozen es ter mah'y one,' I holler out."

"Oh, Uncle Isam! No wonder Aunt Eve was angry. Here we are—'Isam, son of Docia, born August 12, 18—.'"

"Lawd, Miss Cynthy, 'twan' me dat mek Eve mad—twuz de preacher, 'caze atter we got back ter de cabin en eat de watermillion ter de rin', she up en tied her bonnet on tight es a chestnut burr en made right fur de do'. De preacher done tole 'er, she sez, dat Eve 'uz in subjection ter her husban', en she'd let 'im see she warn' gwine be subjected unner no man, she warn't. 'Fo' de Lawd, Miss Cynthy, dat ar Eve sutney wuz a high-sperited 'ooman!"

"But, Uncle Isam, it was so silly. Why, she'd been married to you already for a lifetime."

"Dat's so, Miss Cynthy, dat's so, 'caze 'twuz dem ar wuds dat rile 'er mos'. She 'low she done been in subjection fur gwine on fifty years widout knowin' hit."

He finished his coffee at a gulp and leaned back in his chair.

"En now des lemme hyear how ole I is," he wound up sorrowfully.

"The twelfth of August, 18— (that's the date of your birth), makes you—let me see—you'll be seventy years old next summer. There, now, since you've found out what you wanted, you'd better spend the night with Uncle Boaz."

"Thanky, ma'am, but I mus' be gwine back agin," responded Uncle Isam, shuffling to his feet, "en ef you don' min', Marse Christopher, I'd like a wud wid you outside de do'."

Laughing, Christopher rose from his chair and, with a patriarchal dignity of manner, followed the old man into the moonlight.

CHAPTER VI

CARRAWAY PLAYS COURTIER

AT TWELVE o'clock the next day, Carraway, walking in the June brightness along the road to the Blake cottage, came suddenly, at the bend of the old ice-pond, upon Maria Fletcher returning from a morning ride. The glow of summer was in her eyes, and though her face was still pale, she seemed to him a different creature from the grave, repressed girl of the night before. He noticed at once that she sat her horse superbly, and in her long black habit all the sinuous lines of her figure moved in rhythm with the rapid pace.

As she neared him, and apparently before she had noticed his approach, he saw her draw rein quickly, and, screened by the overhanging boughs of a blossoming chestnut, send her glance like a hooded falcon across the neighbouring field. Following the aim of her look, he saw Christopher Blake walking idly among the heavy furrows, watching, with the interest of a born agriculturist, the busy transplanting of Fletcher's crop. He still wore his jean clothes, which, hanging loosely upon his impressive figure, blended harmoniously with the dull-purple tones of the upturned soil. Beyond him there was a background of distant wood, still young in leaf, and his bared head, with the strong, sunburned line of his profile, stood out as distinctly as a portrait done in early Roman gold.

That Maria had seen in him some higher possibility than that of a field labourer was soon evident to Carraway, for her horse was still standing on the slight incline, and as he reached her side she turned with a frank question on her lips.

"Is that one of the labourers—the young giant by the fence?"

"Well, I dare say he labours, if that's what you mean. He's young Blake, you know."

"Young Blake?" She bent her brows, and it was clear that the name suggested only a trivial recollection to her mind. "There used to be some Blake children in the old overseer's house—is this one of them."

"Possibly; they live in the overseer's house."

She leaned over, fastening her heavy gauntlet. "They wouldn't play with me, I remember; I couldn't understand why. Once I carried my dolls over to their yard, and the boy set a pack of hounds on me. I screamed so that an old negro ran out and drove them off, and all the time the boy stood by, laughing and calling me names. Is that he, do you think?"

"I dare say. It sounds like him."

"Is he so cruel?" she asked a little wistfully.

"I don't know about that—but he doesn't like your people. Your grandfather had some trouble with him a long time ago."

"And he wanted to punish me?—how cowardly."

"It does sound rather savage, but it isn't an ordinary case, you know. He's the kind of person to curse 'root and branch,' from all I hear, in the good old Biblical fashion.''

"Oh, well, he's certainly very large, isn't he?"

"He's superb," said Carraway, with conviction.

"At a distance—so is that great pine over there," she lifted her whip and pointed across the field; then as Carraway made no answer, she smiled slightly and rode rapidly toward the Hall.

For a few minutes the lawyer stood where she had left him, watching in puzzled thought her swaying figure on the handsome horse. The girl fretted him, and yet he felt that he liked her almost in spite of himself—liked something fine and fearless he found in her dark eyes; liked, too, even while he sneered her peculiar grace of manner. There was the making of a woman in her after all, he told himself, as he turned into the sunken road, where he saw Christopher already moving homeward. He had meant to catch up with him and join company on the way, but the young man covered ground so quickly with his great strides that at last Carraway, losing sight of him entirely, resigned himself to going leisurely about his errand.

When, a little later, he opened the unhinged white-washed gate before the cottage, the place, as he found it, seemed to be tenanted solely by a family of young turkeys scratching beneath the damask rose-bushes in the yard. From a rear chimney a dark streak of smoke was rising, but the front of the house gave no outward sign of life, and as there came no answer to his insistent knocks he at last ventured to open the door and pass into the narrow hall. From the first room on the right a voice spoke at his entrance, and following the sound he found himself face to face with Mrs. Blake in her massive Elizabethan chair.

"There is a stranger in the room," she said rigidly, turning her sightless eyes; "speak at once."

"I beg pardon most humbly for my intrusion," replied Carraway, conscious of stammering like an offending schoolboy, "but as no one answered my knock, I committed the indiscretion of opening a closed door."

Awed as much by the stricken pallor of her appearance as by the inappropriate grandeur of her black brocade and her thread lace cap, he advanced slowly and stood awaiting his dismissal.

"What door?" she demanded sharply, much to his surprise.

"Yours, madam."

"Not answer your knock?" she pursued, with indignation. " So that was the noise I heard, and no wonder that you entered. Why, what is the matter with the place? Where are the servants?"

He humbly replied that he had seen none, to be taken up with her accustomed quickness of touch.

"Seen none! Why, there are three hundred of them, sir. Well, well, this is really too much. I shall put a butler over Boaz this very day."

For an instant Carraway felt strangely tempted to turn and run as fast as he could along the sunken road—remembering, as he struggled with the impulse, that he had once been caught at the age of ten and whipped for stealing apples. Recovering with an effort his sense of dignity, he offered the suggestion that Boaz, instead of being seriously in fault, might merely have been engaged in useful occupations "somewhere at the back."

"What on earth can he have to do at the back, sir?" inquired the irrepressible old lady; "but since you were so kind as to overlook our inhospitable reception, will you not be equally good and tell me your name?"

"I fear it won't enlighten you much," replied the lawyer modestly, "but my name happens to be Guy Carraway."

"Guy—Guy Carraway," repeated Mrs. Blake, as if weighing each separate letter in some remote social scales. "I've known many a Guy in my day—and that part, at least, of your name is quite familiar. There was Guy Nelson, and Guy Blair, and Guy Marshall, the greatest beau of his time—but I don't think I ever had the pleasure of meeting a Carraway before."

"That is more than probable, ma'am, but I have the advantage of you, since, as a child, I was once taken out upon the street corner merely to see you go by on your way to a fancy ball, where you appeared as Diana."

Mrs. Blake yielded gracefully to the skilful thrust. "Ah, I was Lucy Corbin then," she sighed. "You find few traces of her in me now, sir."

"Unfortunately, your mirror cannot speak for me." She shook her head.

"You're a flatterer—a sad flatterer, I see," she returned, a little wistfully; "but it does no harm, as I tell my son, to flatter the old. It is well to strew the passage to the grave with flowers."

"How well I remember that day," said Carraway, speaking softly. "There was a crowd about the door,

waiting to see you come out, and a carpenter lifted
me upon his shoulder. Your hair was as black as
night, and there was a circle round your head——"

"A silver fillet," she corrected, with a smile in
which there was a gentle archness.

"A fillet, yes; and you carried a bow and a quiver
full of arrows. I declare, it seems but yesterday."

"It was more than fifty years ago," murmured the
old lady. "Well, well, I've had my day, sir, and it
was a merry one. I am almost seventy years old—
I'm half dead, and stone blind into the bargain, but I
can say to you that this is a cheerful world in spite of
the darkness in which I linger on. I'd take it over
again and gladly any day—the pleasure and the pain,
the light and the darkness. Why, I sometimes think
that my present blindness was given me in order that
I might view the past more clearly. There's not a
ball of my youth, nor a face I knew, nor even a dress
I wore, that I don't see more distinctly every day.
The present is a very little part of life, sir; it's the past
in which we store our treasures."

"You're right, you're right," replied Carraway,
drawing his chair nearer the embroidered ottoman
and leaning over to stroke the yellow cat; "and I'm
glad to hear so cheerful a philosophy from your lips."

"It is based on a cheerful experience—I've been as
you see me now only twenty years."

Only twenty years! He looked mutely round the
soiled whitewashed walls, where hung a noble gathering of Blake portraits in massive old gilt frames.
Among them he saw the remembered face of Lucy
Corbin herself, painted under a rose-garland held by
smiling Loves.

"Life has its trials, of course," pursued Mrs. Blake, as if speaking to herself. "I can't look out upon the June flowers, you know, and though the pink crape-myrtle at my window is in full bloom I cannot see it."

Following her gesture, Carraway glanced out into the little yard; no myrtle was there, but he remembered vaguely that he had seen one in blossom at the Hall.

"You keep flowers about you, though," he said, alluding to the scattered vases of June roses.

"Not my crape-myrtle. I planted it myself when I first came home with Mr. Blake, and I have never allowed so much as a spray of it to be plucked."

Forgetting his presence, she lapsed for a time into one of the pathetic day-dreams of old age. Then recalling herself suddenly, her tone took on a sprightliness like that of youth.

"It's not often that we have the pleasure of entertaining a stranger in our out-of-the-way house, sir— so may I ask where you are staying—or perhaps you will do us the honour to sleep beneath our roof. It has had the privilege of sheltering General Washington."

"You are very kind," replied Carraway, with a gratitude that was from his heart, "but to tell the truth, I feel that I am sailing under false colours. The real object of my visit is to ask a business interview with your son. I bring what seems to me a very fair offer for the place."

Grasping the carved arms of her chair, Mrs. Blake turned the wonder in her blind eyes upon him.

"An offer for the place! Why, you must be dreaming, sir! A Blake owned it more than a hundred years before the Revolution."

At the instant, understanding broke upon Carraway like a thundercloud, and as he rose from his seat it seemed to him that he had missed by a single step the yawning gulf before him. Blind terror gripped him for the moment, and when his brain steadied he looked up to meet, from the threshold of the adjoining room, the enraged flash of Christopher's eyes. So tempestuous was the glance that Carraway, impulsively falling back, squared himself to receive a physical blow; but the young man, without so much as the expected oath, came in quietly and took his stand behind the Elizabethan chair.

"Why, what a joke, mother," he said, laughing; "he means the old Weatherby farm, of course. The one I wanted to sell last year, you know."

"I thought you'd sold it to the Weatherbys, Christopher."

"Not a bit of it—they backed out at the last; but don't begin to bother your head about such things; they aren't worth it. And now, sir," he turned upon Carraway, "since your business is with me, perhaps you will have the goodness to step outside."

With the feeling that he was asked out for a beating, Carraway turned for a farewell with Mrs. Blake, but the imperious old lady was not to be so lightly defrauded of a listener.

"Business may come later, my son," she said, detaining them by a gesture of her heavily ringed hand. "After dinner you may take Mr. Carraway with you into the library and discuss your affairs over a bottle of burgundy, as was your grandfather's custom before you; meanwhile, he and I will resume our very pleasant talk which you interrupted. He remembers seeing me in the old days when we were all in the United States, my dear."

Christopher's brow grew black, and he threw a sharp and malignant glance of sullen suspicion at Carraway, who summoned to meet it his most frank and open look.

"I saw your mother in the height of her fame," he said, smiling, "so I may count myself one of her oldest admirers, I believe. You may assure yourself," he added softly, "that I have her welfare very decidedly at heart."

At this Christopher smiled back at him, and there was something of the June brightness in his look.

"Well, take care, sir," he answered, and went out, closing the door carefully behind him, while Carraway applied himself to a determined entertaining of Mrs. Blake.

To accomplish this he found that he had only to leave her free, guiding her thoughts with his lightest touch into newer channels. The talk had grown merrier now, and he soon discovered that she possessed a sharpened wit as well as a ready tongue. From subject to subject she passed with amazing swiftness, bearing down upon her favourite themes with the delightful audacity of the talker who is born, not made. She spoke of her own youth, of historic flirtations in the early twenties, of great *beaux* she had known, and of famous recipes that had been handed down for generations. Everywhere he felt her wonderful keenness of perception—that intuitive understanding of men and manners which had kept her for so long the reigning belle among her younger rivals.

As she went on he found that her world was as different from his own as if she dwelt upon some undiscovered planet—a world peopled with shades and governed by an ideal group of abstract laws. She lived upon lies, he saw, and thrived upon the sweetness she extracted from them. For her the Confederacy had never fallen, the quiet of her dreamland had been disturbed by no invading army, and the three hundred slaves, who had in reality scattered like chaff before the wind, she still saw in her cheerful visions tilling her familiar fields. It was as if she had fallen asleep with the great blow that had wrecked her body, and had dreamed on steadily throughout the years. Of real changes she was as ignorant as a new-born child. Events had shaken the world to its centre, and she, by her obscure hearth, had not felt so much as a sympathetic tremor. In her memory there was no Appomattox, news of the death of Lincoln had never reached her ears, and president had peacefully succeeded president in the secure Confederacy in which she lived. Wonderful as it all was, to Carraway the most wonderful thing was the intricate tissue of lies woven around her chair. Lies —lies—there had been nothing but lies spoken within her hearing for twenty years.

CHAPTER VII

In Which a Stand Is Made

THE wonder was still upon him when Docia appeared bearing her mistress's dinner-tray, and a moment later Cynthia came in and paused uncertainly near the threshold.

"Do you wish anything, mother?"

"Only to present Mr. Carraway, my child. He will be with us at dinner."

Cynthia came forward smiling and held out her hand with the cordial hospitality which she had inherited with the family portraits and the good old name. She wore this morning a dress of cheap black calico, shrunken from many washings, and beneath the scant sleeves Carraway saw her thin red wrists, which looked as if they had been soaking in harsh soapsuds. Except for a certain ease of manner which she had not lost in the drudgery of her life, she might have been sister to the toilworn slattern he had noticed in one of the hovels across the country.

"We shall be very glad to have you," she said, with quiet dignity. "It is ready now, I think."

"Be sure to make him try the port, Cynthia," called Mrs. Blake, as Carraway followed the daughter across the threshold.

In the kitchen they found Tucker and Lila and a

75

strange young man in overalls, who was introduced
as "one of the Weatherbys who live just up the
road." He was evidently one of their plainer neighbours, for Carraway detected at once a constraint in
Cynthia's manner which Lila did not appear to share.
The girl, dressed daintily in a faded muslin, with an
organdy kerchief crossed over her swelling bosom,
flashed upon Carraway's delighted vision like one of
the maidens hanging, gilt-framed, in the old lady's
parlour. That she was the particular pride of the
family—the one luxury they allowed themselves
besides their costly mother—the lawyer realised upon
the instant. Her small white hands were unsoiled by
any work, and her beautiful, kindly face had none of
the nervous dread which seemed always lying behind
Cynthia's tired eyes. With the high devotion of a
martyr, the elder sister must have offered herself a
willing sacrifice, winning for the younger an existence
which, despite its gray monotony, showed fairly
rose-coloured in comparison with her own. She
herself had sunk to the level of a servant, but through
it all Lila had remained "the lady," preserving an
equable loveliness to which Jim Weatherby hardly
dared lift his wistful gaze.

As for the young man himself, he had a blithe, open
look which Carraway found singularly attractive—
the kind of look it warms one's heart to meet in the
long road on a winter's day. Leaning idly against
the lintel of the door, and fingering a bright axe which
he was apparently anxious that they should retain,
he presented a pleasant enough picture to the attentive eyes within the kitchen.

"You'd as well keep this axe as long as you want it,"

he protested earnestly. "It's an old one, anyway, that I sharpened when you asked for it, and we've another at home; that's all we need."

"It's very kind of you, Jim, but ours is mended now," replied Cynthia, a trifle stiffly.

"If we need one again, we'll certainly borrow yours," added Lila, smiling as she looked up from the glasses she was filling with fresh buttermilk.

"Sit down, Jim, and have dinner with us; there's no hurry," urged Tucker hospitably, with a genial wave toward the meagerly spread table. "Jim's a great fellow, Mr. Carraway; you ought to know him. He can manage anything from a Sunday-school to the digging of a well. I've always said that if he'd had charge of the children of Israel's journey to the promised land he'd have had them there, flesh-pots and all, before the week was up."

"I can see he is a useful neighbour," observed Carraway, glancing at the axe.

"Well, I'm glad I come handy," replied Jim in his hearty way; "and are you sure you don't want me to split up that big oak log at the woodpile? I can do it in a twinkling."

Cynthia declined his knightly offer, to be overruled again by Lila's smiling lips.

"Christopher will have to do it when he comes in," she said; "poor Christopher, he never has a single moment of his own."

Jim Weatherby looked at her eagerly, his blue eyes full of sparkle. "Why, I can do it in no time," he declared, shouldering his axe, and a moment afterward they heard his merry strokes from the woodpile.

"Are you interested in tobacco, Mr. Carraway?"

inquired Tucker, as they seated themselves at the
pine table without so much as an apology for the
coarseness of the fare or an allusion to their fallen
fortunes. "If so, you've struck us at the time when
every man about here is setting out his next winter's
chew. Sol Peterkin, by the way, has planted every
square inch of his land in tobacco, and when I
asked him what market he expected to send it to he
answered that he only raised a little for his own use."

"Is that the Peterkin who has the pretty daughter?"
asked Cynthia, slicing a piece of bacon. "May I
help you to turnip salad, Mr. Carraway?" Uncle
Boaz, hobbling with rheumatism, held out a quaint
old tray of inlaid woods; and the lawyer, as he placed
his plate upon it, heaved a sigh of gratitude for the
utter absence of vulgarity. He could fancy dear old
Miss Saidie puffing apologies over the fat bacon, and
Fletcher profanely deploring the sloppy coffee.

"The half-grown girl with the bunch of flaxen curls
tied with a blue ribbon?" returned Tucker, while
Lila cut up his food as if he were a child. "Yes,
that's Molly Peterkin, though it's hard to believe she's
any kin to Sol. I shouldn't wonder if she turned
into a bouncing beauty a few years further on."

"It was her father, then, that I walked over with
from the cross-roads," said Carraway. "He struck
me as a shrewd man of his sort."

"Oh, he's shrewd enough," rejoined Tucker, "and
the proof of it is that he's outlived three wives and is
likely to outlive a fourth. I met him in the road
yesterday, and he told me that he had just been off
again to get married. 'Good luck to you this time,
Sol', said I. 'Wall, it ought to be, sir,' said he, 'see-

ing as marrying has got to be so costly in these days. Why, my first wife didn't come to more than ten dollars, counting the stovepipe hat and all, and this last one 's mounted up to 'most a hundred.' 'Try and take good care of her, then,' I cautioned; 'they come too high to throw away.' 'That's true, sir,' he answered, with a sorrowful shake of his head. 'But the trouble is that as the price goes up the quality gets poorer. My first one lasted near on to thirty years, and did all the chores about the house, to say nothing of the hog-pen; and if you'll believe me, sir, the one before this struck at the hog-feeding on her wedding day, and then wore out before twelve months were up.'"

He finished with his humorous chuckle and lifted his fork skilfully in his left hand.

"I dare say he overvalues himself as a husband," remarked Carraway, joining in the laugh, "but he has at least the merit of being loyal to your family."

"Well, I believe he has; but then, he doesn't like new folks or new things, I reckon. There's a saying that his hatred of changes keeps him from ever changing his clothes."

Christopher came in at the moment, and with a slight bow to Carraway, slipped into his place.

"What's Jim Weatherby chopping up that log for?" he asked, glancing in the direction of the ringing strokes.

Cynthia looked at him almost grimly, and there was a contraction of the muscles about her determined mouth.

"Ask Lila," she responded quietly. As Christopher's questioning gaze turned to her, Lila flushed rose-pink and played nervously with the bread-crumbs on the table.

"He said he had nothing else to do," she answered, with an effort, "and he knew you were so busy—that was all."

"Well, he's a first rate fellow," commented Christopher, as he reached for the pitcher of buttermilk, "but I don't see what makes him so anxious to do my work."

"Oh, that's Jim's way, you know," put in Tucker with his offhand kindliness. "He's the sort of old maid who would undertake to straighten the wilderness if he could get the job. Why, I actually found him once chopping off dead boughs in the woods, and when I laughed he excused himself by saying that he couldn't bear to see trees look so scraggy."

As he talked, his pleasant pale blue eyes twinkled with humour, and his full double chin shook over his shirt of common calico. He had grown very large from his long inaction, and it was with a perceptible effort that he moved himself upon his slender crutches. Yet despite his maimed and suffering body he was dressed with a scrupulous neatness which was almost like an air of elegance. As he chatted on easily, Carraway forgot, in listening to him, the harrowing details in the midst of which he sat—forgot the over-heated, smoky kitchen, the common pine table with its broken china, and the sullen young savage whom he faced.

For Christopher was eating his dinner hurriedly, staring at his plate in a moodiness which he did not take the trouble to conceal. With all the youthful beauty of his face, there was a boorishness in his ill-humour which in a less commanding figure would have been repellent—an evident pride in the sincerity of the scowl upon his brow.

When his meal was over he rose with a muttered excuse and went out into the yard, where a few minutes afterward Carraway was bold enough to follow him.

The afternoon was golden with sunshine, and every green leaf on the trees seemed to stand out clearly against the bright blue sky. In the rear of the house there was a lack of the careful cleanliness he had noticed at the front, and rotting chips from the woodpile strewed the short grass before the door, where a clump of riotous ailanthus shoots was waging a desperate battle for existence. Beside the sunken wooden step a bare brown patch showed where the daily splashes of hot soapsuds had stripped the ground of even the modest covering that it wore. Within a stone's throw of the threshold the half of a broken wheelbarrow, white with mould, was fast crumbling into earth, and a little farther off stood a disorderly group of chicken coops before which lay a couple of dead nestlings. On the soaking plank ledge around the well-brink, where fresh water was slopping from the overturned bucket, several bedraggled ducks were paddling with evident enjoyment. The one pleasant sight about the place was the sturdy figure of Jim Weatherby, still at work upon the giant body of a dead oak tree.

When Carraway came out, Christopher was feeding a pack of hounds from a tin pan of coarse corn bread, and to the lawyer's surprise he was speaking to them in a tone that sounded almost jocular. Though born of a cringing breed, the dogs looked contented and well fed, and among them Carraway recognised his friend Spy, who had followed at the heels of Uncle Boaz.

"Here, Miser, this is yours," the young man was saying. "There, you needn't turn up your nose; it's as big as Blister's. Down, Spy, I tell you; you've had twice your share; you think because you're the best looking you're to be the best fed, too."

As Carraway left the steps the dogs made an angry rush at him, to be promptly checked by Christopher.

"Back, you fools; back, I say. You'd better be careful how you walk about here, sir," he added; "they'd bite as soon as not—all of them except Spy."

"Good fellow, Spy," returned Carraway, a little nervously, and the hound came fawning to his feet. "I assure you I have no intention of treading upon their preserves," he hastened to explain; "but I should like a word with you, and this seems to be the only opportunity I'll have, as I return to town to-morrow."

Christopher threw the remaining pieces of corn bread into the wriggling pack, set the pan in the doorway, and wiped his hands carelessly upon his overalls.

"Well, I don't see what you've got to say to me," he replied, walking rapidly in the direction of the well, where he waited for the other to join him.

"It's about the place, of course," returned the lawyer, with an attempt to shatter the awkward rustic reserve. "I understand that it has passed into your possession."

The young man nodded, and, drawing out his clasp-knife, fell to whittling a splinter which he had broken from the well-brink.

"In that case," pursued Carraway, feeling as if he were dashing his head against a wall, "I shall address myself to you in the briefest terms. The place, I suppose, as it stands, is not worth much to-day. Even good land is cheap, and this is poor."

Again Christopher nodded, intent upon his whittling. "I reckon it wouldn't bring more than nine hundred," he responded coolly.

"Then my position is easy, for I am sure you will consider favourably the chance to sell at treble its actual value. I am authorised to offer you three thousand dollars for the farm."

For a moment Christopher stared at him in silence, then, "What in the devil do you want with it?" he demanded.

"I am not acting for myself in the matter," returned the lawyer, after a short hesitation. "The offer is made through me by another. That it is to your advantage to accept it is my honest conviction."

Christopher tossed the bit of wood at a bedraggled drake that waddled off, quacking angrily.

"Then it's Fletcher behind you," he said in the same cool tones.

"It seems to me that is neither here nor there. Naturally Mr. Fletcher is very anxious to secure the land. As it stands, it is a serious inconvenience to him, of course.

Laughing, Christopher snapped the blade of his knife.

"Well, you may tell him from me," he retorted,

"that just as long as it is 'a serious inconvenience to him' it shall stand as it is. Why, man, if Fletcher wanted that broken wheelbarrow enough to offer me three thousand dollars for it, I wouldn't let him have it. The only thing I'd leave him free to take, if I could help it, is the straight road to damnation!"

His voice, for all the laughter, sounded brutal, and Carraway, gazing at him in wonder, saw his face grow suddenly lustful like that of an evil deity. The beauty was still there, blackened and distorted, a beauty that he felt to be more sinister than ugliness. The lawyer was in the presence of a great naked passion, and involuntarily he lowered his eyes.

"I don't think he understands your attitude," he said quietly; "it seems to him—and to me also, I honestly affirm—that you would reap an advantage as decided as his own."

"Nothing is to my advantage, I tell you, that isn't harm to him. He knows it if he isn't as big a fool as he is a rascal."

"Then I may presume that you are entirely convinced in your own mind that you have a just cause for the stand you take?"

"Cause!" the word rapped out like an oath. "He stole my home, I tell you; he stole every inch of land I owned, and every penny. Where did he get the money to buy the place—he a slave-overseer? Where did he get it, I ask, unless he had been stealing for twenty years?"

"It looks ugly, I confess," admitted Carraway; "but were there no books—no accounts kept?"

"Oh, he settled that, of course. When my father died, and we asked for the books, where were they?

Burned, he said—burned in the old office that the
Yankees fired. He's a scoundrel, I tell you,
sir, and I know him to the core. He's a rotten
scoundrel!"

Carraway caught his breath quickly and drew
back as if he had touched unwittingly a throbbing
canker. To his oversensitive nature these primal
emotions had a crudeness that was vulgar in its unre-
straint. He beheld it all—the old wrong and the
new hatred—in a horrid glare of light, a disgraceful
blaze of trumpets. Here there was no cultured
evasion of the conspicuous vice—none of the refinements even of the Christian ethics—it was all raw
and palpitating humanity.

"Then my mission is quite useless," he confessed.
"I can only add that I am sorrier than I can say—
sorry for the whole thing, too. If my services could
be of any use to you I should not hesitate to offer
them, but so far as I see there is absolutely nothing
to be done. An old crime, as you know, very often
conforms to an appearance of virtue."

He held out his hand, Christopher shook it, and
then the lawyer went back into the house to bid
good-by to Mrs. Blake. When he came out a few
moments later, and passed through the whitewashed
gate into the sunken road, he saw that Christopher
was still standing where he had left him, the golden
afternoon around him, and the bedraggled ducks
paddling at his feet.

burial places, but he climbed the old moss-grown
wall, where poisonous ivy grew rank and venomous,
and landing deep in the periwinkle that carpeted
the ground, made his way rapidly to the flat oblong
slab beneath which his father lay. The marble was
discoloured by long rains and stained with bruised
periwinkle, and the shallow lettering was hidden
under a fall of dried needles from a little stunted
fir-tree; but, leaning over, he carefully swept the
dust away and loosened the imprisoned name which
seemed to hover like a spiritual presence upon the
air.

"HERE LIES ALL THAT IS MORTAL

OF

CHRISTOPHER BLAKE,

WHO DIED IN THE HOPE OF A JOYFUL

RESURRECTION,

APRIL 12, 186–, AGED 70 YEARS.

INTO THY HANDS, O LORD, I COMMIT MY SPIRIT."

Around him there were other graves—graves of
all dead Blakes for two hundred years, and the flat
tombstones were crowded so thickly together that it
seemed as if the dead must lie beneath them row on
row. It was all in deep shadow, fallen slabs, rank
periwinkle, dust and mould—no cheerful sunshine
had ever penetrated through the spreading cedars
overhead. Life was here, but it was the shy life of
wild creatures, approaching man only when he had
returned to earth. A mocking-bird purled a love
note in the twilight of a great black cedar, a lizard
glided like a gray shadow along one of the overturned

slabs, and at his entrance a rabbit had started from the ivy on his father's grave. To climb the overgrown wall and lie upon the periwinkle was like entering, for a time, the world of shades—a world far removed from the sunny meadow and the low green hill.

With his head pillowed upon his father's grave, Christopher stretched himself at full length on the ground and stared straight upward at the dark-browed cedars. It was such an hour as he allowed himself at long intervals when his inheritance was heavy upon him and his disordered mind needed to retreat into a city of refuge. As a child he had often come to this same spot to dream hopefully of the future—unboylike dreams in which the spirit of revenge wore the face of happiness. Then, with the inconsequence of childhood, he had pictured Fletcher gasping beneath his feet—trampled out like a worm, when he was big enough to take his vengeance and come again into his own. Mere physical strength seemed to him at that age the sole thing needed—he wanted then only the brawny arm and the heart bound by triple brass.

Now, as he stretched out his square, sunburned hand, with its misshapen nails, he laughed aloud at the absurdity of those blunted hopes. To-day he stood six feet three inches from the ground, with muscles hard as steel and a chest that rang sound as a bell, yet how much nearer his purpose had he been as a little child! He remembered the day that he had hidden in the bushes with his squirrel gun and waited with fluttering breath for the sound of Fletcher's footsteps along the road. On that day it had seemed

to him that the hand of the Lord was in his own—
Godlike vengeance nerving his little wrist.   He had
meant to shoot—for that he had saved every stray
penny from his sales of hogs and cider, of water-
melons and chinkapins; for that he had bought
the gun and rammed the powder home.   Even when
the thud of footsteps beat down the sunny road
strewn with brown honeyshucks, he had felt neither
fear nor hesitation as he crouched amid the under-
brush.   Rather there was a rare exhilaration, warm
blood in his brain and a sharp taste in his mouth like
that of unripe fruit—as if he had gorged himself upon
the fallen honeyshucks.   It was the happiest moment
of his life, he knew, the one moment when he seemed
to measure himself inch by inch with fate; and like
all such supreme instants, it fell suddenly flat among
the passing hours.   For even as the gun was lifted,
at the very second that Fletcher's heavy body swung
into view, he heard a crackling in the dead bushes at
his back, and Uncle Boaz struck up his arm with a
palsied hand.

"Gawd alive, honey, you don' wanter be tucken
out an' hunged?" the old man cried in terror.

The boy rose in a passion and flung his useless gun
aside.   " Oh, you've spoiled it ! you've spoiled it !" he
sobbed, and shed bitter tears upon the ground.

To this hour, lying on his father's grave, he knew
that he regretted that wasted powder—that will to
slay which had blazed up and died down so soon.
Strangely enough, it soothed him now to remember
how near to murder he had been, and as he drank the
summer air in deep drafts he felt the old desire
rekindle from its embers.   While he lived it was still

possible—the one chance that awaits the ready hand, the final answer of a sympathetic heaven that deals out justice. His god was a pagan god, terrible rather than tender, and there had always been within him the old pagan scorn of everlasting mercy. There were moods even when he felt the kinship with his savage forefathers working in his blood, and at such times he liked to fit heroic tortures to heroic crimes— to imagine the lighted stake and his enemy amid the flames.

Over him as he lay at full length the ancient cedars, touched here and there with a younger green, reared a dusky tent that screened him alike from the hot sunshine and the bright June sky. Somewhere in the deepest shadow the mocking-bird purled over its single note, and across the lettering on the marble slab beside him a small brown lizard was gliding back and forth. The clean, fresh smell of the cedars filled his nostrils like a balm.

For a moment the physical pleasure in his surroundings possessed his thoughts; then gradually, in a state between waking and sleeping, the curious boughs above took fantastic shapes and were interwoven before his eyes with his earlier memories.

There was a great tester bed, with carved posts and curtains of silvery damask, that he had slept in as a child, and it was here that he had once had a terrible dream—a dream which he had remembered to this day because it was so like a story of Aunt Delisha's, in which the devil comes with a red-hot scuttle to carry off a little boy. On that night he had been the little boy, and he had seen the scuttle with its leaping flames so plainly that in his terror he had struggled up and screamed aloud. A moment later he had awakened fully, to find a lighted candle in his face and his father in a flowered dressing-gown sitting beside the bed and looking at him with his sad, bloodshot eyes.

"Is the devil gone, father, and did you drive him away?" he asked; and then the tall, white-haired old man, whose mind was fast decaying, did a strange and a pitiable thing, for he fell upon his knees beside the bed and cried out upon Christopher for forgiveness for the sefishness of his long life.

"You came too late, my son," he said; "you came twenty years too late. I had given you up long ago and grown hopeless. You came like Isaac to Abraham, but too late—too late!"

The boy sat up in bed, huddling in the bedclothes, for the night was chilly. He grew suddenly afraid of his father, the big, beautiful old man in the flowered dressing-gown, and he wished that his mother would come in and take him away.

"But I came twins with Lila, father," he replied, trying to speak bravely.

"With Lila! Oh, my poor children! my poor children!" cried the old man, and, taking up his candle, tottered to the door. Then Christopher stopped his ears in the pillows, for he heard him moaning to himself as he went back along the hall. He felt all at once terribly frightened, and at last, slipping down the tall bed-steps, he stole on his bare feet to Cynthia's door and crept in beside her.

After this, dim years went by when he did not see his father, and the great closed rooms on the north side of the house were as silent as if a corpse lay there awaiting burial. His beautiful, stately mother, who, in spite of her gray hair, had always seemed but little older than himself, vanished as mysteriously from his sight—on a thrilling morning when there were many waving red flags and much hurried marching by of gray-clad troops. Young as he was, he was already beginning to play his boy's share in a war which was then fighting slowly to a finish; and in the wild flutter of events he forgot, for a time, to do more than tip softly when he crossed the hall. She was ill, they told him—too ill to care even about the battles that were fought across the river. The sound of the big guns sent no delicious shivers through her limbs, and there was only Lila to come with him when he laid his ear to the ground and thrilled with the strong shock which seemed to run around the earth. When at last her door was opened again and he went timidly in, holding hands with Lila, he found his mother sitting stiffly erect among her cushions— as she would sit for the remainder of her days— blind and half-dead, in her Elizabethan chair. His beautiful, proud mother, with the smiling Loves painted above her head!

For an instant he shut his eyes beneath the cedars, seeing her on that morning as a man sees in his dreams the face of his first love. Then another day dawned slowly to his consciousness—a day which stood out clear-cut as a cameo from all the others of his life. For weeks Cynthia's eyes had been red and swollen, and he commented querulously upon them, for they made her homelier than usual. When he had finished, she looked at him a moment without replying, then, putting her arm about him, she drew him out upon the lawn and told him why she wept. It was a mellow autumn day, and they passed over gold and russet leaves strewn deep along the path. A light wind was blowing in the tree-tops, and the leaves were still falling, falling, falling! He saw Cynthia's haggard face in a flame of glowing colours. Through the drumming in his ears, which seemed to come from the clear sky, he heard the ceaseless rustle beneath his feet; and to this day he could not walk along a leaf-strewn road in autumn without seeing again the blur of red-and-gold and the gray misery in Cynthia's face.

"It will kill mother!" he said angrily. "It will kill mother! Why, she almost died when Docia broke her Bohemian bowl."

"She must never know," answered Cynthia, while the tears streamed unheeded down her cheeks. "When she is carried out one day for her airing, she shall go back into the other house. It is a short time now at best—she may die at any moment from any shock—but she must die without knowing this. There must be quiet at the end, at least. Oh, poor mother! poor mother!"

She raised her hands to her convulsed face, and Christopher saw the tears trickle through her thin fingers.

"She must never know," repeated the boy. "She must never know if we can help it."

"We must help it," cried Cynthia passionately. "We must work our fingers to the bone to help it, you and I."

"And Lila?" asked the boy, curiously just even in

the intensity of his emotion. "Mustn't Lila work, too?"

Cynthia sobbed—hard, strangling sobs that rattled like stones within her bosom.

"Lila is only a girl," she said, "and so pretty, so pretty."

The boy nodded.

"Then don't let's make Lila work," he responded sturdily.

Selfish in her supreme unselfishness, the woman turned and kissed his brow, while he struggled, irritated, to keep her off.

"Don't let's, dear," she said, and that was all.

CHAPTER IX

CYNTHIA

As soon as Christopher had passed out of sight, Cynthia came from the kitchen with an armful of wet linen and began spreading it upon some scrubby lilac bushes in a corner of the yard. After fifteen years it still made her uncomfortable to have Christopher around when she did the family washing, and when it was possible she waited to dry the clothes until he had gone back to the field. In her scant calico dress, with the furrows of age already settling about her mouth, and her pale brown hair strained in thin peaks back from her forehead, she might have stood as the world-type of toil-worn womanhood, for she was of the stuff of martyrs, and the dignity of their high resolve was her one outward grace. Life had been revealed to her as something to be endured rather than enjoyed, and the softer adornments of her sex had not withstood the daily splashes of harsh soapsuds—they had faded like colours too delicate to stand the strain of ordinary use.

As she lifted one of her mother's full white petticoats and turned to wring it dry with her red and blistered hands, a look that was perilously near disgust was on her face—for though she had done her duty heroically and meant to do it until the end, there

were brief moments when it sickened her to desperation. She was the kind of woman whose hands per-
form the more thoroughly because the heart revolts
against the task.

Lila, in her faded muslin which had taken the colours of November leaves, came to the kitchen doorway and stood watching her with a cheerful face.

"Has Jim Weatherby gone, Cynthia?"

Cynthia nodded grimly, turning her squinting gaze
upon her. "Do you think I'd let him see me hanging out the clothes?" she snapped. Supreme as her
unselfishness was, there were times when she appeared
to begrudge the least of her services; and after the
manner of all affection that comes as a bounty, the
unwilling spirit was more impressive than the ready
hand.

"I do wish you would make Docia help you," said
Lila, in a voice that sounded as if she were speaking
in her own defense.

Cynthia wrung out a blue jean shirt of Christopher's,
spread it on an old lilac-bush, and pushed a stray lock
of hair back with her wrist.

"There's no use talking like that when you know
Docia has heart disease and can't scrub the clothes
clean," she responded. "If she'd drop down dead
I'd like to know what we'd do with mother."

"Well, I'd help you if you'd only let me," protested
Lila, on the point of tears. "I've darned your
lavender silk the best I could, and I'd just as soon
iron as not."

"And get your hands like mine in a week. No, I
reckon it's as well for one of us to keep decent. My
hands are so knotted I had to tell mother it was gout

in the joints, and she said I must have been drinking too much port." She laughed, but her eyes filled with tears, and she wiped them with hard rubs on a twisted garment, which she afterward shook in the air to dry.

"Well, you're a saint, Cynthia, and I wish you weren't," declared Lila almost impatiently. "It makes me feel uncomfortable, as if it were somehow my fault that you had to be so good."

"Being a saint is a good deal like being a woman, I reckon," returned Cynthia dryly. "There's a heap in having been born to it. Aunt Polly, have you put the irons on the fire? The first batch of clothes is almost dry."

Aunt Polly, an aged crone, already stumbling into her dotage, hobbled from the kitchen and gathered up an armful of resinous pine from a pile beside the steps. "Dey's 'mos' es hot es de debbil's wooden-iron shovel," she replied, with one foot on the step; adding in a piercing whisper: "I know dat ar shovel, honey, 'caze de debbil he done come fur me in de daid er de night, lookin' moughty peart, too; but I tole 'im he des better bide a,w'ile 'caze I 'uz leanin' sorter favo'bly to'ad de Lawd."

"Aunt Polly, you ought to be ashamed of yourself. Take those irons off and let them cool."

"Dat's so, Miss Cynthy, en I'se right down 'shamed er myse'f, sho' 'nough, but de shame er hit cyarn tu'n de heart er 'ooman. De debbil he sutney did look young en peart, dat he did—en de Lawd He knows, Miss Cynthy, I allers did like 'em young! I 'uz done had nine un um in all, countin' de un—en he wuz Cephus—dat run off 'fo' de mah'age wid my bes' fedder baid made outer de gray goose fedders ole miss done throwed away 'caze dey warn' w'ite. Yes, Lawd, dar's done been nine un um, black en yaller, en dar ain' nuver been en ole 'un in de hull lot. Whew! I ain' nuver stood de taste er nuttin' ole lessen he be a 'possum, en w'en hit comes ter en ole man, I d'clar hit des tu'ns my stomick clean inside out."

"But, Aunt Polly, you're old yourself—it's disgraceful."

Aunt Polly chuckled with flattered vanity.

"I know I is, honey—I know I is, but I'se gwine ter hev a young husban' at de een ef hit tecks de ve'y las' cent I'se got. De las' un he come monst'ous high, en mo'n dat, he wuz sech en outlandish nigger dat he'd a-come high ef I'd got 'im as a Christmas gif'. I had ter gin 'im dat burey wid de bevel glass I bought wid all my savin's, en des es soon es I steps outside de do' he up en toted hit all de way ter de cabin er dat low-lifeted, savigorous, yaller hussy Delphy. Men sutney are tuh'ble slippery folks, Miss Cynthy, en y'all des better look out how you monkey wid 'em, 'caze I'se done hed nine, en I knows 'em thoo en thoo. De mo' you git, de likelier 'tis you gwine git one dat's worth gittin', dat's w'at I 'low."

Cynthia gathered up the scattered garments, which had been left carelessly from the day before, and carried them into the kitchen, where a pine ironing-board was supported by two empty barrels. Lila was busily preparing a bowl of gruel for one of the sick old negroes who still lived upon the meager charity of the Blakes.

"Mother wants you, Cynthia," she said. "I won't do at all, for she can't be persuaded that I'm really grown up, you know. Here, give me some of those clothes. It won't hurt my hands a bit."

Cynthia piled the clothes upon the board, and moistening her finger, applied it to the bottom of the iron. Then she handed it to Lila with a funny little air of anxiety. "This is just right," she said; "be careful not to get your fingers burned, and remember to sprinkle the clothes well. Do you know what mother wants?"

"I think it's about taking something to Aunt Dinah. Docia told her she was sick."

"Then I wish Docia would learn to hold her tongue," commented Cynthia, as she left the kitchen.

She found Mrs. Blake looking slightly irritated as she wound a ball of white yarn from a skein that Docia was holding between her outstretched hands.

"I hear Dinah is laid up with a stitch in her chest, Cynthia," she said. "You must look in the medicine closet and give her ten grains of quinine and a drink of whisky. Tell her to keep well covered up, and see that Polly makes her hot flaxseed tea every two hours."

"Lila is fixing her some gruel now, mother."

"I said flaxseed tea, my dear. I am almost seventy years old, and I have treated three hundred servants and seen sixty laid in their graves, but if you think you are a better doctor than I am, of course there's nothing to be said. Docia, hold the yarn a little tighter."

"We'll make the flaxseed tea at once, and I'll carry it right over—a breath of air will do me good."

Mrs. Blake sighed. "You mustn't stay too closely with me," she said; "you will grow old before your

time, I fear.   As it is you have given up your young
life to my poor old one."

"I had nothing to give up, mother," replied Cynthia
quietly, and in the few words her heart's tragedy was
written—since of all lives, the saddest is the one that
can find nothing worthy of renouncement.   There
were hours when she felt that any bitter personal
past—that the recollection of a single despairing
kiss or a blighted love would have filled her days with
happiness.   What she craved was the conscious
dignity of a broken heart—some lofty memory that
she might rest upon in her hours of weakness.

"Well, you might have had, my child," returned her
mother.

Cynthia's only answer was to smooth gently the
pillows in the old lady's chair.   "If you could learn
to lean back, dearest, it would rest you so," she
said.

"I have never slouched in my life," replied Mrs.
Blake decisively, "and I do not care to fall into the
habit in my seventieth year.   When my last hour
comes, I hope at least to meet my God in the attitude
becoming a lady, and in my day it would have been
considered the height of impropriety to loll in a chair
or even to rock in the presence of gentlemen.   Your
Great-aunt Susannah, one of the most modest women
of her time, has often told me that once, having
unfortunately crossed her knees in the parlour after
supper, she suffered untold tortures from "budges"
for three mortal hours rather than be seen to do
anything so indelicate as to uncross them.   Well,
well, ladies were ladies in those days, and now Lila
tells me it is quite customary for them to sit like

men. My blindness has spared me many painful sights, I haven't a doubt."

"Things have changed, dear. I wish they hadn't. I liked the old days, too."

"I'm glad at least to hear you say so. Your Aunt Susannah—and she was the one who danced a minuet with General Lafayette, you know—used to say that patience and humility became a gentle-woman better than satin and fine lace. She was a lady of fashion and a great beauty, so I suppose her opinion counts for something—especially as she was noted for being the proudest woman of her day, and it was said that she never danced with a gentleman who hadn't fought a duel on her account. When she went to a ball it took six small darkies to carry her train, and her escort was always obliged to ride on top of the coach to keep from rumpling the flounces of her petticoat. They always said that I had inherited something of her face and step."

"I'm sure she was never so beautiful as you, mother."

"Ah, well, every one to his taste, my child: and I have heard that she wore a larger shoe. However, this is foolish chatter, and a waste of time. Go and carry Dinah the medicine, and let me see Christopher as soon as he comes in. By the way, Cynthia, have you noticed whether he seeks the society of ladies? Do you think it likely that his affections are engaged?"

"No, no, not at all. He doesn't care for girls; I'm sure of it."

"That seems very strange. Why, at his age, his father had been the object of a dozen love affairs, and been jilted twice, report went, though I had my suspicion from the first that it was the other way. Certainly Miss Peggie Stuart (and he had once been engaged to her) went into a decline immediately after our marriage—but in affairs of the heart, as I have mentioned often before, the only reliable witnesses are those who never tell what they know. Now, as for Christopher, are you quite sure he is as handsome as you say?"

"Quite, quite, he's splendid—like the picture of the young David in the Bible."

"Then there's something wrong. Does he cough?"

"His health seems perfect."

"Which proves conclusively that he cherishes a secret feeling. For a man to go twenty-six years without falling in love means that he's either a saint or an imbecile, my dear; and for my part, I declare I don't know which character sits worse upon a gentleman. Can it be one of the Morrisons, do you think? The youngest girl used to be considered something of a beauty by the family; though she was always too namby-pamby for my taste."

"She's fifty by now, if she's a day, mother, and the only thing I ever saw Christopher do for her was to drive a strange bull out of her road."

"Well, that sounds romantic; but I fear, as you say, she's really too old for him. How time does fly!"

Cynthia stooped and carefully arranged the old lady's feet upon the ottoman. "There, now—I'll carry the medicine to Aunt Dinah," she said, "and be back in plenty of time to dress for supper."

She found the quinine in an old medicine chest in the adjoining room, and went with it to one of the crumbling cabins which had formed part of the "quarters" in the prosperous days of slavery.

Aunt Dinah insisted upon detaining her for a chat, and it was half an hour afterward that she came out again and walked slowly back along the little falling path. The mild June breeze freshened her hot cheeks, and as she passed thoughtfully between the coarse sprays of yarrow blooming along the ragged edges of the fields she felt her spirit freed from the day's burden of unrest. What she wanted just then was to lie for an hour close upon the ground, to renew the vital forces within her by contact with the invigorating earth—to feel Nature at friendly touch with her lips and hands. She would have liked to run like a wild thing through the golden sunshine lying upon the yarrow, following the shy cries of the partridges that scattered at her approach—but there was work for her inside the house, so she went back patiently to take it up.

As she entered the little yard, she saw Tucker basking in the sunshine on an old bench beside one of the damask rose-bushes, and she crossed over and stood for a moment in the tall grass before him.

"You look so happy, Uncle Tucker. How do you manage it?"

"By keeping so, I reckon, my dear. I tell you, this sun feels precious good on the back."

She dropped limply on the bench beside him. "Yes, it is pleasant, but I hadn't thought of it."

"Well, you'd think of it often enough if you were in my place," pursued Tucker, always garrulous, and grateful for a listener. "I didn't notice things much myself when I was young. The only sights that seemed to count, somehow, were those I saw inside my head, and if you'll believe me, I used to be moody and out of sorts half the time, just like Christopher. Times have changed now, you'll say, and it's true. Why, I've got nothing to do these days but to take a look at things, and I tell you I see a lot now where all was a blank before. You just glance over that old field and tell me what you find."

Cynthia followed the sweep of his left arm. "There's first the road, and then a piece of fallow land that ought to be ploughed," she said.

"Bless my soul, is that all you see? Why, there is every shade of green on earth in that old field, and almost every one of blue, except azure, which you'll find up in the sky. That little bit of white cloud, no bigger than my hand, is shaped exactly like an eagle's wing. I've watched it for an hour, and I never saw one like it. As for that old pine on top the little knoll, if you look at it long enough you'll see that it's a great big green cross raised against the sky."

"So it is," said Cynthia, in surprise; "so it is."

"Then to come nearer, look at that spray of turtle-head growing by that gray stone—the shadow it throws is as fine as thread lace, and it waves in the breeze just like the flower."

"Oh, it is beautiful, and I never should have seen it."

"And best of all," resumed Tucker, as if avoiding an interruption, "is that I've watched a nestful of young wrens take flight from under the eaves. There's not a play of Shakespeare's greater than that, I tell you."

"And it makes you happy—just this?" asked

Cynthia wistfully, as the pathos of his maimed figure drove to her heart.

"Well, I reckon happiness is not so much in what comes as in the way you take it," he returned, smiling. "There was a time, you must remember, when I was the straightest shot of my day, and something of a lady-killer as well, if I do say it who shouldn't. I've done my part in a war and I'm not ashamed of it. I've taken the enemy's cannon under a fire hot enough to roast an ox, and I've sent more men to eternity than I like to think of; but I tell you honestly there's no battle-field under heaven worth an hour of this old bench. If I had my choice to-day, I'd rather see the flitting of those wrens than kill the biggest Yankee that ever lived. The time was when I didn't think so, but I know now that there's as much life out there in that old field as in the tightest-packed city street I ever saw—purer life, praise God, and sweeter to the taste. Why, look at this poplar leaf that blew across the road: I've studied the pattern of it for half an hour, and I've found out that such a wonder is worth going ten miles to see."

"Oh, I can't understand you," sighed Cynthia hopelessly. "I wish I could, but I can't—I was born different—so different."

"Bless your heart, honey, I was born different myself, and if I'd kept my leg and my arm I dare say I'd be strutting round on one and shaking the other in the face of God Almighty just as I used to do. A two-legged man is so busy getting about the world that he never has time to sit down and take a look around him. I tell you I see more in one hour as I am now than I saw in all the rest of my life when I was sound and whole. Why, I could sit here all day long and stare up at that blue sky, and then go to bed feeling that my twelve hours were full and brimming over. If I'd never seen anything in my life but that sky above the old pine, I should say at the end 'Thank God for that one good look.'"

"I can't understand—I can't understand," repeated Cynthia, in a broken voice, though her face shed a clear, white beam. "I only know that we are all in awful straights, and that to-morrow is the day when I must get up at five o'clock and travel all the way to town to get my sewing."

He laid his large pink hand on hers.

"Why not let Lila go for you?"

"What! to wait like a servant for the bundle and walk the streets all day—I'd go twenty times first!"

"My dear, you needn't envy me," he responded, patting her knotted hand. "I took less courage with me when I stormed my heights."

CHAPTER X

SENTIMENTAL AND OTHERWISE

IN THE gray dawn Cynthia came softly downstairs and, passing her mother's door on tiptoe, went
out into the kitchen to begin preparations for her
early breakfast. She wore a severe black alpaca
dress, made from a cast-off one of her mother's, and
below her white linen collar she had pinned a cameo
brooch bearing the head of Minerva, which had once
belonged to Aunt Susannah. On the bed upstairs
she had left her shawl and bonnet and a pair of carefully mended black silk mitts, for her monthly visits
to the little country town were endured with something of the frozen dignity which supported Marie
Antoinette in the tumbrel. It was a case where
family pride was found more potent than Christian
resignation.

When she opened the kitchen door, with her arms
full of resinous pine from the pile beside the steps,
she found that Tucker had risen before her and was
fumbling awkwardly in the safe with his single hand.

"Why, Uncle Tucker!" she exclaimed in surprise,
"what on earth has happened?"

Turning his cheerful face upon her, he motioned to
a little wooden tobacco box on the bare table.

"A nest full of swallows tumbled down my chimney

in the night," he explained, "and they cried so lo[ud]
I couldn't sleep, so I thought I might as well get [up]
and dig 'em a worm or two. Do you happen [to]
know where a bit of wool is?"

Cynthia threw her bundle of kindling-wood on the
hearth and stood regarding him with apathetic
eyes. "You'd much better wring their necks," she
responded indifferently; "but there's a basketful
of wool Aunt Polly has just carded in the closet.
How in the world did you manage to dress yourself?"

"Oh, it's wonderful what one hand can do when
it's put to it. Would you mind fastening my collar,
by the way, and any buttons that you happen to
see loose?"

She glanced over him critically, pulling his clothes
in place and adjusting a button here and there. "I
do hate to see you in this old jean suit," she said;
"you used to look so nice in your other clothes."

With a laugh he settled his empty sleeve. "Oh,
they're good for warm weather," he responded; "and
they wash easily, which is something. Think, too,
what a waste it would be to dress half a man in a
whole suit of broadcloth."

"Oh, don't, don't," she protested, on the point of
tears, but he smiled and patted her bowed shoulder.
"I got over that long ago, honey," he said gently.
"I kicked powerful hard with my one foot at first,
but the dust I raised wasn't a speck in the face of
God Almighty. There, there, we'll have a fine
sunrise, and I'm going out to watch it from my old
bench—unless you'll find something for a single
hand to do."

She shook her head, smiling with misty eyes.

"You'll have breakfast with me, I suppose," she said. "I got up early because I couldn't sleep, but it's not yet four o'clock."

For an instant he looked at her gravely. "Worrying about the day?"

"A little."

"If I could only manage to hobble along with you."

"Oh, but you couldn't, dear—and the worst of it is having to wait so long in town for the afternoon stage. I get my sewing, and then I eat my lunch on the old church steps, and then there are four mortal hours when I walk about aimlessly in the sun."

"And you wouldn't go to see anybody?"

"With my bundle of work, and in this alpaca? Not for worlds!"

He sighed, not reproachfully, but with the sympathy which projects itself into states of feeling other than its own.

"Well, I wish all the same you'd let Lila go in with you. I think you make a mistake about her, Cynthia; she wouldn't feel the strain of it half so much as you do."

"But I'd feel it for her. No, no, it's better as it is; and she does walk to the cross-roads with me, you know. Old Jacob Weatherby brings her back in his wagon. Christopher can't get off, but he'll come for me at sundown."

"Are you sure it isn't young Jim who fetches Lila?"

She frowned. "If it were young Jim, her going would be impossible—but the old man knows his place and keeps it."

"It's a better place than ours to-day, I reckon,"

returned Tucker, smiling. "To an observer across the road I dare say the odds would seem considerably in his favour. I met him in the turnpike last Sunday in a brand new broadcloth."

"Oh, I can't bear to hear you," returned Cynthia passionately. "If we must go to the dogs, for heaven's sake, let's go remembering that we are Blakes—or Corbins, if you like."

"Bless your heart, child, I'd just as lief remember I was a Blake—or even a Weatherby, for that matter. Why, Jacob Weatherby's grandfather was an honest, self-respecting tiller of the soil when mine used to fish his necktie out of the punch-bowl every Saturday night, people said."

She lifted her black skirt above her knees, and pinned it tightly at her back with a large safety pin she had taken from her bosom. Then kneeling on the hearth, she laid the knots of resinous pine on a crumpled newspaper in the great stone fireplace.

"I don't mind your picking flaws in me," she said dryly, "but I do wish you would let my great grandfather rest in his grave. He's about all I've got."

"Well, I beg his pardon for speaking the truth about him," returned Tucker penitently; "and now my swallows are so noisy I must stop their mouths."

He went out humming a tune, while Cynthia hung the boiler from the crane and mixed the corn-meal dough in a wooden tray.

When breakfast was on the table Lila appeared with a reproachful face, hurriedly knotting her kerchief as she entered.

"Oh, Cynthia, you promised to let me get breakfast," she said. "Mother was very restless all night—she dreamed that she was being married over again—so I slept too late."

"It didn't matter, dear; I was awake, and I didn't mind getting up.   Are you ready to go?"

"All except my hat." Yawning slightly, she raised her hands and pushed up her clustering hair that was but a shade darker than Christopher's. Trivial as the likeness was, it began and ended with her heavy curls, for her hazel eyes held a peculiar liquid beam, and her face, heart-shaped in outline, had none of the heaviness of jaw which marred the symmetry of his. A little brown mole beside the dimple in her cheek gave the finishing touch of coquetry to the old-world quaintness of her appearance.

As she passed the window on her way to the table she threw a drowsy glance out into the yard.

"Why, there's Uncle Tucker sitting on the ground," she said; "he must be crazy."

Cynthia was pouring the hastily made coffee from the steaming boiler, and she did not look up as she answered.

"You'd better go out and help him up. He's digging worms for some swallows that fell down his chimney."

"Well, of all the ideas!" exclaimed Lila, laughing, but she went out with cheerful sweetness and assisted him to his crutches.

A half-hour later, when the meal was over and Christopher had gone out to the stable, the two women tied on their bonnets and went softly through the hall. As they passed Mrs. Blake's door she awoke and called out sharply.

"Cynthia, is that you? What are you doing up so early?"

Cynthia paused at strained attention on the threshold.

"I'm going to the Morrisons', mother, to spend the day. You know I told you Miss Martha had promised to teach me that new fancy stitch."

"But, my dear, surely it is bad manners to arrive before eleven o'clock. I remember once when I was a girl that we went over to Meadow Hall before ten in the morning, and found old Mrs. Dudley just putting on her company cap."

"But they begged me to come to breakfast, dear."

"Well, customs change, of course; but be sure to take Mrs. Morrison a jar of the green tomato catchup. You know she always fancied it."

"Yes, yes; good-by till evening."

She moved on hurriedly, her clumsy shoes creaking on the bare planks, and a moment afterward as the door closed behind them they passed out into the first sunbeams. Beyond the whitewashed fence the old field was silvered by the heavy dew, and above it the great pine towered like a burnished cross upon the western sky. To the eastward a solitary thrush was singing—a golden voice straight from out the sunrise.

"This is worth getting up for!" said Lila, with a long, joyful breath; and she broke into a tender carolling as spontaneous as the bird's. The bloom of the summer was in her face, and as she moved with her buoyant step along the red clay road she was like a rare flower blown lightly by the wind. To Cynthia's narrowed eyes she seemed, indeed, a heroine descended from old romance—a maiden to whom, even in these degenerate modern days, there must at last arrive a noble destiny. That Lila at the end of her twenty-six years should have wearied of her long waiting and grown content to compromise with fate would have appeared to her impossible —as impossible as the transformation of young Jim Weatherby into the fairy prince.

"Hush!" she said suddenly, shifting her bundle of sewing from one arm to the other; "there's a wagon turning from the branch road."

They had reached the first bend beyond the gate, and as they rounded the long curve, hidden by honey-locusts, a light spring wagon came rapidly toward them, with Jim Weatherby, in his Sunday clothes, on the driver's seat.

"Father's rheumatism is so bad he couldn't get out to-day," he explained, as he brought the horses to a stand; "so as long as I had to take the butter over, I thought I might save you the five miles." He spoke to Cynthia, and she drew back stiffly.

"It is a pleasant day for a walk," she returned dryly.

"But it's going to be hot," he urged; "I can tell by the way the sun licks up the dew." A feathery branch of the honey-locust was in his face, and he pushed it impatiently aside as he looked at Lila. "I waited late just to take you," he added wistfully, jumping from his seat and going to the horses' heads. "Won't you get in?"

"You will be so tired, Cynthia," Lila persuaded. "Think of the walking you have to do in town."

As Jim Weatherby glanced up brightly from the strap he was fastening, the smile in his blue eyes was like a song of love; and when the girl met it she heard again the solitary thrush singing in the sunrise. "You will come?" he pleaded, and this time he looked straight at her.

"Well, I reckon I will, if you're going anyway," said Cynthia at last; "and if I drive with you there'll be no use for Lila to go—she can stay with mother."

"But mother doesn't need me," said Lila, in answer to Jim's wistful eyes; "and it's such a lovely day—after getting up so early I don't want to stay indoors."

Without a word Jim held out his hand to Cynthia, and she climbed, with unbending dignity, to the driver's seat. "You know you've got that dress to turn, Lila," she said, as she settled her stiff skirt primly over her knees.

"I can do it when I get home," answered Lila, laying her hand on the young man's arm and stepping upon the wheel. "Where shall I sit, Jim?"

Cynthia turned and looked at her coldly.

"You'd be more comfortable in that chair at the back," she suggested, and Lila sat down obediently in the little split-bottomed chair between a brown stone jar of butter and a basket filled with new-laid eggs. The girl folded her white hands in the lap of her faded muslin and listened patiently to the pleasant condescension in Cynthia's voice as she discussed the belated planting of the crops. As the spring wagon rolled in the shade of the honey-locusts between the great tobacco fields, striped with vivid green, the June day filled the younger sister's eyes with a radiance that seemed but a reflection of its own perfect beauty. Not once did her lover turn from

Cynthia to herself, but she was conscious, sitting quietly beside the great brown jar, that for him she filled the morning with her presence—that he saw her in the blue sky, in the sunny fields, and in the long red road with the delicate shadowing of the locusts. In her cramped life there had been so little room in which her dreams might wander that gradually the romantic devotion of her old playmate had grown to represent the measure of her emotional ideal. In spite of her poetic face she was in thought soundly practical, and though the plain Cynthia might send a fanciful imagination in pursuit of the impossible, to Lila the only destiny worth cherishing at heart was the one that drew its roots deep from the homely soil about her. The stern class-distinctions which had always steeled Cynthia against the friendly advances of her neighbours troubled the younger sister not at all. She remembered none of the past grandeur, the old Blake power of rule, and the stories of gallant indiscretions and powdered *beaux* seemed to her as worthless as the moth-eaten satin rags which filled the garret. She loved the familiar country children, the making of fresh butter, and honest admiration of her beauty; and except for the colourless poverty in which they lived, she might easily have found her placid happiness on the little farm. With ambition—the bitter, agonised ambition that Cynthia felt for her—she was as unconcerned as was her blithe young lover chatting so merrily in the driver's seat. The very dulness of her imagination had saved her from the awakening that follows wasted hopes.

"The tobacco looks well," Cynthia was saying in

her formal tones; "all it needs now is a rain to start it growing. You've got yours all in by now, I suppose."

"Oh, yes; mine was put in before Christopher's," responded Jim, feeling instantly that the woman beside him flinched at his unconscious use of her brother's name.

"He is always late," she remarked with forced politeness, and the conversation dragged until they reached the cross-roads and she climbed into the stage.

"Be sure to hurry back," were her last words as she rumbled off; and when, in looking over her shoulder at the first curve, she saw Lila lift her beaming eyes to Jim Weatherby's face, the protest of all the dust in the old graveyard was in the groan that hovered on her lips. She herself would have crucified her happiness with her own loyal hands rather than have dishonoured by so much as an unspoken hope the high excellences inscribed upon the tombstones of those mouldered dead.

In her shabby black dress, with her heavy bundle under her arm, she passed, a lonely, pathetic figure, through the streets of the little town. The strange smells fretted her, the hot bricks tired her feet, and the jarring noises confused her hazy ideas of direction. On the steps of the old church, where she ate her lunch, she found a garrulous blind beggar with whom she divided her slender meal of bacon and corn-bread. After a moment's hesitation, she bought a couple of bananas for a few cents from a fruit-stand at the corner, and coming back, gave the larger one to the beggar who sat complaining in the sun. Then, withdrawing to a conventional distance in the shadow of the steeple, she waited patiently for the slow hours to wear away. Not until the long shadow pointed straight from west to east did the ancient vehicle rattle down the street and the driver pull up for her at the old church steps. Then it was that with her first sigh of relief she awoke to the realisation that through all the trying day her heaviest burden was the memory of Lila's morning look into the face of the man whose father had been a common labourer at Blake Hall.

Three hours later, when, pale and exhausted, with an aching head, she found the stage halting beneath the blasted pine, her pleasantest impression was of Christopher standing in the yellow afterglow beside the old spring wagon. The driver spoke to him, and then, as the horses stopped, turned to toss the weather-beaten mail-bag to the porch of the country store, where a group of men were lounging. Among them Cynthia saw the figure of a girl in a riding habit, who, as the stage halted, gathered up her long black skirt and ran hastily to the roadside to speak to some one who remained still seated in the vehicle.

That Christopher's eyes followed the graceful figure in its finely fitting habit Cynthia noticed with a sudden jealous pang, detecting angrily the warmth of the admiration in his gaze. The girl had met his look, she knew, for when she lifted her face to her companion it was bright with a winter's glow, though the day was warm. She spoke almost breathlessly, too, as if she had been running, and Cynthia overhearing her first low words, held her prim skirt aside, and descended awkwardly over the wheel. She

stumbled in reaching the ground, and the girl with a
kindly movement turned to help her.

"I hope you aren't hurt," she said in crisp, clear-
cut tones; but the elder woman, recovering herself
with an effort, passed on after an ungracious bow.

When she reached Christopher he was still standing
motionless beside the wagon, and at her first words
he started like one awaking from a pleasant day-
dream.

"So you came, after all," he remarked in an
absent-minded manner.

"Of course I came." She was conscious that she
almost snapped the reply. "Did you expect me to
spend the night in town?"

"In town? Hardly." He laughed gaily as he
helped her into the wagon; then, with the reins in his
hands, he turned for a last glance at the stage.
"Why, what did you think I was waiting for?"

"What you are waiting for now is more to the
purpose," she retorted, pressing her fingers upon her
aching temples. "The afterglow is fading; come,
get in."

Without a word he seated himself beside her, and
as he touched the horses lightly with the whip the
wagon rolled between the green tobacco fields.

"How delicious the wild grape is!" exclaimed
Cynthia, drawing her breath, "I hope the horses
aren't tired.   Have they been at the plough?"

"Not since dinner time." It was clear that his
mind was still abstracted, and he kept his face
turned toward the pale red line that lingered on the
western horizon.

"This is a queer kind of life," he said presently,

still looking away from her. "We are so poor and so shut in that we have no idea what people of the world are really like. That girl out there at the cross-roads, now, she was different from any one I'd ever seen. Did you hear where she came from?"

"I didn't ask," Cynthia replied, compressing her lips. "I didn't like the way she stared."

"Stared? At you?"

"No, at you. I'm glad you didn't notice it. It was bold, to say the least."

Throwing back his head, he laughed with boyish merriment; and she saw, as he turned his face toward her, that his heavy hair had fallen low across his forehead, giving him a youthful look that became him strangely. At the instant she softened in her judgment of the unknown woman at the cross-roads.

"Why, she thought I was some queer beast of burden, I reckon," he returned—"some new farm animal that made her a little curious. Well, whoever she may be, she walked as if she felt herself a princess."

Cynthia snorted. "Her habit fitted her like a glove," was her comment, to which she added after a pause: "As things go, it's just as well you didn't hear what she said, I reckon."

"About me, do you mean?"

"She came down to meet another girl," pursued Cynthia coolly. "I was getting out, so I don't suppose they noticed me—a shabby old creature with a bundle. At any rate, when she kissed the other, she whispered something I didn't hear, and then, 'I've seen that man before—look!' That was when I stumbled, and that made me catch the next:

'Where?' her friend asked her quickly, and she answered——"

There was a pause, in which the warm dusk was saturated with the fragrance of the grape blossoms on the fence.

"She answered?" repeated Christopher slowly.

Cynthia looked up and down the road, and then gave the words as if they were a groan:

"In my dreams."

Book Two
The Temptation

THE TEMPTATION

CHAPTER I

THE ROMANCE THAT MIGHT HAVE BEEN

WITH July there came a long rain, and in the burst of sunshine which followed it the young tobacco shot up fine and straight and tall, clothing the landscape in a rich, tropical green.

From morning till night the men worked now in the great fields, removing the numerous "suckers" from the growing plants, and pinching off the slender tops to prevent the first beginnings of a flower, except where, at long spaces, a huge pink cluster would be allowed to blossom and come to seed.

Christopher, toiling all day alone in his own field, felt the clear summer dawn break over him, the golden noon gather to full heat, and the coming night envelop him like a purple mist. Living, as he did, so close to the earth, himself akin to the strong forces of the soil, he had grown gradually from his childhood into a rare physical expression of the large freedom of natural things.

It was an unusually hot day in mid-August—the

time of the harvest moon and of the dreaded tobacco fly—that he came home at the dinner hour to find Cynthia standing, spent and pale, beside the well.

"The sun is awful, Christopher; I don't see how you bear it—but it makes your hair the colour of ripe wheat."

"Oh, I don't mind the sun," he answered, laughing as he wiped the sweat from his face and stooped for a drink from the tilted bucket. "I'm too much taken up just now with fighting those confounded tobacco flies. They were as thick as thieves last night."

"Uncle Boaz is going to send the little darkies out to hunt them at sundown," returned Cynthia. "I've promised them an apple for every one they catch."

Her gaze wandered over the broad fields, rich in promise, and she added after a moment, "Fletcher's crop has come on splendidly."

"The more's the pity."

For a long breath she looked at him in silence— at the massive figure, the face burned to the colour of terra-cotta, the thick, wheaten-brown hair— then, with an impulsive gesture, she spoke in her wonderful voice, which held so many possibilities of passion:

"I didn't tell you, Christopher, that I'd found out the name of the girl at the cross-roads. She went away the day afterward and just got back yesterday."

Something in her tone made the young man look up quickly, his face paling beneath the sunburn.

All the boyish cheerfulness he had worn of late faded suddenly from his look.

"Who is she?" he asked.

"Jim Weatherby knew. He had seen her several times on horseback, and he says she's Maria Fletcher, that ugly little girl, grown up. She hates the life here, he says, and they think she is going to marry before the winter. Fletcher was talking down at the store about a rich man who is in love with her."

Christopher stooped to finish his drink, and then rose slowly to his full height.

"Well, one Fletcher the less will be a good riddance," he said harshly, as he went into the house.

In the full white noon he returned to the field, working steadily on his crop until the sunset. Back and forth among the tall green plants, waist deep in their rank luxuriance, he passed with careful steps and attentive eyes, avoiding the huge "sand leaves" spreading upon the ground and already yellowing in the August weather. As he searched for the hidden "suckers" along the great juicy stalks, he removed his hat lest it should bruise the tender tops, and the golden sunshine shone full on his bared head.

Around him the landscape swept like an emerald sea, over which the small shadows rippled in passing waves, beginning at the rail fence skirting the red clay road and breaking at last upon the darker green of the far-off pines. Here and there a tall pink blossom rose like a fantastic sail from the deep and rocked slowly to and fro in the summer wind.

When at last the sun dropped behind the distant wood and a red flame licked at the western clouds, he still lingered on, dreaming idly, while his hands followed their accustomed task. Big green moths hovered presently around him, seeking the deep rosy tubes of the clustered flowers, and alighting finally to leave their danger-breeding eggs under the drooping leaves. The sound of laughter floated suddenly from the small negro children, who were pursuing the tobacco flies between the furrows. He had ceased from his work, and come out into the little path that trailed along the edge of the field, when he saw a woman's figure, in a gown coloured like April flowers, pass from the new road over the loosened fence-rails. For a breathless instant he wavered in the path; then turning squarely, he met her questioning look with indifferent eyes. The new romance had shrivelled at the first touch of the old hatred.

Maria, holding her skirt above her ruffled petti-coat, stood midway of the little trail, a single tobacco blossom waving over her leghorn hat. She was no longer the pale girl who had received Carraway with so composed a bearing, for her face and her gown were now coloured delicately with an April bloom.

"I followed the new road," she explained, smiling, "and all at once it ended at the fence. Where can I take it up again?"

He regarded her gravely. "The only way you can take it up again is to go back to it," he answered. "It doesn't cross my land, you know, and—I beg your pardon—but I don't care to have you do so.

Besides staining your dress, you will very likely bruise my tobacco."

He had never in his life stood close to a woman who wore perfumed garments, and he felt, all at once, that her fragrance was going to his brain. Delicate as it was, he found it heady, like strong drink.

"But I could walk very close to the fence," said the girl, surprised.

"Aren't you afraid of the poisonous oak?"

"Desperately. I caught it once as a child. It hurt so."

He shook his head impatiently.

"Apart from that, there is no reason why you should come on my land. All the prettiest walks are on the other side—and over here the hounds are taught to warn off trespassers."

"Am I a trespasser?"

"You are worse," he replied boorishly; "you're a Fletcher."

"Well, you're a savage," she retorted, angered in her turn. "Is it simply because I happen to be a Fletcher that you become a bear?"

"Because you happen to be a Fletcher," he repeated, and then looked calmly and coolly at her dainty elegance.

"And if I were anybody else, I suppose, you would let me walk along that fence, and even be polite enough to keep the dogs from eating me up?"

"If you were anybody else and didn't injure my tobacco—yes."

"But as it is I must keep away?"

"All I ask of you is to stay on the other side."

"And if I don't?" she questioned, her spirit flaring up to match with his, "and if I don't?"

All the natural womanhood within her responded to the appeal of his superb manhood; all the fastidious refinement with which she was overlaid was alive to the rustic details which marred the finished whole —to the streak of earth across his forehead, to the coarseness of his ill-fitting clothes, to the tobacco juice staining his finger nails bright green.

On his side, the lady of his dreams had shrunken to a witch; and he shook his head again in an effort to dispel the sweetness that so strangely moved him.

"In that case you will meet the hounds one day and get your dress badly torn, I fear."

"And bitten, probably."

"Probably."

"Well, I don't think it would be worth it," said the girl, in a quiver of indignation. "If I can help it, I shall never set my foot on your land again."

"The wisest thing you can do is to keep off," he retorted

Turning, with an angry movement, she walked rapidly to the fence, heedless of the poisonous oak along the way; and Christopher, passing her with a single step, lowered the topmost rails that she might cross over the more easily.

"Thank you," she said stiffly, as she reached the other side.

"It was a pleasure," he responded, in the tone his father might have used when in full Grecian dress at the fancy ball.

"You mean it is a pleasure to assist in getting rid of me?"

"What I mean doesn't matter," he answered irritably, and added, "I wish to God you were anybody else!"

At this she turned and faced him squarely as he held the rails.

"But how can I help being myself?" she demanded.

"You can't, and there's an end of it."

"Of what?"

"Oh, of everything—and most of all of the evening at the cross-roads."

"You saw me then?" she asked.

"You know I did," he answered, retreating into his rude simplicity.

"And you liked me then?"

"Then," he laughed—"why, I was fool enough to dream of you for a month afterward."

"How dare you!" she cried.

"Well, I shan't do it again," he assured her insolently.

"You can't possibly dislike me any more than I do you," she remarked, drawing back step by step. "You're a savage, and a mean one at that—but all the same, I should like to know why you began to hate me."

He laid the topmost rail along the fence and turned away. "Ask your grandfather!" he called back, as he passed into the tobacco field, with her fragrance still in his nostrils.

Maria, on the other side, walked slowly homeward along the new road that had ended so abruptly. Her lip trembled, and, letting her skirt drag in the dust, she put up her hand to suppress the first hint of emotion. It angered her that he had had the power to provoke her so, and for the moment the encounter seemed to have bereft her of her last shreds of womanly reserve. It was as if a strong wind had blown over her, laying her bosom bare, and she flushed at the knowledge that he had heard the fluttering of her breath and seen the indignant tears gather to her eyes—he a boorish stranger who hated her because of her name. For the first time in her life she had run straight against an impregnable prejudice—had felt her feminine charm ineffectual against a stern masculine resistance. She was at the age when the artificial often outweighs the real—when the superficial manner with a woman is apt to be misunderstood, and so to her Christopher Blake now appeared stripped even of his physical comeliness: the interview had left her with an impression of mere vulgar incivility.

As she entered the house she met Fletcher passing through the hall with the mail-bag in his hand, and a little later, while she sat in a big chair by her chamber window, Miss Saidie came in and laid a letter in her lap.

"It's from Mr. Wyndham, I think, Maria. Shall I light a candle?"

"Not yet; it is so warm I like the twilight."

"But won't you read the letter?"

"Oh, presently. There's time enough."

Miss Saidie came to the window and leaned out to sniff the climbing roses, her shapeless figure outlined against the purple dusk spangled with fireflies. Her presence irritated the girl, who stirred restlessly in her chair.

"Is he coming, Maria, do you think?"

"If I let him—yes."

"And he wants to marry you?"

The girl laughed bitterly. "He hasn't seen me in my home yet," she answered, "and our vulgarity may be too much for him. He's very particular, you know."

The woman at the window flinched as if she had been struck.

"But if he loves you, Maria?"

"Oh, he loves me for what isn't me," she answered, "for my 'culture,' as he calls it—for the gloss that has been put over me in the last ten years."

"Still if you care for him, dear——"

"I don't know—I don't know," said Maria, speaking in the effort to straighten her disordered thoughts rather than for the enlightenment of Miss Saidie. "I was sure I loved him before I came home—but this place upsets me so—I hate it. It makes me feel raw, crude, unlike myself. When I come back here I seem to lose all that I have learned, and to grow vulgar, like Jinnie Spade, at the store."

"Not like her, Maria."

"Well, I ought to know better, of course, but I don't believe I do—not when I'm here."

"Then why not go away? Don't think of us; we can get along as we used to do."

"I don't think of you," said the girl. "I don't think of anybody in the world except myself—and that's the awful part—that's the part I hate. I'm selfish to the core, and I know it."

"But you do love Jack Wyndham?"

"Oh, I love him to distraction! Light the candle, Aunt Saidie, and let me read his letter. I can tell

you, word for word, what is in it before I break
the seal. Six months ago I went into a flutter at
the sight of his handwriting. Six months before
that I was madly in love with Dick Bright—and six
months from to-day—— Oh, well, I suppose I really
haven't much heart to know—and if I ever care for
anybody it must be for Jack—that's positive."

Standing beside the lighted candle on the bureau,
she read the letter twice over, and then turning
away, wrote her answer kneeling beside the big
chair at the window.

CHAPTER II

The Romance That Was

WAKING in the night she said again, "I love him to distraction," and slipping under the dimity curtains of the bed, sought his letter where she had left it on the bureau. The full light of the harvest moon was in the room—a light so soft that it lay like a yellow fluid upon the floor. It seemed almost as if one might stoop and fill the open palms.

She found the letter thrown carelessly upon the pincushion, and holding it to her lips, paused a moment beside the window, looking beyond the shaven lawn and the clustered oaks to where the tobacco fields lay golden beneath the moon. It was such a night as seemed granted by some kindly deity for the fulfilment of lovers' vows, and the girl, standing beside the open window, grew suddenly sad, as one who sees a vision with the knowledge that it is not life. When presently she went back to bed it was to lie sleepless until dawn, with the love letter held tightly in her hands.

The next day a restlessness like that of fever worked in her blood, and she ran from turret to basement of the roomy old house, calling Will to come and help her find amusement.

"Play ball with me, Will," she said; "I feel as if I were a child to-day."

"Oh, it's no fun playing with a girl," replied the boy; "besides, I am going fishing in the river with Zebbadee Blake; I shan't be back till supper," and shouldering his fishing-rod he flung off with his can of worms.

Miss Saidie was skimming big pans of milk in the spring-house, and Maria watched her idly for a time, growing suddenly impatient of the leisurely way in which the spoon travelled under the yellow cream.

"I don't see how you can be so fond of it," she said at last.

"Lord, child, I never could abide dairy work," responded Miss Saidie, setting the skimmed pan aside and carefully lifting another from the flat stones over which a stream of water trickled.

"And yet you've done nothing else all your long life," wondered Maria.

"When it comes to doing a thing in this world," returned the little woman, removing a speck of dust from the cream with the point of the spoon, "I don't ask myself whether I like it or not, but what's the best way to get it done. I've spent sixty years doing things I wasn't fond of, and I don't reckon I'm any the less happy for having done 'em well."

"But I should be," asserted Maria, and then, with her white parasol over her bared head, she started for a restless stroll along the old road under the great chestnuts.

She had reached the abandoned ice-pond, and was picking her way carefully in the shadow of the trees, when the baying of a pack of hounds in full cry broke on her ears, and with the nervous tremor

she had associated from childhood with the sound,
she stopped short in the road and waited anxiously
for the hunt to pass.   Even as she hesitated, feeling
in imagination all the blind terror of the pursuit,
and determined to swing into a chestnut bough in
case of an approach, a small animal darted suddenly
from around the bend in the sunken road, and an
instant afterward the hounds in hot chase broke
from the cover.   For a single breath the girl,
dropping her parasol, looked at the lowered branch;
then as the small animal neared her her glance
fell, and she saw that it was a little yellow dog,
with hanging red tongue and eyes bulging in terror.
From side to side of the red clay road the creature
doubled for a moment in its anguish, and then
with a spring, straight as the flight of a homing
bird, fled to the shelter of Maria's skirts.   Quick
as a heart-beat the girl's personal fears had vanished,
and as an almost savage instinct of battle awoke
in her, she stooped with a protecting movement
and, picking the small dog from the ground, held
him high above her head as the hounds came on.
A moment before her limbs had shaken at the
distant cries; now facing the immediate presence of
the danger, she felt the rage of her pity flow like
an infusion of strong blood through her veins.   Until
they dashed her to the ground she knew that she
would stand holding the hunted creature above
her head.

Like a wave the pack broke instantly upon her,
forcing her back against the body of the chestnut,
and tearing her dress, at the first blow, from her
bosom to the ground.   She had felt their weight

upon her breast, their hot breath full in her face, when, in the midst of the confused noises in her ears, she heard a loud oath that rang out like a shot, followed by the strokes of a rawhide whip on living flesh. So close came the lash that the curling end smote her cheek and left a thin flame from ear to mouth. The lessening sounds became all at once like the silence; and when the hounds, beaten back, slunk, whimpering, to heel, she lowered her eyes until she looked straight into the face of Christopher Blake.

"My God! You have pluck!" he said, and his face was like that of a dead man.

Still holding the dog above her head, she lay motionless against the body of the tree. "Drive the beasts away," she pleaded like a frightened child. Without a word he turned and ordered the hounds home, and they crawled obediently back along the sunken road. Then he looked at her again.

"I saw them start the dog on my land," he said, "and I ran across the field as soon as I could find my whip. If I hadn't come up when I did they would have torn you to pieces. Not another man in the world could have brought them in. Look at your dress."

Glancing down, she followed the long slit from bosom to hem.

"I hate them!" she exclaimed fiercely.

"So it was your dog they started?"

"Mine!" She lowered the yellow cur, holding him close in her arms, where he nestled shivering. "I never saw him before, but he's mine now; I

saved him. I shall name him Agag, because the
bitterness of death is past."

"Well, rather—— Look here," he burst out impulsively, "you've got the staunchest pluck I ever
saw. I never knew a man brave enough to stand
up against those hounds—and you—why, I don't
believe you flinched an eyelash, and—by George—
the dog wasn't yours after all."

"As if that made a difference!" she flashed out.
"Why, he ran to me for help—and they might
have killed me, but I'd never have given him up."

"I believe you," he declared.

She was conscious of a slight thrill that passed
quickly, leaving her white and weak. "I feel
tired," she said, pressing hard against the tree.
"Will you be so good as to pick up my parasol?"

"Tired!" he exclaimed, and after a moment,
"Your face is hurt—did the dogs do it?"

She shook her head. "You struck me with your
whip."

"Is that so? I can't say after this that I never
lifted my hand against a woman—but harsh measures
are sometimes necessary, I reckon. Does it smart?"

She touched the place lightly. "Oh, it's no
matter!" she returned. "I suppose I ought really
to thank you for taking the trouble to save my life—
but I don't, because, after all, the hounds are yours,
you know."

"Yes, I know; and they're good hounds, too, in
their way. The dog had no business on their land."

"And they're taught to warn off trespassers?
Well, I hardly fancy their manner of conveying
the hint."

"It is sometimes useful, all the same."

"Ah, in case of a Fletcher, I presume."

"In case of a Fletcher," he repeated, his face darkening. "Do you know I had entirely forgotten who you were?"

"It's time you were remembering it," she returned, "for I am most decidedly a Fletcher."

For an instant he scowled upon her.

"Then you are most decidedly a devil," was his retort, as he stooped to pick up her parasol from the road. "There's not much left of it," he remarked, handing it to her.

"As things go, I dare say I ought to be grateful that they spared the spokes," she said impatiently. "It does seem disagreeable that I can't go for a short stroll along my own road without the risk of having my clothes torn from my back. You really must keep your horrid beasts from becoming a public danger."

"They never chase anything that keeps off my farm," he replied coolly. "There's not so well trained a pack anywhere in the county. No other dogs around here could have been beaten back at the death."

"I fear that doesn't afford me the gratification you seem to feel—particularly as the death you allude to would have been mine. I suppose I ought to be overpowered with gratitude for the whole thing, but unfortunately I'm not. I have had a very unpleasant experience and I can't help feeling that I owe it to you."

"You're welcome to feel about it anyway you please," he responded, as Maria, tucking the dog under her arm, started down the road to the Hall, the tattered parasol held straight above her head.

At the house she carried Agag to her room, where she spent the afternoon in the big chair by the window. Miss Saidie, coming in with her dinner, inquired if she were sick, and then picked up the torn dress from the bed.

"Why, Maria, how on earth did you do it?"

"Some hounds jumped on me in the road."

"Well, I never! They were those dreadful Blake beasts, I know. I declare, I'll go right down and speak to Brother Bill about 'em."

"For heaven's sake, don't," protested the girl. "We've had quarrelling enough as it is—and, tell me, Aunt Saidie, have you ever known what it was all about?"

Miss Saidie was examining the rent with an eye to a possible mending, and she did not look up as she answered. "I never understood exactly myself, but your grandpa says they squandered all their money and then got mad because they had to sell the place. That's about the truth of it, I reckon."

"The Hall belonged to them once, didn't it?"

"Oh, a long time ago, when they were rich. Sakes alive, Maria, what's the matter with your face?"

"I struck it getting away from the hounds. It's too bad, isn't it? And Jack coming so soon, too. Do I look very ugly?"

"You're a perfect fright now, but I'll fix you a liniment to draw the bruise away. It will be all right in a day or two. I declare, if you haven't gone and brought a little po'-folksy yellow dog into the house."

Maria was feeding Agag with bits of chicken from her plate, bending over him as he huddled against her dress.

"I found him in the road," she returned, "and I'm going to keep him. I saved him from the hounds."

"Well, it seems to me you might have got a prettier one," remarked Miss Saidie, as she went down to mix the liniment.

It was several mornings after this that Fletcher, coming into the dining-room where Maria sat at a late breakfast, handed her a telegram, and stood waiting while she tore it open.

"Jim Weatherby brought it over from the cross-roads," he said. "It got there last night."

"I hope there's nobody dead, child," observed Miss Saidie, from the serving-table, where she was peeling tomatoes.

"More likely it points to a marriage, eh, daughter?" chuckled Fletcher jocosely.

The girl folded the paper and replaced it carefully in the envelope. "It's from Jack Wyndham," she said, "and he comes this evening. May I take the horses to the cross-roads, grandpa?"

"Well, I did have a use for them," responded Fletcher, in high good-nature, "but, seeing as your young fellow doesn't come every day, I reckon I'll let you have 'em out."

Maria flinched at his speech; and then as the clear pink spread evenly in her cheeks, she spoke in her composed tones. "I may as well tell you, grandpa, that we shall marry almost immediately," she said.

CHAPTER III

Fletcher's Move and Christopher's Counter-stroke

Not until September, when he lounged one day with a glass of beer in the little room behind Tom Spade's country store, did Christopher hear the news of Maria's approaching marriage. It was Sol Peterkin who delivered it, hiccoughing in the enveloping smoke from several pipes, as he sat astride an overturned flour barrel in one corner.

"I jest passed a wagonload of finery on the way to the Hall," he said, bulging with importance. "It's for the gal's weddin', I reckon; an' they do say she's a regular Jezebel as far as clothes go. I met her yestiddy with her young man that is to be, an' the way she was dressed up wasn't a sight for modest eyes. Not that she beguiled me, suh, though the devil himself might have been excused for mistakin' her for the scarlet woman—but I'm past the time of life when a man wants a woman jest to set aroun' an' look at. I tell you a good workin' pair of hands goes to my heart a long ways sooner than the blackest eyes that ever oggled."

"Well, my daughter Jinnie has been up thar sewin' for a month," put in Tom Spade, a big, greasy man, who looked as if he had lived on cabbage from his infancy, "an' she says that sech a sight of lace she never laid eyes on. Why, her very stockin's have got lace let in 'em, Jinnie says."

"Now, that's what I call hardly decent," remarked Sol, as he spat upon the dirty floor. "Them's the enticin' kind of women that a fool hovers near an' a wise man fights shy of. Lace in her stockin's! Well, did anybody ever?"

"She's got a pretty ankle, you may be sho'," observed Matthew Field, a long wisp of a man who had married too early to repent it too late, "an' I must say, if it kills me, that I always had a sharp eye for ankles."

"It's a pity you didn't look as far up as the hand," returned Tom Spade, with boisterous mirth. "I have heard that Eliza lays hers on right heavy."

"That's so, suh, that's so," admitted Matthew, puffing smoke like a shifting engine, "but that's the fault of the marriage service, an' I'll stand to it at the Judgment Day—yes, suh, in the very presence of Providence who made it. I tell you, 'twill I led that woman to the altar she was the meekest-mouthed creetur that ever wiggled away from a kiss. Why, when I stepped on her train jest as I swung her up the aisle, if you believe me, all she said was, 'I hope you didn't hurt yo' foot'; an', bless my boots, ten minutes later, comin' out of church, she whispered in my year, 'You white-livered, hulkin' hound, you, get off my veil!' Well, well, it's sad how the ceremony can change a woman's heart."

"That makes it safer always to choose a widow," commented Sol. "Now, they do say that this is a fine weddin' up at the Hall—but I have my doubts. Them lace let in stockin's ain't to my mind."

"What's the rich young gentleman like?" inquired Tom Spade, with interest. "Jinnie says he's the kind of man that makes kissin' come natural—but I can't say that that conveys much to the father of a family."

"Oh, he's the sort that looks as if God Almighty had put the finishin' touches an' forgot to make the man," replied Sol. "He's got a mustache that you would say went to bed every night in curl papers."

Christopher pushed back his chair and drained his glass standing, then with a curt nod to Tom Spade he went out into the road.

It was the walk of a mile from the store to his house, and as he went on he fell to examining the tobacco, which appeared to ripen hour by hour in the warm, moist season. There was no danger of frost as yet, and though a little of Fletcher's crop had already been cut, the others had left theirs to mature in the favourable weather. From a clear emerald the landscape had changed to a yellowish green, and the huge leaves had crinkled at the edges like shirred silk. Here and there pale-brown splotches on a plant showed that it had too quickly ripened, or small perforations revealed the destructive presence of a hidden tobacco worm.

As Christopher neared the house the hounds greeted him with a single bay, and the cry brought Cynthia hastily out upon the porch and along the little path. At the gate she met him, and slipping her hand under his arm, drew him across the road to the rail fence that bordered the old field. At sight of her tearless pallor his ever-present fear shot up, and without waiting for her words he cried out quickly: "Is mother ill?"

"No, no," she answered, "oh, no; but, Christopher, it is the next worse thing."

He thought for a breath. "Then she has found out?"

"It's not that either," she shook her head. "Oh, Christopher, it's Fletcher!"

"It's Fletcher! What in thunder have we to do with Fletcher?"

"You remember the deed of trust on the place— —the three hundred dollars we borrowed when mother was sick. Fletcher has bought it from Tom Spade and he means to foreclose it in a week. He has advertised the farm at the cross-roads."

He paled with anger. "Why, I saw Tom about it three days ago," he said, striking the rotten fence-rail until it broke and fell apart; "he told me it could run on at the same interest."

"It's since then that Fletcher has bought it. He meant it as a surprise, of course, to drive us out whether or no, but Sam Murray came straight up to tell you."

He stood thinking hard, his eyes on the waving goldenrod in the old field.

"I'll sell the horses," he said at last.

"And starve? Besides, they wouldn't bring the money."

"Then we'll sell the furniture—every last stick! We'll sell the clothes from our backs—I'll sell myself into slavery before Fletcher shall beat me now!"

"We've sold all we've got." said Cynthia; "the old furniture is too heavy—all that's left; nobody about here wants it."

"I tell you I'll find those three hundred dollars if I have to steal them. I'd rather go to prison than have Fletcher get the place."

"Then he'd have it in the end," remarked Cynthia hopelessly; adding after a pause, "I've thought it all out, dear, and we must steal the money—we must steal it from mother."

"From mother!" he echoed, touched to the quick.

"You know her big diamond," sobbed the woman, "the one in her engagement ring, that she never used to take off, even at night, till her fingers got so thin."

"Oh, I couldn't!" he protested.

"There's no other way," pursued Cynthia, without noticing him. "Surely, it is better than having her turned out in her old age—surely, anything is better than that. We can take the ring to-night after she goes to bed, and pry the diamond from the setting; it is held only by gold claws, you know. Then we will put in it the piece of purple glass from Docia's wedding ring—the shape is the same; and she will never find it out—— Oh, mother! mother!"

"I can't," returned Christopher stubbornly; "it is like robbing her, and she so blind and helpless. I cannot do it."

"Then I will," said Cynthia quietly, and, turning from him, she walked rapidly to the house.

Later that night, when he had gone up to his little garret loft, she came to him with the two rings in her outstretched hand—the superb white diamond and the common purple setting in Docia's brass hoop.

"Lend me your knife," she said, kneeling beside the smoky oil lamp; and without a word he drew his clasp-knife from his pocket, opened the blade, and held the handle toward her. She took it from him, and then knelt motionless for an instant looking at the diamond, which shone like a star in her hollowed palm. Presently she stooped and kissed it, and then taking the fine point of the blade, carefully pried the gold claws back from the imprisoned stone.

"She has worn it for fifty years," she said softly, seeing the jewel contract and give out a deeper flame to her misty eyes.

"It is robbery," he protested.

"It is robbery for her sake!" she flashed out angrily.

"All the same, it seems bitterly cruel."

With deft fingers she removed the bit of purple glass from Docia's ring and inserted it between the gold claws, which she pressed securely down. "To the touch there is no difference," she said, closing her eyes. "She will never know."

Rising from her knees, she gazed steadily at the loosened diamond lying in her hand; then, wrapping it in cotton, she placed it in a little wooden box from a jeweller of fifty years ago. "You must get up to-morrow and take it to town," she went on. "Carry it to Mr. Withers—he knows us. There is no other way," she added hastily.

"There is no other way, I know," he repeated, as he held out his hand.

"And you'll be back after sundown."

"Not until night. I shall walk over from the cross-roads."

For a time they were both silent, and he, walking to the narrow window, looked out into the moist darkness. The smell of the oil lamp oppressed the atmosphere inside, and the damp wind in his face revived in a measure his lowered spirits. He seemed suddenly able to cope with life—and with Fletcher.

Far away there was a faint glimmer among the trees, now shining clear, now almost lost in mist, and he knew it to be a lighted window at Blake Hall. The thought of Maria's lace stockings came to him all at once, and he was seized with a rage that was ludicrously large for so small a cause. Confused questions whirled in his brain, struggling for recognition: "I am here and she is there, and what is the meaning of it all? I know in spite of everything I might have loved her, and yet I know still better that it is not love, but hate I now feel. What is the difference, after all? And why this eternal bother of possibilities?" He turned presently and spoke: "And you got this without her suspecting it?"

"She was sleeping like a child, and Lila was in the little bed in her chamber. Often she is restless, disturbed by her dreams, but to-night she lies very quiet, and she smiled once as if she were so happy."

"And to-morrow she will wear the ring with its setting of purple glass."

"She will never know—see, it fits perfectly. I have fastened it carefully. After all, what does it matter to her—the ring is still the same, and the value of it was for her in the association."

Again he looked out of the window, and the distant glimmer gathered radiance and shone brightly among the trees. "I am here and she is there, and what is the meaning of it all?"

CHAPTER IV

A Gallant Deed That Leads to Evil

Two days later Christopher met Fletcher in the little room behind the store and paid down the three hundred dollars in the presence of Sam Murray. Several loungers, who had been seasoning their drinks with leisurely stories, hastily drained their glasses and withdrew at Fletcher's entrance, and when the three men came together to settle the affair of the mortgage they were alone in the presence of the tobacco-stained walls, the square pine table with its dirty glasses, and the bills of notice posted beside the door. Among them Christopher had seen the public advertisement of his farm—a rambling statement in large letters, signifying that the place would be sold for debt on Monday, the twenty-fifth of September, at twelve o'clock.

"I want the money right flat down. Are you sure you've got it?" were Fletcher's first words after his start of angry surprise.

For answer Christopher drew the roll of bills from his pocket and counted them out upon the table.

"Here it is," he said, "and I am done with you for good and all—with you and your rascally cheating ways."

"Come, come, let's go easy," warned Sam Murray, a fat, well-to-do farmer, who was accustomed to act the part of a lawyer in small transactions.

Fletcher flushed purple and threw off his rage in a sneering guffaw.

"Now that sounds well from him, doesn't it?" he inquired—"when everybody knows he hasn't a beggarly stitch on earth but that strip of land he thinks so much of."

"And whose fault is that, Bill Fletcher?" demanded the young man, throwing the last note down.

"Oh, well, I don't bear you any grudge," responded Fletcher, with an abrupt assumption of good-natured tolerance; "and to show I'm a well-meaning man in spite of abuse, I'll let the debt run on two years longer at the same interest if you choose."

Christopher laughed shortly. "That's all right, Sam," he said, without replying directly to the offer. "I owe him too much already to hope to pay it back in a single lifetime."

"Well, you're a cantankerous, hard-headed fool, that's all I've got to say," burst out Fletcher, swallowing hard, "and the sooner you get to the poorhouse along your own road the better it'll be for the rest of us."

"You may be sure I'll take care not to go along yours. I'll have honest men about me, at any rate."

"Then it's more than you've got a right to expect."

Christopher grew pale to the lips. "What do you mean, you scoundrel?" he cried, taking a single step forward.

"Come, come, let's go easy," said Sam Murray

persuasively, rising from his chair at the table. "Now that this little business is all settled there's no need for another word. I haven't much opinion of words myself, anyhow. They're apt to set fire to a dry tongue, that's what I say."

"What do you mean?" repeated Christopher, without swerving from his steady gaze.

Tom Spade glanced in at the open door, and, catching Fletcher's eye, hurriedly retreated. A small boy with a greasy face came in and gathered up the glasses with a clanking noise.

"What do you mean, you coward?" demanded Christopher for the third time. He had not moved an inch from the position he had first assumed, but the circle about his mouth showed blue against the sunburn on his face.

Fletcher raised his hand and spoke suddenly with a snort.

"Oh, you needn't kick so about swallowing it," he said. "Everybody knows that your grandfather never paid a debt he owed, and your father was mighty little better. He was only saved from becoming a thief by being a drunkard."

He choked over the last word, for Christopher, with an easy, almost leisurely movement, had struck him full in the mouth.

The young man's arm was raised again, but before it fell Sam Murray caught it back.

"I say, Tom, there's the devil to pay here!" he shouted, and Tom Spade rushed hurriedly through the doorway.

"Now, now, that'll never do, Mr. Christopher," he reasoned, with a deference he would never have wasted upon Fletcher. "Why, he's old enough to be yo' pa twice over."

A white fleck was on Fletcher's beard, and as he wiped it away he spoke huskily. "It's a clear case of assault and I'll have the law on him," he said. "Sam Murray, you saw him hit me square in the face."

"Bless your life, I wasn't looking, suh," responded Sam pleasantly. "I miss a lot in this life by always happening to look the other way."

"I'll have the law on you," cried Fletcher again, shaking back his heavy eyebrows.

"You're welcome to have every skulking hound in the county on me," Christopher replied, loosening Sam Murray's restraining grasp. "If I can settle you I reckon I can settle them; but the day you open your lying mouth to me again I'll shoot you down as I would a mad dog—and wash my hands clean afterward!"

He looked round for his harvest hat, picked it up from the floor where it had fallen, and walked slowly out of the room.

In the broad noon outside he staggered an instant, dazzled by the glare.

"Had a drop too much, ain't you, Mr. Christopher?" a voice inquired at his side, and, looking down, he saw Sol Peterkin sitting on a big wooden box just outside the store.

"Not too much to mind my own business," was his curt reply.

"Oh, no harm's meant, suh, an' I hope none's taken," responded the little man good-naturedly. "I saw you walk kinder crooked, that was all, an'

it came to me that you might be needin' an arm
toward home. Young gentlemen will be gentlemen, that's the truth, suh, an' in my day I reckon
I've steadied the legs of mo' young beaux than
you could count on your ten fingers. Good Lord,
when it comes to thinkin' of those Christmas Eve
frolics that we had befo' the war! Why, they
use to say that you couldn't get to the Hall unless
you swam your way through apple toddy. Jest
to think! an' here I've been settin' an' countin'
the bundles goin' up thar now——"

"I'm looking for a box, Tom," said a clear voice
at Christopher's back, "a big paper hat-box that
ought to have come by express——"

He turned quickly and saw Maria Fletcher in a
little cart in the road, with a strange young man
holding the reins. As Christopher swung round,
she nodded pleasantly, but with a cool stare he
passed down the steps and out into the road, carrying with him a distasteful impression of the strange
young man. Yet from that first hurried glimpse
he had brought away only the picture of a brown
mustache.

"By George, I'd like to see that fellow in the prize
ring," he heard the stranger remark as he went by.
"Do they have knock-outs around here, I wonder?"

"Oh, I dare say he'd oblige you with one if you
took the trouble to tread on his preserves," was
the girl's laughing rejoinder.

A massive repulsion swept over Christopher,
pervading his entire body—a repulsion that was
but a recoil from his exhausted rage. In this new
emotion there were both weariness and self-pity,

and to his mental vision there showed clearly, with an impersonal detachment, his own figure in relation to the scenes among which he moved. "That is I yonder," he might have said had he been able to disentangle thought from sensation, "plodding along there through the red mud in the road. Look at the coarse clothes, smelling of axle-grease, the hands knotted by toil and stained with tobacco juice, the face soiled with sweat and clay. That is I, who was born with the love of ease and the weakness to temptation in my blood, with the love, too, of delicate food, of rare wines, and of beautiful women. Once I craved these things; now the thought of them troubles me no longer, for I work in the sun all day and go home to enjoy my coarse food. Is it because I have been broken to my life as a young horse is broken to the plough, or have all the desires I have known been swallowed up in a single hatred—a hatred as jealous and as strong as love?"

It was his nightly habit, lying upon his narrow bed in the little loft, to yield some moments before sleeping to his idle dreams of vengeance—to plan exquisite punishments and impossible retaliations. In imagination he had so often seen Fletcher drop dead before him, had so often struck the man down with his own hand, that there were hours when he almost believed the deed to have been done—when something like madness gripped him, and his hallucinations took the snape and colour of life itself. At such times he was conscious of the exhilaration that comes in the instants of swift action, when events move quickly, and one rises beyond the ordinary level of experience. When the real moment came—the supreme chance—he wondered if he would meet it as triumphantly as he met his dreams? Now, plodding along the rocky road, he went over again all the old schemes for the great revenge.

The small cart whirled past him, scattering dried mud-drops in his face, and he caught the sound of bright girlish laughter. Looking after it, he saw the flutter of cherry-coloured ribbons coiling outward in the wind, and he remembered, watching the gay streamers, that the only woman he had ever kissed was eating cherries at the moment. Trivial as the recollection was, it started other associations, and he followed the escaping memory of that boyish romance, blithe and short-lived, which was killed at last by a single yielded kiss. At sixteen it had seemed to him that when he caught the girl of the cherries in his arms he should hold veritable happiness; and yet afterward there was only a great heaviness and something of the repulsion that he felt to-day. Happiness was not to be found on a woman's lips: he had learned this in his boyhood; and then even as the knowledge returned to him he found himself savagely regretting that he had not kissed Maria Fletcher the day he found her on his land—a kiss of anger, not of love, which she would have loathed all her life—and have remembered! To have her utterly forget him—pass on serenely into her marriage, hardly remembering that he hated her— this was the bitterest thing he had to face; but with the brutal wish, he softened in recalling the tremor of her lip as she turned away—the indignant quiver of her eyelashes. Again came the thought: "I know in spite of everything I might have loved her, and yet I know still better that it is not love, but hate I now feel." Her fragrance, floating in the sunshine, filled his nostrils, and involuntarily he glanced over his shoulder, half expecting to find a dropped handkerchief in the road. None was there —only a scattered swarm of butterflies drifting like yellow rose-leaves on the wind.

Upon reaching the house he found that his mother had asked for him, and running hastily up to change his clothes, he came down and bent over the upright Elizabethan chair.

"I have been worrying a good deal about you, my son," she said, with a sprightly gesture in which the piece of purple glass struck the dominant note. "Are you quite sure that you are feeling perfectly well? No palpitations of the heart when you go upstairs? and no particular heaviness after meals? I dreamed about you all night long, and though there's not a woman in the world freer from superstition, I can't help feeling uneasy."

Taking her hand, he gently caressed the slender fingers.

"Why, I'm a regular ox, mother," he returned, laughing, "my muscle is like iron, and I assure you I'm ready for my meals day or night. There's no use worrying about me, so you'd as well give it up."

"I can't understand it, I really can't," protested Mrs. Blake, still unconvinced. "I am an old woman, you know, and I am anxious to have you settled in life before I die—but there seems to be a most extraordinary humour in the family with regard to marriage. I'm sure your poor father would turn in his grave at the very idea of his having no grand-children to come after him."

"Well, there's time yet, mother; give us breathing space."

"There's not time in my day, Christopher, for I am very old, and half dead as it is—but it does seem hard that I am never to be present at the marriage of a child. As for Cynthia, she is out of the question, of course, which is a great pity. I have very little patience with an unmarried woman —no, not if she were Queen Elizabeth herself— though I do know that they are sometimes found very useful in the dairy or the spinning-room. As for an old bachelor, I have never seen the spot on earth—and I've lived to a great age—where he wasn't an encumbrance. They really ought to be taught some useful occupation, such as skimming milk or carding wool."

"I hardly think either of those pursuits would be to my taste," protested Christopher, "but I give you leave to try your hand on Uncle Tucker."

"Tucker has been a hero, my son," rejoined the old lady in a stately voice, "and the privilege of having once been a hero is that nobody expects you to exert yourself again. A man who has taken the enemy's guns single-handed, or figured prominently in a society scandal, is comfortably settled in his position and may slouch pleasantly for the remainder of his life. But for an ordinary gentleman it is quite different, and as we are not likely to have another war, you really ought to marry. You are preparing to go through life too peacefully, my son."

"Good Lord!" exclaimed Christopher, "are you hankering after squabbles? Well, you shan't drag me into them, at any cost. There's Uncle Tucker to your hand, as I said before."

"I'm sure Tucker might have married several times had he cared about it," replied Mrs. Blake reprovingly. "Miss Matoaca Bolling always had a sentiment for him, I am certain, and even after his misfortune she went so far as to present him with a most elaborate slipper of red velvet ornamented with steel beads. I remember well her consulting me as to whether it would be better to seem unsympathetic and give him two or to appear indelicate and offer him one. I suggested that she should make both for the same foot, which, I believe, she finally decided to do."

"Well, well, this is all very interesting, mother," said Christopher, rising from his seat, "but I've promised old Jacob Weatherby to pass my word on his tobacco. On the way down, however, I'll cast my eyes about for a wife."

"Between here and the Weatherbys' farm? Why, Christopher!"

"That's all right, but unless you expect me to pick up one on the roadside I don't see how we'll manage. I'll do anything to oblige you, you know, even marry, if you'll find me a good, sensible woman."

The old lady's eyelids dropped over her piercing black eyes, which seemed always to regard some far-off, ecstatic vision. Three small furrows ran straight up and down her forehead, and she lifted one delicate white hand to rub them out.

"I don't like joking on so serious a subject, my

son," she said. "I'm sure Providence expects every man to do his duty, and to remain unmarried seems like putting one's personal inclination before the intentions of the Creator. Your grandfather Corbin used to say he had so high an opinion of marriage that if his fourth wife—and she was very sickly—were to die at once, he'd marry his fifth within the year. I remember that Bishop Deane remarked it was one of the most beautiful tributes ever paid the marriage state—especially as it was no idle boast, for, as it happened, his wife died shortly afterward, and he married Miss Polly Blair before six months were up."

"What a precious old fool he was!" laughed the young man, as he reached the door, passing out with a horrified "What, Christopher! Your own grandfather?" ringing in his ears.

In the yard he found Cynthia drawing water at the well, and he took the heavy bucket from her and carried it into the kitchen. "You'd better change your clothes," she remarked, eying him narrowly, "if you're going back to the field."

"But I'm not going back; the axe handle has broken again and I'll have to borrow Jim Weatherby's. There's no use trying to mend that old handle any more. It'll have to lie over till after tobacco cutting, when I can make a new one."

"Oh, you might as well keep Jim's altogether," returned Cynthia irritably, loath to receive favours from her neighbours. "The first thing we know he will be running this entire place."

"I reckon he'd make a much better job of it," replied Christopher, as he swung out into the road.

On the whitewashed porch of the Weatherbys' house he found old Jacob—a hale, cleanly old man with cheeks like frosted winter apples—gazing thoughtfully over his fine field of tobacco, which had grown almost to his threshold.

"The weather's going to have a big drop to-night," he said reflectively; "I smell it on the wind. Lord! Lord! I reckon I'd better begin on that thar tobaccy about sunup—and yet another day or so of sun and September dew would sweeten it consider'ble. How about yours, Mr. Christopher?"

"I'll cut my ripest plants to-morrow," answered Christopher, sniffing the air. "A big drop's coming, sure enough, but I don't scent frost as yet—the pines don't smell that way."

They discussed the tobacco for a time—the rosy, genial old man, whom age had mellowed without souring—listening with a touching deference to his visitor's casual words; and when at last Christopher, with the axe on his shoulder, started leisurely homeward, "the drop" was already beginning, and the wind blew cool and crisp across the misty fields, beyond which a round, red sun was slowly setting. Level, vast and dark, the tobacco swept clear to the horizon.

Between Weatherby's and the little store there was an abrupt bend in the road, where it shot aside from a steep descent in the ground; and Christopher had reached this point when he saw suddenly ahead of him a farm wagon driven forward at a reckless pace. As it neared him he heard the wheels thunder on the rocky bed of the road, and saw that the driver's seat was vacant, the man evidently having

been thrown some distance back. The horses—
a young pair he had never seen before—held the
bits in their mouths; and it was with a hopelessness
of checking their terrible speed that he stepped out
of the road to give them room. The next instant
he saw that they were making straight for the
declivity from which the road shot back, seeing in
the same breath that the driver of the wagon, not
falling clear, had entangled himself in the long reins
and was being dragged rapidly beneath the wheels.

Tossing his axe aside, he sprang instantly at the
horses' heads, hanging with his whole powerful
weight upon their mouths. Life or death was nothing
to him at the moment, and he seemed to have only
an impersonal interest in the multiplied sensations.
What followed was a sense of incalculable swiftness,
a near glimpse of blue sky, the falling of stars
around him in the road, and after these things a
great darkness.

.   .   .   .

When he came to himself he was lying in a patch
of short grass, with a little knot of men about him,
among whom he recognised Jim Weatherby.

"I brought them in, didn't I?" he asked, struggling
up; and then he saw that his coat sleeves were rent
from the armholes, leaving his arms bare beneath
his torn blue shirt. Cynthia's warning returned to
him, and he laughed shortly.

"Well, I reckon you could bring the devil in if
you put all your grip on him," was Jim's reply; "as
it is, you're pretty sore, ain't you?"

"Oh, rather, but I wish I hadn't spoiled my coat."
He was still thinking of Cynthia.

"God alive, man, it's a mercy you didn't spoil your life. Why, another second and the horses would have been over that bank yonder, with you and young Fletcher under the wagon."

Christopher rose slowly from the ground and stood erect.

"With me—and who under the wagon?—and who?" he asked in a throaty voice.

Jim Weatherby whistled. "Why, to think you didn't know all along!" he exclaimed. "It was Fletcher's boy; he made Zebbadee let him take the reins. Fletcher saw it all and he was clean mad when he got here—it took three men to hold him. He thinks more of that boy than he does of his own soul. What's the matter, man, are you hurt?"

Christopher had gone dead white, and the blue circle came out slowly around his mouth. "And I saved him!" he gasped. "I saved him! Isn't there some mistake? Maybe he's dead anyway!"

"Bless you, no," responded Jim, a trifle disconcerted. "The doctor's here and he says it's a case of a broken leg instead of a broken neck, that's all."

Looking about him, Christopher saw that there was another group of men at a little distance, gathered around something that lay still and straight on the grass. The sound of a hoarse groan reached him suddenly—an inarticulate cry of distress—and he felt with a savage joy that it was from Fletcher. He looked down, drawing together his tattered sleeves. For a time he was silent, and when he spoke it was with a sneering laugh.

"Well, I've been a fool, that's all," was what he said.

CHAPTER V

The Glimpse of a Bride

THE next morning he awoke with stiffened limbs
and confusion in his head, and for a time he lay idly
looking at his little window-panes, beyond which
the dawn hung like a curtain. Then, as a long finger
of sunlight pointed through the glass, he rose with
an effort and, dressing himself hastily, went downstairs to breakfast. Here he found that Zebbadee
Blake, who had promised to help him cut his crop,
had not yet appeared, owing probably to the
excitement of Fletcher's runaway. The man's
absence annoyed him at first; and then, as the day
broke clear and cold, he succumbed to his ever-
present fear of frost and, taking his pruning-knife
from the kitchen mantelpiece, went out alone to
begin work on his ripest plants.

The sun had already tempered the morning chill
in the air, and the slanting beams stretched over
the tobacco, which, as the dew dried, showed a vivid
green but faintly tinged with yellow—a colour that
even in the sparkling sunlight appeared always
slightly shadowed. To attempt alone the cutting
of his crop, small as it was, seemed, with his stiffened
limbs, a particularly trying task, and for a moment
he stood gazing wearily across the field. Presently,

with a deliberate movement as if he were stooping to shoulder a fresh burden, he slit the first ripe stalk from its flaunting top to within a hand's-breadth of the ground; then, cutting it half through near the roots, he let it fall to one side, where it hung, slowly wilting, on the earth. Gradually, as he applied himself to the work, the old zest of healthful labour returned to him, and he passed buoyantly through the narrow aisle, leaving a devastated furrow on either side. It was a cheerful picture he presented, when Tucker, dragging himself heavily from the house, came to the ragged edge of the field and sat down on an old moss-grown stump.

"Where's Zebbadee, Christopher?"

"He didn't turn up. It was that affair of the accident, probably. Fletcher berated him, I reckon."

"So you've got to cut it all yourself. Well, it's a first-rate crop—the very primings ought to be as good as some top leaves."

"The crop's all right," responded Christopher, as his knife passed with a ripping noise down the juicy stalk. "You know I made a fool of myself yesterday, Uncle Tucker," he said suddenly, drawing back when the plant fell slowly across the furrow, "and I'm so stiff in the joints this morning I can hardly move. I met one of Fletcher's farm wagons running away, with his boy dragged by the reins, and—I stopped it."

Tucker turned his mild blue eyes upon him. Since the news of Appomattox nothing had surprised him, and he was not surprised now—he was merely interested. "You couldn't have helped it, I suspect," he remarked.

"I didn't know whose it was, you see," answered Christopher; "the horses were new."

"You'd have done it anyway, I reckon. At such moments it's a man's mettle that counts, you know, and not his emotions. You might have hated Fletcher ten times worse, but you'd have risked your life to stop the horses all the same—because, after all, what a man is is something different from how he feels about things. It's in your blood to dare everything whenever a chance offers, as it was in your father's before you. Why, I've seen him stop on the way to a ball, pull off his coat, and go up a burning ladder to save a woman's pet canary, and then, when the crowd hurrahed him, I've laughed because I knew he deserved nothing of the kind. With him it wasn't courage so much as his inborn love of violent action—it cleared his head, he used to say."

Christopher stopped cutting, straightened himself, and held his knife loosely in his hand.

"That's about it, I reckon," he returned. "I know I'm not a bit of a hero—if I'd been in your place I'd have shown up long ago for a skulking coward—but it's the excitement of the moment that I like. Why, there's nothing in life I'd enjoy so much as knocking Fletcher down—it's one of the things I look forward to that makes it all worth while."

Tucker laughed softly. It was a peculiarity of his never to disapprove.

"That's a good savage instinct," he said, with a humorous tremor of his nostrils, "and it's a saying of mine, you know, that a man is never really civilised until he has turned fifty. We're all born mighty near to the wolf and mighty far from the dog, and it takes a good many years to coax the wild beast to lie quiet by the fireside. It's the struggle that the Lord wants, I reckon; and anyhow, He makes it easier for us as the years go on. When a man gets along past his fiftieth year, he begins to understand that there are few things worth bothering about, and the sins of his fellow mortals are not among 'em."

"Bless my soul!" exclaimed Christopher in disgust, rapping his palm smartly with the flat blade of his knife. "Do you mean to tell me you've actually gone and forgiven Bill Fletcher?"

"Well, I wouldn't go so far as to water the grass on his grave," answered Tucker, still smiling, "but I've not the slightest objection to his eating, sleeping, and moving on the surface of the earth. There's room enough for us both, even in this little county, and so long as he keeps out of my sight, as far as I am concerned he absolutely doesn't exist. I never think of him except when you happen to call his name. If a man steals my money, that's his affair. I can't afford to let him steal my peace of mind as well."

With a groan Christopher went back to his work.

"It may be sense you're talking," he observed, "but it sounds to me like pure craziness. It's just as well, either way, I reckon, that I'm not in your place and you in mine—for if that were so Fletcher would most likely go scot free."

Tucker rose unsteadily from the stump.

"Why, if we stood in each other's boots," he said,

" . . . stood, bareheaded, gazing over the broad field."

with a gentle chuckle, "or, to be exact, if I stood in your two boots and you in my one, as sure as fate, you'd be thinking my way and I yours. Well, I wish I could help you, but as I can't I'll be moving slowly back."

He shuffled off on his crutches, painfully swinging himself a step at a time, and Christopher, after a moment's puzzled stare at his pathetic figure, returned diligently to his work.

His passage along the green aisle was very slow, and when at last he reached the extreme end by the little beaten path and felled the last stalk on his left side he straightened himself for a moment's rest, and stood, bareheaded, gazing over the broad field, which looked as if a windstorm had blown in an even line along the edge, scattering the outside plants upon the ground. The thought of his work engrossed him at the instant, and it was with something of a start that he became conscious presently of Maria Fletcher's voice at his back. Wheeling about dizzily, he found her leaning on the old rail fence, regarding him with shining eyes in which the tears seemed hardly dried.

"I have just left Will," she said; "the doctor has set his leg and he is sleeping. It was my last chance —I am going away to-morrow—and I wanted to tell you—I wanted so to tell you how grateful we feel."

The knife dropped from his hand, and he came slowly along the little path to the fence.

"I fear you've got an entirely wrong idea about me," he answered. "It was nothing in the world to make a fuss over—and I swear to you if it were the last word I ever spoke—I did not know it was your brother."

"As if that mattered!" she exclaimed, and he remembered vaguely that he had heard her use the words before. "You risked your life to save his life: we know that. Grandpa saw it all—and the horses dragged you, too. You would have been killed if the others hadn't run up when they did. And you tell me—as if that made it any the less brave—that you didn't know it was Will."

"I didn't," he repeated stubbornly. "I didn't."

"Well, he does," she responded, smiling; "and he wants to thank you himself when he is well enough."

"If you wish to do me a kindness, for heaven's sake tell him not to," he said irritably. "I hate all such foolishness—it makes me out a hypocrite!"

"I knew you'd hate it; I told them so," tranquilly responded the girl. "Aunt Saidie wanted to rush right over last night, but I wouldn't let her. All brave men dislike to have a fuss made over them, I know."

"Good Lord!" ejaculated Christopher, and stopped short, impatiently desisting before the admiration illumining her eyes. From her former disdain he had evidently risen to a height in her regard that was romantic in its ardour. It was in vain that he told himself he cared for one emotion as little as for the other—in spite of his words, the innocent fervour in her face swept over the barrier of his sullen pride.

"So you are going away to-morrow," he said at last; "and for good?"

"For good, yes. I go abroad very unexpectedly for perhaps five years. My things aren't half ready, but business is of more importance than a woman's clothes."

"Will you be alone?"

"Oh, no."

"Who goes with you?" he insisted bluntly.

As she reddened, he watched the colour spread slowly to her throat and ear.

"I am to be married, you know," she answered, with her accustomed composure of tone.

His lack of gallantry was churlish.

"To that dummy with the brown mustache?" he inquired.

A little hysterical laugh broke from her, and she made a hopeless gesture of reproof. "Your manners are really elementary," she remarked, adding immediately: "I assure you he isn't in the least a dummy—he is considered a most delightful talker."

He swept the jest impatiently aside.

"Why do you do it?" he demanded.

"Do what?"

"You know what I mean. Why do you marry him?"

Again she bit back a laugh. It was all very primitive, very savage, she told herself; it was, above all, different from any of the life that she had known, and yet, in a mysterious way, it was familiar, as if the unrestrained emotion in his voice stirred some racial memory within her brain.

"Why do I marry him?" She drew a step away, looking at sky and field. "Why do I marry him?" She hesitated slightly, "Oh, for many reasons, and all good ones—but most of all because I love him."

"You do not love him."

"I beg your pardon, but I do."

For the first time in her life, as her eyes swept over the landscape, she was conscious of a peculiar charm in the wildness of the country, in the absence of all civilising influences—in the open sky, the red road, the luxuriant tobacco, the coarse sprays of yarrow blooming against the fence; in the homely tasks, drawing one close to the soil, and the harvesting of the ripened crops, the milking of the mild-eyed cows, and in the long still days, followed by the long still nights.

Their eyes met, and for a time both were silent. She felt again the old vague trouble at his presence, the appeal of the rustic tradition, the rustic temperament; of all the multiplied inheritances of the centuries, which her education had not utterly extinguished.

"Well, I hope you'll live to regret it," he said suddenly, with bitter passion.

The words startled her, and she caught her breath with a tremor.

"What an awful wish!" she exclaimed lightly.

"It's an honest one."

"I'm not sure I shouldn't prefer a little polite lying."

"You won't get it from me. I hope you'll live to regret it. Why shouldn't I?"

"Oh, you might at least be decently human. If you hadn't been so brave yesterday, I might almost think you a savage to-day."

"I didn't do that on purpose, I told you," he returned angrily.

"You can't make me believe that—it's no use trying."

"I shan't try—though it's the gospel truth—and you'll find it out some day."

"When?"

"Oh, when the time comes, that's all."

"You speak in riddles," she said, "and I always hated guessing." Then she held out her hand with a pleasant, conventional smile. "I am grateful to you in spite of everything," she said; "and now good-by."

His arms hung at his side. "No, I won't shake hands," he answered. "What's the use?"

"As you please—only, it's the usual thing at parting."

"All the same, I won't do it," he said stubbornly. "My hands are not clean." He held them out, soiled with earth and the stains from the tobacco.

For an instant her eyes dwelt upon him very kindly.

"Oh, I shan't mind the traces of honest toil," she said; but as he still hung back, she gave a friendly nod and went quickly homeward along the road. As her figure vanished among the trees, a great bitterness oppressed him, and, picking up his knife, he went back doggedly to his work.

In the kitchen, when he returned to dinner some hours later, he found Cynthia squinting heavily over the torn coat.

"I must say you ruined this yesterday," she remarked, looking up from her needle, "and if you'd listened to me you could have stopped those horses just as well in your old jean clothes. I had a feeling that something was going to happen, when I saw you with this on."

"I don't doubt it," he responded, wofully eying the garment spread on her knees, "and I may as well admit right now that I made a mess of the whole thing. To think of my wasting the only decent suit I had on a Fletcher—after saving up a year to buy it, too."

Cynthia twitched the coat inside out and placed a square patch over the ragged edges of the rent. "I suppose I ought to be thankful you saved the boy's life," she observed, "but I can't say that I feel particularly jubilant when I look at these arm-holes. Of course, when I first heard of it the coat seemed a mere trifle, but when I come to the mending I begin to wish you'd been heroic in your every-day clothes. There'll have to be a patch right here, but I don't reckon it will show much. Do you mind?"

"I'd rather wear a mustard plaster than a patch any time," he replied gravely; "but as long as there's no help for it, lay them on—don't slight the job a bit because of my feelings. I can stand pretty well having my jean clothes darned and mended, but I do object to dressing up on Sundays in a bed-quilt."

"Well, you'll have to, that's all," was Cynthia's reassuring rejoinder. "It's the price you pay for being a hero when you can't afford it."

CHAPTER VI

SHOWS FLETCHER IN A NEW LIGHT

RESPONDING to a much-distracted telegram from Fletcher, Carraway arrived at the Hall early on the morning of Maria's marriage, to arrange for the transfer to the girl of her smaller share in her grandfather's wealth. In the reaction following the hysterical excitement over the accident, Fletcher had grown doubly solicitous about the future of the boy—feeling, apparently, that the value of his heir was increased by his having so nearly lost him. When Carraway found him he was bustling noisily about the sick-room, walking on tiptoe with a tramp that shook the floor, while Will lay gazing wearily at the sunlight which filtered through the bright-green shutters. Somewhere in the house a canary was trilling joyously, and the cheerful sound lent a pleasant animation to the otherwise depressing atmosphere. On his way upstairs Carraway had met Maria running from the boy's room, with her hair loose upon her shoulders, and she had stopped long enough to show a smiling face on the subject of her marriage. There were to be only Fletcher, Miss Saidie and himself as witnesses, he gathered—Wyndham's parents having held somewhat aloof from the connection—and within three hours at the

175

most it would be over and the bridal pair beginning their long journey. Looking down from the next landing, he had further assurance of the sincerity of Maria's smile when he saw the lovers meet and embrace within the shadow of the staircase; and the sight stirred within his heart something of that wistful pity with which those who have learned how little emotion counts in life watch the first exuberance of young passion. A bright beginning whatever be the ending, he thought a little sadly, as he turned the handle of the sick-room door.

The boy's fever had risen and he tossed his arms restlessly upon the counterpane. "Stand out of my sunshine, grandpa," he said fretfully, as the lawyer sat down by his bedside.

Fletcher shuffled hastily from before the window, and it struck Carraway almost ludicrously that in all the surroundings in which he had ever seen him the man had never appeared so hopelessly out of place—not even when he had watched him at prayer one Sunday in the little country church.

"There, you're in it again," complained the boy in his peevish tones.

Fletcher lifted a cup from the table and brought it over to the bed.

"Maybe you'd like a sip of this beef tea now," he suggested persuasively. "It's most time for your medicine, you know, so jest a little taste of this beforehand."

"I don't like it, grandpa; it's too salt."

"Thar, now, that's jest like Saidie," blurted Fletcher angrily. "Saidie, you've gone and made his beef tea too salt."

Miss Saidie appeared instantly at the door of the adjoining room, and without seeking to diminish the importance of her offense, mildly offered to prepare a fresh bowl of the broth.

"I'm packing Maria's clothes now," she said, "but I'll be through in a jiffy, and then I'll make the soup. I've jest fixed up the parlour for the marriage. Maria insists on having a footstool to kneel on—she ain't satisfied with jest standing with jined hands before the preacher, like her pa and ma did before she was born."

"Well, drat Maria's whims," retorted Fletcher impatiently; "they can wait, I reckon, and Will's got to have his tea, so you'd better fetch it."

"But I don't want it, grandpa," protested the boy, flushed and troubled. "You worry me so, that's all. Please stop fooling with those curtains— I like the sunshine."

"A nap is what he needs, I suspect," observed Carraway, touched, in spite of himself, by the lumbering misery of the man.

"Ah, that's it," agreed Fletcher, catching readily at the suggestion. "You jest turn right over and take yo' nap, and when you wake up—well, I'll give you anything you want. Here, swallow this stuff down quick and you'll sleep easy."

He brought the medicine glass to the bedside, and, slipping his great hairy hand under the pillow, gently raised the boy's head.

"I reckon you'd like a brand new saddle when you git up," he remarked in a coaxing voice.

"I'd rather have a squirrel gun, grandpa; I want to go hunting."

Fletcher's face clouded.

"I'm afraid you'd git shot, sonny."

With his lips to the glass, Will paused to haggle over the price of his obedience.

"But I want it," he insisted; "and I want a pack of hounds, too, to chase rabbits."

"Bless my boots! You ain't going to bring any driveling beasts on the place, air you?"

"Yes, I am, grandpa. I won't swallow this unless you say I may."

"Oh, you hurry up and git well, and then we'll see—we'll see," was Fletcher's answer. "Gulp this stuff right down now and turn over."

The boy still hesitated.

"Then I may have the hounds," he said; "that new litter of puppies Tom Spade has, and I'll get Christopher Blake to train 'em for me."

The pillow shook under his head, and as he opened his mouth to drink, a few drops of the liquid spilled upon the bedclothes.

"I reckon Zebbadee's a better man for hounds," suggested Fletcher, setting down the glass.

"Oh, Zebbadee's aren't worth a cent—they can't tell a rabbit from a watering-pot. I want Christopher Blake to train 'em, and I want to see him about it to-day. Tell him to come, grandpa."

"I can't, sonny—I can't; you git your hounds and we'll find a better man. Why, thar's Jim Weatherby; he'll do first rate."

"His dogs are setters," fretted Will. "I don't want him; I want Christopher Blake—he saved my life, you know."

"So he did, so he did," admitted Fletcher; "and

he shan't be a loser by that, suh," he added, turning
to Carraway. "When you go over thar, you can
carry my check along for five hundred dollars."

The lawyer smiled. "Oh, I'll take it," he answered,
"and I'll very likely bring it back."

The boy looked at Carraway. "You tell him to
come, sir," he pleaded. His eyes were so like
Fletcher's—small, sparkling, changing from blue to
brown—that the lawyer's glance lingered upon the
other's features, seeking some resemblance in them,
also. To his surprise he found absolutely none—
the high, blue-veined forehead beneath the chestnut
hair; the straight, delicate nose; the sensitive, almost
effeminate curve of the mouth, must have descended
from the "worthless drab" whom he had beheld
in the severe white light of Fletcher's scorn. For
the first time it occurred to Carraway that the
illumination had been too intense.

"I'll tell him, certainly," he said quietly after a
moment; "but I don't promise that he'll come, you
understand."

"Oh, I won't thank him," cried the boy eagerly.
"It isn't for that I want him—tell him so. Maria
says he hates a fuss."

"I'll deliver your message word for word," responded the lawyer. "Not only that, I'll add my
own persuasion to it, though I fear I have little
influence with your neighbour."

"Tell him I beg him to come," insisted the boy,
and the urgent voice remained with Carraway
throughout the day.

It was not until the afternoon, however, when
he had tossed his farewell handful of rice at the

departing carriage and met Maria's last disturbed look at the Hall, that he found time to carry Will's request and Fletcher's check to Christopher Blake. The girl had shown her single trace of emotion over the boy's pillow, where she had shed a few furtive tears, and the thought of this was with Carraway as he walked meditatively along the red clay road, down the long curves of which he saw the carriage rolling leisurely ahead of him. As a bride, Maria puzzled him no less than she had done at their first meeting, and the riddle of her personality he felt to be still hopelessly unsolved. Was it merely repression of manner that annoyed him in her? he questioned, or was it, as he had once believed, the simple lack of emotional power? Her studied speech, her conventional courtesy, seemed to confirm the first impression she had made; then her dark, troubled gaze and the sullen droop of her mouth returned to give the lie to what he could but feel to be a possible misjudgment. In the end, he concluded wisely enough that, like the most of us, she was probably but plastic matter for the mark of circumstance— that her development would be, after all, according to the events she was called upon to face. The possibility that Destiny, which is temperament, should have already selected her as one of those who come into their spiritual heritage only through defeat, did not enter into the half-humorous consideration with which he now regarded her.

Turning presently into the sunken road by the ice-pond, he came in a little while to the overgrown fence surrounding the Blake farm. In the tobacco field beyond the garden he saw Christopher's blue-

clad figure rising from a blur of green, and, following the ragged path amid the yarrow, he joined the
young man where he stood at work.

As the lawyer reached his side Christopher glanced
up indifferently to give a nod of welcome. His
crop had all been cut, and he was now engaged in
hanging the wilting plants from long rails supported
by forked poles. At his feet there were little green
piles of tobacco, and around him from the sunbaked
earth rose a headless army of bruised and bleeding
stubble.

So thriftless were the antiquated methods he
followed that the lawyer, as he watched him, could
barely repress a smile. Two hundred years ago
the same crop was probably raised, cut and cured
on the same soil in the same careless and primitive
fashion. Beneath all the seeming indifference to
success or failure Carraway discerned something
of that blind reliance upon chance which is apt to
be the religious expression of a rural and isolated
people.

"Yes, I'll leave it out awhile, I reckon, unless the
weather changes," replied Christopher, in answer
to the lawyer's inquiry.

"Well, it promises fair enough," returned Carraway
pleasantly. "They tell me, by the way, that the
yellow, sun-cured leaf is coming into favour in the
market. You don't try that, eh?"

Christopher shook his head, and, kneeling on the
ground, carelessly sorted his pile of plants. "I
learned to cure it indoors," he answered, "and I
reckon I'll keep to the old way. The dark leaf is
what the people about here like—it makes the

sweeter chew, they think. As for me, I hate the very smell of it."

"That's odd, and I'll wager you're the only man in the county who neither smokes nor chews."

"Oh, I handle it, you see. The smell and the stain of it are well soaked in. I sometimes wonder if all the water in the river of Jordan could wash away the blood of the tobacco worm."

With a laugh in which there was more bitterness than mirth, he stretched out his big bronzed hands, and Carraway saw that the nails and finger-tips were dyed bright green.

"It does leave its mark," observed the lawyer, and felt instantly that the speech was inane.

Christopher went on quietly with his work, gathering up the plants and hanging the slit stalks over the long poles, while the peculiar heavy odour of the freshly cut crop floated unpleasantly about them.

For a time Carraway watched him in silence, his eyes dwelling soberly upon the stalwart figure. In spite of himself, the mere beauty of outline touched him with a feeling of sadness, and when he spoke at last it was in a lowered tone.

"You have, perhaps, surmised that my call is not entirely one of pleasure," he began awkwardly; "that I am, above all, the bearer of a message from Mr. Fletcher."

"From Fletcher?" repeated Christopher coolly. "Well, I never heard a message of his yet that wasn't better left undelivered."

"I am sure I am correct in saying," Carraway went on steadily and not without definite purpose, "that he hopes you will be generous enough to let bygones be bygones."

Christopher nodded.

"He feels, of course," pursued the lawyer, "that his obligation to you is greater than he can hope to repay. Indeed, I think if you knew the true state of the case your judgment of him would be softened. The boy who so nearly lost his life is the one human being whom Fletcher loves better than himself—better than his own soul, I had almost said."

Christopher looked up attentively. "Who'd have thought it," he muttered beneath his breath.

Judging that he had at last made a beginning at the plastering over of old scars, Carraway went on as if the other had not spoken. "So jealous is his affection in this instance, that I believe his grand-daughter's marriage is something of a relief to him. He is positively impatient of any influence over the boy except his own—and that, I fear, is hardly for good."

Picking up a clod of earth, Christopher crumbled it slowly to dust. "So the little chap comes in for all this, does he?" he asked, as his gaze swept over the wide fields in the distance. "He comes in for all that is mine by right, and Fletcher's intention is, I dare say, that he'll reflect honour upon the theft?"

"That he'll reflect honour upon the name—yes. It is the ambition of his grandfather, I believe, that the lad should grow up to be respected in the county—to stand for something more than he himself has done."

"Well, he'll hardly stand for more of a rascal,"

remarked Christopher quietly; and then, as his eyes rested on the landscape, he appeared to follow moodily some suggestion which had half escaped him. "Then the way to touch the man is through the boy, I presume," he said abruptly.

Arrested by the words, the lawyer looked down quickly, but the other, still kneeling upon the ground, was fingering a plant he had just picked up. "Fine leaves, eh?" was the remark that met Carraway's sudden start.

"To touch him, yes," replied the lawyer thoughtfully. "Whatever heart he has is given to his grandson, and when you saved the lad's life the other day you placed Fletcher in your debt for good. Of his gratitude I am absolutely sure, and as a slight expression of it he asked me to hand you this."

He drew the check from his pocket, and leaning over, held it out to Christopher. To his surprise, the young man took it from him, but the next moment he had torn it roughly in two and handed it back again. "So you may as well return it to him," he said, and, rising slowly from the ground, he stood pushing the loose plants together with his foot.

"I feared as much," observed Carraway, placing the torn slip of paper in his pocket. "Your grudge is of too long standing to mend in a day. Be that as it may, I have a request to make of you from the boy himself which I hope you will not refuse. He has taken a liking to you, it appears, and as he will probably be ill for some weeks, he begs that you will come back with me to see him."

He finished a little wistfully, and stood looking up

at the young man who towered a good head and shoulders above him.

"I may as well tell you once for all," returned Christopher, choking over the words, "that you've given me as much of Fletcher as I can stand and a long sight more than I want. If anybody but you had brought me that piece of paper with Bill Fletcher's name tagged to it I'd have rammed it down his throat before this. As it is, you may tell him from me that when I have paid him to the last drop what I owe him—and not till then—will I listen to any message he chooses to send me. I hate him, and that's my affair; I mean to be even with him some day, and I reckon that's my affair, too. One thing I'm pretty sure of, and that is that it's not yours. Is your visit over, or will you come into the house?"

"I'll be going back now," replied the lawyer, shrinking from before the outburst, "but if I may have the pleasure, I'll call upon your mother in the morning."

Christopher shook the hand which he held out, and then spoke again in the same muffled voice. "You may tell him one thing more," he pursued, "and that is, that it's the gospel truth I didn't know it was his grandson in the wagon. Why, man, there's not a Fletcher on this earth whose neck I'd lift my little finger to save!"

Then, as Carraway passed slowly along the ragged path to the sunken road, he stood looking after him with a heavy frown upon his brow. His rage was at white heat within him, and, deny it as he would, he knew now that within the last few weeks his hatred had been strengthened by the force of a newer passion which had recoiled upon itself. Since his parting with Maria Fletcher the day before, he had not escaped for a breath from her haunting presence. She was in his eyes and in the air he breathed; the smell of flowers brought her sweetness to him, and the very sunshine lying upon the September fields thrilled him like the warmth of her rare smile. He found himself fleeing like a hunted animal from the memory which he could not put away, and despite the almost frenzied haste with which he presently fell to work, he saw always the light and gracious figure which had come to him along the red clay road. The fervour which had shone suddenly in her eyes, the quiver of her mouth as she turned away, the poise of her head, the gentle, outstretched hand he had repulsed, the delicate curve of her wrist beneath the falling sleeve, the very lace on her bosom fluttering in the still weather as if a light wind were blowing—these things returned to torture him like the delirium of fever. Appealing as the memory was, it aroused in his distorted mind all the violence of his old fury, and he felt again the desire for revenge working like madness in his blood. It was as if every emotion of his life swept on, to empty itself at last into the wide sea of his hatred.

CHAPTER VII

IN WHICH HERO AND VILLAIN APPEAR AS ONE

A MONTH later Christopher's conversation with Carraway returned to him, when, coming one morning from the house with his dogs at his heels and his squirrel gun on his shoulder, he found Will Fletcher and a troop of spotted foxhound puppies awaiting him outside the whitewashed gate.

"I want to speak to you a moment, Mr. Blake," began the boy, in the assured tones of the rich man to the poor. The Blake hounds made a sudden rush at the puppies, to be roughly ordered to heel by their master.

"Well, fire away," returned the young man coolly. "But I may as well warn you that it's more than likely it will be a clear waste of breath. I'll have nothing to do with you or your sort." He leaned on his gun and looked indifferently over the misty fields, where the autumn's crop of life-everlasting shone silver in the sunrise.

"I don't see why you hate me so," said the boy wonderingly, checking the too frolicsome adventures of the puppies in the direction of the hounds. "I've always liked you, you know, even before you saved my life—because you're the straightest shot and the best trainer of hounds about here. Grandpa says I mustn't have anything to do with you, but I will anyway, if I please."

"Oh, you will, will you?" was Christopher's rejoinder, as he surveyed him with the humorous contempt which the strong so often feel for the weak of the same sex. "Well, I suppose I'll have my say in the matter, and strangely enough I'm on your grandfather's side. The clearer you keep of me the better it will be for you, my man."

"That's just like grandpa all over again," protested the boy; "and when it comes to that, he needn't know anything about it—he doesn't know half that I do, anyway; he blusters so about things."

Christopher's gaze returned slowly from the landscape and rested inquiringly upon the youthful features before him, seeking in them some definite promise of the future. The girlish look of the mouth irritated him ludicrously, and half-forgotten words of Carraway's awoke within his memory.

"Fletcher loves but one thing on this earth, and his ambition is that the boy shall be respected in the county." A Fletcher respected in the very stronghold of a Blake! He laughed aloud, and then spoke hurriedly as if to explain the surprising mirth in his outburst.

"So you came to pay a visit to your nearest neighbour and are afraid your grandfather will find it out? Then you'll get a spanking, I dare say."

Will blushed furiously, and stood awkwardly scraping up a pile of sand with the sole of his boot. "I'm not a baby," he blurted out at last, "and I'll go where I like, whatever he says."

"He keeps a pretty close watch over you, I reckon.

Perhaps he's afraid you'll become a man and step into his shoes before he knows it."

"Oh, he can't find me out, all the same," said the boy slyly. "He thinks I've gone over to Mr. Morrison's now to do my Greek—he's crazy about my learning Greek, and I hate it—and, you bet your life, he'll be hopping mad if he finds I've given him the slip."

"He will, will he?" remarked Christopher, and the thought appeared to afford him a peculiar satisfaction. For the first time the frown left his brow and his tone lost its insolent contempt. Then he came forward suddenly and laid his hand upon the gate. "Well, I can't waste my morning," he said. "You'd better run back home and play the piano. I'm off."

"I don't play the piano—I'm not a girl," declared the boy; "and what I want is to get you to train my hounds for me. I'd like to go hunting with you to-day."

"Oh, I can't be bothered with babies," sneered Christopher in reply. "You'd fall down, most likely, and scratch your knees on the briers, and then you'd run straight home to blab to Fletcher."

"I won't!" cried Will angrily. "I'll never blab. He'd be too mad, I tell you, if he found it out."

"Well, I don't want you anyhow, so get out of my way. You'd better look sharp after your pups or the hounds will chew them up."

The boy stood midway of the road, kicking the dust impatiently ahead of him. His lips quivered with disappointment, and the expression gave them a singularly wistful beauty.

"I'll give you all my pocket money if you'll take me with you," he pleaded suddenly, stretching out a handful of silver.

With a snarl Christopher pushed his arm roughly aside. "Put up your money, you fool," he said; "I don't want it."

"Oh, you don't, don't you?" taunted the other, raging with wounded pride. "Why, grandpa says you're as poor as Job's turkey after it was plucked."

It was an old joke of Fletcher's, who, in giving utterance to it, little thought of the purpose it would finally be made to serve, for Christopher, halting suddenly at the words, swung round in the cloud of dust and stood regarding the grandson of his enemy with a thoughtful and troubled look. The lawyer's words sounded so distinctly in his ears that he glanced at the boy with a start, fearing that they had been spoken aloud: "His grandson is the sole living thing that Fletcher loves." Again the recollection brought a laugh from him, which he carelessly threw off upon the frolics of the puppies. Then the frown settled slowly back upon his brow, and the brutal look, which Carraway had found so disfiguring, crept out about his mouth.

"I tell you honestly," he said gruffly, "that if you knew what was good for you, you'd scoot back along that road a good deal faster than you came. If you're such a headstrong fool as to want to come with me, however, I reckon you may do it. One thing, though, I'll have no puling ways."

The boy jumped with pleasure. "Why, I knew all the time I'd get around you," he answered.

"I always do when I try; and may I shoot some with your shotgun?"

"I'll teach you, perhaps."

"When? Shall we start now? Call the dogs together—they're nosing in the ditch."

Without taking the trouble to reply, Christopher strode off briskly along the road, and after waiting a moment to assemble his scattered puppies, Will caught up with him and broke into a running pace at his side. As they swung onward the two shadows —the long one and the short one—stretched straight and black behind them in the sunlight.

"You're the biggest man about here, aren't you?" the boy asked suddenly, glancing upward with frank admiration.

"I dare say. What of it?"

"Oh, nothing; and your father was the biggest man of his time, Sol Peterkin says; and Aunt Mehitable remembers your grandfather, and he was the tallest man alive in his day. Who'll be the biggest when you die, I wonder? And, I say, isn't it a pity that such tall men had to live in such a little old house—I don't see how they ever got in the doors without stooping. Do you have to stoop when you go in and out.

Christopher nodded.

"Well, I shouldn't like that," pursued Will; "and I'm glad I don't live in such a little place. Now, the doors at the Hall are so high that I could stand on your shoulders and go in without bending my head. Let's try it some day. Grandpa wouldn't know."

Christopher turned and looked at him suddenly.

"What would you say to going 'possum hunting one night?" he asked in a queer voice.

"Whoopee!" cried the boy, tossing his hat in the air. "Will you take me?"

"Well, it's hard work, you know," went on the other thoughtfully. "You'd have to get up in the middle of the night and steal out of the window without your grandfather's knowing it."

"I should say so!"

"We'd tramp till morning, probably, with the hounds, and Tom Spade would come along to bring his lanterns. Then when it was over we'd wind up for drinks at his store. It's great sport, I tell you, but it takes a man to stand it."

"Oh, I'm man enough by now."

"Not according to your grandfather's thinking."

"What does he know about it? He's just an old fogy himself."

"We'll see, we'll see. If he wants to keep you tied to nurse's strings too long, we must play him a trick. Why, when I was fourteen I could shoot with any man about here—and drink with him, too, for that matter. Nobody kept me back, you see."

The boy looked up at Christopher with sparkling eyes, in which the eternal hero-worship of youth was already kindled.

"Oh, you're splendid!" he exclaimed, "and I'm going to be just like you. Grandpa shan't keep me a baby any longer, I can tell you. All this Greek, now—he's crazy about my learning it—and I hate it. Do you know Greek?"

Christopher laughed shortly. "Where does he live?" he inquired mockingly.

For a moment the boy looked at him perplexed.
"It's a language," he replied gravely; "and grandpa
says it comes handy in a bargain, but I won't learn
it. I hate school, anyway, and he swears he's going
to send me back in two weeks. I hope I'll fall ill,
and then he can't."

"In two weeks," repeated the other reflectively;
"well, a good deal may happen, I reckon, in two
weeks."

"Oh, lots!" agreed the boy with enthusiasm;
"you'll let me chase rabbits with you every day—
won't you? and teach me to shoot? and we'll go
'possum hunting one night and not get home till
morning. It will be easy enough to fool grandpa.
I'll take care of that, and if Aunt Saidie finds it
out she'll never tell him—she never does tell on me.
Here, let me take the gun awhile, will you?"

Christopher handed him the gun, and they went
on rapidly along the old road under the honey
locusts that grew beyond the bend. They were
nearing the place where Christopher, as a child of
twelve, had waited with his bird-gun in the bushes to
shoot Fletcher when he came in sight, and now as
the recollection returned to him he unconsciously
slackened his pace and cast his eyes about for the
spot where he had stood. It was all there just as
it had been that morning—the red clumps of sumach
covered with gray dust, the dried underbrush piled
along the fence, and the brown honeyshucks strewn
in the sunny road. For the first time in his life he
was glad at this instant that he had not killed Fletcher
then—that his hand had been stayed that day to fall
the heavier, it might be, at the appointed time.

The boy still chatted eagerly, and when presently the hounds scented a rabbit in the sassafras beyond the fence, he started with a shout at the heels of the pursuing pack. Swinging himself over the brushwood, Christopher followed slowly across the waste of life-everlasting, tearing impatiently through the flowering net which the wild potato vine cast about his feet.

Through the brilliant October day they hunted over the ragged fields, resting at noon to eat the slices of bread and bacon which Christopher had brought in his pocket. As they lay at full length in the sunshine upon the life-everlasting, the young man's gaze flew like a bird across the landscape— where the gaily decorated autumn fallows broke in upon the bare tobacco fields like gaudy patches on a homely garment—to rest upon the far-off huddled chimneys of Blake Hall. For a time he looked steadily upon them; then, turning on his side, he drew his harvest hat over his eyes and began a story of his early adventures behind the hounds, speaking in half-gay, half-bitter tones.

In the mild autumn weather a faint haze overhung the landscape, changing from violet to gray as the shadows rose or fell. Around them the unploughed wasteland swept clear to the distant road, which wound like a muddy river beside the naked tobacco fields. Lying within the slight depression of a hilltop, the two were buried deep amid the life-everlasting, which shed its soft dust upon them and filled their nostrils with its ghostly fragrance.

As he went on, Christopher found a savage delight in mocking the refinements of the boy's language, in tossing him coarse expressions and brutal oaths much as he tossed scraps to the hounds, in touching with vulgar scorn all the conventional ideals of the household—obedience, duty, family affection, religion even. While he sank still lower in that defiant self-respect to which he had always clung doggedly until to-day, there was a fierce satisfaction in the knowledge that as he fell he dragged Will Fletcher with him—that he had sold himself to the devil and got his price.

This unholy joy was still possessing him when at nightfall, exhausted, dirty, brier-scratched, and bearing their strings of game, they reached Tom Spade's, and Christopher demanded raw whisky in the little room behind the store. Sol Peterkin was there, astride his barrel, and as they entered he gave breath to a low whistle of astonishment.

"Why, your grandpa's been sweepin' up the county for you!" he exclaimed to Will.

"So he's found out I wasn't at the Morrisons'," said the boy a little nervously. "I'd better be going home, I reckon, and get it over."

Christopher drained his glass of whisky, and then, refilling it, pushed it across the table.

"What! Aren't you man enough to swallow a thimbleful?" he asked, with a laugh. His face was flushed, and the dust of the roads showed in streaks upon his forehead, where the crown of his straw hat had drawn a circle around his moist fair hair. The hand with which he touched the glass trembled slightly, and his eyes were so reckless that, after an instant's frightened silence, Peterkin cried out in alarm:

"For the Lord's sake, Mr. Christopher, you're not yourself—it's the way his father went, you know!"

"What of it?" demanded Christopher, turning his dangerous look upon the little man. "If there's a merrier way to go, I'd like to know it."

Peterkin drew over to the table and laid a restraining hold on the boy's arm. "Put that down, sonny," he said. "I couldn't stand it, and you may be sure it'll do you no good. It will turn your stomach clean inside out."

"He took it," replied the boy stubbornly, "and I'll drink it if he says so." He lifted the glass and stood looking inquiringly at the man across from him. "Shall I drink it?" he asked, and waited with a boyish swagger.

Christopher gave a short nod. "Oh, not if you're afraid of it," he responded roughly; and then, as Will threw back his head and the whisky touched his lips, the other struck out suddenly and sent the glass shivering to the floor. "Go home, you fool!" he cried, "and keep clear of me for good and all."

A moment afterward he had passed from the room, through the store, and was out upon the road.

CHAPTER VIII

Between the Devil and the Deep Sea

There was a cheerful blaze in the old lady's parlour, and she was sitting placidly in her Elizabethan chair, the yellow cat dozing at her footstool. Lila paced slowly up and down the room, her head bent a little sideways, as she listened to Tucker's cheerful voice reading the evening chapter from the family Bible. His crutch, still strapped to his right shoulder, trailed behind him on the floor, and the smoky oil lamp threw his eccentric shadow on the whitewashed wall, where it hung grimacing like a grotesque from early Gothic art.

"*Many waters cannot quench love, neither can the floods drown it,*" he read in his even tones; "*if a man would give all the substance of his house for love, it would utterly be contemned.*"

The old lady tapped the arm of her chair and turned her sightless eyes upon the Bible, as if Solomon in person stood there awaiting judgment.

"I always liked that verse, brother," she remarked, "though I am not sure that I consider it entirely proper reading for the young. Aren't you tired walking, Lila?"

"Oh, no, mother."

"Well, we mustn't take the Scriptures literally,

you know, my child; if we did, I fear a great deal of trouble would come of it—and surely it is a pity to magnify the passion of love when so very many estimable persons get along quite comfortably without it. You remember my remarking how happy Miss Belinda Morrison always appeared to be, and so far as I know she never had a suitor in her life, though she lived to be upward of eighty."

"Oh, mother! and yet you were so madly in love with father—you remember the fancy ball."

"The fancy ball occupied only one night, my dear, and I've had almost seventy years. I married for love, as you certainly know—at my age, I suppose I might as well admit it—but the marriage happened to be also entirely suitable, and I hope that I should never have been guilty of anything so indelicate as to fall in love with a gentleman who wasn't a desirable match."

Lila flushed and bit her lip.

"I don't care about stations in life, nor blood, nor anything like that," she protested

The old lady sighed. "We won't have any more of Solomon, Tucker," she observed. "I fear he will put notions into the child's head. Not care about blood, indeed! What are we coming to, I wonder? Well, well, I suppose it is what I deserve for allowing myself to fall so madly in love with your father. When I look back now it seems to me that I could have achieved quite as much with a great deal less expenditure of emotion."

"Now, now, Lucy," said Tucker, closing the gilt clasps of the Bible, "you're not yet seventy, and by the time you reach eighty you will see things

clearer. I'm a good deal younger than you, but
I'm two-thirds in the grave already, which makes
a difference. My life's been long and pleasant as
it is, but when I glance back upon it now I tell you
the things I regret least in it are my youthful follies.
A man must be very far in his dotage, indeed, when he
begins to wear a long face over the sharp breaths that
he drew in youth. I came very near ruining myself
for a woman once, and the fact that I was ready
to do it—even though I didn't—is what in the past
I like best to recall to-day. It makes it all easier
and better, somehow, and it seems to put a zest
into the hours I spend now on my old bench. To
have had one emotion that was bigger than you
or your universe is to have had life, my dear."

The old lady wiped her eyes. "It may be so,
brother, it may be so," she admitted; "but not
before Lila. Is that you, Christopher?"

The young man came in and crossed slowly to the
fire, bending for an instant over her chair. He was
conscious suddenly that his clothes smelled of the
fields and that the cold water of the well had not
cleansed his face and hands. All at once it came
to him with something of a shock that this bare,
refined poverty was beyond his level—that about
himself there was a coarseness, a brutality even, that
made him shrink from contact with these others—
with his mother, with Lila, with poor, maimed Tucker
in his cotton suit. Was it only a distinction in
manner, he wondered resentfully, or did the difference
lie still deeper in some unlikeness of soul? For the
first time in his life he felt ill at ease in the presence
of those he loved, and as his eyes dwelt moodily on

Lila's graceful figure—upon the swell of her low bosom, her swaying hips, and the free movement of her limbs—he asked himself bitterly if he had aught in common with so delicate and rare a thing? And she? Was her blithe acquiescence, after all, but an assumed virtue, to whose outward rags she clung? Was it possible that there was here no inward rebellion, none of that warfare against Destiny which at once inspirited and embittered his heart?

His face grew dark, and Uncle Boaz, coming in to stir the fire, glanced up at him and sighed.

"You sho' do look down in de mouf, Marse Chris," he observed.

Christopher started and then laughed blankly. "Well, I'm not proof against troubles, I reckon," he returned. "They're things none of us can keep clear of, you know."

Uncle Boaz chuckled under his breath. "Go 'way f'om yer, Marse Chris; w'at you know 'bout trouble—you ain' even mah'ed yet."

"Now, now, Boaz, don't be putting any ideas against marriage in his head," broke in the old lady. "He has remained single too long as it is, for, as dear old Bishop Deane used to say, it is surely the duty of every gentleman to take upon himself the provision of at least one helpless female. Not that I wish you to enter into marriage hastily, my son, or for any merely sentimental reasons; but I am sure, as things are, I believe one may have a great many trials even if one remains single, and though I know, of course, that I've had my share of trouble, still I never blamed your poor father one instant —not even for the loss of my six children, which certainly would not have happened if I had not married him. But, as I've often told you, my dear, I think marriage should be rightly regarded more as a duty than as a pleasure. Your Aunt Susannah always said it was like choosing a partner at a ball; for my part, I think it resembles more the selecting of a brand of flour."

"And to think that she once cried herself sick because Christopher went hunting during the honeymoon!" exclaimed Tucker, with his pleasant laugh.

"Ah, life is long, and one's honeymoon is only a month, brother," retorted the old lady; "and I'm not saying anything against love, you know, when it comes to that. Properly conducted, it is a very pleasant form of entertainment. I've enjoyed it mightily myself; but I'm nearing seventy, and the years of love seem very small when I look back. There are many interesting things in a long life, and love for a man is only one among them; which brings me, after all, to the conclusion that the substance of anybody's house is a large price to pay for a single feeling."

Christopher leaned over her and held out his arms.

"It is your bedtime, mother—shall I carry you across?" he asked; and as the old lady nodded, he lifted her as if she were a child and held her closely against his breast, feeling his tenderness revive at the clasp of her fragile hands. When he placed her upon her bed, he kissed her good-night and went up the narrow staircase, stooping carefully to avoid the whitewashed ceiling above.

Once in his room, he threw off his coat and sat down upon the side of his narrow bed, glancing con-

temptuously at his bare brown arms, which showed
through the openings in his blue shirt sleeves. He
was still smarting from the memory of the sudden
self-consciousness he had felt downstairs, and a
pricking sensitiveness took possession of him, piercing
like needles through the boorish indifference he had
worn. All at once he realised that he was ashamed
of himself—ashamed of his ignorance, his awkward-
ness, his brutality—and with the shame there awoke
the slow anger of a sullen beast. Fate had driven
him like a whipped hound to the kennel, but he
could still snarl back his defiance from the shadow
of his obscurity. The strong masculine beauty of
his face—the beauty, as Cynthia had said, of the
young David—confronted him in the little greenish
mirror above the bureau, and in the dull misery of
the eyes he read those higher possibilities, which
even to-day he could not regard without a positive
pang. What he might have been seemed forever
struggling in his look with what he was, like the
Scriptural wrestle between the angel of the Lord
and the brute. The soul, distorted, bruised, defeated,
still lived within him, and it was this that brought
upon him those hours of mortal anguish which he
had so vainly tried to drown in his glass. From
the mirror his gaze passed to his red and knotted
hand, with its blunted nails, and the straight furrow
grew deeper between his eyebrows. He remembered
suddenly that his earliest ambition—the ambition
of his childhood—had been that of a gentlemanly
scholar of the old order. He had meant to sit in a
library and read Horace, or to complete the laborious
translation of the "Iliad" which his father had left

unfinished. Then his studies had ended abruptly with the Greek alphabet, and from the library he had passed out to the plough. In the years of severe physical labour which followed he had felt the spirit of the student go out of him forever, and after a few winter nights, when he fell àsleep over his books, he had sunk slowly to the level of the small tobacco growers among whom he lived. With him also was the curse of apathy—that hereditary instinct to let the single throw decide the issue, so characteristic of the reckless Blakes. For more than two hundred years his people had been gay and careless livers on this very soil; among them all he knew of not one who had gone without the smallest of his desires, nor of one who had permitted his left hand to learn what his right one cast away. Big, blithe, mettlesome, they passed before him in a long, comely line, flushed with the pleasant follies which had helped to sap the courage in their descendants' veins.

At first he had made a pitiable attempt to remain "within his class," but gradually, as time went on, this, too, had left him, and in the end he had grown to feel a certain pride in the ignorance he had formerly despised—a clownish scorn of anything above the rustic details of his daily life. There were days even when he took a positive pleasure in the degree of his abasement, when but for his blind mother he would have gone dirty, spoken in dialect, and eaten with the hounds. What he dreaded most now were the rare moments of illumination in which he beheld his degradation by a blaze of light—moments such as this when he seemed to stand alone upon the edge of the world, with the devil awaiting him when he should turn at last. Years ago he had escaped these periods by strong physical exertion, working sometimes in the fields until he dropped upon the earth and lay like a log for hours. Later, he had yielded to drink when the darkness closed over him, and upon several occasions he had sat all night with a bottle of whisky in Tom Spade's store. Both methods he felt now to be ineffectual; fatigue could not deaden nor could whisky drown the bitterness of his soul. One thing remained, and that was to glut his hatred until it should lie quiet like a gorged beast.

Steps sounded all at once upon the staircase, and after a moment the door opened and Cynthia entered.

"Did you see Fletcher's boy, Christopher?" she asked. "His grandfather was over here looking for him."

"Fletcher over here? Well, of all the impudence!"

"He was very uneasy, but he stopped long enough to ask me to persuade you to part with the farm. He'd give three thousand dollars down for it, he said."

She dusted the bureau abstractedly with her checked apron and then stood looking wistfully into the mirror.

"Is that so? If he'd give me three million I wouldn't take it," answered Christopher.

"It seems a mistake, dear," said Cynthia softly; "of course, I'd hate to oblige Fletcher, too, but we are so poor, and the money would mean so much to us. I used to feel as you do, but somehow I seem all worn out now—soul as well as body. I haven't the strength left to hate."

"Well, I have," returned Christopher shortly,

"and I'll have it when I'm gasping over my last breath. You needn't bother about that business, Cynthia; I can keep up the family record on my own account. What's the proverb about us—'a Blake can hate twice as long as most men can love'—that's my way, you know."

"You didn't finish it," said Cynthia, turning from the bureau; "it's all downstairs in the 'Life of Bolivar Blake'; you remember Colonel Byrd got it off in a toast at a wedding breakfast, and Great-grandfather Bolivar was so proud of it he had it carved above his library door."

"High and mighty old chap, wasn't he? But what's the rest?"

"What he really said was: 'A Blake can hate twice as long as most men can love, and love twice as long as most men can live.'"

Christopher looked down suddenly at his great bronzed hands. "Oh, he needn't have stuck the tail of it on," he remarked carelessly; "but the first part has a bully sound."

When Cynthia had gone, he undressed and threw himself on the bed, but there was a queer stinging sensation in his veins, and he could not sleep. Rising presently, he opened the window, and in the frosty October air stood looking through the darkness to the light that twinkled in the direction of Blake Hall. Faint stars were shining overhead, and against the indistinct horizon something obscure and black was dimly outlined—perhaps the great clump of oaks that surrounded the old brick walls. Somewhere by that glimmer of light he knew that Fletcher sat hugging his ambition like a miser, gloating over the grandson who would grow up to redeem his name. For the weak, foolish-mouthed boy Christopher at this moment knew neither tolerance nor compassion; and if he stooped to touch him, he felt that it was merely as he would grasp a stick which Fletcher had taken for his own defense. The boy himself might live or die, prosper or fail, it made little difference. The main thing was that in the end Bill Fletcher should be hated by his grandson as he was hated by the man whom he had wronged.

CHAPTER IX

As the Twig Is Bent

It was two weeks after this that Fletcher, looking up from his coffee and cakes one morning, demanded querulously:

"Whar's Will, Saidie? It seems to me he sleeps late these days."

"Oh, he was up hours ago," responded Miss Saidie, from behind the florid silver service. "I believe he has gone rabbit hunting with that young Blake."

Fletcher laid down his knife and fork and glowered suspiciously upon his sister, the syrup from his last mouthful hanging in drops on his coarse gray beard.

"With young Blake! Why, what's the meaning of that?" he inquired.

"It's only that Will's taken to him, I think. Thar's no harm in this hunting rabbits that I can see, and it keeps the child out of doors, anyway. Fresh air is what the doctor said he needed, you know."

"I don't like it; I don't like it," protested Fletcher; "those Blakes are as bad as bulldogs, and they've been so as far back as I can remember. The sooner a stop's put to this thing the better it'll be. How long has it been going on, I wonder?"

"About ten days, I believe, and it does seem to give the boy such an interest. I can't help feeling it's a pity to break it up."

"Oh, bother you and your feelings!" was Fletcher's retort. "If you'd had the sense you ought to have had, it never would have started; but you've always had a mushy heart, and I ought to have allowed for it, I reckon. Thar're two kind of women in this world, the mulish and the pulish, an' when it comes to a man's taking his pick between 'em, the Lord help him. As for that young Blake—well, if I had to choose between him and the devil, I'd take up with the devil mighty fast, that's all."

"Oh, Brother Bill, he saved the child's life!"

"Well, he didn't do it on purpose; he told me so himself. I tried to settle that fair and square with him, you know, and he had the face to tear my check in half and send it back. Oh, I don't like this thing, I tell you, and I won't have it. I've no doubt it's at the bottom of all Will's cutting up about school, too. He was not well enough to go yesterday, he said, and here he's getting up this morning at daybreak and streaking, heaven knows whar, with a beggar. You may as well pack his things— I'll ship him off to-morrow if I'm alive."

"I hope you won't scold him, anyway; he's not strong, you know, and it's good for him to have a little pleasure. I'm sure I can't see what you have against the Blakes, as far as that goes. I remember the old gentleman when I was a child—so fine, and clean, and pleasant, it was a sight just to see him ride by on his dappled horse. He always lifted his hat to me, too, when he passed me in the road, and once he gave me some peaches for opening the red gate for him. I never could help liking him, and I was sorry when he lost his money and they had to sell the Hall."

Fletcher choked over his coffee and grew purple in the face.

"Hang your puling!" he cried harshly. "I'll not stand it, do you hear? The old man was a beggarly, cheating spendthrift, and the young one is a long sight worse. I'd rather wring Will's neck than have him mixed up with that batch of paupers."

Miss Saidie shrunk back, frightened, behind the silver service.

"Of course you know best, brother," she hastened to acknowledge, with her unfailing good-humour. "I'm as fond of the child as you are, I reckon—and of Maria, too, for that matter. Have you seen this photograph she sent me yesterday, taken at some outlandish place across the water? I declare, I had no idea she was half so handsome. She has begun to wear her hair low and has filled out considerable."

"Well, there was room for it," commented Fletcher, as he glanced indifferently at the picture and laid it down. "Get Will's clothes packed to-day, remember. He starts off to-morrow morning, rain or shine."

Pushing back his chair, he paused to gulp a last swallow of coffee, and then stamped heavily from the room.

At dinner Will did not appear, and when at last the supper bell jangled in the hall and Fletcher strode in to find the boy's place still empty, the shadow upon his brow grew positively black. As they rose from the table there were brisk, light steps along the hall, and Will entered hurriedly, warm and dusty after the day's hunt. Catching sight of his grandfather, he started nervously, and the boyish animation he had brought in from the fields faded quickly from his face, which took on a sly and dogged look.

"Whar in the devil's name have you been, suh?" demanded Fletcher bluntly.

The boy hesitated, seeking the inevitable defenses of the weak pitted against the strong. "I've been teaching my hounds to hunt rabbits," he replied, after a moment. "Zebbadee was with me."

"So you were too sick to start for school this morning, eh?" pursued Fletcher, hurt and angry. "Only well enough to go traipsing through the bushes after a pack of brutes?"

"I had a headache, but it got better. May I go up now to wash my hands?"

For an instant Fletcher regarded him in a brooding silence; then, with that remorseless cruelty which is the strangest manifestation of wounded love, he loosened upon the boy's head all the violence of his smothered wrath.

"You'll do nothing of the kind! I ain't done with you yet, and when I am I reckon you will know it. Mark my words, if you warn't such a girlish-looking chap I'd take my horsewhip to your shoulders in a jiffy. So this is the return I get, is it, for all my trouble with you since the day you were born! Tricks and lies are all the reward I'm to expect, I reckon. Well, you'll learn—once for all, now—that when you undertake to fool me it's a clear waste of time. I've found out whar you've been to-day, and I know you've been sneaking across the county with that darn Blake!"

The boy looked at him steadily, first with speechless terror, then with a cowed and sullen rage. The glare in Fletcher's eyes fascinated him, and he stood motionless on his spot of carpet as if he were held there in an invisible vise. Weakling as he was, he had been humoured too long to bear the lash submissively at last, and beneath the tumult of words that overwhelmed him he felt his anger flow like an infusion of courage in his veins. The greater share of love was still on his grandfather's side, and the knowledge of this lent a sullen defiance to his voice.

"You bluster so I can't hear," he said, blinking fast to shut out the other's eyes. "If I did go with Christopher Blake, what's the harm in it? I only lied because you make such a fuss it gives me a headache."

"It's the first fuss I ever made with you, I reckon," returned Fletcher, softening before the accusation. "If I ever fussed with you before, sonny, you may make mighty certain you deserved it."

"You frighten me half to death when you rage so," persisted the boy, snatching craftily at his advantage.

"There, there, we'll get it over," said Fletcher, quieting instantly. "I didn't mean to scare you that way, but the truth is it put me in a passion to hear of you mixing up with that scamp Blake. Jest keep clear of him and I'll ask nothing more of you. You may chase all your rabbits between here and kingdom come for aught I care, but if I ever see you alongside of Christopher Blake again, I tell you, I'll lick you until you're black and blue. And now hurry up and git your supper and go to bed, for you start to school to-morrow morning at sunrise."

Will flushed, and stood blinking his eyes in the lamplight.

"I don't want to go to school, grandpa," he said persuasively.

"That's a pity, sonny, because you've got to go whether you like it or not. Your Aunt Saidie has gone and packed your things, and I'll give you a month's pocket money to start with."

"But I'd rather stay at home and study with Mr. Morrison. Then I could follow after the hounds in the afternoon and keep out in the fresh air, as the doctor said I must."

"Now, now, we've had enough of this," said Fletcher decisively. "You'll do what I say, mind you, and you'll do it quick. No haggling over it, do you hear?"

Will looked at him sullenly, nerved by that reckless anger which so often passes for pure daring.

"If you make me go you'll be sorry, grandpa," he said, choking.

Fletcher swallowed an uneasy laugh, strangled over it, and finally spat it out with a wad of tobacco.

"Why, what blamed maggot have you got in your head, son?" he inquired, laying his heavy hand on the boy's shoulder. "You didn't use to hate school so, and, as sure as you're born, you'll find it first rate sport when you get back. It's this Blake business, that's what it is—he's gone and stuffed you plum full of notions. Look here, now, you don't want to grow up to be a dunce like him, do you?"

He had touched the raw at last, and Will broke out passionately in revolt, inflamed by a boyish admiration for his own bravado.

"He's got a lot more sense than anybody about here," he cried, backing against the door and holding tightly to the handle; "and if he doesn't know that plaguey Greek it's because he says there isn't any use in it. Why, he can shoot a bird on the wing over his shoulder, and mount a horse at full gallop, and tell stories that make you creep all over. He's not a dunce, grandpa; he's my friend, and I like him!"

The last words came in a sudden spurt, for, feeling his artificial courage ooze out of him, the boy had started in a run from the room. He had barely crossed the threshold, however, when Fletcher reached out with a strong grip and pulled him back, swinging him slowly round until the two stood face to face.

"Now, here's one thing flat," said the man in a husky voice, "if I ever see or hear of you opening your mouth to that rascal again, I'll thrash you until you haven't a sound bone in your body. You'd better go up now and say your prayers."

As he released his grasp, the boy struck out at him with a nerveless gesture and then shot like an arrow through the hall and out into the twilight. At the moment his terror of Fletcher was forgotten in the paroxysm of his anger. Short sobs broke from him as he ran, and presently his breath came in pants like those of an overdriven horse; but still, without slackening his pace, he sped on to the old ice-pond and then wheeled past the turning into the sunken road. Not until he had reached the long gate before the Blake cottage did he stop short suddenly and stand, grasping his moist shirt collar, in an effort to quiet his convulsed breathing.

The hounds greeted him with a single bay, and at the noise Cynthia came out upon the porch and then down into the gravelled path between the old rose-bushes.

"What do you wish?" she demanded stiffly, standing severe and erect in her faded silk.

"I must speak to Christopher—I must!" gasped the boy, breathing hard. "I am going away to-morrow, and this is my last chance."

"Well, he's in the stable, I believe," replied Cynthia coolly. "If you want him, you must go there to look for him, and be sure not to make a noise when you pass the house." Then, as he darted away, her eyes followed him with a weary aversion.

Will passed the kitchen and the woodpile and, turning into a little path that led from the well, came to the open door of the rudely built stable. A dim light fell in a square across the threshold, and looking inside he saw that a lantern was hanging from a nail above the nearest stall and that within the circle of its illumination Christopher was busily currying the old gray mare.

At the boy's entrance he paused for an instant, glanced carelessly over the side of the stall, and then went on with his work.

"Playing night-owl, eh?" he remarked indifferently. "There's no rubbing-down for you to do, I reckon."

"There's a darn sight worse," returned the boy,

throwing out the oath with a conscious swagger as he braced himself against the ladder that ran up to the loft.

His tone arrested Christopher's hand, and, lifting his head, the young man stood attentively regarding him, one arm lying upon the broad back of the old mare.

"Why, what's up now?" he questioned with a smile. Some fine chaff, which he had brought down from the loft, still clung to his hair and clothes and darkened his upper lip like a mustache.

"Grandpa's found it out and he's hopping," said the boy. "I always told you he would be, you know, and now it's come. If he ever catches me with you again he swears he'll give it to me like hell." He pressed tightly against the ladder and wagged his head defiantly. "But he needn't think he can bully me like that—not if I know it!"

"Well, he mustn't catch you again," returned Christopher, not troubling to soften his scorn of such cheap heroics; "we must manage better next time. Did you think to remind him, by the way, that I once took the trouble to save your life?"

"That's a fact, I didn't think of it. What would he have said, I wonder?"

Christopher raised his eyebrows. "Knocked your front teeth out, perhaps. He's like that, isn't he?"

"Oh, he's awfully fond of me, you know," protested the boy; "but it's his meddling ways that I can't stand. What business is it of his who my friends are? He hasn't got to take up with 'em, has he? Why, what he hates is for me to want to be with anybody but himself or Aunt Saidie. He'd like to keep me dangling all day to his coat tails, but it's not fair, and I won't have it. I'll show him whether I'm to be kept a kid forever or not!"

"There's spirit for you!" drawled Christopher with a laugh, as he applied the currycomb to the mare's flank.

"You just wait till you hear the worst," returned the other, with evident pride in the thunderbolt about to be delivered. "He swears he's going to send me to school to-morrow at sunrise."

"You don't say so?" ejaculated Christopher.

"Oh, but he'll do it, too—the only way to get around him is to fall ill, and I can't work that to-morrow. I played the trick last week and he saw through it. I've got to go, that's certain; but I'm going to make him sorry enough before he's done. Why couldn't he let me keep on studying with Mr. Morrison, as the doctor said I ought to? What's the use of this blamed old Latin and Greek, anyway? Nobody about here knows them, and why should I set myself up for a precious numbskull of a scholar? I'd rather be a crack shot like you any day! I tell you one thing," he finished, sucking in his breath in a way that had annoyed Christopher from the first, "I've half a mind to run away or fall ill after I get there!"

Christopher turned suddenly, slapped the mare on the flank, and came out of the stall, the curry-comb still in his hand. His shirt sleeves were rolled above his elbows, and the muscles of his arms stood out like cords under the sunburned skin, which showed a paler bronze from the wrists up. He was flushed from leaning over, and his clothes smelled strongly of the stable.

"If you do, come to me," he said lightly, "and I'll hide you in the barn till the storm blows over. It wouldn't last long, I reckon."

"Bless you, no; when he's scared I can do anything with him. Why, he was as soft as mush after the horses ran away with me, though he'd threatened to thrash me if I touched the reins. Oh, I say it's a shame we never had that 'possum hunt!"

Christopher turned down his shirt sleeves and brushed the chaff from his face.

"What do you say about to-night?" he inquired, with something like a sneer. "We couldn't go far, of course, and we'd have to borrow Tom Spade's hounds—mine are tired out—but we might have a short run about midnight, get a 'possum or so, and be in our beds before daybreak. Shall we try it?"

The boy wavered, struggling between his desire for the chase and his fear of Fletcher.

"Of course, if you're afraid——" added Christopher slowly.

"I'm not afraid," broke out Will angrily. "I'm not afraid and you know it. You be at the store by eleven, and I'll get out of the window and join you. Grandpa will never know, and if he does—well, I'll settle him!"

"Then be quick about it," was Christopher's retort, and as the boy ran out into the darkness he followed him to the door and stood gazing moodily down upon the yellow circle that his lantern cast on the bare ground. A massive fatigue oppressed him, and his hands and feet had become like leaden weights. There was a heaviness, too, about his head, and his eyeballs burned as if he had looked

too long at a bright light.   At the moment he felt
like a man who, being bound upon a wheel, is whirled
so rapidly around that he is dazed by the continuous
revolutions.   What did it all mean, anyway—the
boy, Fletcher, himself, and the revenge which he
now saw so clearly before him?   Was it a great
divine judgment or a great human cruelty?

Question as he would, the wheel still turned, and
he knew that for good or evil he was bound upon
it until the end.

CHAPTER X

Powers of Darkness

OCTOBER dragged slowly along, and Christopher followed his work upon the farm with the gloomy indifference which had become the settled expression of his attitude toward life. Since the morning when he had seen Will drive by to the cross-roads he had heard nothing of him, and gradually, as the weeks went on, that last reckless night behind the hounds had ceased to represent a cause either of rejoicing or of regret. He had not meant to goad the boy into drinking—of this he was quite sure— and yet when the hunt was over and the two stood just before dawn in Tom Spade's room he had felt the devil enter into him and take possession. The old mad humour of his blood ran high, and as the raw whisky fired his imagination he was dimly conscious that his talk grew wilder and that the surrounding objects swam before his gaze as if seen through a fog. Life, for the time at least, lost its relative values; the moment loomed larger in his vision than the years, and he beheld the past and the future dwarfed by the single radiant instant that was his own. It was as if he could pay back the score of a lifetime in that one minute.

"Is it possible that what was so difficult yesterday

should have grown so easy to-day?" he asked himself, astonished. "Why have I never seen so clearly before? Why, until this evening, have I gone puling about my life as if such things as disgrace and poverty were sufficient to crush the strength out of a man? Let me put forth all my courage and nothing is impossible—not even the attainment of success nor the punishment of Fletcher. It is only necessary to begin at once—to hasten about one's task—and in a few short years it will be accomplished and done with. All will be as I wish, and I shall then be as happy as Tucker."

Following this came the questions, How? When? Where shall I begin?—but he put them angrily aside and refilled his glass. A great good-humour possessed him, and, as he drank, all the unpleasant things of life—loss, unrest, heavy labour—vanished in the roseate glow that pervaded his thoughts.

What came of it was not quite clear to him next day, and this caused the uneasiness that lasted for a week. He had a vague recollection that Tom Spade took the boy home and rolled him through the window, and that he himself went whistling to his bed with the glorious sensation that he was riding the crest of a big wave. With the morning came a severe headache and the ineffectual effort to remember just how far it had all gone, and then a sharp anxiety, which vanished when he saw Will pass on his way to school.

"The boy was none the worse for it," Tom Spade told him later; "he had a drop too much, to be sure, but his legs were as steady as mine, an' he slept it off in an hour. He's a ticklish chap, Mr. Christopher," the storekeeper added after a moment, "an' I'd keep my hands from meddlin' with him, if I was you. That thing shan't happen agin at my place, an' it wouldn't have happened then if I'd been around at the beginnin'. You may tamper with yo' own salvation as much as you please—that's my gospel, but I'll be hanged if you've got a right to tamper with anybody else's."

Christopher wheeled suddenly about and gave him a keen glance from under his lowered eyelids. For the first time he detected a lack of deference in Tom Spade's tone, and a suspicion shot through him that the words were meant to veil a reprimand.

"Well, I reckon the boy's got as good a right to drink as I have," he retorted sneeringly, and a moment afterward went gaily whistling through the store. At the time he felt a certain pleasure in defying Tom's opinion—in setting himself so boldly in opposition to the conventional morality of his neighbours. The situation gave him several sharp breaths and that dizzy sense of insecurity in which his mood delighted. It had needed only the shade of disapproval expressed in the store-keeper's voice to lend a wonderful piquancy to his enjoyment—to cause him to toy in imagination with his hatred as a man does with his desire. Before Tom spoke he had caught himself almost regretting the affair—wondering, even, if his error were past retrieving—but with the first mere suggestion of outside criticism his humour underwent a startling change.

Between Fletcher and himself the account was still open, and the way in which he meant to settle it concerned himself alone—least of all did it concern Tom Spade.

He was groping confusedly among these reflections when, one evening in early November, he went upstairs after a hasty supper to find Cynthia already awaiting him in his room. At his start of displeased surprise she came timidly forward and touched his arm.

"Are you sick, Christopher? or has anything happened? You are so unlike yourself."

He shook his head impatiently and her hand fell from his sleeve. It occurred to him all at once, with an aggrieved irritation, that of late his family had failed him in sympathy—that they had ceased to value the daily sacrifices he made. Almost with horror he found himself asking the next instant whether the simple bond of blood was worth all that he had given—worth his youth, his manhood, his ambition? Until this moment his course had seemed to him the one inevitable outcome of circumstances—the one appointed path for him to tread; but even as he put the question he saw in a sudden illumination that there might have been another way—that with the burden of the three women removed he might have struck out into the world and at least have kept his own head above water. With his next breath the horror of his thought held him speechless, and he turned away lest Cynthia should read his degradation in his eyes.

"Happened! Why, what should have happened?" he inquired with attempted lightness. "Good Lord! After a day's work like mine you can hardly expect me to dance a hornpipe. Since sunrise I've done a turn at fall ploughing, felled and chopped a tree, mended the pasture fence, brought the water for the washing, tied up some tobacco leaves, and looked after the cattle and the horses—and now you find fault because I haven't cut any extra capers!"

"Not find fault, dear," she answered, and the hopeless courage in her face smote him to the heart. In a bitter revulsion of feeling he felt that he could not endure her suffering tenderness.

"Find fault with you! Oh, Christopher! It is only that you have been so different of late, so brooding, and you seem to avoid us at every instant. Even mother has noticed it, and she imagines that you are in love."

"In love!" he threw back his head with a loud laugh. "Oh, I'm tired, Cynthia—dog-tired, that's the matter."

"I know, I know," replied Cynthia, rubbing her eyes hard with the back of her hand. "And the worst is that there's no help for it—absolutely none. I think about it sometimes until I wonder that I don't go mad."

He turned at this from the window through which he had been gazing and fixed upon her a perplexed and moody stare. The wistful patience in her face, like the look he had seen in the eyes of overworked farm animals, aroused in him a desire to prod her into actual revolt—into any decisive rebellion against fate. To accept life upon its own terms seemed to him, at the instant, pure cowardliness—the enforced submission of a weakened will; and he questioned almost angrily if the hereditary instincts were alive in her also? Did she, too, have her secret battles and her silent capitulations? Or was her pious resignation, after all, only a new form of the old Blake malady—of that fatal apathy which seized them, like disease, when events demanded strenuous endeavour? Could the saintly fortitude he had once so envied be, when all was said, merely the outward expression of the inertia he himself had felt—of the impulse to drift with the tide, let it carry one where it would?

"Well, I'm glad it's no worse," said Cynthia, with a sigh of relief, as she turned toward the door. "Since you are not sick, dear, things are not so bad as they might be. I'll let mother fancy you have what she calls 'a secret sentiment.' It amuses her, at any rate. And now I'm going to stir up some buckwheat cakes for your breakfast. We've got a jug of black molasses."

"That's pleasant, at least," he returned, laughing; and then as she reached the door he went toward her and laid his hand awkwardly upon her shoulder. "Don't worry about me, Cynthia," he added; "there's a lot of work left in me yet, and a change for the better may come any day, you know. By next year the price of tobacco may shoot sky-high."

Her face brightened and a flush smoothed out all the fine wrinkles on her brow, but with the pathetic shyness of a woman who has never been caressed she let his hand fall stiffly from her arm and went hurriedly from the room.

For a few minutes Christopher stood looking abstractedly at the closed door. Then shaking his head, as if to rid himself of an accusing thought, he turned away and began rapidly to undress. He had thrown off his coat, and was stooping to remove his boots, when a slight noise at the window startled him, and straightening himself instantly he awaited attentively a repetition of the sound. In a moment it came again, and hastily crossing the room and raising the sash, he looked out into the full moonlight and saw Will Fletcher standing in the gravelled path below. At the first glance surprise held him motionless, but as the boy waved to him he responded to the signal, and, catching up his coat from the bed, ran down the staircase and out into the yard.

"What in the devil's name——" he exclaimed, aghast.

Will was trembling from exhaustion, and his face glimmered like a pallid blotch under the shadow of the aspen. When the turkeys stirred on an overhanging bough above him he started nervously and sucked in his breath with a hissing sound. He was run to death; this Christopher saw at the first anxious look.

"Get me something to eat," said the boy; "I'm half starved—but bring it to the barn, for I'm too dead tired to stand a moment. Yes, I ran away, of course," he finished irritably. "Do I look as if I'd come in grandpa's carriage?"

With a last spurt of energy he disappeared into the shadows behind the house, and Christopher, going into the kitchen, began searching the tin safe for the chance remains of supper. On the table was the bowl of buckwheat which Cynthia had been preparing when she was called away by some imperious demand of her mother's, and near it he saw the open prayer-book from which she had been reading.

From the adjoining room he heard Tucker's voice
—those rich, pleasant tones that translated into sound
the courageous manliness of the old soldier's face—
and for an instant he yearned toward the cheerful
group sitting in the firelight beyond the whitewashed
wall—toward the blind woman in her old oak chair,
listening to the evening chapter from the Scriptures.
Then the feeling passed as quickly as it had come,
and securing a plate of bread and a dried ham-bone,
he filled a glass with fresh milk, and, picking up his
lantern, went out of doors and along the little
straggling path to the barn.

The yard was frosted over with moonlight, but
when he reached the rude building where the farm
implements and cattle fodder were sheltered he saw
that it was quite dark inside, only a few scattered
moonbeams crawling through the narrow doorway.
To his first call there was no answer, and it was
only after he had lighted his lantern and swung it
round in the darkness that he discovered Will lying
fast asleep upon a pile of straw.

As the light struck him full in the face the boy
opened his eyes and sprang up.

"Why, it's you," he said in a relieved voice.
"I thought it was grandpa. If he comes you've
got to keep him out, you know!"

He spoke in an excited whisper, and his eyes
plunged beyond the entrance with a look of pitiable
and abject terror. Once or twice he shivered as
if from cold, and then, turning away, cowered into
the pile of straw in search of warmth.

For a time Christopher stood gazing uneasily down
upon him. "Look here, man, this can't keep up,"

he said. "You'd better go straight home, that's my opinion, and get into a decent bed."

Will started up again. "I won't see him! I won't!" he cried angrily. "If you bring him here I'll get up and hide. I won't see him! Why, he almost killed me after that 'possum hunt we had, and if he found this out so soon he'd kill me outright. There was an awful rumpus at school. They wrote him and he said he was coming, so I ran away. It was all his fault, too; he had no business to send me back again when he knew how I hated it. I told him he'd be sorry."

"Well, he shan't get in here to-night," returned Christopher soothingly. "I'll keep him out with a shotgun, bless him, if he shows his face. Come, now, sit up and eat a bit, or there won't be any fight left in us."

Will took the food obediently, but before it touched his lips the hand in which he held it dropped limply to the straw.

"I can't eat," he complained, with a gesture of disgust. "I'm too sick—I've been sick for days. It was all grandpa's doing, too. When I heard he was coming I went out and got soaking wet, and then slept in my clothes all night. I knew he'd never make a fuss if I could only get ill enough, but the next morning I felt all right, so I came away."

Kneeling upon the floor, Christopher held the glass to his lips, gently forcing him to drink a few swallows. Then dipping his handkerchief in the cattle-trough outside, he bathed the boy's face and hands, and, loosening his clothes, made him as comfortable as he could. "This won't do, you know," he urged presently, alarmed by Will's difficult breathing. "You are in for a jolly little spell, and I must get you home. Your grandfather will never bother you while you're sick."

At the words the boy clung to him deliriously, breaking into frightened whimpers such as a child makes in the dark. "I won't go back! I won't go back!" he repeated wildly; "he'll never believe I'm ill, and I won't go back!"

"All right; that settles it. Lie quiet and I'll fetch you some bedding from my room. Then I'll fix you a pallet out here, and we'll put up as best we can till morning."

"Don't stay; don't stay," pleaded Will, as the other, leaving his lantern on the floor, ran out into the moonlight.

Returning in a quarter of an hour, he threw a small feather-bed down upon the straw and settled the boy comfortably upon it. Then he covered him with blankets, and, after closing the door, came back and stood watching for him to fall asleep. A slight draught blew from the boarded window, and, taking off his coat, he hung it carefully across the cracks, shading the lantern with his hand that its light might not flash in the sleeper's face.

At his step Will gave a stifled moan and looked up in terror.

"I thought you'd left me. Don't go," he begged, stretching out his hand until it grasped the other's. With the hot, nerveless clutch upon him, Christopher was conscious of a quick repulsion, and he remembered the sensation he had felt as a boy when he had once suddenly brought his palm down on a little green snake that was basking in the sunshine on an old log. Yet he did not shake the hand off, and when presently the blanket slipped from Will's shoulders he stooped and replaced it with a strange gentleness. The disgust he felt was so evenly mingled with compassion that, as he stood there, he could not divide the one emotion from the other. He hated the boy's touch, and yet, almost in spite of himself, he suffered it.

"Well, I'm not going, so you needn't let that worry you," he replied. "I'll stretch myself alongside of you in the straw, and if you happen to want me, just yell out, you know."

The weak fingers closed tightly about his wrist.

"You promise?" asked the boy.

"Oh, I promise," answered the other, raising the lantern for a last look before he blew it out.

By early daybreak Will's condition was still more alarming, and leaving him in a feverish stupor upon the pallet, Christopher set out hurriedly shortly after sunrise to carry news of the boy's whereabouts to Fletcher.

It was a clear, cold morning, and the old brick house, set midway of the autumn fields, appeared, as he approached it, to reflect the golden light that filled the east. Never had the place seemed to him more desirable than it did as he went slowly toward it along the desolate November roads. The sombre colours of the landscape, the bared majesty of the old oaks where a few leaves still clung to the topmost boughs, the deserted garden filled with wan spectres of summer flowers, were all in peculiar harmony with his own mood as with the stern gray walls wrapped in naked creepers. That peculiar sense of ownership was strongly with him as he ascended the broad steps and lifted the old brass knocker, which still bore the Blake coat of arms.

To his astonishment the door opened instantly and Fletcher himself appeared upon the threshold. At sight of Christopher he fell back as if from a blow in the chest, ripping out an oath with a big downward gesture of his closed fist.

"So you are mixed up in it, are you! Whar's the boy?" From the dusk of the hall his face shone dead white about the eyes.

"If you want to get anything out of me you'd better curb your tongue, Bill Fletcher," replied Christopher coolly, feeling an animal instinct to prolong the torture. "If you think it's any satisfaction to me to have your young idiot thrown on my hands you were never more mistaken in your life. I've been up half the night with him, and the sooner you take him away the better I'll like it."

"Oh, you leave him to me and I'll settle him," responded Fletcher, reaching for his hat. "Jest show me whar he is and I'll git even with him befo' sundown. As for you, young man, I'll have the sheriff after you yit."

"In the meantime, you'd better have the doctor. The boy's ill, I tell you. He came to me last evening, run to death and with a high fever. He slept in the barn, and this morning he is decidedly worse. If you come, bring Doctor Cairn with you, and I warn you now you've got to use a lot of caution. Your grandson is mortally afraid of you, and he threatens to run away if I let you know where he is. He wants me to sit at the door with a shotgun and keep you off."

He delivered his blows straight out from the shoulder, lingering over each separate word that he might enjoy to the full its stupendous effect.

"This is your doing," repeated Fletcher hoarsely; "it's your doing, every blamed bit of it."

Christopher laughed shortly. "Well, I'm through with my errand," he said, moving toward the steps and pausing with one hand on a great white column. "The sooner you get him out of my barn the better riddance it will be. There's one thing certain, though, and that is that you don't lay eyes on him without the doctor. He's downright ill, on my oath."

"Oh, it's the same old trick, and I see through it," exclaimed Fletcher furiously. "It's pure shamming."

"All the same, I've got my gun on hand, and you don't go into that barn alone." He hung for an instant upon the topmost step, then descended hurriedly and walked rapidly back along the broad white walk. It would be an hour, at least, before Fletcher could follow him with Doctor Cairn, and after he had returned to the barn and given Will a glass of new milk he fed and watered the horses and did the numberless small tasks about the house. He was at the woodpile, chopping some lightwood splinters for Cynthia, when the sound of wheels reached him, and in a little while more the head of Fletcher's mare appeared around the porch. Doctor Cairn, a frousy, white-bearded old man, crippled from rheumatism, held out his hand to Christopher as he descended with some difficulty between the wheels of the buggy.

Christopher motioned to the barn, and then, taking the reins, fastened the horse to the branch of a young ailanthus tree which grew near the wood-pile. As he watched the figures of the two men pass along the little path between the fringes of dead yarrow he drew an uneasy breath and dug his boot into the rotting mould upon the ground. The barn door opened and closed; there was a short silence, and then a sudden despairing cry as of a rabbit caught in the jaws of a hound. When he heard it he turned impulsively from the horse's head and went quickly along the path the men had taken. There was no definite intention in his mind, but as he reached the barn door it shot open and Fletcher put out a white face.

"The Doctor wants you, Mr. Christopher," he cried; "Will has gone clean mad!"

Without a word, Christopher pushed by him and went into the great dusky room, where the boy was struggling like a madman to loosen the doctor's grasp. He was conscious at the moment that the air was filled with fine chaff and that he sucked it in when he breathed.

At his entrance Will lay quiet for a moment and looked at him with dazed, questioning eyes.

"Keep them out, Christopher!" he cried, in anguish.

Christopher crossed the room and laid his hand with a protecting gesture on the boy's head.

"Why, to be sure I will," he said heartily; "the devil himself won't dare to touch you when I am by."

Book Three
The Revenge

THE REVENGE

CHAPTER I

IN WHICH TOBACCO IS HERO

ON an October afternoon some four years later, at the season of the year when the whole county was fragrant with the curing tobacco, Christopher Blake passed along the stretch of old road which divided his farm from the Weatherbys', and, without entering the porch, called for Jim from the little walk before the flat whitewashed steps. In response to his voice, Mrs. Weatherby, a large, motherly looking woman, appeared upon the threshold, and after chatting a moment, directed him to the log tobacco barn, where the recently cut crop was "drying out."

"Jim and Jacob are both over thar," she said; "an' a few others, for the matter of that, who have been helpin' us press new cider an' drinkin' the old. I'm sure I don't see why they want to lounge out thar in all that smoke, but thar's no accountin' for the taste of a man that ever I heard tell of— an' I reckon they kin fancy pretty easy that they are settin' plum in the bowl of a pipe. It beats me, though, that it do. Why, one mouthful of it is enough to start me coughin' for a week, an' those men thar jest swallow it down for pure pleasure."

Clean, kindly, hospitable, she wandered garrulously on, remembering at intervals to press the young man to "come inside an' try the cakes an' cider."

"No; I'll look them up out there," said Christopher, resisting the invitation to enter. "I want to get a pair of horseshoes from Jim; the gray mare cast hers yesterday, and Dick Boxley is laid up with a sprained arm. Oh, no, thanks; I must be going back." With a friendly nod he turned from the steps and went rapidly along the path which led to the distant barn.

As Mrs. Weatherby had said, the place was like the bowl of a pipe, and it was a moment before Christopher discovered the little group gathered about the doorway, where a shutter hung loosely on wooden hinges.

The ancient custom of curing tobacco with open fires, which had persisted in Virginia since the days of the early settlers, was still commonly in use; and it is possible that had one of Christopher's colonial ancestors appeared at the moment in Jacob Weatherby's log barn it would have been difficult to convince him that between his death and his resurrection there was a lapse of more than two hundred years. He would have found the same square, pen-like structure, built of straight logs carefully notched at the corners; the same tier-poles rising at intervals of three feet to the roof; the same hewn plates to support the rafters; the same "daubing" of the chinks with red clay; and the same crude door cut in the south wall. From the roof the tobacco hung in a fantastic decoration, shading from dull green to deep bronze, and appearing,

when viewed from the ground below, to resemble a
numberless array of small furled flags. On the hard
earth floor there were three parallel rows of "un-
seasoned" logs which burned slowly day and night,
filling the barn with gray smoke and the pungent
odour of the curing tobacco.

"It takes a heap of lookin' arter, an' no mistake,"
old Jacob was remarking, as he surveyed the fine
crop with the bland and easy gaze of ownership.
"Why, in a little while them top leaves thar will be
like tinder, an' the first floatin' spark will set it all
afire. That's the way Sol Peterkin lost half a crop
last year, an' it's the way Dick Moss lost his whole
one the year before." At Christopher's entrance he
paused and turned his pleasant, ruddy face from
the fresh logs which he had been watching. "So
you want to have a look at my tobaccy, too?" he
added, with the healthful zest of a child. "Well,
it's worth seein', if I do say so; thar hasn't been
sech leaves raised in this county within the memory
of man."

"That's so," said Christopher, with an appreciative
glance. "I'm looking for Jim, but he's keeping up
the fires, isn't he?" Then he turned quickly, for
Tom Spade, who with young Matthew Field had
been critically weighing the promise of Jacob's crop,
broke out suddenly into a boisterous laugh.

"Why, I declar', Mr. Christopher, if you ain't
lost yo' shadow!" he exclaimed.

Christopher regarded him blankly for a moment,
and then joined lightly in the general mirth. "Oh,
you mean Will Fletcher," he returned. "There
was a pretty girl in the road as we came up, and I

couldn't get him a step beyond her. Heaven knows what's become of him by now!"

"I bet my right hand that was Molly Peterkin," said Tom. "If anybody in these parts begins to talk about 'a pretty gal,' you may be sartain he's meanin' that yaller-headed limb of Satan. Why, I stopped my Jinnie goin' with her a year ago. Sech women, I said to her, are fit for nobody but men to keep company with."

"That's so; that's so," agreed old Jacob, in a charitable tone; "seein' as men have most likely made 'em what they are, an' oughtn't to be ashamed of thar own handiwork."

"Now, when it comes to yaller hair an' blue eyes," put in Matthew Field, "she kin hold her own agin any wedded wife that ever made a man regret the day of his birth. Many's the time of late I've gone a good half-mile to git out of that gal's way, jest as I used to cut round old Fletcher's pasture when I was a boy to keep from passin' by his red-heart cherry-tree that overhung the road. Well, well, they do say that her young man, Fred Turner, went back on her, an' threw her on her father's hands two days befo' the weddin'."

"It was hard on Sol, now you come to think of it," said Tom. "He told me himself that he tried to git the three who ought to marry her to draw straws for the one who was to be the happy man, but they all backed out an' left her high an' dry an' as pretty as a peach. Fred Turner would have taken his chance, he said, like an honest man, an' he was terrible down in the mouth when I saw him, for he was near daft over the gal."

"Well, he was right," admitted Matthew, after reflection. "Why, the gal sins so free an' easy you might almost fancy her a man."

He drew back, coughing, for Jim came in with a long green log and laid it on the smouldering fire, which glowed crimson under the heavy smoke.

"Here's Sol," said the young man, settling the log with his foot. "I told him you were on your way to the house, pa, but he said he had only a minute, so he came out here."

"Oh, I've jest been to borrow some Jamaica ginger from Mrs. Weatherby," explained Sol Peterkin, carefully closing the shutter after his entrance. "My wife's took so bad that I'm beginnin' to fear she'll turn out as po' a bargain as the last. It's my luck—I always knew I was ill-fated—but, Lord a-mercy, how's a man goin' to tell the state of a woman's innards from the way she looks on top? All the huggin' in the world won't make her wink an eyelash, an' then there'll crop out heart disease or dropsy befo' the year is up. When I think of the trouble I had pickin' that thar woman it makes me downright sick. It ain't much matter about the colour or the shape, I said—a freckled face an' a scrawny waist I kin stand—only let it be the quality that wears. If you believe it, suh, I chose the very ugliest I could find, thinkin' that the Lord might be mo' willin' to overlook her—an' now this is what's come of it. She's my fourth, too, an' I'll begin to be a joke when I go out lookin' for a fifth. Naw, suh; if Mary dies, pure shame will keep me a widower to my death."

"Thar ain't but one thing sartain about marriage,

in my mind," commented Matthew Field, "an' that is that it gits most of its colour from the distance that comes between. The more your mouth waters for a woman, the likelier 'tis that 'tain't the woman for you—that's my way of thinkin'. The woman a man don't git somehow is always the woman he ought to have had. It's a curious, mixed-up business, however you look at it."

"That's so," said Tom Spade; " I always noticed it. The woman who is your wife may be a bouncin' beauty, an' the woman who ain't may be as ugly as sin, but you'd go twice as far to kiss her all the same. Thar is always a sight more spice about the woman who ain't."

"Jest look at Eliza, now," pursued Matthew, wrapped in the thought of his own domestic infelicities. "What I could never understand about Eliza was that John Sales went clean to the dogs because he couldn't git her. To think of sech a thing happenin', jest as if I was to blame, when if I'd only known it I could hev turned about an' taken her sister Lizzie. Thar were five of 'em in all, an' I settled on Eliza, as it was, with my eyes blindfold. Poor John—poor John! It was sech a terrible waste of wantin'."

"Well, it's a thing to stiddy about," said old Jacob, with a sigh. "They tell me now that that po' young gal of Bill Fletcher's has found it a thorny bed, to be sho'. Her letters are all bright an' pleasant enough, they say, filled with fine clothes an' the names of strange places, but a gentleman who met her somewhar over thar wrote Fletcher that her husband used her like a dumb brute."

Christopher started and looked up inquiringly.

"Have you heard anything about that, Jim?" he asked in a queer voice.

"Nothin' more. Fletcher told me he had written to her to come home, but she answered that she would stick to Wyndham for better or for worse. It's a great pity—the marriage promised so well, too."

"Oh, the gal's got a big heart; I could tell it from her eyes," said old Jacob. "When you see those dark, solemn eyes, lookin' out of a pale, peaked face, it means thar's a heart behind 'em, an' a heart that bodes trouble some day, whether it be in man or woman."

Christopher passed his hand across his brow and stood staring vacantly at the smouldering logs. He could not tell whether the news saddened or rejoiced him, but, at least, it brought Maria's image vividly before his eyes. The spell of her presence was over him again, and he felt, as he had felt on that last evening, the mysterious attraction of her womanhood. So intense was the visionary appeal that it had for the moment almost the effect of hallucination; it was as if she still entreated him across all the distance. The brooding habit of his mind had undoubtedly done much to conserve his emotion, as had the rural isolation in which he lived. In a city life the four years would probably have blotted out her memory; but where comparison was impossible, and lighter distractions almost unheard of, what chance was there for him to forget the single passionate experience he had known? Among his primitive neighbours Maria had flitted for a time like a bewildering vision; then the great distant world had caught her up into its brightness, and the desolate waste country was become the guardian of the impression she had left.

"If thar's a man who has had bad luck with his children, it's Bill Fletcher," old Jacob was saying thoughtfully. "He's been a hard man an' a mean one, too, an' when he couldn't beg or borrow it's my opinion that he never hesitated to put forth his hand an' steal. Thar's a powerful lot of judgment in dumb happenin's, an' when you see a family waste out an' run to seed like that it usually means that the good Lord is havin' His way about matters. It takes a mighty sharp eye to tell the difference between judgment an' misfortune, an' I've seen enough in this world to know that, no matter how skilfully you twist up good an' evil, God Almighty may be a long time in the unravelling, but He'll straighten 'em out at last. Now as to Bill Fletcher, his sins got in the bone an' they're workin' out in the blood. Look at his son Bill—didn't he come out of the army to drink himself to death? Then his granddaughter Maria has gone an' mismarried a somebody, an' this boy that he'd set his heart on is goin' to the devil so precious fast that he ain't got time to look behind him."

"Oh, he's young yet," suggested Tom Spade, solemnly wagging his head, "an' Fletcher says, you know, that he's all right so long as he keeps clear of Mr. Christopher. It's Mr. Christopher, he swears, that's been the ruin of him."

Christopher met this with a sneer.

"Why does he let him dog my footsteps, then?"

he inquired with a laugh. "I never go to the Hall, and yet he's always after me."

"Bless you, suh, it ain't any question of lettin'— an' thar never has been sence the boy first put on breeches. Why, when I refused to sell him whisky at my sto', what did he do but begin smugglin' it out from town! Fletcher found it out an' blew him sky-high, but in less than a month it was all goin' on agin."

"An' the funny part is," said Jim Weatherby, "that you can't dislike Will Fletcher, however much you try. He's a kind-hearted, jolly fellow, in spite of the devil."

"Or in spite of Mr. Christopher," added Tom, with a guffaw.

Frowning heavily, Christopher turned toward the door.

"Oh, you ask Will Fletcher who is his best friend," he said, "and let me hear his answer."

With an abrupt nod to Jacob, he went out of the tobacco barn and along the little path to the road. He had barely reached the gate, however, when Jim Weatherby ran after him with the horse-shoes, and offered eagerly to come over in the morning and see that the gray mare was properly shod.

"I'm handy at that kind of thing, you know," he explained, with a blush.

"Well, if you don't mind, I wish you would come," Christopher replied, "but to save my life I can't see why you are so ready with other people's jobs."

Then, taking the horseshoes, he opened the gate and started rapidly toward home. His mind was still absorbed by old Jacob's news, and upon reaching the house he was about to pass up to his room, when Cynthia called him from the little platform beyond the back door, and going out, he found her standing pale and tearful on the kitchen threshold. Looking beyond her, he saw that Lila and Tucker were in the room, and from the intense and resolute expression in the younger sister's face he judged that she was the central figure in what appeared to be a disturbing scene.

"Christopher, you can't imagine what has happened," Cynthia began in her beautiful, tragic voice. "Lila went to church yesterday—with whom, do you suppose?"

Christopher thought for a moment.

"Not with Bill Fletcher?" he gave out at last.

"Come, come, now, it's a long ways better than that, you'll admit, Cynthia," broke in Tucker, with a peaceful intention. "I can't help reminding you, my dear, to be thankful that it wasn't so unlikely a person as Bill Fletcher."

With a decisive gesture such as he had never believed her capable of, Lila came up to Christopher and stood facing him with beaming eyes. He had never before seen her so lovely, and he realised at the instant that it was this she had always needed to complete her beauty. From something merely white and warm and delicate she had become suddenly as radiant as a flame.

"I went with Jim Weatherby, Christopher," she said slowly, "and I'm not ashamed of it."

The admission wrung a short groan from Cynthia, who stood twisting her gingham apron tightly about her fingers.

"Oh, Lila, who was his grandfather?" she cried.

"Well, there's one thing certain, she doesn't want to marry his grandfather," put in Tucker, undaunted by the failure of his former attempts at peace-making. "Not that I have anything against the old chap, for that matter; he was an honest, well-behaved old body, and used to mend my boots for me up to the day of his death. Jim gets his handy ways from him, I reckon."

Cynthia turned upon him angrily.

"Uncle Tucker, you will drive me mad," she exclaimed, the tears starting to her lashes. "It does seem to me that you, at least, might show some consideration for the family name. It's all we've left."

"And it's a good enough relic in its way," returned Tucker amicably, "though if you are going to make a business of sacrificing yourself, for heaven's sake let it be for something bigger than a relic. A live neighbour is a much better thing to make sacrifices for than a dead grandfather."

"I don't care one bit what his grandfather was or whether he ever had any or not!" cried Lila, in an outburst of indignation; "and more than that, I don't care what mine was, either. I am going to marry him—I am—I am! Don't look at me like that, Cynthia. Do you want to spoil my whole life?"

Cynthia threw out her hands with a despairing grasp of the air, as if she were reaching for the broken remnants of the family pride. "To marry a Weatherby!" she gasped. "Oh, mother! mother! Lila, is it possible that you can be so selfish?"

But Lila had won her freedom too dearly to surrender it to an appeal.

"I want to be selfish," she said stubbornly. "I have never been selfish in my life, and I want to see what it feels like. Oh, you are cruel, all of you, and you will break my heart."

Christopher's face paled and grew stern.

"We must all think of mother's wishes, Lila," he said gravely.

For the first time the girl lost her high fortitude, and a babyish quiver shook her lips. Her glance wavered and fell, and with a pathetic gesture she turned from Christopher to Cynthia and from Cynthia to Tucker.

"Oh, you can't understand, Christopher!" she cried; "you have never been in love, nor has Cynthia. None of you can understand but Uncle Tucker!"

She ran to him sobbing, and he, steadying himself on a single crutch, folded his arm about her.

"I understand, child, thank God," he said softly.

CHAPTER II

Between Christopher and Will

An hour later Christopher was at work in the stable, when he heard a careless whistle outside, and Will Fletcher looked in at the open door.

"I say, Chris, take a turn off and come down to Tom Spade's," he urged.

Christopher, who was descending from the loft with an armful of straw, paused midway of the ladder and regarded his visitor with perceptible hesitation.

"I can't this evening," he answered; "the light is almost gone, and I've a good deal to get through with after dark. I'll manage better to-morrow, if I can. By the way, why didn't you show up at Weatherby's?"

Will came in and sat down on the edge of a big wooden box which contained the harness. In the four years he had changed but little in appearance, though his slim figure had shot up rapidly in height. His chestnut hair grew in high peaks from his temples and swept in a single lock above his small, sparkling eyes, which held an expression of intelligent animation. On the whole, it was not an unpleasing face, despite the tremulous droop of the mouth, already darkened by the faint beginning of a brown mustache.

"Oh, Molly Peterkin stopped me in the road," he replied readily. "I'd caught her eye once or twice before, but this was the first chance we'd had to speak. I tell you she's a peach, Christopher."

Christopher came down from the ladder and spread the straw evenly in the horses' stalls.

"So they say," he responded; "but I haven't much of an eye for women, you know. Now, when it comes to judging a leaf of tobacco, I'm a match for any man."

"Well, one can't be everything," remarked Will consolingly. He snatched at a piece of straw that had fallen on the lowest rung of the ladder and began idly chewing it. "As for me, I know a blamed sight more about women than I do about tobacco," he added, with a swagger.

Christopher glanced up, and at sight of the boyish figure burst into a hearty laugh.

"Oh, you're a jolly old sport, I know, and to think that Tom Spade has been accusing me of leading you astray! Why, you are already twice the man that I am."

"Pshaw! That's just grandpa's chatter! The old man rails at me day and night about you until it's a mortal wonder he doesn't drive me to the dogs outright. I'd like to see another fellow that would put up with it for a week. Captain Morrison told him, you know, that I hadn't done a peg of study for a year, and it brought on a scene that almost shook the roof. Now he swears I'm to go to the university next fall or hang."

"Well, I'd go, by all means."

"What under heaven could I do there? All

those confounded languages Morrison poured into my head haven't left so much as a single letter of the alphabet. *Ad nauseam* is all I learned of Latin. I tell you I'd rather be a storekeeper any time than a scholar—books make me sick all over—and, when it comes to that, I don't believe I know much more to-day than you do."

A smile crossed Christopher's face, leaving it very grim. The words recalled to him his own earlier ambition—that of the gentlemanly scholar of the old order—and there flickered before his eyes the visionary library, suffused with firelight, and the translation of the "Iliad" he had meant to finish.

"I always told you it wasn't worth anything," he said roughly. "Not worth so much as Molly Peterkin's little finger. Do you think she'd love you any better if you could spurt Greek?"

Will broke into a pleased laugh, his mind dwelling upon the fancy the other had conjured up so skilfully.

"Did you ever see such lips in your life?" he inquired.

Christopher shook his head. "I haven't noticed them, but Sol's have a way of sticking in my memory."

"Oh, you brute! It's a shame that she should have such a father. He's about the worst I ever met."

"Some think the shame is on the other side, you know."

"That's a lie—she told me so. Fred Turner started the whole thing because she refused to marry him at the last moment. She found out suddenly that she wasn't in love with him. Girls are like that, you see. Why, Maria——"

Christopher looked up quickly.

"I've nothing to do with your sister," he observed.

"I know that; but it's true, all the same. Maria couldn't tell her own mind any better. Why, one day she was declaring that she was over head and ears in love with Jack, and the next she was wringing her hands and begging him to go away."

"What are you going to do down at the store?" asked Christopher abruptly.

"Oh, nothing in particular—just lounge, I suppose; there's never anything to do. By the way, can't we have a hunt to-morrow?"

"I'll see about it. Look here, is your grandfather any worse than usual? He stormed at me like mad yesterday because I wouldn't turn my team of oxen out of the road."

"It's like blasting rock to get a decent word out of him. The only time he's been good-humoured for four years was the week we were away together. He offered me five thousand dollars down if I'd never speak to you again."

"You don't say so!" exclaimed Christopher. He bent his head and stood looking thoughtfully at the matted straw under foot. "Well, you had a chance to turn a pretty penny," he said, in a tone of gentle raillery.

"Oh, hang it! What do you mean?" demanded Will. "Of course, I wasn't going back on you like that just to please grandpa. I'd have been a confounded sneak if I had!"

"You're a jolly good chap and no mistake! But the old man would have been pleased, I reckon?"

Will grinned.

"You bet he would! I could twist him round my finger but for you, Aunt Saidie says."

"It will be all the same in the end, though. The whole thing will come to you some day."

"Oh, yes. Maria got her share, and Wyndham has made ducks and drakes of it."

"Your grandfather's aging, too, isn't he?"

"Rather," returned Will, with a curious mixture of amiable lightness and cool brutality. "He's gone off at least twenty years since that time I had pneumonia in your barn. That wrecked him, Aunt Saidie says, and all because he knew he'd have to put up with you when the doctor told him to let me have my way. His temper gets worse, too, all the time. I declare, he sometimes makes me wish he were dead and buried."

"Oh, he'll live long enough yet, never fear—those wiry, cross-grained people are as tough as lightwood knots. It's a pity, though, he wants to bully you like that—it would kill me in a day."

A flush mounted to Will's forehead. "I knew you'd think so," he said, "and it's what I tell him all the time. He's got no business meddling with me so much, and I won't stand it."

"He ought to get a dog," suggested Christopher indifferently.

"Well, I'm not a dog, and I'll make him understand it yet. Oh, you think I'm an awful milksop, of course, but I'll show you otherwise some day. I'd like to know if you could have done any better in my place?"

"Done! Why, I shouldn't have been in your place long, that's all."

"I shan't, either, for that matter; but I've got to humour him a little, you see, because he holds the purse-strings."

"He'd never go so far as to kick you out, would he?"

"Well, hardly. I'm all he has, you know. He doesn't like Maria because of her fine airs, much as he thinks of education. I've got to be a gentleman, he says; but as for him, he wouldn't give up one of his vulgar habits to save anybody's soul. His trouble with Maria all came of her reproving him for drinking out of his saucer. Now, I don't mind that kind of thing so much, but Maria used to say she'd rather have him steal, any day, than gulp his coffee. Why are you laughing so?"

"Oh, nothing. Are you going to Tom's now? I've got to work."

Will slid down from the big box and sauntered toward the door, pausing on the little wooden step to light a cigarette.

"Drop in if you get a chance," he threw back over his shoulder, with a puff of smoke.

In a few moments Christopher finished his work, and, coming outside, closed the stable door. Then he walked a few paces along the little path, stopping from time to time to gaze across the darkening landscape. A light mist was wreathed about the tops of the old lilac-bushes, where it glimmered so indistinctly that it seemed as if one might dispel it by a breath; and farther away the soft evening colours had settled over the great fields, beyond which a clear yellow line was just visible above the distant woods. The wind was sharp with an edge of frost, and as it blew into his face he raised his head and drank long, invigorating drafts. From the cattle-pen hard by he smelled the fresh breath of the cows, and around him were those other odours, vague, familiar, pleasant, which are loosened at twilight in the open country.

The time had been when the mere physical contact with the air would have filled him with a quiet satisfaction, but during the last four years he had lost gradually his sensitiveness to external things—to the changes of the seasons as to the beauties of an autumn sunrise. A clear morning had ceased to arouse in him the old buoyant energy, and he had lost the zest of muscular exertion which had done so much to sweeten his labour in the fields. It was as if a clog fettered his simplest no less than his greatest emotion; and his enjoyment of nature had grown dull and spiritless, like his affection for his family. With his sisters he was aware that a curious constraint had become apparent, and it was no longer possible for him to meet his mother with the gay deference she still exacted. There were times, even, when he grew almost suspicious of Cynthia's patience, and at such moments his irritation was manifested in a sullen reserve. To himself he could give no explanation of his state of mind; he knew merely that he retreated day by day farther into the shadow of his loneliness, and that, while in his heart he still craved human sympathy, an expression of it even from those he loved was, above all, the thing he most bitterly resented.

A light flashed in the kitchen, and he went on slowly toward the house. As he reached the back porch he saw that Lila was sitting at the kitchen window looking wearily out into the dusk. The firelight scintillated in her eyes, and as she turned quickly at a sound within the room he noticed with a pang that the sparkles were caused by teardrops on her lashes. His heart quickened at the sight of her drooping figure, and an impulse seized him to go in and comfort her at any cost. Then his severe constraint laid an icy hold upon him, and he hesitated with his hand upon the door.

"If I go in and speak to her, what is there for me to say?" he thought, overcome by his horror of any uncontrolled emotion. "We will merely go over the old complaints, the endless explanations. She will probably weep like a child, and I shall feel a brute when I look on and keep silent. In the first place, if I speak to her, what is there for me to say? If I simply beg her to stop crying, or if I rush in and urge her to marry Jim Weatherby to-morrow, what good can come of either course? She doesn't wait for my consent to the marriage, for she is as old as I am, and knows her own heart much better than I know mine. It is true that she is too beautiful to waste away like this, but how can I prevent it, or what is there for me to do?"

Again came the impulse to go in and fold her in his arms, but before he had taken the first step he yielded, as always, to his strange reserve, and he realised that if he entered it would be but to assume his customary unconcern, from the shelter of which he would probably make a few commonplace remarks on trivial subjects. The emotional situation would be ignored by them all, he knew; they would treat it absolutely as if it had no existence, as if its voice was not speaking to them in the silence, and they would break their bread and drink their coffee in apparent unconsciousness that supper was not the single thing that engrossed their thoughts. And all the time they would be face to face with the knowledge that they had demanded that Lila should sacrifice her life.

Presently Cynthia came out and called him, and he went in carelessly and sat down at the table. Lila left the window and slipped into her place, and when Tucker joined them she cut up his food as usual and prepared his coffee.

"Uncle Tucker's cup has no handle, Cynthia," she said with concern. "Let me take this one and give him another."

"Well, I never!" exclaimed Cynthia, bending over to examine the break with her near-sighted squint. "We'll soon have to begin using Aunt Susannah's set, if this keeps up. Uncle Boaz, you've broken another cup to-day."

Her tone was sharp with irritation, and the fine wrinkles caused by ceaseless small worries appeared instantly between her eyebrows. Christopher, watching her, remembered that she had worn the same expression during the scene with Lila, and it annoyed him unspeakably that she should be able to descend so readily, and with equal energy, upon so insignificant a grievance as a bit of broken china.

Uncle Boaz hobbled round the table and peered contemptuously at the cup which Lila held.

"Dar warn' no use bruckin' dat ar one," he observed, "'caze 'twuz bruck a'ready."

"Oh, there won't be a piece left presently," pursued Cynthia indignantly; and Christopher felt suddenly that there was something contemptible in the passion she expended upon trifles. He wondered if Tucker noticed how horribly petty it all was— to lament a broken cup when the tears were hardly dried on Lila's cheeks.

Finishing hurriedly, he pushed back his chair and rose from the table, shaking his head in response to Cynthia's request that he should go in to see his mother.

"Not now," he said impatiently, with that nervous avoidance of the person he loved best. "I'll be back in time to carry her to bed, but I've got to take a half-hour off and look in on Tom Spade."

"She really ought to go to bed before sundown," responded Cynthia, "but nothing under heaven will persuade her to do so. It's her wonderful will that keeps her alive, just as it keeps her sitting bolt upright in that old chair. I don't believe there's another woman on earth who could have done it for more than twenty years."

Taking down his hat from a big nail in the wall, Christopher stood for a moment abstractedly fingering the brim.

"Well, I'll be back shortly," he said at last, and went out hurriedly into the darkness.

At the instant he could not tell why he had so suddenly decided to follow Will Fletcher to the store, but, as usual, when the impulse came to him he proceeded to act promptly as it directed. Strangely enough, the boy was the one human being whom he felt no inclination to avoid, and the least oppressive moments that he knew were the reckless ones they spent together. While his daily companion was mentally and morally upon a lower plane than his own, the association was not without a balm for his wounded pride; and the knowledge that it was still possible to assume superiority to Fletcher's heir was, so far as he himself admitted, the one consolation that his life contained. As for his feeling toward Will Fletcher as an individual, it was the outcome of so curious a mixture of attraction and repulsion that he had long ceased from any attempt to define it as pure emotion. For the last four years the boy had been, as Tom Spade put it, "the very shadow on the man's footsteps," and yet at the end of that time it was almost impossible for Christopher to acknowledge either his liking or his hatred. He had suffered him for his own end, that was all, and he had come at last almost to enjoy the tolerance that he displayed. The hero-worship—the natural imitation of youth—was at least not unpleasant, and there had been days during a brief absence of the boy when Christopher had, to his surprise, become aware of a positive vacancy in his surroundings. So long as Will made no evident attempt to rise above him—so long, indeed, as Fletcher's grandson kept to Fletcher's level, it was possible that the companionship would continue as harmoniously as it had begun.

In the store he found Tom Spade and his wife— an angular, strong-featured woman, in purple calico, who carried off the reputation of a shrew with noisy honours. When he asked for Will, the store-keeper turned from the cash-drawer which he was emptying and nodded toward the half-open door of the adjoining room.

"Several of the young fellows are in thar now," he remarked offhand, "an' I've jest had to go in an' git between Fred Turner an' Will Fletcher. They came to out-an'-out blows, an' I had to shake 'em both by the scuff of thar necks befo' they'd hish snarlin'. Bless yo' life, all about a woman, too, every last word of it. Well, well, meanin' no disrespect to you, Susan, it's a queer thing that a man can't be born, married, or buried without a woman gittin' herself mixed up in the business. If she ain't wrappin' you in swaddlin' bands, you may be sho' she's measurin' off yo' windin'-sheet. Mark my words, Mr. Christopher, I don't believe thar's ever been a fight fought on this earth—be it a battle or a plain fisticuff—that it warn't started in the brain of somebody's mother, wife, or sweetheart— an' it's most likely to have been the sweetheart. It is strange, when you come to study 'bout it, how sech peaceable-lookin' creaturs as women kin have sech hearty appetites for trouble."

"Well, trouble may be born of a woman, but it generally manages to take the shape of a man," observed Mrs. Spade from behind the counter, where she was filling a big glass jar with a fresh supply of striped peppermint candy. "And as far as that goes, ever sence the Garden of Eden, men have taken a good deal mo' pleasure in layin' the blame on thar wives than they do in layin' blows on the devil. It's a fortunate woman that don't wake up the day after the weddin' an' find she's married an Adam instid of a man. However, they are as the Lord made 'em, I reckon," she finished charitably, "which ain't so much to thar credit as it sounds, seein' they could have done over sech a po' job with precious little trouble."

"Oh, I warn't aimin' at you, Susan," Tom hastened to assure her, aware from experience that he entered an argument only to be worsted. "You've been a good wife to me, for all yo' sharp tongue, an' I've never had to git up an' light the fire sence the day I married you. Yes, you've been a first-rate wife to me, an' no mistake."

"I'm the last person you need tell that to," was Mrs. Spade's retort. "I don't reckon I've b'iled inside an' sweated outside for mo' than twenty years without knowin' it. Lord! Lord! If it took as hard work to be a Christian as it does to be a wife, thar'd be mighty few but men in the next world—an' they'd git thar jest by followin' like sheep arter Adam——"

"I declar', Susan, I didn't mean to rile you," urged Tom, breaking in upon the flow of words with an appealing effort to divert its course. "I was merely crackin' a joke with Mr. Christopher, you know."

"I'm plum sick of these here jokes that's got to have a woman on the p'int of 'em," returned Mrs. Spade, tightly screwing on the top of the glass jar. "I've always noticed that thar ain't nothin' so funny in this world but it gits a long sight funnier if a man kin turn it on his wife——"

"Now, my dear——" helplessly expostulated Tom.

"My name's Susan, Tom Spade, an' I'll have you

call me by it or not at all. If thar's one thing I
hate on this earth it's a 'dear' in the mouth of a
married man that ought to know better. I'd every
bit as lief you'd shoot a lizard at me, an' you ain't
jest found it out. If you think I'm the kind of
person to git any satisfaction out of improper speeches
you were never mo' mistaken in yo' life; an' I kin
p'int out to you right now that I ain't never heard
one of them words yit that I ain't had to pay for it.
A 'dear' the mo' is mighty apt to mean a bucket of
water the less. Oh, you can't turn my head with
yo' soft tricks, Tom Spade. I'm a respectable woman,
as my mother was befo' me, an' I don't want familiar
doin's from any man, alive or dead. The woman
who does, whether she be married or single, ain't
no better than a female—that's my opinion!"

She paused to draw breath, and Tom was quick
to take advantage of the intermission. "Good
Lord, Mr. Christopher, those darn young fools are
at it agin!" he exclaimed, darting toward the adjoining room.

With a stride, Christopher pushed past him and,
opening the door, stopped uncertainly upon the
threshold.

At the first glance he saw that the trouble was
between Will and Fred Turner, and that Will,
because of his slighter weight, had got very much
the worst of the encounter. The boy stood now,
trembling with anger and bleeding at the mouth,
beside an overturned table, while Fred—a stout,
brawny fellow—was busily pummelling his shoulders.

"You're a sneakin', puny-livered liar, that's what
you are!" finished Turner with a vengeance.

Christopher walked leisurely across the room.

"And you're another," he observed in a quiet voice—the voice of his courtly father, which always came to him in moments of white heat. "You are exactly that—a sneaking, puny-livered liar." His manner was so courteous that it came as a surprise when he struck out from the shoulder and felled Fred as easily as he might have knocked over a wooden tenpin. "You really must learn better manners," he remarked coolly, looking down upon him.

Then he wiped his brow on his blue shirt-sleeve and called for a glass of beer.

CHAPTER III

Mrs. Blake Speaks Her Mind on Several Matters

Breakfast was barely over the next morning when Jim Weatherby appeared at the kitchen door carrying a package of horseshoe nails and a small hammer.

"I thought perhaps Christopher might want to use the mare early," he explained to Cynthia, who was clearing off the table. There was a pleasant precision in his speech, acquired with much industry at the little country school, and Cynthia, despite her rigid disfavour, could not but notice that when he glanced round the room in search of Lila he displayed the advantage of an aristocratic profile. Until to-day she could not remember that she had ever seen him directly, as it were; she had looked around him and beyond him, much as she might have obliterated from her vision a familiar shrub that chanced to intrude itself into her point of view. The immediate result of her examination was the possibility she dimly acknowledged that a man might exist as a well-favoured individual and yet belong to an unquestionably lower class of life.

"Well, I'll go out to the stable," added Jim, after a moment in which he had patiently submitted to her

263

squinting observation. "Christopher will be somewhere about, I suppose?"

"Oh, I suppose so," replied Cynthia indifferently,
emptying the coffee-grounds into the kitchen sink.
The asperity of her tone was caused by the entrance
of Lila, who came in with a basin of corn-meal dough
tucked under her bared arm, which showed as round
and delicate as a child's beneath her loosely rolled-
up sleeve.

"Cynthia, I can't find the hen-house key," she
began; and then, catching sight of Jim, she flushed
a clear pink, while the little brown mole ran a race
with the dimple in her cheek.

"The key is on that nail beside the dried hops,"
returned Cynthia sternly. "I found it in the lock
last night and brought it in. It's a mercy that the
chickens weren't all stolen."

Without replying, Lila took down the key, strung
it on her little finger, and, going to the door, passed
with Jim out into the autumn sunshine. Her soft
laugh pulsed back presently, and Cynthia, hearing
it, set her thin lips tightly as she carefully rinsed
the coffee-pot with soda.

Christopher, who had just come up to the well-
brink, where Tucker sat feeding the hounds from a
plate of scraps, gave an abrupt nod in the direction
of the lovers strolling slowly down the hen-house
path.

"It will end that way some day, I reckon," he
said with a sigh, "and you know I'm almost of a
mind with Cynthia about it. It does seem a downright pity. Not that Jim isn't a good chap and
all that, but he's an honest, hard-working farmer

and nothing more—and, good heavens! just look at Lila! Why, she's beautiful enough to set the world afire."

Smiling broadly, Tucker tossed a scrap of corn-bread into Spy's open jaws; then his gaze travelled leisurely to the hen-house, which Lila had just unlocked. As she pushed back the door there was a wild flutter of wings, and the big fowls flew in a swarm about her feet, one great red-and-black rooster craning his long neck after the basin she held beneath her arm. While she scattered the soft dough on the ground she bent her head slightly sideways, looking up at Jim, who stood regarding her with enraptured eyes.

"Well, I don't know that much good ever comes of setting anything afire," answered Tucker with his amiable chuckle; "the danger is that you're apt to cause a good deal of trouble somewhere, and it's more than likely you'll get singed yourself in putting out the flame. You needn't worry about Lila, Christopher; she's the kind of woman—and they're rare—who doesn't have to have her happiness made to order; give her any fair amount of the raw material and she'll soon manage to fit it perfectly to herself. The stuff is in her, I tell you; the atmosphere is about her—can't you feel it?—and she's going to be happy, whatever comes. A woman who can make over a dress the sixth time as cheerfully as she did the first has the spirit of a Cæsar, and doesn't need your lamentations. If you want to be a Jeremiah, you must go elsewhere."

"Oh, I dare say she'll grow content, but it does seem such a terrible waste. She's the image of that

Saint-Memin portrait of Aunt Susannah, and if she'd only been born a couple of generations ago she would probably have been the belle of two continents. Such women must be scarce anywhere."

"She's pretty enough, certainly, and I think Jim knows it. There's but one thing I've ever seen that could compare with her for colour, and that's a damask rose that blooms in May on an old bush in the front yard. When all is said, however, that young Weatherby is no clodhopper, you know, and I'm not sure that he isn't worthier of her than any high-sounding somebody across the water would have been. He can love twice as hard, I'll wager, and that's the chief thing, after all; it's worth more than big titles or fine clothes—or even than dead grand-fathers, with due respect to Cynthia. I tell you, Lila may never stir from the midst of these tobacco fields; she may be buried alive all her days between these muddy roads that lead heaven knows where, and yet she may live a lot bigger and fuller life than she might have done with all London at her feet, as they say it was at your Greataunt Susannah's. The person who has to have outside props to keep him straight must have been made mighty crooked at the start, and Lila's not like that."

Christopher stooped and pulled Spy's ears.

"That's as good a way to look at it as any other, I reckon," he remarked; "and now I've got to hurry the shoeing of the mare."

He crossed over and joined Lila and Jim before the hen-house door, where he put the big fowls to noisy flight.

"Well, you're a trusty neighbour," he cried good-humoredly, striking Jim a friendly blow that sent him reeling out into the path.

Lila passed her hand in a sweeping movement round the inside of the basin and flirted the last drops of dough from her finger-tips.

"A few of your pats will cripple Jim for a week," she observed, "so you'd better be careful; he's too useful a friend to lose while there are any jobs to do."

"Why, if I had that muscle I could run a farm with one hand," said Jim. "Give a plough a single push, Christopher, and I believe it would run as long as there was level ground."

Cynthia, standing at the kitchen window with a cup-towel slung across her arm, watched the three chatting merrily in the sunshine, and the look of rigid resentment settled like a mask upon her face. She was still gazing out upon them when Docia opened the door behind her and informed her in a whisper that "Ole miss wanted her moughty quick."

"All right, Docia. Is anything the matter?"

"Naw'm, 'tain' nuttin' 'tall de matter. She's des got fidgetty."

"Well, I'll come in a minute. Are you better to-day? How's your heart?"

"Lawd, Miss Cynthia, hit's des bruised all over. Ev'y breaf I draw hits it plum like a hammer. I hyear hit thump, thump, thump all de blessed time."

"Be careful, then. Tell mother I'm coming at once."

She hung the cup-towel on the rack, and, taking off her blue checked apron, went along the little

platform to the main part of the house and into the
old lady's parlour, where the morning sunshine fell
across the faces of generations of dead Blakes. The
room was still furnished with the old rosewood
furniture, and the old damask curtains hung before
the single window, which gave on the overgrown
front yard and the twisted aspen. Though the rest
of the house suggested only the direst poverty, the
immediate surroundings of Mrs. Blake revealed
everywhere the lavish ease so characteristic of the
old order which had passed away. The carving on
the desk, on the book-cases, on the slender sofa,
was all wrought by tedious handwork; the delicate
damask coverings to the chairs were still lustrous
after almost half a century; and the few vases
scattered here and there and filled with autumn
flowers were, for the most part, rare pieces of old
royal Worcester. While it was yet Indian summer,
there was no need of fires, and the big fireplace was
filled with goldenrod, which shed a yellow dust
down on the rude brick hearth.

The old lady, inspired by her indomitable energy,
was already dressed for the day in her black brocade,
and sat bolt upright among the pillows in her great
oak chair.

"Some one passed the window whistling, Cynthia.
Who was it? The whistle had a pleasant, cheery
sound."

"It must have been Jim Weatherby, I think:
old Jacob's son."

"Is he over here?"

"To see Christopher—yes."

"Well, be sure to remind the servants to give him

something to eat in the kitchen before he goes back, and I think, if he's a decent young man, I should like to have a little talk with him about his family. His father used to be one of our most respectable labourers."

"It would tire you, I fear, mother. Shall I give you your knitting now?"

"You have a most peculiar idea about me, my child. I have not yet reached my dotage, and I don't think that a little talk with young Weatherby could possibly be much of an ordeal. Is he an improper person?"

"No, no, of course not; you shall see him whenever you like. I was only thinking of you."

"Well, I'm sure I am very grateful for your consideration, my dear, but there are times, occasionally, you know, when it is better for one to judge for oneself. I sometimes think that your only fault, Cynthia, is that you are a little—just a very little bit, you understand—inclined to manage things too much. Your poor father used to say that a domineering woman was like a kicking cow; but this doesn't apply to you, of course."

"Shall I call Jim now, mother?"

"You might as well, dear. Place a chair for him, a good stout one, and be sure to make him wipe his feet before he comes in. Does he appear to be clean?"

"Oh, perfectly."

"I remember his father always was—unusually so for a common labourer. Those people sometimes smell of cattle, you know; and besides, my nose has grown extremely sensitive in the years since I lost my eyesight. Perhaps it would be as well to hand me the bottle of camphor. I can pretend I have a headache."

"There's no need, really; he isn't a labourer at all, you know, and he looks quite a gentleman. He is, I believe, considered a very handsome young man."

Mrs. Blake waved toward the door and the piece of purple glass flashed in the sunlight. "In that case, I might offer him some sensible advice," she said. "The Weatherbys, I remember, always showed a very proper respect for gentle people. I distinctly recall how well Jacob behaved when on one occasion Micajah Blair—a dreadful, dissolute character, though of a very old family and an intimate friend of your father's—took decidedly too much egg-nog one Christmas when he was visiting us, and insisted upon biting Jacob's cheek because it looked so like a winesap. Jacob had come to see your father on business, and I will say that he displayed a great deal of good sense and dignity; he said afterward that he didn't mind the bite on his cheek at all, but that it pained him terribly to see a Virginia gentleman who couldn't balance a bowl of egg-nog. Well, well, Micajah was certainly a rake, I fear; and for that matter, so was his father before him."

"Father had queer friends," observed Cynthia sadly. "I remember his telling me when I was a little girl that he preferred that family to any in the county."

"Oh, the family was all right, my dear. I never heard a breath against the women. Now you may fetch Jacob. Is that his name?"

"No; Jim."

"Dear me; that's very odd. He certainly should

have been called after his father. I wonder how they could have been so thoughtless."

Cynthia drew forward an armchair, stooped and carefully arranged the ottoman, and then went with stern determination to look for Jim Weatherby.

He was sitting in the stable doorway, fitting a shoe on the old mare, while Lila leaned against an overturned barrel in the sunshine outside. At Cynthia's sudden appearance they both started and looked up in amazement, the words dying slowly on their lips.

"Why, whatever is the matter, Cynthia?" cried Lila, as if in terror.

Cynthia came forward until she stood directly at the mare's head, where she delivered her message with a gasp:

"Mother insists upon talking to Jim. There's no help for it; he must come."

Weatherby dropped the mare's hoof and raised a breathless question to Cynthia's face, while Lila asked quickly:

"Does she know?"

"Know what?" demanded Cynthia, turning grimly upon her. "Of course she knows that Jim is his father's son."

The young man rose and laid the hammer down on the overturned barrel; then he led the mare back to her stall, and coming out again, washed his hands in a tub of water by the door.

"Well, I'm ready," he observed quietly. "Shall I go in alone?"

"Oh, we don't ask that of you," said Lila, laughing. "Come; I'll take you."

She slipped her hand under his arm and they went gaily toward the house, leaving Cynthia to pick up the horseshoe nails lying loose upon the ground.

Hearing the young man's step on the threshold, Mrs. Blake turned her head with a smile of pleasant condescension and stretched out her delicate yellowed hand.

"This is Jim Weatherby, mother," said Lila in her softest voice. "Cynthia says you want to talk to him."

"I know, my child; I know," returned Mrs. Blake, with an animated gesture. "Come in, Jim, and don't trouble to stand. Find him a chair, Lila. I knew your father long before you were born," she added, turning to the young man, "and I knew only good of him. I suppose he has often told you of the years he worked for us?"

Jim held her hand for an instant in his own, and then, bending over, raised it to his lips.

"My father never tires of telling us about the old times, and about Mr. Blake and yourself," he answered in his precise English, and with the simple dignity which he never lost. Lila, watching him, prayed silently that a miracle might open the old lady's eyes and allow her to see the kind, manly look upon his face.

Mrs. Blake nodded pleasantly, with evident desire to put him wholly at his ease.

"Well, his son is becoming quite courtly," she responded, smiling, "and I know Jacob is proud of you—or he ought to be, which amounts to the same thing. There's nothing I like better than to see a good, hard-working family prosper in life and raise its station. Not that I mean to put ideas into your head, of course, for it is a ridiculous sight to see a person dissatisfied with the position in which the good Lord has placed him. That was what I always liked about your mother, and I remember very well her refusing to wear some of my old finery when she was married, on the ground that she was a plain, honest woman, and wanted to continue so when she was a wife. I hope, by the way, that she is well."

"Oh, quite. She does not walk much, though; her joints have been troubling her."

To Lila's surprise, he was not the least embarrassed by the personal tone of the conversation, and his sparkling blue eyes held their usual expression of blithe good-humour.

"Indeed!" Mrs. Blake pricked at the subject in her sprightly way. "Well, you must persuade her to use a liniment of Jamestown weed steeped in whisky. There is positively nothing like it for rheumatism. Lila, do we still make it for the servants? If so, you might send Sarah Weatherby a bottle."

"I'll see about it, mother. Aren't you tired? Shall I take Jim away?"

"Not just yet, child. I am interested in seeing what a promising young man he has become. How old are you, Jim?"

"Twenty-nine next February. There are two of us, you know—I've a sister Molly. She married Frank Granger and moved ten miles away."

"Ah, that brings me to the very point I was driving at. Above all things, let me caution you most earnestly against the reckless marriages so common in your station of life. For heaven's sake,

don't marry a woman because she has a pretty face
and you cherish an impracticable sentiment for her.
If you take my advice, you will found your marriage
upon mutual respect and industry. Select a wife
who is not afraid of work, and who expects no fol-
derol of romance. Love-making, I've always main-
tained, should be the pastime of the leisure class
exclusively."

"I'm not afraid of work myself," replied Jim,
laughing as he looked boldly into the old lady's
sightless eyes, "but I'd never stand it for my wife—
not a—a lick of it!"

"Tut, tut! Your mother does it."

Jim nodded. "But I'm not my father," he mildly
suggested.

"Well, you're a fine, headstrong young fool, and
I like you all the better for it," declared Mrs. Blake.
"You may go now, because I feel as if I needed a
doze; but be sure to come in and see me the next
time you're over here. Lila, put the cat on my
knees and straighten my pillows."

Lila lifted the cat from the rug and placed it in
the old lady's lap; then, as she arranged the soft
white pillows, she bent over suddenly and kissed the
piece of purple glass on the fragile hand.

CHAPTER IV

In Which Christopher Hesitates

Following his impulsive blow in defense of Will Fletcher, Christopher experienced, almost with his next breath, a reaction in his feeling for the boy; and meeting him two days later at the door of the tobacco barn, he fell at once into a tone of contemptuous raillery.

"So you let Fred smash you up, eh?" he observed, with a sneer.

Will flushed.

"Oh, you needn't talk like that," he answered; "he's the biggest man about here except you. By the way, you're a bully friend to a fellow, you know, and it's not a particle of use pretending you don't like me, because you can't help hitting back jolly quick when anybody undertakes to give me a licking."

"Why were you such a fool as to go at him?" inquired Christopher, glancing up at his evenly hanging rows of tobacco, and then coming outside to lock the door. "You'll never get a reputation as a fighter if you are always jumping on men over your own size. Now, next time I should advise you to try your spirit on Sol Peterkin."

"Oh, it was all about Molly," explained Will frankly. "I told Fred that he was a big blackguard to use the girl so, and then he called me a 'white-livered liar.'"

"I heard him," remarked Christopher quietly.

"Well, I don't care what he says—he is a black-guard. I'm glad you knocked him down, too; it was no more than he deserved."

"I didn't do it on Molly Peterkin's account, you know. Tobacco takes up quite enough of my time without my entering the lists as a champion of light women. But if you aren't man enough to fight your own battles, I suppose I'll have to keep my muscle in proper shape."

Will smarted from the words, and the corners of his mouth took a dogged droop.

"I don't see how you expect me to be a match for Fred Turner," he returned angrily.

"Why, I don't expect it," replied Christopher coolly, as he turned the key in the padlock, drew it out, and slipped it into his pocket. "I expect you merely to keep away from him, that's all."

Will stared at him in perplexity. "What a devil of a humour you are in!" he exclaimed.

"Am I?" Christopher broke into a laugh. "You are accustomed to the sunny temper of your grand-father. How is he to-day? In his usual cheerful vein?"

"Oh, he's awful," answered the boy, relieved at the change of subject. "If you could only have heard him yesterday! Somebody told him about the fight at the store, and, as luck would have it, he found out that Molly Peterkin was at the bottom of it all. When he called me into his room and locked the door I knew something was up; and sure enough, we had blood and thunder for two mortal hours. He threatened to sell the horses and the hounds, and to put me at the plough, if I ever so much as looked at the girl again—'gal,' he called her, and a 'brazen wench.' That is the way he talks, you know."

"I know," Christopher nodded gravely.

"But the funny part is, that the thing that made him hottest was your knocking over Fred Turner. That he simply couldn't stand. Why, he'd have paid Fred fifty dollars down to thrash me black and blue, he said. He called you—— Oh, he has a great store of pet names!"

"What?" asked Christopher, for the other caught himself up suddenly.

"Nothing much—he's always doing it, you know."

"You needn't trouble yourself on my account. I'm familiar with his use of words."

"Oh, he called you 'a crazy pauper who ought to be in gaol.'"

"He did, did he? Well, for once in his life he drew it mild." Then he gave a long whistle and kicked away a rock in the path. "'A crazy pauper who ought to be in gaol.' I've a pretty good-sized debt to settle with your grandfather, when I come to think of it."

"Just suppose you were in my place now," insisted Will. "Then I reckon you'd have cause for swearing, sure enough. I tell you I couldn't get out of that room yesterday until I promised him I'd turn over a new leaf—that I'd start in with Mr. Morrison to-morrow, and dig away at Latin and Greek until I go to the university next fall."

Christopher turned quickly.

"To-morrow?" he repeated. "Why, that's the day I had planned we'd go hunting. Make Morrison's Friday."

The boy wavered.

"Can't we go another day?" he asked. "He's so awfully set on to-morrow. I'd have to be mighty sharp to fool him again."

"Oh, well, but it's the only day I've free. There's a lot of fall ploughing to do; then the apples are ready to be gathered; and I must take some corn to the mill before the week's up. I've wasted too much time with you as it is. It's the only wealth I have, you see."

"Then I'll go—I'll go," declared Will, jumping to a decision. "There'll be a terrific fuss if he finds it out, but perhaps he won't. I'll bring my gun over to the barn to-night, and get Zebbadee to meet us with the hounds at the bend in the road. Well, I must get back now. I don't want him to suspect I've seen you to-day."

He started off at a rapid pace, and Christopher, turning in the other direction, went to bring the horses from the distant pasture. It was a mellow afternoon, and a golden haze wrapped the broad meadow, filled with autumn wild flowers, and the little bricked-up graveyard on the low, green hill. As he swung himself over the bars at the end of the path he saw Lila and Jim Weatherby gathering goldenrod in the center of the field. When they caught sight of him, Jim laid his handful of blossoms in a big basket on the ground and came to join him on his way to the pasture.

"They are for Mrs. Blake's fireplace," he remarked with a friendly smile, as he glanced back at Lila standing knee-deep amid the October flowers.

"It's a queer idea," observed Christopher, finding himself at a loss for a reply.

Jim strolled on leisurely, snatching at the heads of wild carrot as he passed.

"There's something I've wanted to tell you, Christopher," he said after a moment, turning his pleasant, manly face upon the other.

"Is that so?" asked Christopher, with a sudden desire to avert the impending responsibility. "Oh, but I hardly think I'm the proper person," he added, laughing.

Jim met his eyes squarely.

"I'm a plain man," he said slowly, "and though I'm not ashamed of it, I know, of course, that my family have always been plain people. As things are, I had no business on earth to fall in love with your sister, but all the same it's what I've gone and done."

Christopher nodded and walked on.

"Well, I suppose it's what I should have done, too, in your place," he returned quietly.

"I've reproached myself for it often enough," pursued Jim; "but when all is said, how can a man prevent a thing like that? I might as well try to shut my eyes to the sun when it is shining straight on me. Why, everybody else seems dull and lifeless when I look at her—and I seem such a brute myself that I hardly dare touch her hand. All I ask is to be her servant until I die."

It took courage to speak such words, and

Christopher, knowing it, stopped midway of the little path and regarded Jim with the rare smile which gave a boyish brightness to his face.

"By George, you are a trump!" he said heartily. "And as far as that goes, you're good enough for Lila or for anybody else. It isn't that, you see; it's only——"

"I know," finished Jim quietly and without resentment; "it's my grandfather. Your sister, Cynthia, told me, and I reckon it's all natural, but somehow I can't make myself ashamed of the old man—nor is Lila, for that matter. He was an honest, upright body as ever you saw, and he never did a mean thing in his life, though he lived to be almost ninety."

"You're right," said Christopher, flushing suddenly; "and as far as I'm concerned, I'd let Lila marry you to-morrow; but as for mother, she would simply never consent. The idea would be impossible to her, and we could never explain things; you must see that yourself."

"I see," replied Jim readily; "but the main point is that you yourself would have no objection to our marriage, provided it were possible."

"Not a bit; not a bit."

He held out his hand, and Jim shook it warmly before he picked up his basket and went to rejoin Lila.

Turning in the path, Christopher saw the girl, who was sitting alone on the lowered bars, rise and wave a spray of goldenrod above her head. Then, as the lovers met, she laid her hand upon Jim's arm and lifted her glowing face as if to read his words before he uttered them. Something in the happy surrender of her gesture, or in the brooding mystery of the Indian summer, when one seemed to hear the earth turn in the stillness, touched Christopher with a sudden melancholy, and it appeared to him when he went on again that a shadow had fallen over the brightness of the autumn fields. Disturbed by the unrest which follows any illuminating vision of ideal beauty, he asked himself almost angrily, in an effort to divert his thoughts, if it were possible that he was weakening in his purpose, since he no longer found the old zest in his hatred of Fletcher. The deadness of his emotions had then affected this one also—the single feeling which he had told himself would be eternal; and the old nervous thrill, so like the thrill of violent love, no longer troubled him when he chanced to meet his enemy face to face. To-day he held Will Fletcher absolutely in his hand, he knew; in a few years at most his debt to Fletcher would probably be cancelled; the man and the boy would then be held together by blood ties like two snarling hounds in the leash—and yet, when all was said, what would the final outcome yield of satisfaction? As he put the question he knew that he could meet it only by evasion, and his inherited apathy enfeebled him even while he demanded an answer of himself.

As the months went on, his indifference to success or failure pervaded him like a physical lethargy, and he played his game so recklessly at last that he sometimes caught himself wondering if it were, after all, worth a single flicker of the candle. He still saw Will Fletcher daily; but when the spring came he ceased consciously, rather from weariness than from any nobler sentiment, to exert an influence which he felt to be harmful to the boy. For four years he had wrought tirelessly to compass the ruin of Fletcher's ambition; and now, when he had but to stretch forth his arm for the final blow, he admitted impatiently that what he lacked was the impulsive energy the deed required.

He was still in this mood when, one afternoon in April, as he was driving his oxen to the store, he met Fletcher in the road behind the pair of bays. At sight of him the old man's temper slipped control, and at the end of a few minutes they were quarrelling as to who should be the one to turn aside.

"Git out of the road, will you?" cried Fletcher, half rising from his seat and jerking at the reins until the horses reared. "Drive your brutes into the bushes and let me pass!"

"If you think I'm going to swerve an inch out of my road to oblige you, Bill Fletcher, you are almost as big a fool as you are a rascal," replied Christopher in a cool voice, as he brought his team to a halt and placed himself at the head of it with his long rawhide whip in his hand.

As he stood there he had the appearance of taking his time as lightly as did the Olympian deities; and it was clear that he would wait patiently until the sun set and rose again rather than yield one jot or tittle of his right upon the muddy road. While he gazed placidly over Fletcher's head into the golden distance, he removed his big straw hat and began fanning his heated face.

There followed a noisy upbraiding from Fletcher,

which ended by his driving madly into the under-brush and almost overturning the heavy carriage. As he passed, he leaned from his seat and slashed his whip furiously into Christopher's face; then he drove on at a wild pace, bringing the horses in a shiver, and flecked with foam, into the gravelled drive before the Hall.

The bright flower-beds and the calm white pillars were all in sunshine, and Miss Saidie, with a little, green watering-pot in her hand, was sprinkling a tub of crocuses beside the steps.

"You look flustered, Brother Bill," she observed, as Fletcher threw the reins to a Negro servant and came up to where she stood.

"Oh, I've just had some words with that darned Blake," returned Fletcher, chewing the end of his mustache, as he did when he was in a rage. "I met him as I drove up the road and he had the impudence to keep his ox-cart standing plumb still while I tore through the briers. It's the third time this thing has happened, and I'll be even with him for it yet."

"I'm sure he must be a very rude person," re-marked Miss Saidie, pinching off a withered blossom and putting it in her pocket to keep from throwing it on the trim grass. "For my part, I've never been able to see what satisfaction people git out of being ill-mannered. It takes twice as long as it does to be polite, and it's not nearly so good for the digestion afterward."

Fletcher listened to her with a scowl. "Well, if you ever get anything but curses from Christopher Blake, I'd like to hear of it," he said, with a coarse laugh.

"Why, he was really quite civil to me the other day when I passed him," replied Miss Saidie, facing Fletcher with her hand resting on the belt of her apron. "I was in the phaeton, and he got down off his wagon and picked up my whip. I declare, it almost took my breath away, but when I thanked him he raised his hat and spoke very pleasantly."

"Oh, you and your everlasting excuses!" sneered Fletcher, going up the steps and turning on the porch to look down upon her. "I tell you I've had as many of 'em as I'm going to stand. This is my house, and what I say in it has got to be the last word. If you squirt any more of that blamed water around here the place will rot to pieces under our very feet."

Miss Saidie placed her watering-pot on the step and lifted to him the look of amiable wonder which he found more irritating than a sharp retort.

"I forgot to tell you that Susan Spade has been waiting to speak to you," she remarked, as if their previous conversation had been of the friendliest nature.

"Oh, drat her! What does she want?"

"She wouldn't tell me—it was for you alone, she said. That was a good half-hour ago, and she's been waiting in your setting-room ever sence. She's such a sharp-tongued woman I wonder how Tom manages to put up with her."

"Well, if he does, I won't," growled Fletcher, as he went in to meet his visitor.

Mrs. Spade, wearing a severe manner and a freshly starched purple calico, was sitting straight and stiff **on** the edge of the cretonne-covered lounge, and as he entered she rose to receive him with a visible unbending of her person. She was a lank woman, with a long, scrawny figure which appeared to have run entirely to muscle, and very full skirts that always sagged below the belt-line in the back. Her face was like that of a man—large-featured, impressive, and not without a ruddy masculine comeliness.

"It's my duty that's brought me, Mr. Fletcher," she began, as they shook hands. "You kin see very well yo'self that it's not a pleasure, as far as that goes, for if it had been I never should have come—not if I yearned and pined till I was sore. I never saw a pleasure in my life that didn't lead astray, an' I've got the eye of suspicion on the most harmless-lookin' one that goes. As I tell Tom—though he won't believe it—the only way to be sartain you're followin' yo' duty in this world is to find out the thing you hate most to do an' then do it with all yo' might. That rule has taken me through life, suh; it married me to Tom Spade, an' it's brought me here to-day. 'Don't you go up thar blabbin' on Will Fletcher,' said Tom, when I was tyin' on my bonnet. 'You needn't say one word mo' about it,' was my reply. 'I know the Lord's way, an' I know mine. I've wrastled with this in pra'r, an' I tell you when the Lord turns anybody's stomach so dead agin a piece of business, it means most likely that it's the very thing they've got to swallow down."

"Oh, Will!" gasped Fletcher, dropping suddenly into his armchair. "Please come to the point at once, ma'am, and let me hear what the rascal has done last."

"I'm comin', suh; I'm comin'," Mrs. Spade hastened to assure him. "Yes, Tom an' I hev talked it all down to the very bone, but I wouldn't trust a man's judgment on morals any mo' than I would on matchin' calico. Right an' wrong don't look the same to 'em by lamplight as they do by day, an' if thar conscience ain't set plum' in the pupils of thar eyes, I don't know whar 'tis, that's sho'. But, thank heaven, I ain't one of those that's always findin' an excuse for people—not even if the backslider be my own husband. Thar's got to be some few folks on the side of decency, an' I'm one of 'em. Virtue's a slippery thing—that's how I look at it—an' if you don't git a good grip on it an' watch it with a mighty stern eye it's precious apt to wriggle through yo' fingers. I'm an honest woman, Mr. Fletcher, an' I wouldn't blush to own it in the presence of the King of England——"

"Great Scott!" exclaimed Fletcher, with a brutal laugh; "do you mean to tell me the precious young fool has fallen in love with you?"

"Me, suh? If he had, a broomstick an' a spar' rib or so would have been all you'd ever found of him agin. I've never yit laid eyes on the man I couldn't settle with a single sweep, an' when a lone woman comes to wantin' a protector, I've never seen the husband that could hold a candle to a good stout broom. That's what I said to Jinnie when she got herself engaged to Fred Boxley. 'Married or single,' I said, 'gal, wife, or widow, a broom is yo' best friend.'"

Fletcher twisted impatiently in his chair.

"Oh, for heaven's sake, stop your drivelling," he

blurted out at last, "and tell me in plain language what the boy has done."

"Oh, I don't know what he's done or what he hasn't," rejoined Mrs. Spade, "but I've watched him courtin' Molly Peterkin till I told Tom this thing had to stop or I would stop it. If thar's a p'isonous snake or lizard in this country, suh, it's that tow-headed huzzy of Sol Peterkin's; an' if thar's a sex on this earth that I ain't go no patience with, it's the woman sex. A man may slip an' slide a little because he was made that way, but when it comes to a woman she's got to w'ar whalebones in her clothes when I'm aroun'. Lord! Lord! What's the use of bein' honest if you can't p'int yo' finger at them that ain't? Virtue gits mighty little in the way of gewgaws in this world, an' I reckon it's got to make things up in the way it feels when it looks at them that's gone astray——"

"Molly Peterkin!" gasped Fletcher, striking the arm of his chair a blow that almost shattered it. "Christopher Blake was bad enough, and now it's Molly Peterkin! Out of the frying-pan right spang into the fire. Oh, you did me a good turn in coming, Mrs. Spade. I'll forgive you the news you brought, and I'll even forgive you your blasted chatter. How long has this thing been going on, do you know?"

"That I don't, suh, that I don't; though I've been pryin' an' peekin' mighty close. All I know is, that every blessed evenin' for the last two weeks I've seen 'em walkin' together in the lane that leads to Sol's. This here ain't goin' to keep up one day mo'; that's what I put my foot down on yestiddy. I'd stop it if I didn't have nothin' agin that gal but the colour of her hair. I don' know how 'tis, suh, but I've always had the feelin' that thar's somethin' indecent about yaller hair, an' if I'd been born with it I'd have stuck my head into a bowl of pitch befo' I'd have gone flauntin' those corn-tassels in the eyes of every man I met. Thar's nothin' in the looks of me that's goin' to make a man regret he's got a wife if I can help it; an' mark my word, Mr. Fletcher, if they had dyed Molly Peterkin's hair black she might have been a self-respectin' woman an' a hater of men this very day. A light character an' a light head go precious well together, an' when you set one a good sober colour the other's pretty apt to follow."

Fletcher rose from his chair and stood gripping the table hard.

"Have you any reason to think—does it look likely—that young Blake has had a hand in this?" he asked.

"Who? Mr. Christopher? Why, I don't believe he could tell a petticoat from a pair of breeches to save his soul. He ain't got no fancy for corn-tassels and blue ribbons, I kin tell you that. It's good honest women that are the mothers of families that he takes to, an' even then it ain't no mo' than 'How are you, Mrs. Spade? A fine mornin'!'"

"Well, thar's one thing you may be sartain of," returned Fletcher, breaking in upon her, "and that is that this whole business is as good as settled. I leave here with the boy to-morrow morning at sunrise, and he doesn't set foot agin in this county until he's gone straight through the university.

I'll drag him clean across the broad ocean before he shall do it.''

Then, as Mrs. Spade took a noisy departure, he stood, without listening to her, gazing morosely down upon the pattern of the carpet.

CHAPTER V

THE HAPPINESS OF TUCKER

EARLY in the following November, Jim Weatherby, returning from the cross-roads one rainy afternoon, brought Christopher a long, wailing letter from Will.

"Oh, I've had to walk a chalk-line, sure enough," he wrote, "since that awful day we left home in a pouring rain, with grandpa wearing a whole thunderstorm on his forehead. It has been cram, cram, cram ever since, I can tell you, and here I am now, just started at the university, with my head still buzzing with the noise of those confounded ancients. If grandpa hadn't gone when he did, I declare I believe he would have ended by driving me clean crazy. Since he left I've had time to take a look about me, and I find there's a good deal of fun to be got here, after all. How I'll manage to mix it in with Greek I don't see, but luck's with me, you know—I've found that out—so I shan't bother.

"By the way, I wish you would make Molly Peterkin understand how it was I came away so hastily. Tell her I haven't forgotten her, and give her the little turquoise pin I'm sending. It just matches her eyes. Be sure to let me know if she's as pretty as ever."

By the next mail the turquoise brooch arrived, and Christopher, putting it in his pocket, went over to Sol Peterkin's to bear the message to the girl. As it happened, she was swinging on the little sagging gate when he came up the lane, and at sight of him her eyebrows shot up under her flaxen curls, which hung low upon her forehead. She was a pretty, soulless little animal, coloured like peach-blossoms, and with a great deal of that soft insipidity which is usually found in a boy's ideal of maiden innocence.

"Why, I couldn't believe my eyes when I first saw you," she said, arranging her curls over her left shoulder with a conscious simper.

The old Blake gallantry rose to meet her challenging eyes, and he regarded her smilingly a moment before he answered.

"Well, I could hardly believe mine, you know," he responded carelessly. "I thought for an instant that a big butterfly had alighted on the gate."

She pouted prettily.

"Won't you come in?" she asked after a moment, with an embarrassed air, as she remembered that he was one of the "real Blakes" for whom her father used to work.

A light retort was on his lips, but while he looked at her a little weary frown darkened her shallow eyes, and with the peculiar sympathy for all those oppressed by man or nature which was but one expression of his many-sided temperament he quickly changed the tone of his reply. At the instant it seemed to him that Molly Peterkin and himself stood together defrauded of their rightful heritage of life; and as his thought broadened he felt suddenly the

pathos of her forlorn little figure, of her foolish blue
eyes, of her trivial vanities, of her girlish beauty
soiled and worn by common handling. A look very
like compassion was in his face, and the girl, seeing
it, reddened angrily and kicked at a loose pebble in
the path. When he went away a moment later
he left a careless message for Sol about the tobacco
crop, and the little white box containing the turquoise
brooch was still in his pocket.

That afternoon the trinket went back to Will with
a curt letter. "If you take my advice, you'll leave
Molly Peterkin alone," he wrote in his big, unformed
hand, "for as far as I can see you are too good a match
to get on well together. She's a fool, you know, and
from the way you're going on just now it looks very
much as if you were one also. At any rate, I'm not your
man for gallantries. I'd rather hunt hares than
women, any day—and game's plentiful just now."

It was a long winter that year, and for the first
time since her terrible illness Mrs. Blake was forced
to keep her bed during a bitter spell of weather,
when the raw winds whistled around the little frame
house, entering the cracks at the doors and the
loosened sashes of the windows. Cynthia grew
drawn and pinched with a sickly, frost-bitten look, and
even Lila's rare bloom drooped for a while like that of a
delicate plant starving for the sunshine. Christopher,
who, as usual, was belated in his winter's work, was
kept busy hauling and chopping wood, shovelling the
snow away from the porch and the paths that led to
the well, the stable, and the barn. Once a day, most
often after breakfast, Jim Weatherby appeared,
smiling gaily beneath his powdering of snow; and

sometimes, in defiance of Cynthia, he would take Lila for a sleigh-ride, from which she would return blossoming like a rose.

Mrs. Blake, from her tester bed, complained bitterly of the cold, and drew from the increasing severity of the winters, which she declared became more unbearable each year, warrant for her belief in the gradual "decline of the world as a dwelling-place."

"You may say what you please, Tucker," she remarked one morning when she had awakened with an appetite to find that her eggs had frozen in the kitchen, "but you can hardly be so barefaced as to compliment this weather. I'm sure I never felt anything like it when I was young."

"Well, at least I have a roof over my head now, and I didn't when I marched to Romney with old Stonewall," remarked Tucker from the hearth, where he was roasting an apple before the big logs. "Many's the morning I waked then with the snow frozen stiff all over me, and I had to crack through it before I could get up."

The old lady made a peevish gesture.

"It may sound ungrateful," she returned, "but I'm sometimes tempted to wish that you had never marched to Romney, or that General Jackson had been considerate enough to choose a milder spell. I really believe when you come to die you will console yourself with the recollection of something worse that happened in the war."

Tucker laughed softly to himself as he watched the apple revolving in the red heat on its bit of string.

"Well, I'm not sure that I shan't, Lucy," he said.

"Habit's mighty strong, you know, and when you come to think of it there's some comfort in knowing that you'll never have to face the worst again. A man doesn't duck his head at the future when he's learned that, let be what will; it can't be so bad as the thing he's gone through with and yet come out on top. It gives him a pretty good feeling, after all, to know that he hasn't funked the hardest knock that life could give. Well, my birds are hungry, I reckon, and I'll hobble out and feed 'em while this apple is roasting to the core."

Raising himself with difficulty, he got upon his crutches and went to scatter his crumbs from the kitchen window.

By the first of March the thaw came, and the snow melted in a day beneath the lavish spring sunshine. It was a week later that Christopher, coming from the woods at midday, saw Tucker sitting on his old bench by the damask rose-bush, in which the sap was just beginning to swell. The sun shone full on the dead grass, and the old soldier, with his chin resting in the crook of his crutch, was gazing straight down upon the earth. The expression of his large, kindly face was so radiant with enjoyment that Christopher quickened his steps and slapped him affectionately upon the shoulder.

"Is Fletcher dead, Uncle Tucker?" he inquired, laughing.

"No, no; nobody's dead that I've heard of," responded Tucker in his cheerful voice; "but something better than Bill Fletcher's death has happened, I can tell you. Why, I'd been sitting out here an hour or more, longing for the spring to come, when suddenly I looked down and there was the first dandelion—a regular miracle—blooming in the mould about that old rose-bush."

"Well, I'll be hanged!" exclaimed Christopher, aghast. "Mark my words, you'll be in an asylum yet."

The other chuckled softly.

"When you put me there you'll shut up the only wise man in the county," he returned. "If your sanity doesn't make you happy, I can tell you it's worth a great deal less than my craziness. Look at that dandelion, now—it has filled two hours chock full of thought and colour for me when I might have been puling indoors and nagging at God Almighty about trifles. The time has been when I'd have walked right over that little flower and not seen it, and now it grows yellower each minute that I look at it, and each minute I see it better than I did the one before. There's nothing in life, when you come to think of it—not Columbus setting out to sea nor Napoleon starting on a march—more wonderful than that brave little blossom putting up the first of all through the earth."

"I can't see anything in a dandelion but a nuisance," observed Christopher, sitting down on the bench and baring his head to the sunshine; "but you do manage to get interest out of life, that's certain."

"Interest! Good Lord!" exclaimed Tucker. "If a man can't find something to interest him in a world like this, he must be a dull fellow or else have a serious trouble of the liver. So long as I have my eyes, and there's a different sky over my head each day, and earth, and trees, and flowers all around

me, I don't reckon I'll begin to whistle to boredom.
If I were like Lucy, now, I sometimes think things
would be up with me, and yet Lucy is one of the
very happiest women I've ever known. Her brain
is so filled with pleasant memories that it's never
empty for an instant."

Christopher's face softened, as it always did at
an allusion to his mother's blindness.

"You're right," he said; "she is happy."

"To be sure, she's had her life," pursued Tucker,
without noticing him. "She's been a beauty, a
belle, a sweetheart, a wife, and a mother—to say
nothing of a very spoiled old woman; but all the
same, I don't think I have her magnificent patience.
Oh, I couldn't sit in the midst of all this and not
have eyes to see."

With a careless smile Christopher glanced about
him—at the bright blue sky seen through the bare
trees, at the dried carrot flowers in the old field
across the road, at the great pine growing on the
little knoll.

"I hardly think she misses much," he said, and
added after a moment, "Do you know I'd give
twenty—no forty, fifty years of this for a single
year of the big noisy world over there. I'm dog-
tired of stagnation."

"Well, it's natural," admitted Tucker gently.
"At your age I doubtless felt the same. The young
want action, and they ought to have it, because it
makes the quiet of middle age seem all the sweeter.
You've missed your duels and your flirtations and
your pomades, and you've been put into breeches and
into philosophy at the same time. Why, one might

as well stick a brier pipe in the mouth of a boy who is crying for his first gun and tell him to go sit in the chimney-corner and be happy. When I was twenty-five I travelled all the way to New York for the latest Parisian waistcoat, but I can't remember that I ever strolled round the corner to see a peach-tree in full bloom. I'm a lot happier now, heaven knows, in my homespun coat, than I was then in that waist-coat of satin brocade, so I sometimes catch myself wishing that I could see again the people I knew then—the men I quarrelled with and the women I kissed. I'd like to apologise for the young fool of thirty years ago."

Christopher stirred restlessly, and, clasping his hands behind his head, stared at a small white cloud drifting slowly above the great pine.

"Well, it's the fool part I envy you, all the same," he remarked.

"You're welcome to it, my boy," answered Tucker; then he paused abruptly and bent his ear. "Ah, there's the bluebird! Do you hear him whistling in the meadow? God bless him; he's a hearty fellow and has spring in his throat."

"I passed one coming up," said Christopher.

"The same, I reckon. He'll be paying me a visit soon, and I've got my crumbs ready." He smiled brightly and then sat with his chin on his crutch, looking steadily across the road. "You haven't had your chance, my boy," he resumed presently; "and a man ought to have several chances to look round him in this world, for otherwise the things he misses will always seem to him the only things worth having. I'm not much of a fellow to preach, you'll say—a hundred and eighty pounds of flesh that can't dress itself or hobble about without crutches that are strapped on—but if it's the last word I speak I wouldn't change a day in my long life, and if it came to going over it again I'd trust it all in the Lord's hands and start blindfolded. And yet, when I look back upon it now, I see that it wasn't much of a life as lives go, and the two things I wanted most in it I never got."

Christopher turned quickly with a question.

"Oh, you think I have always been a contented, prosaic chap," pursued Tucker, smiling, "but you were never more mistaken since you were born. Twice in my life I came mighty near blowing out my brains —once when I found that I couldn't go to Paris and be an artist, and the second time when I couldn't get the woman I wanted for my wife. I wasn't cut out for a farmer, you see, and I had always meant from the time I was a little boy to go abroad and study painting. I'd set my heart on it, as people say, but when the time came my father died and I had to stay at home to square his debts and run the place. For a single night I was as clean crazy as a man ever was. It meant the sacrifice of my career, you know, and a career seemed a much bigger thing to me then than it does to-day."

"I never heard that," said Christopher, lowering his voice.

"There's a lot we don't know even about the people we live in a little house with. You never heard, either, I dare say, that I was so madly in love once that when the woman threw me over for a better man I shut myself up in a cabin in the woods and

did not speak to a human being for six months. I
was a rare devil, sure enough, though you'd never
believe it to see me now. It took two blows like
that, a four years' war, and the surgeon's operating
table to teach me how to be happy."

"It was Miss Matoaca Bolling, I suppose?"
suggested Christopher, with a mild curiosity.

The old soldier broke into his soft, full laugh.

"Matoaca! Bless your soul, no. But to think
that Lucy should have kept a secret for more than
thirty years! Never talk to me again about a
woman's letting anything out. If she's got a secret
that it mortifies her to tell it will be buried in the
grave with her, and most likely it will never see the
light at Judgment Day. Lucy was always ashamed
of my being jilted, you know."

"It's a new story then, is it?"

"Oh, it's as old as the hills by now. What's the
funny part, though, is that Lucy has always tried
to persuade herself it was really Matoaca I cared
for. You know, I sometimes think that a woman
can convince herself that black is white if she only
keeps trying hard enough—and it's marvellous that
she never sees the difference between wanting to
believe a thing and believing it in earnest. Now,
if Matoaca had been the last woman on this earth,
and I the last man, I could never have fallen in love
with her, though I may as well confess that I had
my share of fancies when I was young. It's no use
attempting to explain a man's feelings, of course.
Matoaca was almost as great a belle as Lucy, and
she was the handsomest creature you ever laid eyes
on—one of those big, managing women who are

forever improving things around them. Why, I don't believe she could stay two seconds in a man's arms without improving the set of his cravat. Some men like that kind of thing, but I never did, and I often think the reason I went so mad about the other woman was that she came restful after Matoaca. She was the comforting kind, who, you might be sure, always saw you at your best; and no matter the mood you were in, she never wanted to pat and pull you into shape. Lucy always said she couldn't hold a candle to Matoaca in looks, and I suppose she was right; but, pretty or plain, that girl had something about her that went straight to my heart more than thirty years ago and stays there still. Strange to say, I've tried to believe that it was half compassion, for she always reminded me of a little wild bird that somebody had caught and shut up in a cage, and it used to seem to me sometimes that I could almost hear the fluttering of her soul. Well, whatever it was, the feeling was the sort that is most worth while, though she didn't think so, of course, and broke her great heart over another man. She married him and had six children and died a few years ago. He was a fortunate fellow, I suppose, and yet I can't help fancying that I've had the better part and the Lord was right. She was not happy, they said, and he knew it, and yet had to face those eyes of hers every day. It was like many other marriages, I reckon; he got used to her body and never caught so much as a single glimpse of her soul. Then she faded away and died to him, but to me she's just the same as when I first saw her, and I still believe that if she could come here and sit on this old bench I should be perfectly happy. It's a lucky man, I tell you, who can keep the same desire for more than thirty years."

He shook his head slowly, smiling as he listened to the bluebird singing in the road. "And now I'll be fetching my crumbs," he added, struggling to his crutches.

When he had helped Tucker to the house, Christopher came back and sat down again on the bench, closing his eyes to the sunshine, the spring sky, and the dandelion blooming in the mould. He was very tired, and his muscles ached from the strain of heavy labour, yet as he lingered there in the warm wind it seemed to him that action was the one thing he desired. The restless season worked in his blood, and he felt the stir of old impulses that had revived each year with the quickening sap since the first pilgrimage man made on earth. He wanted to be up and away while he was still young, and his heart beat high, and at the moment he would have found positive delight in any convulsion of the natural order, in any excuse for a headlong and impetuous plunge into life.

He heard the door open again, and Tucker shuffled out into the path and began scattering his crumbs upon the gravel. When Christopher passed a moment later, on his way to the house, the old soldier was merrily whistling an invitation to a glimpse of blue in a tree-top by the road.

The spring dragged slowly, and with June came the transplanting of the young tobacco. This was the busiest season of the year with Christopher, and so engrossed was he in his work that for a week

at the end of the month he did not go down for the
county news at Tom Spade's store. Fletcher was
at home, he knew, but he had heard nothing of
Will, and it was through the storekeeper at last
that he learned definitely of the boy's withdrawal
from the university. Returning from the field one
afternoon at sunset, he saw Tom sitting beside Tucker
in the yard, and in response to a gesture he crossed
the grass and stopped beside the long pine bench.

"I say, Mr. Christopher, I've brought you a bit
of news," called the storekeeper at the young man's
approach.

"Well, let's have it," returned Christopher,
laughing. "If you're going to tell me that Uncle
Tucker has discovered a rare weed, though, I warn
you that I can't support it."

"Oh, I'm not in this, thank heaven," protested
Tucker; "but to tell the truth, I'm downright sorry
for the boy—Fletcher or no Fletcher."

"Ah," said Christopher under his breath, "so it's
Will Fletcher?"

"He's in a jolly scrape this time, an' no mistake,"
replied Tom. "He's been leadin' a wild life at the
university, it seems, an' to-day Fletcher got a
telegram saying that the boy had been caught
cheatin' in his examinations. The old man left
on the next train, as mad as a hornet, I can tell
you. He swore he'd bring the young scamp back
an' put him to the plough. Well, well, thar are
worse dangers than a pretty gal, though Susan won't
believe it."

"Then he'll bring him home?" asked Christopher,
blinking in the sunlight. At the instant it seemed

to him that sky and field whirled rapidly before his eyes, and a strange noise started in his ears which he found presently to be the throbbing of his arteries.

"Oh, he's been given a hard push down the wrong road," answered Tom, "an' it's more than likely he'll never pull up till he gits clean to the bottom."

CHAPTER VI

THE WAGES OF FOLLY

Two days later Fletcher's big new carriage crawled over the muddy road, and Christopher, looking up from his work in the field, caught a glimpse of the sullen face Will turned on the familiar landscape. The younger Fletcher had come home evidently nursing a grievance at his heart; his eyes held a look of dogged resentment, and the hand in which he grasped the end of the linen dust-robe was closed in an almost convulsive grip. When he met Christopher's gaze he glanced angrily away without speaking, and then finding himself face to face with his grandfather's scowl he jerked impatiently in the opposite direction. It was clear that the tussle of wills had as yet wrung only an enforced submission from the younger man.

Lifting his head, Christopher stood idly watching the carriage until it disappeared between the rows of flowering chestnuts; then, returning in a half-hearted fashion to his work, he found himself wondering curiously if Fletcher's wrath and Will's indiscretions were really so great as public rumour might lead one to suppose.

An answer to his question came the next evening, when he heard a light, familiar whistle outside the stable where he was at work, and a moment afterward Will appeared in the shadow of the doorway.

"So it wasn't a cut, after all?" said Christopher with a laugh, as he held out his hand.

"I'll be hanged if I know what it was," was Will's response, turning away after a limp grasp and seating himself upon the big box in the corner. "To tell the truth, grandpa has put me into such a fluster that I hardly know my head from my heels. There's one thing certain, though; if he doesn't take his eye off me for a breathing space he'll send me to the dogs before he knows it."

His face had lost its boyish freshness of complexion and his weak mouth had settled into lines of sullen discontent. Even his dress displayed the carelessness which is one of the outward marks of a disordered mind, and his bright blue tie was loosely knotted in unequal lengths.

"What's the trouble now?" demanded Christopher, coming from the stall and hanging his lantern from a nail beside the ladder, where the light fell full on Will's face. "Out with it and have done. I thought yesterday that you had been driving a hard bargain with the old man on my account."

"Oh, it's not you this time, thank heaven," returned Will. "It's all about that confounded scrape I got into at the university. I told him it would mean trouble if he sent me there, but he would do it whether or no. He dragged me away from here, you remember, and had me digging at my books with a scatter-brained tutor for a good six months; then when I knew just about enough to start at the university he hauled me there with

his own hands and kept watch over me for several
weeks. I'm quick at most things like that, so after
he went away I thought I'd have a little fun and
trust luck to make it up to me at the end—but
it all went against me somehow, and then they
stirred up that blamed rumpus about the examinations."

Yawning more in disgust than in drowsiness, he
struck a match on the edge of the box and lighted
a cigarette. His flippant manner was touched with
the conscious resentment which still lingered in his
eyes, and from the beginning to the end of his account
he betrayed no hint of a regret for his own shabby
part in the affair. When it was not possible to
rest the blame upon his grandfather, he merely
shrugged his shoulders and lightly tossed the responsibility to fate.

"This is one of the things I daren't do at the house,"
he remarked after a moment, inhaling a cloud of
smoke and blowing it in spirals through his nostrils;
"the old man won't tolerate anything more decent
than a pipe, unless it happens to be a chew. Oh,
I'm sick to death of the whole business," he burst
out suddenly. "When I woke up this morning I
had more than half a mind to break loose and go
abroad to Maria. By the way, Wyndham's dead,
you know; he died last fall just after we went away."

"Ah, is that so!" exclaimed Christopher. "She'll
come home, then, will she?"

"That's the queer part—she won't, and nobody
knows why. Wyndham turned out to be a regular
scamp, of course; he treated her abominably and all
that, but he no sooner died than she turned about

and picked up one of his sisters to nurse and coddle. Oh, it's all foolishness, but I've half a mind to run away, all the same. A life like this will drive me crazy in six months, and I'll be hanged if it is my fault, after all. He knew I never had a head for books, but he drove me at them as if I were no better than a black slave. Things have all been against me from the start, and yet I used to think that I was born to be lucky——"

"What does he mean to do with you now?" inquired Christopher.

"Put me to the plough, he says; but I can't stand it—I haven't the strength. Why, this morning he made me hang around that tobacco field in the blazing sun for two mortal hours, minding those shiftless darkies. If I complain, or even go off to sit down in a bit of shade, he rushes up and blusters about kicking me out of doors unless I earn my bread. Oh, his temper is simply awful, and he gets worse every day. He's growing stingy, too, and makes us live like beggars. All the vegetables go to market now, and most of the butter, and this morning he blew Aunt Saidie's head off because she had spring chickens on the breakfast table. I don't dare ask him for a penny, and yet he's rich— one of the richest men in the State, they say."

"Well, it sounds jolly," observed Christopher, smiling.

"Oh, you can't imagine the state of things, and you'd never believe it if I told you. It's worse than any fuss you ever heard of or ever saw. I used to be able to twist him round my finger, you know, and now he hates me worse than he does a snake.

He hasn't spoken a word to me since that scene we had at the university, except to order me to go out and watch the Negroes plant tobacco. If he finds out I want a thing he'll move heaven and earth to keep me from getting it—and then sit by and grin. He's got a devil in him, that's the truth, and there's nothing to do except keep out of his way as much as possible. I'm patient, too—Aunt Saidie knows it —and the only time I ever hit back was when he jumped on you the other day. Then I got mad and struck out hard, I tell you."

Christopher leaned over and began buckling and unbuckling a leather strap in the harness-box.

"Don't get into hot water on my account," he returned; "the more he abuses me, you know, the better I like it. But it's odd that after all these years he should want to turn you into an overseer."

"Well, he shan't do it; that's certain. It will be a cold day when he gets me masquerading in the family character. Let him go just one step too far and I'll shake him off for good, and strike out on a freight-train. Life couldn't be any worse than it is now, and it might be a great deal better. As to my hanging round like this much longer and swearing at a pack of worthless darkies—well, it's more than I bargain for, that's all."

"There's not much excitement in it, to be sure. I would rather be a freight-hand myself, I think, when all is said."

"Oh, you needn't joke. You were brought up to it and it doesn't come so hard."

"Doesn't it?"

"Not so hard as it does to me, at any rate. There's

got to be some dash about life, I tell you, to make
it suit my taste. I wasn't born to settle down and
count my money and my tobacco from morning
till night. It's spice I want in things, and—hang
it! I don't believe there's a pretty woman in the
county."

For a moment Christopher stared silently down
at the matted straw. His face had grown dark,
and the reckless lines about his mouth became
suddenly prominent.

"Why, where's Molly Peterkin?" he asked
abruptly, with a laugh that seemed to slip from him
against his will.

The other broke into a long whistle and tossed
the end of his cigarette through the doorway.

"You needn't think I've forgotten her," he replied;
"she's the one bright spot I see in this barren hole.
By the way, why do you think her a fool?"

"Because she is one."

"And you're a brute. What does a man want
with brains in a woman, anyway. Maria had them
and they didn't keep her from coming to shipwreck."

Christopher reached for the lantern.

"Well, I've got to go now," he broke in, "and
you'd better be trotting home or you'll have the
old man and the hounds out after you."

With the lantern swinging from his hand, he went
to the door and waited for Will; then passing out,
he turned the key in the lock, and with a short
"Good-night!" started briskly toward the house.

Will followed him to the kitchen steps, and then
keeping to the path that trailed across the yard, he
passed through the whitewashed gate and went on

along the sunken road which led by the abandoned ice-pond. Here he turned into the avenue of chestnuts, and with the lighted windows of the Hall before him, walked slowly toward the impending interview with his grandfather.

As he entered the house, Miss Saidie looked out from the dining-room doorway and beckoned in a stealthy fashion with the hen-house key.

"He has been hunting everywhere for you," she whispered, "and I told him you'd gone for a little stroll along the road."

An expression of anger swept over Will's face, and he made a helpless gesture of revolt.

"I won't stand it any longer," he answered, with a spurt of resolution which was exhausted in the feeble speech.

Miss Saidie put up her hand and straightened his necktie with an affectionate pat.

"Only for a little while, dear," she urged; "he's in one of his black humours, and it will blow over, never fear. Things are never so bad but there's hope of a mending some day. Try to please him and go to work as he wants you to do. It all came of the trouble at the university—he had set his heart on your carrying off the honours."

"It was his fault," said Will stubbornly. "I begged him not to send me there. It was his fault."

"Well, that can't be helped now," returned the little woman decisively. "All we can do is to make things as easy as we can, and if thar's ever to be any peace in this house again you must try to humour him. I never saw him in such a state before, and I've known him for sixty years and slept in a trundle-bed with him as a baby. The queerest thing about it, too, is that he seems to get closer and closer every day. Just now thar was a big fuss because I hadn't sent all the fresh butter to market, and I thought he'd have a fit when he found I was saving some asparagus for dinner to-morrow."

"Where is he now?" asked Will in a whisper.

"Complaining over some bills in his setting-room; and he actually told me a while ago, when I went in, that he had been a fool to give Maria so much money for Wyndham to throw away. Poor Maria! I'm sure she has had a hard enough time without being abused for something she couldn't help. But it really is a passion with him, thar's no use denying it. He spends his whole time adding up the cost of what we eat."

Then, as the supper-bell rang in the hall, she finished hurriedly, and assuming a cheerful manner, took her place behind the silver service.

Fletcher entered with a heavy step, his eyes lowering beneath his bushy eyebrows. The weight of his years appeared to have fallen upon him in a night, and he was no longer the hale, ruddy man of middle age, with his breezy speeches and his occasional touches of coarse humour. The untidiness of his clothes was still marked—his coat, his cravat, his finger nails, all showed the old lack of neatness.

"Won't you say grace, Brother Bill?" asked Miss Saidie, as he paused abstractedly beside his chair.

Bending his head, he mumbled a few hurried words, and then cast a suspicious glance over the long table.

"I told you to use the butter with onions in it,"
he said, helping himself and tasting a little on the
end of his knife. "This brings forty cents a pound
in market, and I'll not have the waste."

"Oh, Brother Bill, the other is so bad," gasped
Miss Saidie nervously.

"It's good enough for you and me, I reckon. We
wan't brought up on any better, and what's good
enough for us is good enough for my grandson."
Then he turned squarely upon Will. "So you're
back, eh? Whar did you go?" he demanded.

Will tried to meet his eyes, failed, and stared
gloomily at the white-and-red border of the table-
cloth.

"I went out for a breath of air," he answered in a
muffled voice. "It's been stifling all day."

"You've got to get used to it, I reckon," returned the old man with a brutal laugh. "I'll
have no idlers and no fancy men about me."

An ugly smile distorted his coarse features, and,
laying down his knife and fork, he sat watching his
grandson with his small, bloodshot eyes.

CHAPTER VII

The Toss of a Coin

A FORTNIGHT passed before Will came to Christopher's again, and then he stole over one evening in the shadow of the twilight. Things were no better, he said; they were even worse than usual; the work in the tobacco field was simply what he couldn't stand, and his grandfather was growing more intolerable every day. Besides this, the very dulness of the life was fast driving him to distraction. He had smuggled a bottle of whisky from the town, and last night, after a hot quarrel with the old man, he had succeeded in drugging himself to sleep. "My nerves have gone all to pieces," he finished irritably, "and it's nothing on earth but this everlasting bickering that has done it. It's more than flesh and blood can be expected to put up with."

His hand shook a little when he lighted a cigarette, and his face, which was burned red from wind and sun, contracted nervously as he talked. It was the wildness in his speech, however, the suppressed excitement which ran in an undercurrent beneath his words, that caused the other to turn sharply and regard him for a moment with gathered brows.

"Well, take my advice and don't try that dodge too often," remarked Christopher in a careless tone.

"What in the deuce does it matter?" returned Will desperately. "It was the only quiet night I've had for three weeks: I slept like a log straight through until the breakfast-bell. Then I was late, of course, and he threatened to take an hour's time from my day's wages. By the way, he pays me now, you know, just as he does the other labourers."

For a time he kept up his rambling complaint, but, breaking off abruptly at last, made some trivial excuse, and started homeward across the fields. Christopher, looking after him, was hardly surprised when he saw him branch off into the shaded lane that led to Sol Peterkin's.

There followed a month when the two met only at long intervals, and then with a curious constraint of manner. Sometimes Christopher, stopping on his way to the pasture, would exchange a few words over the rail fence with Will, who lounged on the edge of his grandfather's tobacco crop; but the old intimacy had ceased suddenly to exist, and it was evident that a newer interest had distracted the boy's ardent fancy.

It was not until August that the meaning of the change was made clear to Christopher, when, coming one day to a short turn in a little woodland road upon his land, he saw Will and Molly Peterkin sitting side by side on a fallen log. The girl had been crying, and at the sight of Christopher she gave a frightened sob and pulled her blue gingham sunbonnet down over her forehead; but Will, inspired at the instant by some ideal of chivalry, drew her hand through his arm and came out boldly into the road.

"You know Molly," he said in a brave voice that was not without pathos, "but you don't know that she has promised to be my wife."

Whatever the purpose of the girl's tears, she had need of them no longer, for with an embarrassed little laugh she flushed and dimpled into her pretty smile.

"Your wife?" repeated Christopher blankly. "Why, you're no better than two children and deserve to be whipped. If I were in your place, I'd start to catching butterflies, and quit fooling."

He passed on laughing merrily; but before the day was over he began to wonder seriously if Will could be really sincere in his intention to marry Molly Peterkin—poor, pretty Molly, whose fame was blown to the four corners of the county.

By night the question had come to perplex him in earnest, and it was almost with relief that he heard a familiar rattle on his window-pane as he undressed, and, looking out, saw Will standing in the long grass by the porch.

"Well, it's time you turned up," he said, when he had slipped cautiously down the staircase and joined him in the yard.

"Get your lantern," returned Will, "and come on to the barn. There's something I must see you about at once," and while the other went in search of the light, he stood impatiently uprooting a tuft of grass as he whistled a college song in unsteady tones.

At the end of a minute Christopher reappeared, bearing the lantern, which he declared was quite unnecessary because of the rising moon.

"Oh, but I must talk indoors," responded Will; "the night makes me creepy—it always did."

"So there is something to say, and it's no nonsense? Are the skies about to fall, or has your grandfather got a grip on his temper?"

"Pshaw! It's not that. Wait till we get inside." And when they had entered the barn, he turned and carefully closed the door, after flashing the light over the trampled straw in the dusky corners. In the shed outside a new-born calf bleated plaintively, and at the sound he started and broke into an apologetic laugh. "You thought I was joking to-day," he said suddenly.

Christopher nodded.

"So I presumed," he answered, wondering if drink or love or both together had produced so extreme an agitation.

"Well, I wasn't," declared Will, and, placing the lantern on the floor, he raised his head to meet the other's look. "I was as dead in earnest as I am this minute—and if it's the last word I ever speak, I mean to marry Molly Peterkin."

His excitable nerves were plainly on the rack of some strong emotion, and as he met the blank amazement in Christopher's face he turned away with a gesture of angry reproach.

"Then you're a fool," said Christopher, with a shrug of his shoulders.

Will quivered as if the words struck him like a whip.

"Because she's Sol Peterkin's daughter?" he burst out.

Christopher smiled.

"It's not her father, but her character, that I was thinking of," he answered, and the next instant fell back in sheer surprise, for Will, flinging himself recklessly upon him, struck him squarely in the mouth.

As they fell breathlessly apart Christopher was conscious that for the first time in his life he felt something like respect for Will Fletcher—or at least for that expression of courageous passion which in the vivid moments of men's lives appears to raise the strong and the weak alike above the ordinary level of their surroundings. For a second he stood swallowing down the anger which the blow aroused in him—an anger as purely physical as the mounting of the hot blood to his cheek—then he looked straight into the other's face and spoke in a pleasant voice.

"I beg your pardon; it was all my fault," he said.

"I knew you'd see it," answered Will, appeased at once by the confession, "and I counted on you to help us; that's why I came."

"To help you?" repeated Christopher, a little startled.

"Well, we've got to be married, you know—there's simply nothing else to do. All this confounded talk about Molly has come near killing her, and the poor child is afraid to look anybody in the face. She's so innocent, you know, that half the time she doesn't understand what their lies are all about."

"Good God!" said Christopher beneath his breath.

"And besides, what use is there in waiting?" urged Will. "Grandpa won't be any better fifty years from now than he is to-day, and by that time we'd be old and gray-haired. This life is more than I can stand, anyway, and it makes mighty little difference whether it ends one way or another. Just so I have Molly I don't care much what happens."

"But you can't marry—it's simply out of the question. Why, you're not yet twenty."

"Oh, we can't marry here, of course, but we're going on to Washington to-morrow—all our plans are made, and that's why I came to see you. I want to borrow your horses to take us to the cross-roads at midnight."

Seizing him by the shoulder, Christopher shook him roughly in a powerful grasp.

"Wake up," he said impatiently; "you are either drunk or asleep, and you're going headlong to the devil. If you do this thing you'll be ashamed of it in two weeks." Then he released him, laughing as he watched him totter and regain his balance. "But if you're bent on being an ass, then, for heaven's sake, go and be one," he added irritably.

A shiver passed through Will, and he stuttered an instant before he could form his words.

"She told me you'd say that," he replied. "She told me you'd always hated her."

"Hate her? Nonsense! She isn't worth it. I'd as soon hate a white kitten. As far as that goes, I've nothing against the girl, and I don't doubt she'd be a much better wife than most men deserve. I'm not prating about virtue, mind you; I'm only urging common sense. You're too young and too big a fool to marry anybody."

"Well, you disapprove of her, at any rate—you're against her, and that's why I haven't talked about her before. She's the most beautiful creature alive,

I tell you, and I wouldn't give her up if to keep her meant I'd be a beggar."

"It will mean that, most likely."

Turning away, Will drew a small flask from his pocket and, unscrewing the stopper, raised the bottle to his lips. "I'd go mad but for this," he said; "that's why I've carried it about with me for the last week. It's the only thing that drives away this horrible depression."

As he drank, Christopher regarded him curiously, noting that the whisky lent animation to his face and an unnatural lustre to his eyes. The sunburn on his forehead appeared to deepen all at once, and there was a bright red flush across his cheeks.

"You won't take my advice," said Christopher at last, "but I can't help telling you that unless you're raving mad you'd better drop the whole affair as soon as possible."

"Not now—not now," protested Will gaily, consumed by an artificial energy. "Don't preach to me while the taste of a drink is still in my mouth, for there's no heart so strong as the one whisky puts into a man. When I feel my courage oozing from my fingers I can reinforce it in less time than it takes to sneak away."

Growing boisterous, he assumed a ridiculous swagger, and broke into a fragment of a college song. Until morning he would not probably become himself again, and, knowing this, Christopher desisted helplessly from his efforts at persuasion.

"You will lend me the horses?" asked Will, keeping closely to his point.

"Are you steady enough?"

"Of course—of course," he stretched out his hands and moved a pace or two away; "and besides, Molly drives like old Nick."

"Well, I'll see," said Christopher, and going to the window, he flung back the rude shutter and looked out into the August night. The warm air touched his face like a fragrant breath, and from the darkness a big white moth flew over his shoulder to where the lantern burned dimly on the floor.

"I may take them?" urged Will again, pulling him by the sleeve.

At the words Christopher turned and walked slowly back across the barn.

"Yes, I'll lend them to you," he answered, without meeting the other's eyes.

"You're a jolly good chap; I always knew it," cried Will heartily. "I'll take them out at midnight, when there's a good moon, and get Jerry Green to drive them back to-morrow. Hurrah! It's the best night's work you ever did!"

He went out hurriedly, still singing his college song, and Christopher, without moving from his place, stood watching the big white moth that circled dizzily about the lantern. At the instant he regretted that Will had appealed to him—regretted even that he had promised him the horses. He wished it had all come about without his knowledge—that Fletcher's punishment and Will's ruin had been wrought less directly by his own intervention. Next he told himself that he would have stopped this thing had it been possible, and then with the thought he became clearly aware that it was still in his power to prevent the marriage. He had but to walk across the fields to Fletcher's door, and before sunrise the foolish pair would be safely home again. Will would probably be sent off to recover, and Molly would go back to making butter and to flirting with Fred Turner. On the other hand, let the marriage but take place—let him keep silent until the morning— and the revenge of which he had dreamed since childhood would be accomplished at a single stroke. Bill Fletcher's many sins would find him out in a night.

The big moth, fluttering aimlessly from the lantern, flew suddenly in his face, and the touch startled him from his abstraction. With a laugh he shook the responsibility from his shoulders, and then, as he hesitated again for a breath, the racial instinct arose, as usual, to decide the issue.

Taking a dime from his pocket, he tossed it lightly in the air and waited for it to fall.

"Heads for me, tails for Fletcher."

The coin spun for an instant in the gloom above him and then dropped noiselessly to the floor. When he lifted the lantern and bent over it he saw that the head lay uppermost.

CHAPTER VIII

IN WHICH CHRISTOPHER TRIUMPHS

WHEN he entered the house a little later Cynthia met him in the kitchen doorway with an anxious frown.

"I heard a noise, Christopher. What was it?"

"A man wanted me about something. How is mother resting?"

"Not well. Her dreams trouble her. She grows weaker every day, and the few hours she insists upon spending in her chair tire her dreadfully."

"There is nothing that she needs, you say?"

"No; nothing. She has never felt our poverty for an instant."

The furrow between his eyebrows grew deeper. "And you?" he asked abruptly, regarding her fixedly with his intent gaze. "What under heaven are you up to at this hour?"

Glancing down at the ironing-board before her, she flushed painfully through the drawn grayness of her face.

"I had a little ironing to do," she answered, "and I wanted it all finished to-night. Mother needs me in the day."

Pushing her aside, he seized the iron and ran it in a few hasty strokes over the rough-dry garment which she had spread on the board. "Go to bed and leave these things alone," he insisted.

"Oh, Christopher, you'll spoil it!" cried Cynthia, clutching his arm.

He returned the iron to the stand and met her reproachful look with a gesture of annoyance. "Well, I'm going to sleep, if you aren't," he said, and treading as lightly as possible in his heavy boots, went along the little platform and upstairs to his garret room.

Once inside, he undressed hastily and flung himself upon the bed, but his thoughts spun like a top, and wild visions of Will, of Fletcher, and of Molly Peterkin whirled confusedly through his brain. When at last he lost consciousness for a time, it was to dream restlessly of the cry of a hare that the hounds had caught and mangled. The scream of the creature came to him from a thick wood, which was intersected by innumerable small green paths, and when he tried vainly to go to the rescue he lost himself again and again in the wilderness of trails. Back and forth he turned in the twilight, crushing down the under-brush and striking in a frenzy at the forked boughs the trees wrapped about him, while suddenly the piteous voice became that of a woman in distress. Then, with a great effort, he fought his way through the wood, to see the mangled hare change slowly into Maria Fletcher, who opened her eyes to ask him why he hunted her to death.

He awoke in a cold sweat, and, sitting up in bed, leaned for air toward the open window. A dull ache gnawed at his heart, and his lips were parched as if from fever. Again it seemed to him that Maria entreated him across the distance.

When he came down at sunrise he found Jerry Green awaiting him with the horses, and learned in answer to his questions that the lovers had taken a light wagon at the cross-roads and driven on to town.

"They were that bent on gittin' thar that they couldn't even wait for the stage," the man told him. "Well, they're a merry pair, an' I hope good will come of it—seein' as 'tain't no harm to hope."

"Oh, they think so now, at any rate," Christopher replied, as he turned away to unharness the patient horses.

At breakfast, an hour or two later, he learned that his mother was in one of her high humours, and that, awaking early and prattling merrily of the past, she insisted that they should dress her immediately in her black brocade. When the meal was over he carried her from her bed to the old oak chair, in which she managed to keep upright among her pillows. Her gallant spirit was still youthful and undaunted, and the many infirmities of her body were powerless to distort the cheerful memories behind her sightless eyes.

Leaving her presently, after a careless chat about the foibles of Bolivar Blake, he took his hoe from an outhouse and went to "grub" the young weeds from the tobacco, which had now reached its luxuriant August height. By noon his day's work on the crop was over, and he was resting for a moment in the shadow of a locust tree by the fence, when he heard rapid footsteps approaching in the new road, and Bill Fletcher threw himself over the crumbling rails and came panting into the strip of shade. At

sight of the man's face Christopher flung his hoe
out into the field, where it bore down a giant plant,
and bracing his body against the tree, prepared
himself to withstand the shock of the first blow;
but the other, after glaring at him for a breathless
instant, fell back and rapped out a single thun-
dering oath.

"You hell-hound! This is all your doing!"

Throwing off the words with a gesture of his arm,
Christopher stared coolly into the other's distorted
face; then, yielding to the moment's vindictive
impulse, he broke into a sneering laugh.

"So you have heard the good news?" he inquired
lightly.

Before the rage in the old man's eyes—before the
convulsed features and the quivering limbs—he felt
a savage joy suddenly take possession of him.

"It's all your doing, every last bit of it," repeated Fletcher hoarsely, "and I'll live to pay you
back if I hang for it in the end!"

"Go ahead, then," retorted Christopher; "you
might as well hang for a sheep as for a lamb, you
know."

"Oh, you think I'm fooling?" said the other,
wiping a fleck of foam from his mouth, "but you'll
find out better some day, unless the devil gets you
mighty quick. You've made that boy a scamp and
a drunkard, and now you've gone and married him
to a ——" He swallowed the words and stood
gasping above his loosened collar.

Christopher paled slightly beneath his sunburn;
then, as he recovered his assurance, a brutal smile
was sketched about his mouth.

"Come, come, go easy," he protested flippantly; "there's such a thing, you remember, as the pot calling the kettle black."

His gay voice fell strangely on the other's husky tones, and for the moment, in spite of his earth-stained hands and his clothes of coarse blue jean, he might have been a man of the world condescending to a peasant. It was at such times, when a raw emotion found expression in the primitive lives about him, that he realised most vividly the gulf between him and his neighbours. To his superficial unconcern they presented the sincerity of naked passion.

"You've made the boy what he is," repeated the old man, in a quiver from head to foot. "You've done your level best to send him to the devil."

"Well, he had a pretty good start, it seems, before I ever laid eyes on him."

"You set out to ruin him from the first, and I watched you," went on Fletcher, choking over each separate word before he uttered it; "my eye was on your game, and if you were anything but the biggest villain on earth I could have stopped it. But for you he'd be a decent chap this very minute."

"And the pattern of his grandfather," sneered Christopher.

Fletcher raised his arm for a blow and then let it fall limply to his side. "Oh, I'm done with you now, and I'm done with your gang," he said. "Play your devil's tricks as much as you please; they won't touch me. If that boy sets foot on my land again I'll horsewhip him as I would a hound. Let him see who'll feed him now when he comes to starve."

Catching his breath, Christopher stared at him an instant in silence; then he spoke in a voice which had grown serious.

"The more fool you, then," he said. "The chap's your grandson, and he's a better one than you deserve. Whatever he is, I tell you now, he's a long sight too good for such as you—and so is Molly Peterkin, for that matter. Heavens above! What are you that you should become a stickler for honesty in others? Do you think I've forgotten that you drove my father to his grave, and that the very land you live on you stole from me? Pshaw! It takes more than twenty years to bury a thing like that, you fool!"

Fletcher looked helplessly round for a weapon, and catching sight of the hoe, raised it in his hands; but Christopher, seizing it roughly from him, tossed it behind him in the little path.

"I'll have none of that," added the young man grimly.

"You're a liar, as your father was before you," burst out Fletcher, swallowing hard; "and as for that scamp you've gone and sent to hell, you can let him starve or not, jest as you please. He has made his choice between us, and he can stick to it till he rots in the poorhouse. Much good you'll do him in the end, I reckon."

"Well, just now it seems he hasn't chosen either of us," remarked Christopher, cooling rapidly as the other's anger grew red hot. "It rather looks as if he'd chosen Molly Peterkin."

"Damn you!" gasped Fletcher, putting up a nerveless hand to tear his collar apart, while a purple flush rose slowly from his throat to his forehead.

"If you name that huzzy to me again I'll thrash you within an inch of your life!"

"Let's try it," suggested Christopher in an irritating drawl.

"Oh, I'm used to bullies like you," pursued the old man. "I know the kind of brute that thinks he can knock his way into heaven. Your father was jest sech another, and if you come to die a crazy drunkard like him it'll be about the end that you deserve!"

An impatient frown drew Christopher's brows together, and, picking up the hoe, he walked leisurely out into the field.

"Well, I can't stop to hear your opinion of me," he observed. "You'll have to keep it until another time," and breaking into a careless whistle, he strode off between the tobacco furrows on his way to bring the old mare from the pasture.

A little later, alone with the broad white noon and the stillness of the meadow, his gay whistle ended abruptly on his lips and the old sullen frown contracted his heavy brows. It was in vain that he tried to laugh away the depression of the moment; the white glare of the fields and the perfume of wild flowers blooming in hot sunshine produced in him a sensation closely akin to physical nausea—a disgust of himself and of the life and the humanity that he had known. What was it all worth, after all? And what of satisfaction was there to be found in the thing he sought? Fletcher's face rose suddenly before him, and when he tried to banish the memory the effort that he made brought but the more distinctly to his eyes the coarse, bloated features with the swollen veins across the nose. Trivial recollections returned to annoy him—the way the man sucked in his breath when he was angry, and the ceaseless twitching of the small muscles above his bloodshot eyes. "Pshaw! What business is it of mine?" he questioned angrily. "What am I to the man, that I cannot escape the disgust that he arouses? Is it possible that I should be haunted forever by a face I hate? There are times when I could kill him simply because of the repulsion that I feel. As for the boy—let him marry a dozen Molly Peterkins —who cares? Not I, surely. When he turns upon his grandfather and they fall to gnawing at each other's bones, the better I shall be pleased." He shook his head impatiently, but the oppression which in some vague way he associated with the white heat and the scent of wild flowers still weighed heavily upon his thoughts. "Is it possible that after all that has happened I am not yet satisfied?" he asked, with annoyance.

For awhile he lingered by the little brook in the pasture, and then slipping the bridle on the old mare, returned slowly to the house. At the bars he met Sol Peterkin, who had hurried over in evident consternation to deliver his news.

"Good Lord, Mr. Christopher! What do you think that gal of mine has gone and done now?"

Christopher slid the topmost bar from its place and lifted his head

"Don't tell me that she's divorced already," he returned. "Why, the last I heard of her she had run off this morning to marry Will Fletcher."

"That's it, suh; that's it," said Sol. "I'm meanin'

the marriage. Well, well, it does seem that you can't settle down an' begin to say yo' grace over one trouble befo' a whole batch lights upon you. To think, arter the way I've sweated an' delved to be honest, that a gal of mine should tie me hand an' foot to Bill Fletcher."

In spite of his moodiness, the humour of the situation struck home to Christopher, and throwing back his head he burst into a laugh.

"Oh, you needn't poke yo' fun, suh," continued Sol. "Money is a mighty good thing, but you can't put it in the blood, like you kin meanness. All Bill Fletcher's riches ain't soaked in him blood an' bone, but his meanness is, an' that thar meanness goes a long sight further than his money. Thar ain't much sto' set by honesty in this here world, suh, an' you kin buy a bigger chaw of tobaccy with five cents than you kin with all the virtue of Moses on his Mount; but all the same it's a mighty good thing to rest yo' head on when you go to bed, an' I ain't sure but it makes easier lyin' than a linen pillow-slip an' a white goose tick——"

"Oh, I dare say," interrupted Christopher; "but now that it's over we must make the best of it. She didn't marry Bill Fletcher, after all, you know——"

He checked himself with a start, and the bridle slipped from his arm to the ground, for his name was called suddenly in a high voice from the house, and as he swung himself over the bars Lila came running barehead across the yard.

"O Christopher!" she cried; "we could not find you, and Bill Fletcher has talked to mother like a madman. Come quickly! She has fainted!"

Before she had finished, he had dashed past her and through the house into the little parlour, where the old lady sat erect and unconscious in her Elizabethan chair.

"I found her like this," said Lila, weeping. "We heard loud voices and then a scream, and when we rushed in the man left, and she sat looking straight ahead like this—like this."

Throwing himself upon his knees beside the chair, Christopher caught his mother to his breast and turned angrily upon the women.

"Has nothing been done? Where is the doctor?" he cried.

"Jim has gone for him. Here, let me take her," said Cynthia, unclasping his arms. "There, stand back. She is not dead. In a little while she will come to herself again."

Rising from the floor, he stood motionless in the center of the room, where the atmosphere was heavy with the fragrance of camphor and tea-roses. A broad strip of sunshine was at his feet, and in the twisted aspen beside the window a catbird was singing. These remained with him for years afterward, and with them the memory of the blind woman sitting stiffy erect and staring vacantly into his face.

"He has told her everything," said Cynthia— "after twenty years."

Book Four
The Awakening

THE AWAKENING

CHAPTER I

THE UNFORESEEN

THE road was steep, and Christopher, descending from the big, lumbering cart, left the oxen to crawl slowly up the incline. It was a windy afternoon in March, and he was returning from a trip to Farrar's mill, which was reached by a lane that branched off a half-mile or so from the cross-roads. A blue sky shone brightly through the leafless boughs above him, and along the little wayside path tufts of dandelion were blooming in the red dust. The wind, which blew straight toward him from the opening beyond the strip of wood in which he walked, brought the fresh scent of the upturned fields and of the swelling buds putting out with the warm sunshine. In his own veins he felt also that the blood had stirred, and that strange, quickening impulse, which comes with the rising sap alike to a man and to a tree, worked restlessly in his limbs at the touch of spring. Nature was alive again, and he felt vaguely that in the resurrection surrounding him he must have his part—that in him as well as in the earth the spirit of life must move and put forth in gladness. A flock of swallows passed suddenly like a streak of smoke on the blue sky overhead, and as his eyes followed them the old roving instinct pulled at his heart. To be up and away, to drink life to its dregs and come home for rest, were among the impulses which awoke with the return of spring.

The oxen moved behind him at a leisurely pace, and outstripping them in a little while, he had turned at a sudden opening in the trees into the main road, when, to his surprise, he saw a woman in black, followed by a small yellow dog, walking in front of him along the grassy path. As he caught sight of her a strong gust of wind swept down the road, wrapping her skirt closely about her and whirling a last year's leaf into her face. For a moment she paused and, throwing back her head, drank the air like water; then, holding firmly to her hat, she started on again at her rapid pace. In the ease with which she moved against the wind, in the self-possession of her carriage, and most of all in the grace with which she lifted her long black skirt, made, he could see, after the fashion of the outside world, he realised at once that she was a stranger to the neighbourhood. No woman whom he had known—not even Lila— had this same light yet energetic walk—a walk in which every line in her body moved in accord with the buoyant impulse that controlled her step. As he watched her he recalled instantly the flight of a swallow in the air, for her passage over the ground was as direct and beautiful as a bird's.

When he neared her she turned suddenly, and, as she flung back her short veil, he saw to his amazement that he faced Maria Fletcher.

"So you have forgotten me?" she said, with a smile. "Or have I changed so greatly that my old friends do not know me?"

She held out her hand, and while a tremor ran through him, he kept her bared palm for an instant in his own.

"You dropped from the sky," he answered, steadying his voice with an effort. "You have taken my breath away and I cannot speak."

Then letting her hand fall, he stood looking at her in a wonder that shone in his face, for to the Maria whom he had known the woman before him now bore only the resemblance that the finished portrait bears to the charcoal sketch; and the years which had so changed and softened her had given her girlish figure a nobility that belonged to the maturity she had not reached. It was not that she had grown beautiful—when he sought for physical changes he found only that her cheek was rounder, her bosom fuller; but if she still lacked the ruddy attraction of mere flesh-and-blood loveliness, she had gained the deeper fascination which is the outward accompaniment of a fervent spirit. Her eyes, her voice, her gestures were all attuned to the inner harmony which he recognised also in the smile with which she met his words; and the charm that she irradiated was that rarest of all physical gifts, the power of the flesh to express the soul that it envelops.

The wind or the meeting with himself had brought a faint flush to her cheek, but without lowering her eyes she stood regarding him with her warm, grave smile. The pale oval of her face, framed in the loosened waves of her black hair, had for him all the remoteness that surrounded her memory; and yet, though he knew it not, the appeal she made to him now, and had made long ago, was that he recognised in her, however dumbly, a creature born, like himself, with the power to experience the fulness of joy or grief.

"So I have taken your breath away," she said; "and you have forgotten Agag."

"Agag?" he turned with a question and followed her glance in the direction of the dog. "It is the brute you saved?"

"Only he is not a brute—I have seen many men who were more of one. Look! He recognises you. He has followed me everywhere, but he doesn't like Europe, and if you could have seen his joy when we got out at the cross-roads and he smelt the familiar country! It was almost as great as mine."

"As yours? Then you no longer hate it?"

"I have learned to love it in the last six years," she answered, "as I have learned to love many things that I once hated. Oh, this wind is good when it blows over the ploughed fields, and yet between city streets it would bring only dust and discomfort."

She threw back her head, looking up into the sky, where a bird passed.

"Will you get into the cart now?" he asked after a moment, vaguely troubled by the silence and by the gentleness of her upward look, "or do you wish to walk to the top of the hill?"

She turned and moved quickly on again.

"It is such a little way, let us walk," she replied, and then with a laugh she offered an explanation of her presence. "I wrote twice, but I had no answer," she said; "then I decided to come, and telegraphed, but they handed me my telegram and my last letter at the cross-roads. Can something have happened, do you think? or is it merely carelessness that keeps them from sending for the mail?"

"I hardly know; but they are all alive, at least. You have come straight from—where?"

"From abroad. I lived there for six years, first in one place, then in another—chiefly in Italy. My husband died eighteen months ago, but I stayed on with his people. It seemed then that they needed me most, but one can never tell, and I may have made a mistake in not coming home sooner."

"I think you did," he said quietly, running the end of his long whip through his fingers.

She flashed a disturbed glance at him.

"Is it possible that you are keeping something from me? Is any one ill?"

"Not that I have heard of; but I never see any of them, you know, except your brother."

"And he is married. They told me so at the cross-roads. I can't understand why they did not let me know."

"It was very sudden—they went to Washington."

"How queer! Who is the girl, I wonder?"

"Her name was Molly Peterkin—old Sol's daughter; you may remember him."

She shook her head. "No; I've lived here so little, you see. What is she like?"

"A beauty, with blue eyes and yellow hair."

"Indeed? And are they happy?"

He laughed. "They are in love—or were, six months ago."

"You are cynical. But do they live at the Hall?"

"Not yet. Your grandfather has not spoken to Will since the marriage, and that was last August."

"Where, under heaven, do they live, then?"

"On a little farm he has given them adjoining Sol's. I believe he means that they shall raise tobacco for a living."

She made a gesture of distress. "Oh, I ought to have come home long ago!"

"What difference would that have made: you could have done nothing. A thunderbolt falling at his feet doesn't sober a man when he is in love."

"I might have helped—one never knows. At least I should have been at my post, for, after all, the ties of blood are the strongest claims we have."

"Why should they be?" he questioned, with sudden bitterness. "You are more like that swallow flying up there than you are like any Fletcher that ever lived."

She smiled. "I thought so once," she answered, "but now I know better. The likeness must be there, and I am going to find it."

"You will never find it," he insisted, "for there is nothing of them in you—nothing."

"You don't like them, I remember."

"Nor do you."

A laugh broke from her and humour rippled in her eyes.

"So you still persist in the truth, and in the plain truth!" she exclaimed.

"Then it is so, you confess it?"

"No, no, no," she protested. "Why, I love them all—all, do you hear, and I love Will more than the rest of them put together."

He looked away from her, and then, turning, waited for the oxen to reach the summit of the hill.

"You'd better get in now, I think," he said; "there is a long walk ahead of us, and if my team is slow it is sure also."

As he brought the oxen to a halt, she laid her hand for an instant on his arm, and, mounting lightly upon the wheel, stepped into the cart.

"Now give me Agag," she said, and he handed her the little dog before he took up the ropes and settled himself beside her on the driver's seat. "You look like one of the disinherited princesses in the old stories mother tells," he observed.

A puzzled wonder was in her face as she turned toward him.

"Who are you? And what has Blake Hall to do with your family?" she asked.

"Only that it was named after us. We used to live there."

"Within your recollection?"

He nodded, with his eyes on the slow oxen.

"Then you have not always been a farmer?"

"Ever since I was ten years old."

"I can't understand, I can't understand," she said, perplexed. "You are like no one about here; you are like no one I have ever seen."

"Then I must be like you," he returned bluntly.

"Like me? Oh, heavens, no; you would make three of me—body, brain, and soul. I believe, when I think of it, that you are the biggest man I've ever known—and by that I don't mean in height—for I have seen men with a greater number of physical inches. Inches, somehow, have very little to do with the impression—and so has muscle, strong as yours is. It is simple bigness that I am talking about, and it was the first thing I noticed in you——"

"At the cross-roads?" he asked, and instantly regretted his words.

"No; not at the cross-roads," she answered, smiling. "You have a good memory, but mine is better. I saw you once on a June morning, when I was riding along the road with the chestnuts and you were standing out in the field."

"I did not see you or I should have remembered," he said quietly.

Silence fell between them, and he was conscious in every fibre of his body that he had never been so close to her before—had never felt the touch of her arm upon his own, nor the folds of her skirt brushing against his knees. A gust of wind whipped the end of her veil into his face, and when she turned to recapture it he felt her warm breath on his cheek. The sense of her nearness pervaded him from head to foot, and an unrest like that produced by the spring wind troubled his heart. He did not look at her, and yet he saw her full dark eyes and the curve of her white throat more distinctly than he beheld the blue sky at which he gazed. Was it possible that she, too, shared his disquietude? he wondered, or was the silence that she kept as undisturbed as her tranquil pose?

"I should not have forgotten it," he repeated presently, turning to meet her glance.

She started and looked away from the landscape. "You have long memories in this county, I know," she said. "So few things happen that it becomes a religion to cherish the little incidents. It may be that I, too, have inherited something of this, for I remember very clearly the few months I spent here."

"You remembered them even while you were away?"

"Why not?" she asked. "It is not the moving about, the strange places one sees, nor the people one meets, that really count in life, you know."

"What is it?" he questioned abruptly.

She hesitated as if trying to put her thoughts more clearly into words.

"I think it is the things one learns," she said; "the places in which we take root and grow, and the people who teach us what is really worth while— patience, and charity, and the beauty there is in the simplest and most common lives when they are lived close to Nature."

"In driving the plough or in picking the suckers from a tobacco plant," he added scornfully.

"In those things, yes; and in any life that is good, and true, and natural."

"Well, I have lived near enough to Nature to hate her with all my might," he answered, not without bitterness. "Why, there are times when I'd like to kick every ploughed field I see out into eternity. Tobacco-growing is one of the natural things, I suppose, but if you want to see any beauty in it you must watch it from a shady road. When you get in the midst of it you'll find it coarse and sticky, and given over generally to worms. I have spent my whole life working on it, and to this day I never look at a plant nor smell a pipe without a shiver of disgust. The things I want are over there," he finished, pointing with his whip-handle to the clear horizon. "I want the excitement that makes one's blood run like wine."

"Battle, murder, and all that, I suppose?" she said, smiling.

"War, and fame, and love," he corrected.

Her face had grown grave, and in the thoughtful look she turned upon him it seemed to him that he saw a purpose slowly take form. So earnest was her gaze that at last his own fell before it, at which she murmured a confused apology, like one forcibly awakened from a dream.

"I was wondering what that other life would have made of you," she said; "the life that I have known and wearied of—a life of petty shams, of sham love, of sham hate, of sham religion. It is all little, you know, and it takes a little soul to keep alive in it. I craved it once myself, and it took six years of artifice to teach me that I loved a plain truth better than a pretty lie."

He had been looking at the strong white hand lying in her lap, and now, with a laugh, he held out his own bronzed and roughened one.

"There is the difference," he said; "do you see it?"

A wave of sympathy swept over her expressive face, and with one of her impulsive gestures, which seemed always to convey some spiritual significance, she touched his outstretched palm with her fingers.

"How full of meaning it is," she replied, "for it

tells of quiet days in the fields, and of a courage
that has not faltered before the thing it hates.   When
I look at it it makes me feel very humble—and yet
very proud, too, that some day I may be your friend."

He shook his head, with his eyes on the sun, which
was slowly setting.

"That is out of the question," he answered.   "You
cannot be my friend except for this single day.   If
I meet you to-morrow I shall not know you."

"Because I am a Fletcher?" she asked, wondering.

"Because you are a Fletcher, and because you
would find me worse than a Fletcher."

"Riddles, riddles," she protested, laughing; "and
I was always dull at guessing—but I may as well
warn you now that I have come home determined
to make a friend of every mortal in the county, man
and beast."

"You'll do it," he answered seriously.   "I'm
the only thing about here that will resist you.   You'll
be everybody's friend but mine."

She caught and held his gaze.   "Let us see," she
responded quietly.

For a time they were silent, and spreading out her
skirt, she made a place for the dog upon it.   The
noise of the heavy wheels on the rocky bed of the
road grew suddenly louder in his ears, and he realised
with a pang that every jolt of the cart carried him
nearer the end.   With the thought there came to
him a wish that life might pause at the instant—that
the earth might be arrested in its passage and leave
him forever aware of the warm contact that thrilled
through him.

They had already passed Weatherby's lane, and

presently the chimneys of Blake Hall appeared above the distant trees. When they reached the abandoned ice-pond Christopher spoke with an attempted carelessness.

"It would perhaps be better for you to walk the rest of the way," he said. "Trouble might be made in the beginning if your grandfather were to know that I brought you over."

"You're right, I think," she said, and rising as the cart stopped, she followed him down into the road. Then with a word or two of thanks, she smiled brightly, and, calling the dog, passed rapidly into the twilight which stretched between him and a single shining window that was visible in the Hall.

After she had quite disappeared he still stood motionless by the ice-pond, staring into the dusk that had swallowed her up from his gaze. So long did he remain there that at last the oxen tired of waiting and began to move slowly on along the sunken road. Then starting abruptly from his meditation, he picked up the ropes that trailed before him on the ground and fell into his accustomed walk beside the cart. At the moment it seemed to him that his whole life was shattered into pieces by the event of a single instant. Something stronger than himself had shaken the foundations of his nature, and he was not the man that he had been before. He was like one born blind, who, when his eyes are opened, is ignorant that the light which dazzles him is merely the shining of the sun.

When he came into the house, after putting up the oxen, Cynthia commented upon the dazed look that he wore.

"You must have fallen asleep on the way home," she remarked.

"It is the glare of the lamp," he answered. "I have just come out of the darkness," and before sitting down to his supper, he opened the door and listened for the sound of his mother's voice.

"She is asleep, then?" he said, coming back again. "Has she recognised either of you to-day?"

"No; she wanders again. The present is nothing to her any longer—it is all blotted out with everything that Fletcher told her. She asks for father constantly, and the only thing that interested her was when Jim went in and talked to her about farming. She is quite rational except that she has entirely forgotten the last twenty years, and just before falling asleep she laughed heartily over some old stories of Grandpa Bolivar's."

"Then I may see her for a minute?"

"If you wish it—yes."

Passing along the hall, he entered the little chamber where the old lady lay asleep in her tester bed. Her fine white hair was brushed over the pillow, and her drawn and yellowed face wore a placid and childlike look. As he paused beside her a faint smile flickered about her mouth and her delicate hand trembled slightly upon the couterpane. Her dreams had evidently brought her happiness, and as he stood looking down upon her the wish entered his heart that he might change his young life for her old one—that he might become, in her place, half dead, and done with all that the future could bring of either joy or grief.

CHAPTER II

MARIA RETURNS TO THE HALL

THROUGH the grove of oaks a single lighted window glimmered now red, now yellow, as lamplight struggled with firelight inside, and Maria, walking rapidly through the dark, felt that the comfortable warmth shining on the panes was her first welcome home. The night had grown chilly, and she gathered her wraps closely together as she hastened along the gravelled drive and ran up the broad stone steps to the closed door. There was no answer to her knock, and, finding that the big silver handle of the door turned easily, she entered the hall and passed cautiously through the dusk that enveloped the great staircase. Her foot was on the first step, when a stream of light issued suddenly from the dining-room, and, turning, she stood for an instant hesitating upon the threshold.

A lamp burned dimly in the centre of the old mahogany table, where a scant supper for two had been hastily laid. In the fireplace a single hickory log sent out a shower of fine sparks, which hovered a moment in the air before they were sucked up by the big stone chimney.

The room was just as Maria had left it six **years** before, and yet in some unaccountable fashion it seemed to have lost the dignity which she remembered as its one redeeming feature. Nothing was changed that she could see—the furniture stood in the same places, the same hard engravings hung on the discoloured walls—but as she glanced wonderingly about her she was aware of a shock greater than the one she had nerved herself to withstand. It was, after all, the atmosphere that depressed her, she concluded with her next thought—the general air of slovenly unrefinement revealed in the details of the room and of the carelessly laid table.

While she still hesitated uncertainly on the threshold, the pantry door opened noiselessly and Miss Saidie appeared, carrying a glass dish filled with preserved watermelon rind. At sight of Maria she gave a start and a little scream, and the dish fell from her hands and crashed upon the floor.

"Sakes alive! Is that you, Maria?"

Hastily crossing the room, Maria caught the little woman in her arms and kissed her twice.

"Why, you poor thing! I've frightened you to death," she said, with a laugh.

"You did give me a turn; that's so," replied Miss Saidie, as she wiped the moisture from her crimson face. "It's been so long since anybody's come here that Malindy—she's the only servant we've got now—was actually afraid to answer your knock. Then when I came in and saw you standing by the door, I declare it almost took my breath clean away. I thought for a moment you were a ghost, you looked so dead white in that long, black dress."

"Oh, I'm flesh and blood, never fear," Maria assured her. "Much more flesh and blood, too, than

I was when I went away—but I've made you spill all your preserves. What a shame!"

Miss Saidie glanced down a little nervously. "I must wipe it up before Brother Bill comes in," she said; "it frets him so to see a waste."

Picking up a dust-cloth she had left on a chair, she got down on her knees and began mopping up the sticky syrup which trickled along the floor. "He hates so to throw away anything," she pursued, panting softly from her exertions, "that if he were to see this I believe it would upset him for a week. Oh, he didn't use to be like that, I know," she added, meeting Maria's amazed look; "and it does seem strange, for I'm sure he gets richer and richer every day—but it's the gospel truth that every cent he makes he hugs closer than he did the last. I declare, I've seen him haggle for an hour over the price of salt, and it turns him positively sick to see anything but specked potatoes on the table. He kinder thinks his money is all he's got, I reckon, so he holds on to it like grim death."

"But it isn't all he has. Where's Will?"

Miss Saidie shook her head, with a glance in the direction of the door.

"Don't mention him if you want any peace," she said, rising with difficulty to her feet. "Your grandpa has never so much as laid eyes on him sence he gave him that little worn-out place side by side with Sol Peterkin—and told him he'd shoot him if he ever caught sight of him at the Hall. You've come home to awful worry, thar's no doubt of it, Maria."

"Oh, oh, oh," sighed Maria, and, tossing her hat

upon the sofa, pressed her fingers on her temples. With the firelight thrown full on the ivory pallor of her face, the effect she produced was almost unreal in its intensity of black and white—an absence of colour which had in it all the warmth and the animation we are used to associate with brilliant hues. A peculiar mellowness of temperament, the expression of a passionate nature confirmed in sympathy, shone in the softened fervour of her look as she bent her eyes thoughtfully upon the flames.

"Something must be done for Will," she said, turning presently. "This can't go on another day."

Miss Saidie caught her breath sharply, and hastened to the head of the table, as Fletcher's heavy footsteps crossed the hall.

"For heaven's sake, be careful," she whispered warningly, jerking her head nervously from side to side.

Fletcher entered with a black look, slamming the door heavily behind him, then, suddenly catching sight of Maria, he stopped short on the threshold and stared at her with hanging jaws.

"I'll be blessed if it ain't Maria!" he broke out at last.

Maria went toward him and held out her cheek for his kiss.

"I've surprised you almost as much as I did Aunt Saidie," she said, with her cheerful laugh, which floated a little strangely on the sullen atmosphere.

Catching her by the shoulder, Fletcher drew her into the circle of the lamplight, where he stood regarding her in gloomy silence.

"You've **filled** out considerable," he remarked, as he released her at the end of his long scrutiny. "But thar was room for it, heaven knows. You'll never be the sort that a man smacks his lips over, I reckon, but you're a plum sight better looking than you were when you went away."

Maria winced quickly as if he had struck her; then, regaining her composure almost instantly, she drew back her chair with a casual retort.

"But I didn't come home to set the county afire," she said. "Why, Aunt Saidie, what queer, coarse china! What's become of the white-and-gold set I used to like?"

A purple flush mounted slowly to Miss Saidie's forehead.

"I was afraid it would chip, so I packed it away," she explained. "Me and Brother Bill ain't used to any better than this, so we don't notice. Things will have to be mighty fine now, I reckon, since you've got back. You were always particular about looks, I remember."

"Was I?" asked Maria curiously, glancing down into the plate before her. For the last few years she had schooled herself to despise what she called the "silly luxuries of living," and yet the heavy white cup which Miss Saidie handed her, and the sound of Fletcher drinking his coffee, aroused in her the old poignant disgust.

"I don't think I'm over particular now," she added pleasantly, "but we may as well get out the other china to-morrow, I think."

"You won't find many fancy ways here—eh, Saidie?" inquired Fletcher, with a chuckle. "Thar's been a precious waste of victuals on this place, but it's got to stop. I ain't so sure you did a wise thing in coming back," he finished abruptly, turning his bloodshot eyes on his granddaughter.

"You aren't? Well, I am," laughed Maria; "and I promise you that you shan't find me troublesome except in the matter of china."

"Then you must have changed your skin, I reckon."

"Changed? Why, I have, of course. Six years isn't a day, you know, and I've been in many places." Then, as a hint of interest awoke in his eyes, she talked on rapidly, describing her years abroad and the strange cities in which she had lived. Before she had finished, Fletcher had pushed his plate away and sat listening with the ghost of a smile upon his face.

"Well, you'll do, I reckon," he said at the end, and, pushing back his chair, he rose from his place and stamped out into the hall.

When he had gone into his sitting-room and closed the door behind him, Miss Saidie nodded smilingly, as she measured out the servant's sugar in a cracked saucer. "He's brighter than I've seen him for days," she said; "and now, if you want to go upstairs, Malindy has jest lighted your fire. She had to carry the wood up while we were at supper, so Brother Bill wouldn't see it. He hates even to burn a log, though they are strewn round loose all over the place."

Maria was feeding Agag on the hearth, and she waited until he had finished before she took up her hat and wraps and went toward the door. "Oh, you needn't bother to light me," she said, waving Miss

Saidie back when she would have followed. "Why, I could find my way over this house at midnight without a candle." Then, with a cheerful "Good-night," she called Agag and went up the dusky staircase.

A wood fire was burning in her room, and she stood for a moment looking pensively into the flames, a faint smile sketched about her mouth. Then throwing off her black dress in the desire for freedom, she clasped her hands above her head and paced slowly up and down the shadowy length of the room. In the flowing measure of her walk; in the free, almost defiant, movement of her upraised arms; and in the ample lines of her throat and bosom, which melted gradually into the low curves of her hips, she might have stood for an incarnation of vital force. One felt instinctively that her personality would be active rather than passive—that the events which she attracted to herself would be profoundly emotional in their fulfilment.

Notwithstanding the depressing hour she had just passed, and the old vulgarity which had shocked her with a new violence, she was conscious, moving to and fro in the shadows, of a strange happiness— of a warmth of feeling which pervaded her from head to foot, which fluttered in her temples and burned like firelight in her open palms. The place was home to her, she realised at last, and the surroundings of her married life—the foreign towns and the enchanting Italian scenery—showed in her memory with a distant and alien beauty. Here was what she loved, for here was her right, her heritage—the desolate red roads, the luxuriant tobacco fields, the primitive and ignorant people. In her heart there was no regret for any past that she had known, for over the wild country stretching about her now there hung a romantic and mysterious haze.

A little later she was aroused from her reverie by Miss Saidie, who came in with a lighted lamp in her hand.

"Don't you need a light, Maria? I never could abide to sit in the dark."

"Oh, yes; bring it in. There, put it on the bureau and sit down by the fire, for I want to talk to you. No, I'm not a bit tired; I am only trying to fit myself again in this room. Why, I don't believe you've changed a pin in the pincushion since I went away."

Miss Saidie dusted the top of the bureau with her apron before she placed the tall glass lamp upon it.

"Thar warn't anybody to stay in it," she answered, as she sat down in a deep, cretonne-covered chair and pushed back the hickory log with her foot. "I declare, Maria, I don't see what you want to traipse around with that little poor-folksy yaller dog for. He puts me in mind of the one that old blind nigger up the road used to have."

"Does he?" asked Maria absently, in the voice of one whose thoughts are hopelessly astray.

She was standing by the window, holding aside the curtain of flowered chintz, and after a moment she added curiously: "There's a light in the fields, Aunt Saidie. What does it mean?"

Crossing the room, Miss Saidie followed the gesture with which Maria pointed into the night.

"That's on the Blake place," she said; "it must be Mr. Christopher moving about with his lantern."

"You call him Mr. Christopher?"

"Oh, it slipped out. His father's name was Christopher before him, and I used to open the gate for him when I was a child. Many and many a time the old gentleman's given me candy out of his pocket, or a quarter to buy a present, and one Christmas he brought me a real wax doll from the city. He wasn't old then, I can tell you, and he was as handsome as if he had stepped out of a fashion plate. Why, young Mr. Christopher can't hold a candle to him for looks."

"He was a gentleman, then? I mean the old man."

"Who? Mr. Christopher's father? I don't reckon thar was a freer or a finer between here and London."

Maria's gaze was still on the point of light which twinkled faintly here and there in the distant field.

"Then how, in heaven's name, did he come to this?" she asked, in a voice that was hardly louder than a whisper.

"I never knew; I never knew," protested Miss Saidie, going back to her chair beside the hearth. "Brother Bill and he hate each other worse than death, and it was Will's fancy for Mr. Christopher that brought on this awful trouble. For a time, I declare it looked as if the boy was really bewitched, and they were together morning, noon, and night. Your grandpa never got over it, and I believe he blames Mr. Christopher for every last thing that's happened—Molly Peterkin and all."

"Molly Peterkin?" repeated Maria inquiringly. "Why, how absurd! And, after all, what is the matter with the girl?" Dropping the curtain, she came over to the fire, and sat listening attentively while Miss

Saidie told, in spasmodic jerks and pauses, the foolish story of Will's marriage.

"Your grandpa will never forgive him—never, never. He has turned him out for good and all, and he talks now of leaving every cent of his money to foreign missions."

"Well, we'll see," said Maria soothingly. "I'll go over there to-morrow and talk with Will, and then I'll try to bring grandfather to some kind of reason. He can't let them starve, rich as he is; there's no sense in that—and if the worst comes, I can at least share the little I have with them. It may supply them with bread, if Molly will undertake to churn her own butter."

"Then your money went, too?"

"The greater part of it. Jack was fond of wild schemes, you know. I left it in his hands."

She had pronounced the dead man's name so composedly that Miss Saidie, after an instant's hesitation, brought herself to an allusion to the girl's loss.

"How you must miss him, dear," she ventured timidly; "even if he wasn't everything he should have been to you, he was still your husband."

"Yes, he was my husband," assented Maria quietly.

"You were so brave and so patient, and you stuck by him to the last, as a wife ought to do. Then thar's not even a child left to you now."

Maria turned slowly toward her and then looked away again into the fire. The charred end of a lightwood knot had fallen on the stones, and, picking it up, she threw it back into the flames. "For a year

before his death his mind was quite gone," she said
in a voice that quivered slightly; "he had to be taken
to an asylum, but I went with him and nursed him
till he died.   There were times when he would allow
no one else to enter his room or even bring him his
meals.   I have sat by him for two days and nights
without sleeping, and though he did not recognise
me, he would not let me stir from my place."

"And yet he treated you very badly—even his
family said so."

"That is all over now, and we were both to blame.
I owed him reparation, and I made it, thank God, at
the last."

As she raised her bare arms to the cushioned back
of her chair Miss Saidie caught a glimpse of a deep
white scar which ran in a jagged line above her elbow.

"Oh, it is nothing, nothing," said Maria hastily,
clasping her hands again upon her knees.   "That
part of my life is over and done with and may rest
in peace.   I forgave him then, and he forgives me
now.   One always forgives when one understands,
you know, and we both understand to-day—he   no
less than I.   The chief thing was that we made a
huge, irretrievable mistake—the mistake that two
people make when they think that love can be
coddled and nursed like a domestic pet—when they
forget that it goes wild and free and comes at no man's
call.   Folly like that is its own punishment, I suppose."

"My dear, my dear," gasped Miss Saidie, in
awe-stricken sympathy before the wild remorse in
Maria's voice.

"I did my duty, as you call it; I even clung to it
desperately, and, much as I hated it, I never rebelled

for a single instant. The nearest I came to loving
him, I think, was when, after our terrible life together,
he lay helpless for a year and I was with him day and
night. If I could have given him my strength then,
brain and body, I would have done it gladly, and that
agonised compassion was the strongest feeling I
ever had for him." She broke off for a long breath,
and sat looking earnestly at the amazed little woman
across from her. "You could never understand!"
she exclaimed impetuously, "but I must tell you—
I must tell you because I can't live with you day
after day and know that there is an old dead lie
between us. I hate lies, I have had so many of them,
and I shall speak the truth hereafter, no matter
what comes of it. Anything is better than a long,
wearing falsehood, or than those hideous little shams
that we were always afraid to touch for fear they
would melt and show us our own nakedness. That
is what I loathe about my life, and that is what I've
done with now forever. I am myself now for the
first time since I was born, and at last I shall let my
own nature teach me how to live."

Her intense pallor was illumined suddenly by a
white flame, whether from the leaping of some inner
emotion or from the sinking firelight which blazed
up fitfully Miss Saidie could not tell. As she turned
her head with an impatient movement her black
hair slipped its heavy coil and spread in a shadowy
mass upon her bared shoulders.

"I'm sure I don't know how it is," said Miss
Saidie, wiping her eyes. "But I can't see that it
makes any difference whether you were what they
call in love or not, so long as you were a good, well-

behaved wife. I don't think a man troubles himself
much about a woman's heart after he's put his
wedding ring on her finger; and though I know, of
course, that thar's a lot of nonsense spoken in courtship, it seems to me they mostly take it out in
talking. The wives that I've seen are generally as
anxious about thar setting hens as they are about thar
husband's hearts, and I reckon things are mighty
near the same the world over."

Without noticing her, Maria went on feverishly,
speaking so low at times that the other almost lost
the words.

"It is such a relief to let it all out," she said,
with a long, sighing breath, "and oh! if I had
loved him it would have been so different—so
different. Then I might have saved him; for what
evil is strong enough to contend against a love
which would have borne all things, have covered all
things?"

Rising from her chair, she walked rapidly up and
down, and pausing at last beside the window, lifted
the curtain and looked out into the night.

"I might have saved him; I know it now," she
repeated slowly: "or had it been otherwise, even in
madness I would not have loosened my arms, and
my service would have been the one passionate
delight left in my life. They could never have torn
him from my bosom then, and yet as it was—as
it was——" She turned quickly, and, coming back,
laid her hand on Miss Saidie's arm. "It is such a
comfort to talk, dear Aunt Saidie," she added,
"even though you don't understand half that I
say. But you are good—so good; and now if you'll

lend me a nightgown I'll go to bed and sleep until my trunks come in the morning."

Her voice had regained its old composure, and Miss Saidie, looking back as she went for the gown, saw that she had begun quietly to braid her hair.

CHAPTER III

The Day Afterward

When Maria awoke, the sun was full in her eyes, and somewhere on the lawn outside the first bluebird was whistling. With a start, she sprang out of bed and dressed quickly by the wood fire which Malindy had lighted. Then, before going downstairs, she raised the window and leaned out into the freshness of the morning, where a white mist glimmered in the hollows of the March landscape. In the distance she saw the smoking chimneys of the Blake cottage, very faint among the leafless trees, and nearer at hand men were moving back and forth in her grandfather's fields. Six years ago she would have found little beauty in so grave and colourless a scene, but to-day as she looked upon it a peace such as she had never known possessed her thoughts. The wisdom of experience was hers now, and with it she had gained something of the deeper insight into nature which comes to the soul that is reconciled with the unknown laws which it obeys.

Going down a few moments later, she found that breakfast was already over, and that Miss Saidie was washing the tea things at the head of the bared table.

"Why, it seems but a moment since I fell asleep,"

said Maria, as she drew back her chair. "How long has grandfather been up?"

"Since before daybreak. He is just starting to town, and he's in a terrible temper because the last batch of butter ain't up to the mark, he says. I'm sure I don't see why it ain't, for I worked every pound of it with my own hands—but thar ain't no rule for pleasing men, and never will be till God Almighty sets the universe rolling upside down. That's the wagon you hear now. Thank heaven, he won't be back till after dark."

With a gesture of relief Maria applied herself to the buttered waffles before her, prepared evidently in her honour, and then after a short silence, in which she appeared to weigh carefully her unuttered words, she announced her intention of paying immediately her visit to Will and Molly.

"Oh, you can't, you can't," groaned Miss Saidie, nervously mopping out the inside of a cup. "For heaven's sake, don't raise another cloud of dust jest as we're beginning to see clear again."

"Now don't tell me I can't when I must," responded Maria, pushing away her plate and rising from the table; "there's no such word as 'can't' when one has to, you know. I'll be back in two hours at the most, and oh! with so much to tell you!"

After tying on her hat in the hall, she looked in again to lighten Miss Saidie's foreboding by a tempting bait of news; but when she had descended the steps and walked slowly along the drive under the oaks, the assumed brightness of her look faded as rapidly as the morning sunshine on the clay road before her. It was almost with dismay that she found herself covering the ground between the Hall and Will's home and saw the shaded lane stretching to the little farm adjoining Sol Peterkin's.

As she passed the store, Mrs. Spade, who was selling white china buttons to Eliza Field, leaned over the counter and stared in amazement through the open window.

"Bless my soul an' body, if thar ain't old Fletcher's granddaughter come back!" she exclaimed—"holdin' her head as high as ever, jest as if her husband hadn't beat her black an' blue. Well, well, times have slid down hill sence I was a gal, an' the women of to-day ain't got the modesty they used to be born with. Why, I remember the time when old Mrs. Beale in the next county used to go to bed for shame, with a mustard plaster, every time her husband took a drop too much, which he did every blessed Saturday that he lived. It tided him over the Sabbath mighty well, he used to say, for he never could abide the sermons of Mr. Grant."

Eliza dropped the buttons she had picked up and turned, craning her neck in the direction of Maria's vanishing figure.

"What on earth has she gone down Sol Peterkin's lane for?" she inquired suspiciously.

"The Lord knows; if it's to visit her brother, I may say it's a long ways mo'n I'd do."

"She was always a queer gal even befo' her marriage —so strange an' far-away lookin' that I declar' it used to scare me half to death to meet her all alone at dusk. I never could help feelin' that she could bewitch a body, if she wanted to, with those solemn black eyes."

"She ain't bewitched me," returned Mrs. Spade decisively; "an' what's mo', she's had too many misfortunes come to her to make me believe she ain't done somethin' to deserve 'em. Thar's mighty few folks gets worse than they deserve in this world, an' when you see a whole flock of troubles settle on a person's head you may rest right sartain thar's a long score of misbehaviours up agin 'em. Yes, ma'am; when I hear of a big misfortune happenin' to anybody that I know, the first question that pops into my head is: 'I wonder if they've broke the sixth this time or jest the common seventh?' The best rule to follow, accordin' to my way of thinkin', is to make up yo' mind right firm that no matter what evil falls upon a person it ain't nearly so bad as the good Lord ought to have made it."

"That's a real pious way of lookin' at things, I reckon," sighed Eliza deferentially, as she fished five cents from the deep pocket of her purple calico and slapped it down upon the counter; "but we ain't all such good church-goers as you, the mo's the pity."

"Oh, I'm moral, an' I make no secret of it," replied Mrs. Spade. "It's writ plain all over me, an' it has been ever sence the day that I was born. 'That's as moral lookin' a baby as ever I saw,' was what Doctor Pierson said to ma when I wan't mo'n two hours old. It was so then, an' it's been so ever sence. 'Virtue may not take the place of beaux,' my po' ma used to say, 'but it will ease her along mighty well without 'em'—— Yes, the buttons are five cents. To be sure, I'll watch out and let you hear if she comes this way again."

Maria, meanwhile, happily unconscious of the judgment of her neighbours, walked thoughtfully along the lane until she came in sight of the small tumbled-down cottage which had been Fletcher's wedding gift to his grandson. A man in blue jean clothes was ploughing the field on the left of the road, and it was only when something vaguely familiar in his dejected attitude caused her to turn for a second glance that she realised, with a pang, that he was Will.

At her startled cry he looked up from the horses he was driving, and then, letting the ropes fall, came slowly toward her across the faint purple furrows. All the boyish jauntiness she remembered was gone from his appearance; his reversion to the family type had been complete, and it came to her with a shock that held her motionless that he stood to-day where her grandfather had stood fifty years before.

"O Will!" she gasped, with an impulsive, motherly movement of her arms. Rejecting her caress with an impatient shrug, he stood kicking nervously at a clod of earth, his eyes wavering in a dispirited survey of her face.

"Well, it seems that we have both made a blamed mess of things," he said at last.

Maria shook her head, smiling hopefully. "Not too bad a mess to straighten out, dear," she answered. "We must set to work at once and begin to mend matters. Ah, if you had only written me how things were!"

"What was the use?" asked Will doggedly. "It was all grandpa—he turned out the devil himself, and there was no putting up with him. He'll live forever, too; that's the worst of it!"

"But you did anger him very much, Will—and you might so easily have waited. Surely, you were both young enough."

"Oh, it wasn't all about Molly, you know, when it comes to that. Long before I married he had made my life a burden to me. It all began with his insane jealousy of Christopher Blake——"

"Of Christopher Blake?" repeated Maria, and fell a step away from him.

"Blake has been a deuced good friend to me," insisted Will; "that's what the old man hates—what he's hated steadily all along. The whole trouble started when I wouldn't choose my friends to please him; and when at last I undertook to pick out my own wife there was hell to pay."

Maria's gaze wandered inquiringly in the direction of the house, which had a disordered and thriftless air.

"Is she here?" she asked, not without a slight nervousness in her voice.

Will followed her glance, and, taking off his big straw hat, pulled at the shoestring tied tightly around the crown.

"Not now; but you'll see her some day, when she's dressed up, and I tell you she'll be worth your looking at. All she needs is a little money to turn her into the most tearing beauty you ever saw."

"And she's not at home?"

"Not now," he replied impatiently; "her mother has just come over and taken her off. I say, Maria," he lowered his voice, and an eager look came into his irresolute face, which already showed the effects of heavy drinking, "this can't keep up, you know; it really can't. We must have money, for there's a child coming in the autumn."

"A child!" exclaimed Maria, startled. "Oh, Will! Will!" She glanced round again at the barren landscape and the squalid little house; "then something must be done at once—there's no time to lose. I'll speak to grandfather about it this very night."

"At least, there's no harm in trying," said Will, catching desperately at the suggestion. "Even if you don't make things better, there's a kind of comfort in the thought that you can't make them worse. We're at the bottom of the hill already. So, if you don't pull us up, at least you won't push us any farther down."

"Oh, I'll pull you up, never fear; but you must give me time."

"Your own affairs are in rather a muddle, I reckon, by now?"

"Hopeless, it seems; but I'll share with you the few hundreds I still have. I brought this to-day, thinking you might be in immediate need."

As she drew the little roll of bills from her pocket, Will reached out eagerly, and, seizing it from her, counted it greedily in her presence. "Well, you're a downright brick, Maria," he remarked, as he thrust it hastily into his shirt.

Disappointment had chilled Maria's enthusiasm a little, but the next instant she dismissed the feeling as ungenerous, and slipped her hand affectionately through his arm as he walked back with her into the road.

"I wish I could see Molly," she said again, her eyes on the house, where she caught a glimpse of a bright head withdrawn from one of the windows.

"She is over at her mother's, I told you," returned Will irritably, and then, stooping to kiss her hurriedly, he added in a persuasive voice: "Bring the old man to reason, Maria; it's life or death, remember."

"I'll do my best, Will; I'll go on my knees to him to-night."

"Does he dislike you as much as ever?"

"No; he rather fancies me, I think. Last evening he grew almost amiable, and this morning Aunt Saidie told me he left me a pound of fresh butter from the market jar. If you only knew how fond he's grown of his money you would realise what it means.'

"Well, keep it up, for God's sake. Humour him for all he's worth. Coddle and coax him into doing something for us, or dying and leaving us his money."

Maria's face grew grave. "That's the serious part, Will; he talks of leaving every penny he has to foreign missions."

"The devil!" cried Will furiously. "If he does, I hope he'll land in hell. Don't let him, Maria. It all rests with you. Why, if he did, you'd starve along with us, wouldn't you?"

"Oh, you needn't think of me—I could always teach, you know, and a little money buys a great deal of happiness with me. I have learned that great wealth is almost as much of an evil as great poverty."

"I'd take the risk of it, every time; and he is beastly rich, isn't he, Maria?"

"One of the very richest men in the State, they told me at the cross-roads."

"Yet he has the insolence to cut me off without a dollar. Look at this petered-out little farm he's given me. Why, it doesn't bring in enough to feed a darkey!"

"We'll hope for better things, dear; but you must learn to be patient—very patient. His anger has been smothered so long that it has grown almost as settled as hate. Aunt Saidie doesn't dare mention your name to him, and she tells me that if I so much as speak of you he'll turn me out of doors."

"Then it's even worse than I thought."

"Perhaps. I can't say, for I haven't approached the subject even remotely as yet. Keep your courage, however, and I promise you to do my best."

She kissed him again, and then, turning her face homeward, started at a rapid walk down the lane. The interview with Will had disturbed her more than she liked to admit, and it was with a positive throb of pain that she forced herself at last to compare the boy of five years ago with the broken and dispirited man from whom she had just parted. Was this tragedy the end of the young ambition which Fletcher had nursed so fondly, this—a nervous, overworked tobacco-grower, with bloodshot eyes, and features already inflamed by reckless drinking? The tears sprang to her lashes, and, throwing up her hands with a pathetic gesture of protest, she hastened on homeward as if to escape the terror that pursued her.

She had turned from the lane into the main road, and was just approaching the great chestnuts which

grew near the abandoned ice-pond, when, looking up
suddenly at the call of a bird above her head, she
saw Christopher Blake standing beside the rail fence
and watching her with a strong and steady gaze.
Involuntarily she slackened her pace and waited,
smiling for him to cross the fence; but, to her amazement, after an instant in which his eyes held her as
if rooted to the spot, he turned hastily away and
walked rapidly in the opposite direction. For a
breath she stood motionless, gazing blankly into
space; then, as she went on again, she knew that
she carried with her not the wonder at his sudden
flight, but the clear memory of that one moment's
look into his eyes. A century of experience, with
its tears and its laughter, its joy and its anguish,
its desire and its fulfilment, seemed crowded into
the single instant that held her immovable in the
road.

CHAPTER IV

The Meeting in the Night

When Christopher turned so abruptly from Maria's gaze he was conscious only of a desperate impulse of flight. At the instant his strength seemed to fail him utterly, and he realised that for the first time in his life he feared to trust himself to face the imminent moment. His one thought was to escape quickly from her presence, and in the suddenness of his retreat he did not weigh the possible effect upon her of his rudeness. A little later, however, when he had put the field between him and her haunting eyes, he found himself returning with remorse to his imaginings of what her scattered impressions must have been.

Between regret and perplexity the day dragged through, and he met his mother's exacting humours and Cynthia's wistful inquiries with a curious detachment of mind. He had reached that middle state of any powerful emotion when even the external objects among which one moves seem affected by the inward struggle between reason and desire— the field in which he worked, the distant landscape, the familiar faces in the house, and those frail, pathetic gestures of his mother's hands, all expressed in outward forms something of the passion which he felt stirring in his own breast. It was in his nature to dare risks blindly—to hesitate at no experience offered him in his narrow life, and there were moments during this long day when he found himself questioning if one might not, after all, plunge headlong into the impossible.

As he rose from the supper table, where he had pushed his untasted food impatiently away, he remembered that he had promised in the morning to meet Will Fletcher at the store, and, lighting his lantern, he started out to keep the appointment he had almost forgotten. He found Will overflowing with his domestic troubles, and it was after ten o'clock before they both came out upon the road and turned into opposite ways at the beginning of Sol Peterkin's lane.

"I'll help you with the ploughing, of course," Christopher said, as they lingered together a moment before parting; "make your mind quite easy about that. I'll be over at sunrise on Monday and put in a whole day's job."

Then, as he fell back into his own road, he found something like satisfaction in the prospect of driving Will Fletcher's plough. The easy indifference with which he was accustomed to lend a hand in a neighbour's difficulty had always marked his association with the man whose ruin, he still assured himself, he had wrought.

It was a dark, moonless night, with only a faint, nebulous whiteness where the clouded stars shone overhead. His lantern, swinging lightly from his hand, cast a shining yellow circle on the ground before him, and it was by this illumination that he saw presently, as he neared the sunken road into which he was about to turn, a portion of the shadow by the ice-pond detach itself from the surrounding blackness and drift rapidly to meet him. In his first start of surprise, he raised the lantern quickly above his head and waited breathlessly while the advancing shape assumed gradually a woman's form. The old ghost stories of his childhood thronged confusedly into his brain, and then, before the thrilling certainty of the figure before him, he uttered a single joyous exclamation:

"You!"

The light flashed full upon Maria's face, which gave back to him a white and tired look. Her eyes were heavy, and there was a strange solemnity about them—something that appealed vaguely to his religious instinct.

"What in heaven's name has happened?" he asked, and his voice escaped his control and trembled with emotion.

With a tired little laugh, she screened her eyes from the lantern.

"I had a talk with grandfather about Will," she answered, "and he got so angry that he locked me out of doors. He had had a worrying day in town, and I think he hardly knew what he was doing—but he has put up the bars and turned out the lights, and there's really no way of getting in."

He thought for a moment. "Will you go on to your brother's, or is it too far?"

"At first I started there, but that must have been hours ago, and it was so dark I got lost by the ice-pond. After all, it would only make matters worse if I saw Will again; so the question is, Where am I to sleep?''

"At Tom Spade's, then—or—'' he hesitated an instant, "if you care to come to us, my sister will gladly find room for you.''

She shook her head. ''No, no; you are very kind, but I can't do that. It is best that I shouldn't leave the place, perhaps, and when the servant comes over at sunrise I can slip up into my room. If you'll lend me your lantern I'll make myself some kind of a bed in the barn. Fortunately, grandfather forgot to lock the door.''

"In the barn?'' he echoed, surprised.

"Oh, I went there first, but after I lay down I suddenly remembered the mice and got up and came away. I'm mortally afraid of mice in the dark; but your lantern will keep them off, will it not?''

She smiled at him from the shining circle which surrounded her like a halo, and for a moment he forgot her words in the wonderful sense of her nearness. Around them the night stretched like a cloak, enclosing them in an emotional intimacy which had all the warmth of a caress. As she leaned back against the body of a tree, and he drew forward that he might hold the lantern above her head, the situation was resolved, in spite of the effort that he made, into the eternal problem of the man and the woman. He was aware that his blood worked rapidly in his veins, and as her glance reached upward from the light to meet his in the shadow he realised with the swiftness of intuition that in her also the appeal of the silence was faced with a struggle. They would ignore it, he knew, and yet it shone in

their eyes, quivered in their voices, and trembled
in their divided hands; and to them both its presence
was alive and evident in the space between them.
He saw her bosom rise and fall, her lips part slightly,
and a tremor disturb the high serenity of her self-
control, and there came to him the memory of their
first meeting at the cross-roads and of the mystery
and the rapture of his boyish love.   He had found her
then the lady of his dreams, and now, after all the
violence of his revolt against her, she was still to him
as he had first seen her—the woman whose soul
looked at him from her face.

For a breathless moment—for a single heart-beat
—it seemed to him that he had but to lean down and
gather her eyes and lips and hands to his embrace,
to feel her awaken to life within his arms and her
warm blood leap up beneath his mouth.   Then the
madness left him as suddenly as it had come, and
she grew strangely white, and distant, and almost
unreal, in the spiritual beauty of her look.   He
caught his breath sharply, and lowered his gaze to
the yellow circle that trembled on the ground.

"But you will be afraid even with the light," he
said, in a voice which had grown almost expressionless.

As if awaking suddenly from sleep, she passed
her hand slowly across her eyes.

"No, I shall not be afraid with the light," she
answered, and moved out into the road.

"Then let me hold it for you—the hill is very
rocky."

She assented silently, and quickened her steps
down the long incline; then, as she stumbled in the
darkness, he threw the lantern over upon her side.

"If you will lean on me I think I can steady you," he suggested, waiting until she turned and laid her hand upon his arm. "That's better now; go slowly and leave the road to me. How in thunder did you come over it in the pitch dark?"

"I fell several times," she replied, with a little unsteady laugh, "and my feet are oh! so hurt and bruised. To-morrow I shall go on crutches."

"A bad night's work, then."

"But not so bad as it might have been," she added cheerfully.

"You mean if I had not found you it would have been worse. Well, I'm glad that much good has come out of it. I have spared you a cold—so that goes down to my credit; otherwise—— But what difference does it make?" he finished impatiently. "We must have met sooner or later even if I had run across the world instead of merely across a tobacco field. After all, the world is no bigger than a tobacco field, when it comes to destiny."

"To destiny?" she looked up, startled. "Then there are fatalists even among tobacco-growers?"

He met her question with a laugh. "But I wasn't always a tobacco-grower, and there were poets before Homer, who is about the only one I've ever read. It's true I've tried to lose the little education I ever had—that I've done my best to come down to the level of my own cattle; but I'm not an ox, after all, except in strength, and one has plenty of time to think when one works in the field all day. Why, the fancies I've had would positively turn your head."

"Fancies—about what?"

"About life and death and the things one wants and can never get. I dream dreams and plot unimaginable evil——"

"Not evil," she protested.

"Whole crops of it; and harvest them, too."

"But why?"

"For pure pleasure—for sheer beastly love of the devilment I can't do."

She shook her head, treating his words as a jest.

"There was never evil that held its head so high."

"That's pride, you know."

"Nor that wore so frank a face."

"And that's hypocrisy."

"Nor that dared to be so rude."

He caught up her laugh.

"You have me there, I grant you.   What a brute I must have seemed this morning."

"You were certainly not a Chesterfield—nor a Bolivar Blake."

With a start he looked down upon her.   "Then you, too, are aware of the old chap?" he asked.

"Of Bolivar Blake—why, who isn't? I used to be taught one of his maxims as a child—'If you can't tell a polite lie, don't tell any.'"

"Good manners, but rather bad morality, eh?" he inquired.

"Unfortunately, the two things seem to run together," she replied; "which encourages me to hope that you will prove to be a pattern of virtue."

"Don't hope too hard. I may merely have lost the one trait without developing the other."

"At least, it does no harm to believe the best," she returned in the same careless tone.

Ahead of them, where the great oaks were massed darkly against the sky, he saw the steep road splotched into the surrounding blackness. Her soft breathing came to him from the obscurity at his side, and he felt his arm burn beneath the light pressure of her hand. For the first time in his lonely and isolated life he knew the quickened emotion, the fulness of experience, which came to him with the touch of the woman whom, he still told himself, he could never love. Not to love her had been so long for him a point of pride as well as of honour that even while the wonderful glow pervaded his thoughts, while his pulses drummed madly in his temples, he held himself doggedly to the illusion that the appeal she made would vanish with the morning. It was a delirium of the senses, he still reasoned, and knew even as the lie was spoken that the charm which drew him to her was, above all things, the spirit speaking through the flesh.

"I fear I have been a great bother to you," said Maria, after a moment, "but you will probably solace yourself with the reflection that destiny would have prepared an equal nuisance had you gone along another road."

"Perhaps," he answered, smiling; "but philosophy sometimes fails a body, doesn't it?"

"It may be. I knew a man once who said he leaned upon two crutches, philosophy and religion. When one broke under him he threw his whole weight on the other—and lo! that gave way."

"Then he went down, I suppose."

"I never heard the end—but if it wasn't quite so dark, you would find me really covered with confusion.

I have not only brought you a good mile out of your road, but I am now prepared to rob you of your light. Can you possibly find your way home in the dark?"

As she looked up, the lantern shone in his face, and she saw that he wore a whimsical smile.

"I have been in the dark all my life," he answered, "until to-night."

"Until to-night?"

"Until now—this very minute. For the first time for ten years I begin to see my road at this instant—to see where I have been walking all along."

"And where did it lead you?"

He laughed at the seriousness in her voice.

"Through a muck-heap—in the steps of my own cattle. I am sunk over the neck in it already."

Her tone caught the lightness of his and carried it off with gaiety.

"But there is a way out. Have you found it?"

"There is none. I've wallowed so long in the filth that it has covered me."

"Surely it will rub off," she said.

For a moment the lantern's flash rested upon his brow and eyes, relieving them against the obscurity which still enveloped his mouth.

The high-bred lines of his profile stood out clear and fine as those of an ivory carving, and their very beauty saddened the look she turned upon him. Then the light fell suddenly lower and revealed the coarsened jaw, with the almost insolent strength of the closed lips. The whole effect was one of reckless power, and she caught her breath with the thought that so compelling a force might serve equally the agencies of good or evil.

They had reached the lawn, and as he responded to her hurried gesture of silence they passed the house quickly and entered the great open door of the barn. Here he hung the lantern from a nail, and then, pulling down some straw from a pile in one corner, arranged it into the rude likeness of a pallet.

"I don't think the mice will trouble you," he said at last, as he turned to go, "but if they do— why, just call out and I'll come to slaughter——"

"You won't go home, then?" she asked, amazed.

He nodded carelessly.

"Not till daybreak. Remember, if you feel frightened, that I'm within earshot. '

Then, before she could protest or detain him for an explanation, he turned from her and went out into the darkness.

CHAPTER V

Maria Stands on Christopher's Ground

A BROAD yellow beam sliding under the door brought Maria into sudden consciousness, and rising hastily from the straw, where her figure had shaped an almost perfect outline, she crossed the dusky floor smelling of trodden grain and went out into the early sunshine, which slanted over the gray fields. A man trundling a wheelbarrow from the market garden, and a milkmaid crossing the lawn with a bucket of fresh milk, were the only moving figures in the landscape, and after a single hurried glance about her she followed the straight road to the house and entered the rear door, which Malindy had unlocked.

Meeting Fletcher a little later at breakfast, she found, to her surprise, that he accepted her presence without question and made absolutely no allusion to the heated conversation of the evening before. He looked sullen and dirty, as if he had slept all night in his clothes, and he responded to Maria's few good-humoured remarks with a single abrupt nod over his coffee-cup. As she watched him a feeling of pity for his loneliness moved her heart, and when he rose hastily at last and strode out into the hall she followed him and spoke gently while he paused to take down his hat from one of the old antlers near the door.

"If I could only be of some use to you, grandfather," she said; "are you sure there is nothing I can do?"

With his hand still outstretched, he hesitated an instant and stood looking down upon her, his heavy features wrinkling into a grin.

"I've nothing against you as a woman," he responded, "but when you set up and begin to charge like a judge, I'll be hanged if I can stand you."

"Then I won't charge any more. I only want to help you and to do what is best. If you would but let me make myself of some account."

He laughed not unkindly, and flecked with his stubby forefinger at some crumbs which had lodged in the folds of his cravat.

"Then I reckon you'd better mix a batch of dough and feed the turkeys," he replied, and touching her shoulder with his hat-brim, he went hurriedly out of doors.

When he had disappeared beyond the last clump of shrubbery bordering the drive, she remembered the lantern she had left hanging in the barn, and, going to look for it, carried it upstairs to her room. In the afternoon, however, it occurred to her that Christopher would probably need the light by evening, and swinging the handle over her arm, she set out across the newly ploughed fields toward the Blake cottage. The stubborn rustic pride which would keep him from returning to the Hall aroused in her a frank, almost tender amusement. She had long ago wearied of the trivial worldliness of

life; in the last few years the shallowness of passion
had seemed its crowning insult, and over the absolute
sincerity of her own nature the primal emotion she
had heard in Christopher's voice exerted a compelling
charm. The makeshift of a conventional marriage
had failed her utterly; her soul had rejected the
woman's usual cheap compromise with externals;
and in her almost puritan scorn of the vanities by
which she was surrounded she had attained the
moral elevation which comes to those who live by
an inner standard of purity rather than by outward
forms. In the largeness of her nature there had
been small room for regret or for wasted passion,
and until her meeting with Christopher on the day
of her homecoming he had existed in her imagination
only as a bright and impossible memory. Now, as
she went rapidly forward along the little path that
edged the field, she found herself wondering if, after
all, she had worn unconsciously his ideal as an
armour against the petty temptations and the
sudden melancholies of the last six years.

As she neared the fence that divided the two farms
she saw him walking slowly along a newly turned
furrow, and when he looked up she lifted the lantern
and waved it in the air. Quickening his steps, he
swung himself over the rail fence with a single
bound, and came to where she stood amid a dried
fringe of last summer's yarrow.

"So you are none the worse for the night in the
barn?" he asked anxiously.

"Why, I dreamed the most beautiful dreams,"
she replied, "and I had the most perfect sleep in the
world."

"Then the mice kept away?"

"At least they didn't wake me."

"I stayed within call until sunrise," he said quietly. "You were not afraid?"

Her rare smile shone suddenly upon him, illumining the delicate pallor of her face. "I knew that you were there," she answered.

For a moment he gazed steadily into her eyes, then with a decisive movement he took the lantern from her hand and turned as though about to go back to his work.

"It was very kind of you to bring this over," he said, pausing beside the fence.

"Kind? Why, what did you expect? I knew it might hang there forever, but you would not come for it."

"No, I should not have come for it," he replied, swinging the lantern against the rails with such force that the glass shattered and fell in pieces to the ground.

"Why, what a shame!" said Maria; "and it is all my fault."

A smile was on his face as he looked at her.

"You are right—it is all your fault," he repeated, while his gaze dropped to the level of her lips and hung there for a breathless instant.

With an effort she broke the spell which had fallen over her, and, turning from him, pointed to the old Blake graveyard on the little hill.

"Those black cedars have tempted me for days," she said. "Will you tell me what dust they guard so faithfully?"

He followed her gesture with a frown.

"I will show you, if you like," he answered. "It is the only spot on earth where I may offer you hospitality."

"Your people are buried there?"

"For two hundred years. Will you come?"

While she hesitated, he tossed the lantern over into his field and came closer to her side. "Come," he repeated gently, and at his voice a faint flush spread slowly from her throat to the loosened hair upon her forehead. The steady glow gave her face a light, a radiance, that he had never seen there until to-day.

"Yes, I will come if you wish it," she responded quietly.

Together they went slowly up the low, brown incline over the clods of upturned earth. When they reached the bricked-up wall, which had crumbled away in places, he climbed over into the bed of periwinkle and then held out his hands to assist her in descending. "Here, step into that hollow," he said, "and don't jump till I tell you. Ah, that's it; now, I'm ready."

At his words, she made a sudden spring forward, her dress caught on the wall, and she slipped lightly into his outstretched arms. For the half of a second he held her against his breast; then, as she released herself, he drew back and lifted his eyes to meet the serene composure of her expression. He was conscious that his own face flamed red hot, but to all outward seeming she had not noticed the incident which had so moved him. The calm distinction of her bearing struck him as forcibly as it had done at their first meeting.

"What a solemn place," she said, lowering her voice as she looked about her.

For answer he drew aside the screening boughs of a cedar and motioned to the discoloured marble slabs strewn thickly under the trees.

"Here are my people," he returned gravely. "And here is my ground."

Pausing, she glanced down on his father's grave, reading with difficulty the inscription beneath the dry dust from the cedars.

"He lived to be very old," she said, after a moment.

"Seventy years. He lived exactly ten years too long."

"Too long?"

"Those last ten years wrecked him. Had he died at sixty he would have died happy."

He turned from her, throwing himself upon the carpet of periwinkle, and coming to where he lay, she sat down on a granite slab at his side.

"One must believe that there is a purpose in it," she responded, raising a handful of fine dust and sifting it through her fingers, "or one would go mad over the mystery of things."

"Well, I dare say the purpose was to make me a tobacco-grower," he replied grimly, "and if so, it has fulfilled itself in a precious way. Why, there's never been a time since I was ten years old when I wouldn't have changed places, and said 'thank you,' too, with any one of those old fellows over there. They were jolly chaps, I tell you, and led jolly lives. It used to be said of them that they never won a penny nor missed a kiss."

"Nor learned a lesson, evidently. Well, may they rest in peace; but I'm not sure that their wisdom would carry far. There are better things than gaming and kissing, when all is said."

"Better things? Perhaps."

"Have you not found them?"

"Not yet; but then, I can't judge anything except tobacco, you know."

For a long pause she looked down into his upturned face.

"After all, it isn't the way we live nor the work we do that matters," she said slowly, "but the ideal we put into it. Is there any work too sordid, too prosaic, to yield a return of beauty?"

"Do you think so?" he asked, and glanced down the hill to his ploughshare lying in the ripped-up field. "But it is not beauty that some of us want, you see—it's success, action, happiness, call it what you will."

"Surely they are not the same. I have known many successful people, and the only three perfectly happy ones I ever met were what the world calls failures."

"Failures?" he echoed, and remembered Tucker.

Her face softened, and she looked beyond him to the blue sky, shining through the interlacing branches of bared trees.

"Two were women," she pursued, clasping and unclasping the quiet hands in her lap, "and one was a Catholic priest who had been reared in a foundling asylum and educated by charity. When I knew him he was on his way to a leper island in the South Seas, where he would be buried alive for the remainder of his life. All he had was an ideal, but it flooded his soul with light. Another was a Russian Nihilist, a girl in years and yet an atheist and a revolutionist in thought, and her unbelief was in its way as beautiful as the religion of my priest. To return to Russia meant death; she knew, and yet she went back, devoted and exalted, to lay down her life for an illusion. So it seems, when one looks about the world, that faith and doubt are dry and inanimate forms until we pour forth our heart's blood which vivifies them."

She fell silent, and he started and touched softly the hem of her black skirt.

"And the other?" he asked.

"The other had a stranger and a longer story, but if you will listen I'll tell it to you. She was an Italian, of a very old and proud family, and as she possessed rare loveliness and charm, a marriage was arranged for her with a wealthy nobleman, who had fallen in love with her before she left her convent. She was a rebellious soul, it seems, for the day before her wedding, just after she had patiently tried on her veil and orange blossoms, she slipped into the dress of her waiting-maid and ran off with a music-teacher—a beggarly fanatic, they told me—a man of red republican views, who put dangerous ideas into the heads of the peasantry. From that moment, they said, her life was over; her family shut their doors upon her, and she fell finally so low as to be seen one evening singing in the public streets. Her story touched me when I heard it: it seemed a pitiable thing that a woman should be wrecked so hopelessly by a single moment of mistaken courage;

and after months of searching I at last found the
place she lived in, and went one May evening up the
long winding staircase to her apartment—two clean,
plain rooms which looked on a little balcony where
there were pots of sweet basil and many pigeons.
At my knock the door opened, and I knew her at
once in the beautiful white face and hands of the
woman who stood a little back in the shadow. Her
forty years had not coarsened her as they do most
Italian women, and her eyes still held the unshaken
confidence of extreme youth. Her husband was
sleeping in the next room, she said; he had but a few
days more to live, and he had been steadily dying
for a year. Then, at my gesture of sympathy, she
shook her head and smiled.

" 'I have had twenty years,' she said, 'and I have
been perfectly happy. Think of that when so many
women die without having even a single day of life.
Why, but for the one instant of courage that saved me,
I myself might have known the world only as a vege-
table knows the garden in which it fattens. My soul
has lived, and though I have been hungry and cold
and poorly clad, I have never sunk to the level of
what they would have made me. He is a dreamer,'
she finished gently, 'and though his dreams were
nourished upon air, and never came true except in
our thoughts, still they have touched even the most
common things with beauty.' While she talked,
he awoke and called her, and we went in to see him.
He complained a little fretfully that his feet were cold,
and she knelt down and warmed them in the shawl
upon her bosom. The mark of death was on him,
and I doubt if even in the fulness of his strength he

were worthy of the passion he inspired—but that, after all, makes little difference. It was a great love, which is the next best thing to a great faith."

As she ended, he raised his eyes slowly, catching the fervour of her glance.

"It was more than that—it was a great deliverance," he said.

Then, as she rose, he followed her from the graveyard, and they descended the low brown hill together.

CHAPTER VI

The Growing Light

By THE end of the week a long rain had set in, and while it lasted Christopher took down the tobacco hanging in the roof of the log barn and laid it in smooth piles, pressed down by boards on the ground. The tobacco was still soft from the moist season when Jim Weatherby, who had sold his earlier in the year, came over to help pack the large casks for market, bringing at the same time a piece of news concerning Bill Fletcher.

"It seems Will met the old man somewhere on the road and they came to downright blows," he said. "Fletcher broke a hickory stick over the boy's shoulders."

Christopher carefully sorted a pile of plants, and then, selecting the finest six leaves, wrapped them together by means of a smaller one which he twisted tightly about the stems.

"Ah, is that so?" he returned, with a troubled look.

"It's a pretty kettle of fish, sure enough," pursued Jim. "Of course, Will has made a fool of himself, and gone to the dogs and all that, but I must say it does seem a shame, when you think that old Fletcher can't take his money with him to the next world.

As for pure stinginess, I don't believe he'd find his match if he scoured the country. Why, they say his granddaughter barely gets enough to eat. Look here! What are you putting in that bad leaf for. It's worm-eaten all over."

"So it is," admitted Christopher, examining it with a laugh. "My eyesight must be failing me. But what good under heaven does his money do Fletcher, after all?"

"Oh, he's saving it up to leave to foreign missions, Tom Spade says. Mr. Carraway is coming down next week to draw up a new will."

"And his grandchildren come in for nothing?"

"It looks that way—but you can't see through Bill Fletcher, so nobody knows. The funny part is that he has taken rather a liking to Mrs. Wyndham, I hear, and she has even persuaded him to raise the wages of his hands. It's a pity she can't patch up a peace with Will—the quarrel seems to distress her very much."

"You have seen her, then?"

"Yesterday, for a minute. She stopped me near the store and asked for news of Will. There was nothing I could tell her except that they dragged along somehow with Sol Peterkin's help. That's a fine woman, Fletcher or no Fletcher."

"Well, she can't help that—it's merely a question of name. There's Cynthia calling us to dinner. We'll have to fill the hogsheads later on."

But when the meal was over and he was returning to his work, Cynthia followed him with a message from his mother.

"She has asked for you all the morning, Christopher; there's something on her mind, though she seems quite herself and in a very lively humour. It is impossible to get her away from the subject of marriage—she harps on it continually."

He had turned to enter the house at her first words, but now his face clouded, and he hung back before the door.

"Do you think I'd better go in?" he asked, hesitating.

"There's no getting out of it without making her feel neglected, and perhaps your visit may divert her thoughts. I'm sure I don't see what she has left to say on the subject."

"All right, I'll go," he said cheerfully; "but for heaven's sake, help me drum up some fresh topics."

Mrs. Blake was sitting up in bed, sipping a glass of port wine, and at Christopher's step she turned her groping gaze helplessly in his direction.

"What a heavy tramp you have, my son; you must be almost as large as your father."

Crossing the room as lightly as his rude boots permitted, Christopher stooped to kiss the cheek she held toward him. The old lady had wasted gradually to the shadow of herself, and the firelight from the hearth shone through the unearthly pallor of her face and hands. Her beautiful white hair was still arranged, over a high cushion, in an elaborate fashion, and her gown of fine embroidered linen was pinned together with a delicate cameo brooch.

"I have been talking very seriously to 'Lila," she began at once, as he sat down by the bedside. "My age is great, you know, and it is hardly probable that the good Lord will see fit to leave me much longer to enjoy the pleasures of this world. Now, what troubles me more than all else is that I am to die feeling that the family will pass utterly away. Is it possible that both Lila and yourself persist in your absurd and selfish determination to remain unmarried?"

"Oh, mother! mother!" groaned Lila from the fireplace.

"You needn't interrupt me, Lila; you know quite well that a family is looked at askance when all of its members remain single. Surely one old maid—and I am quite reconciled to poor Cynthia's spinsterhood—is enough to leaven things, as your father used to say——"

Her memory slipped from her for a moment; she caught at it painfully, and a peevish expression crossed her face.

"What was I saying, Lila? I grow so forgetful."

"About father, dear."

"No, no; I remember now—it was about your marrying. Well, well, as I said before, I fear your attitude is the result of some sentimental fancies you have found in books. My child, there was never a book yet that held a sensible view of love, and I hope you will pay no attention to what they say. As for waiting until you can't live without a man before you marry him—tut-tut! the only necessary question is to ascertain if you can possibly live with him. There is a great deal of sentiment talked in life, my dear, and very little lived—and my experience of the world has shown me that one man is likely to make quite as good a husband as another—provided he remains a gentleman and you don't expect him to become a saint. I've had a long marriage, my children, and a happy one. Your father fell in love with me at his first glance, and he did not hate me at his last, though the period covered an association of thirty years. We were an ideal couple, all things considered, and he' was a very devoted husband; but to this day I have not ceased to be thankful that he was never placed in the position where he had to choose between me and his dinner. Honestly, I may as well confess among us three, it makes me nervous when I think of the result of such a pass."

"Oh, mother," protested Lila reproachfully; "if I listened to you I should never want to marry any man."

"I'm sure I don't see why, my dear. I have always urged it as a duty, not advised it as a pleasure. As far as that goes, I hold to this day the highest opinion of matrimony and of men, though I admit, when I consider the attention they require, I sometimes feel that women might select a better object. When the last word is said, a man is not half so satisfactory a domestic pet as a cat, and far less neat in his habits. Your poor father would throw his cigar ashes on the floor to the day of his death, and I could never persuade him to use an ash-tray, though I gave him one regularly every Christmas that he lived. Do you smoke cigars, Christopher? I detect a strong odour of tobacco about you, and I hope you haven't let Tucker persuade you into using anything so vulgar as a pipe. The worst effect of a war, I am inclined to believe, is the excuse it offers every man who fought in it to fall into bad habits."

"Oh, it's Uncle Tucker's pipe you smell," replied Christopher, with a laugh, as he rose from his chair. "I detest the stuff and always did."

"I suppose I ought to be thankful for it," said Mrs. Blake, detaining him by a gesture, "but I can't help recalling a speech of Micajah Blair's, who said that a woman who didn't flirt and a man who didn't smoke were unsexed creatures. It is a commendable eccentricity, I suppose, but an eccentricity, good or bad, is equally to be deplored. Your grandfather always said that the man who was better than his neighbours was quite as unfortunate as the man who was worse. Who knows but that your dislike of tobacco and your aversion to marriage may result from the same peculiar quirk in your brain?"

"Well, it's there and I can't alter it, even to please you, mother," declared Christopher from the door. "I've set my face square against them both, and there it stands."

He went out laughing, and Mrs. Blake resigned herself with a sigh to her old port.

The rain fell heavily, whipping up foaming puddles in the muddy road and beating down the old rose-bushes in the yard.

As Christopher paused for a moment in the doorway before going to the barn he drew with delight the taste of the dampness into his mouth and the odour of the moist earth into his nostrils. The world had taken on a new and appealing beauty, and yet the colourless landscape was touched with a sadness which he had never seen in external things until to-day.

His ears were now opened suddenly, his eyes

unbandaged, and he heard the rhythmical fall of the rain and saw the charm of the brown fields with a vividness that he had never found in his enjoyment of a summer's day. Human life also moved him to responsive sympathy, and he felt a great aching tenderness for his blind mother and for his sisters, with their narrowed and empty lives. His own share in the world, he realised, was but that of a small, insignificant failure; he had been crushed down like a weed in his tobacco field, and for a new springing-up he found neither place nor purpose. The facts of his own life were not altered by so much as a shadow, yet on the outside life that was not his own he beheld a wonderful illumination.

His powerful figure filled the doorway, and Cynthia, coming up behind him, raised herself on tiptoe to touch his bared head.

"Your hair is quite wet, Christopher; be sure to put on your hat and fasten the oilcloth over your shoulders when you go back to the barn. You are so reckless that you make me uneasy. Why, the rain has soaked entirely through your shirt."

"Oh, I'm a pine knot; you needn't worry."

She sighed impatiently and went back to the kitchen, while his gaze travelled slowly along the wet gray road to the abandoned ice-pond, and he thought of his meeting with Maria in the darkness and of the light of the lantern shining on her face. He remembered her white hands against her black dress, her fervent eyes under the grave pallor of her brow, her passionate, kind voice, and her mouth with the faint smile which seemed never to fade utterly away. Love, which is revealed usually as a pleasant dis-

turbing sentiment resulting from the ordinary pur-
poses of life, had come to him in the form of a great
regenerating force, destroying but that it might
rebuild anew.

CHAPTER VII

In Which Carraway Speaks the Truth to Maria

During the first week in April Carraway appeared at the Hall in answer to an urgent request from Fletcher that he should, without delay, put the new will into proper form.

On the morning after his arrival, Carraway had a long conversation with the old man in his sitting-room, and when it was over he came out with an anxious frown upon his brow and went upstairs to the library which Maria had fitted up in the spare room next her chamber. It was the pleasantest spot in the house, he had concluded last evening, and the impression returned to him as he entered now and saw the light from the wood fire falling on the shining floor, which reflected the stately old furniture, and the cushions, and the window curtains of faded green. Books were everywhere, and he noticed at once that they were not the kind read by the women whom he knew—big leather volumes on philosophy, yellow-covered French novels, and curled edges of what he took to be the classic poets. It was almost with relief that he noticed a dainty feminine touch here and there—a work-bag of flowered silk upon the sofa, a bowl of crocuses among the papers on the old mahogany desk, and clinging to each bit of well-worn drapery in the room a faint and delicate fragrance.

Maria was lying drowsily in a low chair before the fire, and as he entered she looked up with a smile and motioned to a comfortable seat across the hearth. A book was on her knees, but she had not been reading, for her fingers were playing carelessly with the uncut leaves. Against her soft black dress the whiteness of her face and hands showed almost too intense a contrast, and yet there was no hint of fragility in her appearance. From head to foot she was abounding with energy, throbbing with life, and though Carraway would still, perhaps, have hesitated to call her beautiful, his eyes dwelt with pleasure on the noble lines of her relaxed figure. Better than beauty, he admitted the moment afterward, was the charm that shone for him in her wonderfully expressive face—a face over which the experiences of many lives seemed to ripple faintly in what was hardly more than the shadow of a smile. She had loved and suffered, he thought, with his gaze upon her, and from both love and suffering she had gained that fulness of nature which is the greatest good that either has to yield.

"So it is serious," she said anxiously, as he sat down.

"I fear so—at least, where your brother is concerned. I can't say just what the terms of the will are, of course, but he made no secret at breakfast of his determination to leave half of his property— which the result of recent investments has made very large—to the cause of foreign missions."

"Yes, he has told me about it."

"Then there's nothing more to be said, unless you can persuade him for your brother's sake to destroy the will when his anger has blown over. I used every argument I could think of, but he simply wouldn't listen to me—swept my advice aside as if it was so much wasted breath——"

He paused as Maria bent her ear attentively.

"He is coming upstairs now!" she exclaimed, amazed.

There was a heavy tread on the staircase, and a little later Fletcher came in and turned to close the door carefully behind him. He had recovered for a moment his air of bluff good-humour, and his face crinkled into a ruddy smile.

"So you're hatching schemes between you, I reckon," he observed, and, crossing to the hearth, pushed back a log with the toe of his heavy boot.

"It looks that way, certainly," replied Carraway, with his pleasant laugh. "But I must confess that I was doing nothing more interesting than admiring Mrs. Wyndham's taste in books."

Fletcher glanced round indifferently.

"Well, I haven't any secrets," he pursued, still under the pressure of the thought which had urged him upstairs, "and as far as that goes, I can tear up that piece of paper and have it done with any day I please."

"So I had the honour to advise," remarked Carraway.

"That's neither here nor thar, I reckon—it's made now, and so it's likely to stand until I die, though I don't doubt you'll twist and split it then as much as you can. However, I reckon the foreign missions will look arter the part that goes to them, and if Maria's got the sense I credit her with she'll look arter hers."

"After mine?" exclaimed Maria, lifting her head to return his gaze. "Why, I thought you gave me my share when I married."

"So I did—so I did, and you let it slip like water through your fingers; but you've grown up, I reckon, sence you were such a fool as to have your head turned by Wyndham, and if you don't hold on to this tighter than you did to the last you deserve to lose it, that's all. You're a good woman—I ain't lived a month in the house with you and not found that out—but if you hadn't had something more than goodness inside your head you wouldn't have got so much as a cent out of me again. Saidie's a good woman and a blamed fool, too, but you're different; you've got a backbone in your body, and I'll be hanged if that ain't why I'm leaving the Hall to you."

"The Hall?" echoed Maria, rising impulsively from her chair and facing him upon the hearthrug.

"The Hall and Saidie and the whole lot," returned Fletcher, chuckling, "and I may as well tell you now, that, for all your spendthrift notions about wages, you're the only woman I ever saw who was fit to own a foot of land. But I like the quiet way you manage things, somehow, and, bless my soul, if you were a man I'd leave you the whole business and let the missions hang."

"There's time yet," observed Carraway beneath his breath.

"No, no; it's settled now," returned Fletcher, "and she'll have more than she can handle as it is.

Most likely she'll marry again, being a woman, and a man will be master here, arter all. If you do," he added, turning angrily upon his granddaughter, "for heaven's sakes, don't let it be another precious scamp like your first!"

With a shiver Maria caught her breath and bent toward him with an appealing gesture of her arms.

"But you must not do it, grandfather; it isn't right. The place was never meant to belong to me."

"Well, it belongs to me, I reckon, and confound your silly puritanical fancies, I'll leave it where I please," retorted Fletcher, and strode from the room.

Throwing herself back into her chair, Maria lay for a time looking thoughtfully at the hickory log, which crumbled and threw out a shower of red sparks. Her face was grave, but there was no hint of indecision upon it, and it struck Carraway very forcibly at the instant that she knew her own mind quite clearly and distinctly upon this as upon most other matters.

"It may surprise you," she said presently, speaking with sudden passion, "but by right the Hall ought not to be mine, and I do not want it. I have never loved it because it has never for a moment seemed home to me, and our people have always appeared strangers upon the land. How we came here I do not know, but it has not suited us, and we have only disfigured a beauty into which we did not fit. Its very age is a reproach to us, for it shows off our newness—our lack of any past that we may call our own. Will might feel himself master here, but I cannot."

Carraway took off his glasses and rubbed patiently at the ridge they had drawn across his nose.

"And yet, why not?" he asked. "The place has been in your grandfather's possession now for more than twenty years."

"For more than twenty years," repeated Maria scornfully, "and before that the Blakes lived here —how long?"

He met her question squarely. "For more than two hundred."

Without shifting her steady gaze which she turned upon his face, she leaned forward, clasping her hands loosely upon the knees.

"There are things that I want to know, Mr. Carraway," she said, "many things, and I believe that you can tell me. Most of all, I want to know why we ever came to Blake Hall? Why the Blakes ever left it? And, above all, why they have hated us so heartily and so long?"

She paused and sat motionless, while she hung with suspended breath upon his reply.

For a moment the lawyer hesitated, nervously twirling his glasses between his thumb and forefinger; then he slowly shook his head and looked from her to the fire.

"Twenty years are not as a day, despite your scorn, my dear young lady, and many facts become overlaid with fiction in a shorter time."

"But you know something—and you believe still more."

"God forbid that I should convert you to any belief of mine."

She put out a protesting hand, her eyes still gravely

insistent. "Tell me all—I demand it. It is my right; you must see that."

"A right to demolish sand houses—to scatter old dust."

"A right to hear the truth. Surely you will not withhold it from me?"

"I don't know the truth, so I can't enlighten you. I know only the stories of both sides, and they resemble each other merely in that they both centre about the same point of interest."

"Then you will tell them to me—you must," she said earnestly. "Tell me first, word for word, all that the Blakes believe of us."

With a laugh, he put on his glasses that he might bring her troubled face the more clearly before him.

"A high spirit of impartiality, I admit," he observed.

"That I should want to hear the other side?"

"That, being a woman, you should take for granted the existence of the other side."

She shook her head impatiently. "You can't evade me by airing camphor-scented views of my sex," she returned. "What I wish to know—and I still stick to my point, you see—is the very thing you are so carefully holding back."

"I am holding back nothing, on my honour," he assured her. "If you want the impression which still exists in the county—only an impression—I must make plain to you at the start (for the events happened when the State was in the throes of reconstruction, when each man was busy rebuilding his own fortunes, and when tragedies occurred without notice and were hushed up without remark)—if you want merely an impression, I repeat, then you may have it, my dear lady, straight from the shoulder."

" Well? " her voice rose inquiringly, for he had paused.

" There is really nothing definite known of the affair," he resumed after a moment, " even the papers which would have thrown light into the darkness were destroyed—burned, it is said, in an old office which the Federal soldiers fired. It is all mystery —grim mystery and surmise; and when there is no chance of either proving or disproving a case I dare say one man's word answers quite as well as another's. At all events, we have your grandfather's testimony as chief actor and eye-witness against the inherited convictions of our somewhat Homeric young neighbour. For eighteen years before the war Mr. Fletcher was sole agent—a queer selection, certainly—for old Mr. Blake, who was known to have grown very careless in the confidence he placed. When the crash came, about three years after the war, the old gentleman's mind was much enfeebled, and it was generally rumoured that his children were kept in ignorance that the place was passing from them until it was auctioned off over their heads and Mr. Fletcher became the purchaser. How this was, of course, I do not pretend to say, but when the Hall finally went for the absurd sum of seven thousand dollars life was at best a hard struggle in the State, and I imagine there was less surprise at the sacrifice of the place than at the fact that your grandfather should have been able to put down the ready money. The making of a fortune is always, I suppose, more inexplicable than the losing of one.

The Blakes had always been accounted people of great wealth and wastefulness, but within five years from the close of the war they had sunk to the position in which you find them now—a change, I dare say, from which it is natural much lingering bitterness should result. The old man died almost penniless, and his children were left to struggle on from day to day as best they could. It is a sad tale, and I do not wonder that it moves you," he finished slowly, and looked down to wipe his glasses.

"And grandfather?" asked the girl quietly. Her gaze had not wavered from his face, but her eyes shone luminous through the tears which filled them.

"He became rich as suddenly as the Blakes became poor. Where his money came from no one asked, and no one cared except the Blakes, who were helpless. They made some small attempts at law suits, I believe, but Christopher was only a child then, and there was nobody with the spirit to push the case. Then money was needed, and they were quite impoverished."

Maria threw out her hands with a gesture of revolt.

"Oh, it is a terrible story," she said, "a terrible story."

"It is an old one, and belongs to terrible times. You have drawn it from me for your own purpose, and be that as it may, I have always believed in giving a straight answer to a straight question. Now such things would be impossible," he added cheerfully; "then, I fear, they were but too probable."

"In your heart you believe that it is true?"

He did not flinch from his response. "In my heart I believe that there is more in it than a lie."

Rising from her chair, she turned from him and walked rapidly up and down the room, through the firelight which shimmered over the polished floor. Once she stopped by the window, and, drawing the curtains aside, looked out upon the April sunshine and upon the young green leaves which tinted the distant woods. Then coming back to the hearthrug, she stood gazing down upon him with a serene and resolute expression.

"I am glad now that the Hall will be mine," she said, "glad even that it wasn't left to Will, for who knows how he would have looked at it. There is but one thing to be done: you must see that yourself. At grandfather's death the place must go back to its rightful owners."

"To its rightful owners?" he repeated in amazement, and rose to his feet.

"To the Blakes. Oh, don't you see it—can't you see that there is nothing else to do in common honesty?"

He shook his head, smiling.

"It is very beautiful, my child, but is it reasonable, after all?" he asked.

"Reasonable?" The fine scorn he had heard before in her voice thrilled her from head to foot. "Shall I stop to ask what is reasonable before doing what is right?"

Without looking at her, he drew a handkerchief from his pocket and shook it slowly out from its folds.

"Well, I'm not sure that you shouldn't," he rejoined.

"Then I shan't be reasonable. I'll be wise," she said; "for surely, if there is any wisdom upon earth, it is simply to do right. It may be many years off, and I may be an old woman, but when the Hall comes to me at grandfather's death I shall return it to the Blakes."

In the silence which followed he found himself looking into her ardent face with a wonder not unmixed with awe. To his rather cynical view of the Fletchers such an outburst came as little less than a veritable thunderclap, and for the first time in his life he felt a need to modify his conservative theories as to the necessity of blue blood to nourish high ideals. Maria, indeed, seemed to him as she stood there, drawn fine and strong against the curtains of faded green, to hold about her something better than that aroma of the past which he had felt to be the intimate charm of all exquisite things, and it was at the moment the very light and promise of the future which he saw in the broad intelligence of her brow. Was it possible, after all, he questioned, that out of the tragic wreck of old claims and old customs which he had witnessed there should spring creatures of even finer fibre than those who had gone before?

"So this is your last word?" he inquired helplessly.

"My last word to you—yes. In a moment I am going out to see the Blakes—to make them understand."

He put out his hand as if to detain her by a feeble pull at her skirt.

"At least, you will sleep a night upon your resolution?"

"How can my sleeping alter things? My waking may."

"And you will sweep the claims of twenty years aside in an hour?"

"They are swept aside by the claims of two hundred."

With a courteous gesture he bent over her hand and raised it gravely to his lips.

"My dear young friend, you are very lovely and very unreasonable," he said.

CHAPTER VIII

Between Maria and Christopher

A LITTLE later, Maria, with a white scarf thrown over her head, came out of the Hall and passed swiftly along the road under the young green leaves which were putting out on the trees. When she reached the whitewashed gate before the Blake cottage she saw Christopher ploughing in the field on the left of the house, and turning into the little path which trailed through the tall weeds beside the "worm" fence, she crossed the yard and stood hesitating at the beginning of the open furrow he had left behind him. His gaze was bent upon the horses, and for a moment she watched him in attentive silence, her eyes dwelling on his massive figure, which cast a gigantic blue-black shadow across the April sunbeams. She saw him at the instant with a distinctness, a clearness of perception, that she had never been conscious of until to-day, as if each trivial detail in his appearance was magnified by the pale yellow sunshine through which she looked upon it. The abundant wheaten-brown hair, waving from the moist ircle drawn by the hat he had thrown aside, the strong masculine profile burned to a faint terra-cotta shade from wind and sun, and the powerful hands knotted and roughened by heavy labour, all stood out vividly in the mental image which remained with her when she lowered her eyes.

Aroused by a sound from the house, he looked up and saw her standing on the edge of the ploughed field, her lace scarf blown softly in the April wind. After a single minute of breathless surprise he tossed the long ropes on the ground, and, leaving the plough, came rapidly across the loose clods of upturned earth.

"Did you come because I was thinking of you?" he asked simply, with the natural directness which had appealed so strongly to her fearless nature.

"Were you thinking of me?" her faint smile shone on him for an instant; "and were your thoughts as grave, I wonder, as my reason for coming?"

"So you have a reason, then?"

"Did you think I should dare to come without one?"

The light wind caught her scarf, blowing the long ends about her head. From the frame of soft white lace her eyes looked dark and solemn and very distant.

"I had hoped that you had no other reason than— kindness." He had lost entirely the rustic restraint he had once felt in her presence, and, as he stood there in his clothes of dull blue jean, it was easy to believe in the gallant generations at his back. Was the fret of their gay adventures in his blood? she wondered.

"You will see the kindness in my reason, I hope," she answered quietly, while the glow of her sudden resolution illumined her face, "and at least you will admit the justice—though belated."

He drew a step nearer. "And it concerns you—and me?" he asked.

"It concerns you—oh, yes, yes, and me also, though very slightly. I have just learned—just a moment ago—what you must have thought I knew all along."

As he fell back she saw that he paled slowly beneath his sunburn.

"You have just learned—what?" he demanded.

"The truth," she replied; "as much of the truth as one may learn in an hour: how it came that you are here and I am there—at the Hall."

"At the Hall?" he repeated, and there was relief in the quick breath he drew; "I had forgotten the Hall."

"Forgotten it? Why, I thought it was your dream, your longing, your one great memory."

Smiling into her eyes, he shook his head twice before he answered.

"It was all that—once."

"Then it is not so now?" she asked, disappointed, "and what I have to tell you will lose half its value."

"So it is about the Hall?"

With one hand she held back the fluttering lace upon her bosom, while lifting the other she pointed across the ploughed fields to the old gray chimneys huddled amid the budding oaks.

"Does it not make you homesick to stand here and look at it?" she asked. "Think! For more than two hundred years your people lived there, and there is not a room within the house, nor a spot upon the land, that does not hold some sacred association for those of your name."

Startled by the passion in her words, he turned from the Hall at which he had been gazing.

"What do you mean?" he demanded imperatively. "What do you wish to say?"

"Look at the Hall and not at me while I tell you. It is this—now listen and do not turn from it for an instant. Blake Hall—I have just found it out— will come to me at grandfather's death, and when it does—when it does I shall return it to your family— the whole of it, every lovely acre. Oh, don't look at me—look at the Hall!"

But he looked neither at her nor at the Hall, for his gaze dropped to the ground and hung blankly upon a clod of dry brown earth. She saw him grow pale to the lips and dark blue circles come out slowly about his eyes.

"It is but common justice; you see that," she urged.

At this he raised his head and returned her look.

"And what of Will?" he asked.

Her surprise showed in her face, and at sight of it he repeated his question with a stubborn insistence: "But what of Will? What has been done for Will?"

"Oh, I don't know; I don't know. The break is past mending. But it is not of him that I must speak to you now—it is of yourself. Don't you see that the terrible injustice has bowed me to the earth? What am I better than a dependent—a charity ward who has lived for years upon your money? My very education, my little culture, the refinements you see in me—these even I have no real right to, for they belong to your family. While you have worked as a labourer in the field I have been busy squandering the wealth which was not mine."

His face grew gentle as he looked at her.

"If the Blake money has made you what you are, then it has not been utterly wasted," he replied.

"Oh, you don't understand—you don't understand," she repeated, pressing her hands upon her bosom, as if to quiet her fluttering breath. "You have suffered from it all along, but it is I who suffer most to-day—who suffer most because I am upon the side of the injustice. I can have no peace until you tell me that I may still do my poor best to make amends—that when your home is mine you will let me give it back to you."

"It is too late," he answered with bitter humour. "You can't put a field-hand in a fine house and make him a gentleman. It is too late to undo what was done twenty years ago. The place can never be mine again—I have even ceased to want it. Give it to Will."

"I couldn't if I wanted to," she replied; "but I don't want to—I don't want to. It must go back to you and to your sisters. Do you think I could ever be owner of it now? Even if it comes to me when I am an old woman, I shall always feel myself a stranger in the house, though I should live there day and night for fifty years. No, no; it is impossible that I should ever keep it for an instant. It must go back to you and to the Blakes who come after you."

"There will be no Blakes after me," he answered. "I am the last."

"Then promise me that if the Hall is ever mine you will take it."

"From you? No; not unless I took it to hand on to your brother. It is an old score that you have brought up—one that lasted twenty years before it was settled. It is too late to stir up matters now."

"It is not too late," she said earnestly. "It is never too late to try to undo a wrong."

"The wrong was not yours: it must never touch you," he replied. "If my life was as clean as yours, it would, perhaps, not be too late for me either. Ten years ago I might have felt differently about it, but not now."

He broke off hurriedly, and Maria, with a hopeless gesture, turned back into the path.

"Then I shall appeal to your sisters when the time comes," she responded quietly.

Catching the loose ends of her scarf, he drew her slowly around until she met his eyes. "And I have said nothing to you—to you," he began, in a constrained voice, which he tried in vain to steady, "because it is so hard to say anything and not say too much. This, at least, you must know—that I am your servant now and shall be all my life."

She smiled sadly, looking down at the scarf which was crushed in his hands.

"And yet you will not grant the wish of my heart," she said.

"How could I? Put me back in the Hall, and I should be as ignorant and as coarse as I am out here. A labourer is all I am and all I am fit to be. I once had a rather bookish ambition, you know, but that is over—I wanted to read Greek and translate 'The Iliad' and all that—and yet to-day I doubt if I could write a decent letter to save my soul. It's partly my fault, of course, but you can't know— you could never know—the abject bitterness and despair of those years when I tried to sink myself to the level of the brutes—tried to forget that I was any better than the oxen I drove. No, there's no pulling me up again; such things aren't lived over, and I'm down for good."

Her tears, which she had held back, broke forth at his words, and he saw them fall upon her bosom, where her hands were still tightly clasped.

"And it is all our fault," she said brokenly.

"Not yours, surely."

"It is not too late," she went on passionately, laying her hand upon his arm and looking up at him with a misty brightness. "Oh, if you would let me make amends—let me help you!"

"Is there any help?" he asked, with his eyes on the hand upon his arm.

"If you will let me, I will find it. We will take up your study where you broke it off—we will come up step by step, even to Homer, if you like. I am fond of books, you know, and I have had my fancy for Greek, too. Oh, it will be so easy—so easy; and when the time comes for you to go back to the Hall, I shall have made you the most learned Blake of the whole line."

He bent quickly and kissed the hand which trembled on his sleeve.

"Make of me what you please," he said; "I am at your service."

For the second time he saw the wonderful light— the fervour—illumine her face, and then fade slowly, leaving a still, soft radiance of expression.

"Then I may teach you all that you haven't learned," she said with a happy little laugh. "How fortunate that I should have been born a bookworm. Shall we begin with Greek?"

He smiled. "No; let's start with English—and start low."

"Then we'll do both; but where shall it be? Not at the Hall."

"Hardly. There's a bench, though, down by the poplar spring that looks as if it were meant to be in school. Do you know the place? It's in my pasture by the meadow brook?"

"I can find it, and I'll bring the books to-morrow at this hour. Will you come?"

"To-morrow—and every day?"

"Every day."

For an instant he looked at her in perplexity. "I may as well tell you," he said at last, "that I'm one of the very biggest rascals on God's earth. I'm not worth all this, you know; that's honest."

"And so are you," she called back gaily, as she turned from him and went rapidly along the little path.

CHAPTER IX

CHRISTOPHER FACES HIMSELF

WHEN she had gone through the gate and across the little patch of trodden grass into the sunken road, Christopher took up the ropes and with a quick jerk of the buried ploughshare began his plodding walk over the turned-up sod. The furrow was short, but when he reached the end of it he paused from sheer exhaustion and stood wiping the heavy moisture from his brow. The scene through which he had just passed had left him quivering in every nerve, as if he had been engaged in some terrible struggle against physical odds. All at once he became aware that the afternoon was too oppressive for field work, and, unhitching the horses from the plough, he led them slowly back to the stable beyond the house. As he went, it seemed to him that he had grown middle-aged within the hour; his youth had departed as mysteriously as his strength.

A little later, Tucker, who was sitting on the end of a big log at the woodpile, looked up in surprise from the ant-hill he was watching.

"Quit work early, eh, Christopher?"

"Yes; I've given out," replied Christopher, stopping beside him and picking up the axe which lay in a scattered pile of chips. "It's the spring weather, I

423

reckon, but I'm not fit for a tougher job than chopping wood."

"Well, I'd leave that off just now, if I were you."

Raising the axe, Christopher swung it lightly over his shoulder; then, lowering it with a nerveless movement, he tossed it impatiently on the ground.

"A queer thing happened just now, Uncle Tucker," he said, "a thing you'll hardly believe even when I tell you. I had a visit from Mrs. Wyndham, and she came to say——" he stammered and broke off abruptly.

"Mrs. Wyndham?" repeated Tucker. "She's Bill Fletcher's granddaughter, isn't she?"

"Maria Fletcher—you may have seen her when she lived here, five or six years ago."

Tucker shook his head.

" Bless your heart, my boy, I haven't seen a woman except Lucy and the girls for twenty-five years. But why did she come, I wonder?"

" That's the strange part, and you won't understand it until you see her. She came because she had just heard—some one had told her—about Fletcher's old rascality."

"You don't say so!" exclaimed Tucker beneath his breath. He gave a long whistle and sat smiling at the little red ant-hill. "And did she actually proffer an apology?" he inquired.

"An amendment, rather. The Hall will come to her at Fletcher's death, and she walked over to say quite coolly that she wanted to give it back to us. Think of that! To part with such a home for the sake of mere right and justice."

"It is something to think about," assented Tucker,

"and to think hard about, too—and yet I cut my teeth on the theory that women have no sense of honour. Now, that is pure, foolish, strait-laced honour, and nothing else."

"Nothing else," repeated Christopher softly; "and if you'll believe it, she cried—she really cried when I told her I couldn't take it. Oh, she's wonderful!" he burst out suddenly, all his awkward reserve dropping from him. "You can't be with her ten minutes without feeling how good she is—good all through, with a big goodness that isn't in the least like the little prudishness of other women——"

He checked himself hastily, but not before Tucker had glanced up with his pleasant smile.

"Well, my boy, I don't misunderstand you. I never knew a man yet to begin a love affair with a panegyric on virtue. She's an estimable woman, I dare say, and I presume she's plain."

"Plain!" gasped Christopher. "Why, she's beautiful—at least, you think so when you see her smile."

"So she smiled through her tears, eh?"

Christopher started angrily. "Can you sit there on that log and laugh at such a thing?" he demanded.

"Come, come," protested Tucker, "an honest laugh never turned a sweet deed sour since the world began—and that was more than sweet; it was fine. I'd like to know that woman, Christopher."

"You could never know her—no man could. She's all clear and bright on the surface, but all mystery beneath."

"Ah, that's it; you see, there was never a fascinating woman yet who was easy to understand. Wasn't it that shrewd old gallant, Bolivar Blake, who said that in love an ounce of mystery was worth a pound of morality?"

"It's like him: he said a lot of nonsense," commented Christopher. "But to think," he added after a moment, "that she should be Bill Fletcher's granddaughter!"

"Well, I knew her mother," returned Tucker, "and she was as honest, God-fearing a body as ever trod this earth. She stood out against Fletcher to the last, you know, and worked hard for her living while that scamp, her husband, drank them both to death. There are some people who are born with a downright genius for honesty, and this girl may be one of them."

"I don't know—I don't know," said Christopher, in a voice which had grown spiritless. Then after an instant in which he stared blankly down at Tucker's ant-hill, he turned hurriedly away and followed the little straggling path to the barn door.

From the restlessness that pricked in his limbs there was no escape, and after entering the barn he came out again and went down into the pasture to the long bench beside the poplar spring. Here, while the faint shadows of the young leaves played over him, he sat with his head bent forward and his hands dropped listlessly between his knees.

Around him there was the tender green of the spring meadows, divided by a little brook where the willows shone pure silver under the April wind. Near at hand a catbird sang in short, tripping notes, and in the clump of briars by the spring a rabbit sat alert for the first sound. So motionless was Christopher that he seemed, sitting there by the pale gray body of a poplar, almost to become a part of the tree against which he leaned—to lose, for the time at least, his share in the moving animal life around him.

At first there was mere blankness in his mind—an absence of light and colour in which his thoughts were suddenly blotted out; then, as the wind raised the hair upon his brow, he lifted his eyes from the ground, and with the movement it seemed as if his life ran backward to its beginning and he saw himself not as he was to-day, but as he might have been in a period of time which had no being.

Before him were his knotted and blistered hands, his long limbs outstretched in their coarse clothes, but in the vision beyond the little spring he walked proudly with his rightful heritage upon him—a Blake by force of blood and circumstance. The world lay before him—bright, alluring, a thing of enchanting promise, and it was as if he looked for the first time upon the possibilities contained in this life upon the earth. For an instant the glow lasted —the beauty dwelt upon the vision, and he beheld, clear and radiant, the happiness which might have been his own; then it grew dark again, and he faced the brutal truth in all its nakedness: he knew himself for what he was—a man debased by ignorance and passion to the level of the beasts. He had sold his birthright for a requital, which had sickened him even in the moment of fulfilment.

To do him justice, now that the time had come for an acknowledgment he felt no temptation to evade the judgment of his own mind, nor to cheat himself with the belief that the boy was marked for ruin before he saw him—that Will had worked out, in vicious weakness, his own end. It was not the weakness, after all, that he had played upon—it was rather the excitable passion and the whimpering fears of the hereditary drunkard. He remembered now the long days that he had given to his revenge, the nights when he had tossed sleepless while he planned a widening of the breach with Fletcher. That, at, least was his work, and his alone—the bitter hatred, more cruel than death, with which the two now stood apart and snarled. It was a human life that he had taken in his hand—he saw that now in his first moment of awakening—a life that he had destroyed as deliberately as if he had struck it dead before him. Day by day, step by step, silent, unswerving, devilish, he had kept about his purpose, and now at the last he had only to sit still and watch his triumph.

With a sob, he bowed his head in his clasped hands, and so shut out the light.

CHAPTER X

By the Poplar Spring

THE next day he watched for her anxiously until she appeared over the low brow of the hill, her arms filled with books, and Agag trotting at her side. As she descended slowly into the broad ravine where he awaited her under the six great poplars that surrounded the little spring, he saw that she wore a dress of some soft, creamy stuff and a large white hat that shaded her brow and eyes. She looked younger, he noticed, than she had done in her black gown, and he recalled while she neared him the afternoon more than six years before when she had come suddenly upon him while he worked in his tobacco.

"So you are present at the roll-call?" she said, laughing, as she sat down on the bench beside him and spread out the books that she had brought.

"Why, I've been sitting here for half an hour," he answered.

"What a shame—that's a whole furrow unploughed, isn't it?"

"Several of them; but I'm not counting furrows now. I'm getting ready to appal you by my ignorance." He spoke with a determined, reckless gaiety that lent a peculiar animation to his face.

"If you are waiting for that, you are going to be

disappointed," she replied, smiling, "for I've put my heart into the work, and I was born and patterned for a teacher; I always knew it. We're going to do English literature and a first book in Latin."

"Are we?" He picked up the Latin grammar and ran his fingers lightly through the pages. "I went a little way in this once," he said. "I got as far as *omnia vincit amor* and stopped. Tobacco conquered me instead."

She caught up his gay laugh. "Well, we'll try it over again," she returned, and held out the book.

An hour later, when the first lesson was over and he had gone back to his work, he carried with him a wonderful exhilaration—a feeling as if he had with a sudden effort burst the bonds that had held him to the earth. By the next day the elation vanished and a great heaviness came in its place, but for a single afternoon he had known what it was to thrill in every fibre with a powerful and pure emotion—an emotion beside which all the cheap sensations of his life showed stale and colourless. While the strangeness of this mood was still upon him he chanced upon Lila and Jim Weatherby standing together by the gate in the gray dusk, and when presently the girl came back alone across the yard he laid his hand upon her arm and drew her over to Tucker's bench beside the rose-bush.

"Lila, I've changed my mind about it all," he said.

"About what, dear?"

"About Jim and you. We were all wrong—all of us except Uncle Tucker—wrong from the very start. You musn't mind mother; you musn't mind anybody. Marry Jim and be happy, if he can make you so."

"Oh, Christopher!" gasped Lila, with a long breath, lifting her lovely, pensive face. "Oh, Christopher!"

"Don't wait; don't put it off; don't listen to any of us," he urged impatiently. "Good God! If you love him as you say you do, why have you let all these years slip away?"

"But you thought it was best, Christopher. You told me so."

"Best! There's nothing best except to be happy if you get the chance."

"He wants me to marry him now," said Lila, lowering her voice. "Mother will never know, he thinks, her mind grows so feeble; he wants me to marry him without any getting ready—after church one Sunday morning."

Putting his arm about her, Christopher held her for a moment against his side. "Then do it," he said gravely, as he stooped and kissed her.

And several weeks later, on a bright first Sunday in May, Lila was married, after morning services, in the little country church, and Christopher watched her almost eagerly as she walked home across the broad meadows powdered white with daisies. To the reproachful countenance which Cynthia presented to him upon his return to the house he gave back a careless and defiant smile.

"So it's all over," he announced gaily, "and Lila's married at last."

"Then you're satisfied, I hope," rejoined Cynthia grimly, "now that you've dragged us down to the level of the Weatherbys and—the Fletchers? There's nothing more to be said about it, I suppose, and you may as well come in to dinner."

She held herself stiffly aloof from the subject, with her head flung back and her chin expressing an indignant protest. There was a kind of rebellious scorn in the way in which she carved the shoulder of bacon and poured the coffee.

"Good Lord! It's such a little thing to make a fuss about," said Tucker, "when you remember, my dear, that our levels aren't any bigger than chalk lines in the eyes of God Almighty."

Cynthia regarded him with squinting displeasure.

"Oh, of course; you have no family pride," she returned; "but I had thought there was a little left in Christopher."

Christopher shook his head, smiling indifferently. "Not enough to want blood sacrifices," he responded, and fell into a detached and thoughtful silence. The vision of Lila in her radiant happiness remained with him like a picture that one has beheld by some rare chance in a vivid and lovely light; and it was still before him when he left the house presently and strolled slowly down to meet Maria by the poplar spring.

The bloom of the meadows filled his nostrils with a delicate fragrance, and from the bough of an old apple-tree in the orchard he heard the low afternoon murmurs of a solitary thrush. May was on the earth, and it had entered into him as into the piping birds and the spreading trees. It was at last good to be alive—to breathe the warm, sweet air, and to watch the sunshine slanting on the low, green hill. So closely akin were his moods to those of the changing seasons that, at the instant, he seemed to feel the current of his being flow from the earth beneath his feet—as if his physical nature drew strength and nourishment from that genial and abundant source.

When he reached the spring he saw Maria appear on the brow of the hill, and with a quick, joyous bound his heart leaped up to meet her. As she came toward him her white dress swept the tall grass from her feet, and her shadow flew like a winged creature straight before her. There was a vivid softness in her face—a look at once bright and wistful —which moved him with a new and strange tenderness.

"I was a little late," she explained, as they met before the long bench and she laid her books upon it, "and I am very warm. May I have a drink?"

"From a bramble cup?"

"How else?" She took off her hat and tossed it on the grass at her feet; then, going to the spring, she waited while he plucked a leaf from the bramble and bent it into shape. When he filled it and held it out, she placed her lips to the edge of the leaf and looked up at him with smiling eyes while she drank slowly from his hand.

"It holds only a drop, but how delicious!" she said, seating herself again upon the bench and leaning back against the great body of a poplar. Then her eyes fell upon his clothes. "Why, how very much dressed you look!" she added.

"Oh, there's a reason besides Sunday—I've just come from a wedding. Lila has married after twelve years of waiting."

"Your pretty sister! And to whom?"

"To Jim Weatherby—old Jacob's son, you know. Now, don't tell me that you disapprove. I count on your good sense to see the wisdom of it."

"So it is your pretty sister," she said slowly, "the woman I passed in the road the other day and held my breath as I did before Botticelli's Venus."

"Is that so? Well, she doesn't know much about pictures, nor does Jim. She has thrown herself away, Cynthia says, but what could she have waited for, after all? Nothing had ever come to her, and she had lived thirty years. Besides, she will be very happy, and that's a good deal, isn't it?"

"It's everything," said Maria quietly, looking down into her lap.

"Everything? And if you had been born in her place?"

"I am not in her place and never could be; but six years ago, if I had been told that I must live here all my life, I think I should have fretted myself to death: that would have happened six years ago, for I was born with a great aching for life, and I thought then that one could live only in the big outside world——"

"And now?" he questioned, for she paused and sat smiling gravely at the book she held.

"Now I know that the fulness of life does not come from the things outside of us, and that we ourselves must create the beauty in which we live. Oh, I have learned so much from misery," she went on softly, "and worst of all, I have learned what it is to starve for bread in the midst of sugar-plums."

"And it was worth learning?"

"The knowledge that I gained? Oh, yes, yes; for it taught me how to be happy. I went down into hell," she said passionately, "and I came out—clean. I saw evil such as I had never heard of; I went close to it, I even touched it, but I always kept my soul very far away, and I was like a person in a dream. The more I saw of sin and ugliness the more I dreamed of peace and beauty. I builded me my own refuge, I fed on my own strength day and night—and I am what I am——"

"The loveliest woman on God's earth," he said.

"You do not know me," she answered, and opened the book before her. "It was the story of the Holy Grail," she added, "and we left off here. Oh, those brave days of King Arthur! It was always May then."

He touched the page lightly with a long blade of grass.

"Read yourself—this once," he pleaded, "and let me listen."

Leaning a little forward, she looked down and slowly turned the pages, her head bent over the book, her long lashes shading the faint flush in her cheeks. Over her white dress fell a delicate lacework from the young poplar leaves, flecked here and there with pale drops of sunshine, which filtered through the thickly clustered boughs. When the wind passed in the high tree-tops, the shadows, soft and fine as cobweb, rippled over her dress, and a loose strand of her dark hair waved gently about her ear. The life—the throbbing vitality within her seemed to vivify the very air she breathed, and he felt all at once that the glad thrill which stirred his blood was but a response to the fervent spirit which spoke in her voice.

"*For it giveth unto all lovers courage, that lusty month of May*," she read, "*in something to constrain him to some manner of thing more in that month than in any other month—for then all herbs and trees renew a man and woman, and in likewise lovers call again to mind old gentleness and old service and many kind deeds that were forgotten by negligence.*"

The words went like wine to his head, and he saw her shadowy figure recede and dissolve suddenly as in a mist. A lump rose in his throat, his heart leaped, and he felt his pulses beating madly in his temples. He drew back, closing his eyes to shut out her face; but the next instant, as she stirred slightly to hold down the rippling leaves, he bent forward and laid his hand upon the one that held the open book.

Her voice fluttered into silence, and, raising her head, she looked up in tremulous surprise. He saw her face pale slowly, her lids quiver and droop above her shining eyes, and her teeth gleam milk white between her parted lips. A tremor of alarm ran through her, and she made a swift movement to escape; then, lifting her eyes again, she looked full into his own, and, stooping quickly, he kissed her on the mouth.

An instant afterward the book fell to the ground, and he rose to his feet and stood trembling against the body of the poplar.

"Forgive me," he said; "forgive me—I have ruined it."

Standing beside the bench, she watched him with a still, grave gentleness before which his gaze dropped slowly to the ground.

"Yes, you have ruined this," she answered, smiling, "but Latin is still left."

"It's no use," he went on breathlessly. "I can't do it; it's no use."

His eyes sought hers and held them while he made a single step forward; then, turning quickly away, he went from her across the meadow to the distant wood.

Book Five
The Ancient Law

THE ANCIENT LAW

CHAPTER I

CHRISTOPHER SEEKS AN ESCAPE

A CLUMP of brambles caught at his feet, and, stumbling like a drunken man, he threw himself at full length upon the ground, pressing his forehead on the young, green thorns. A century seemed to have passed since his flight from the poplar spring, and yet the soft afternoon sunshine was still about him and the low murmurs of the thrush still floated from the old apple-tree. All the violence of his undisciplined nature had rushed into revolt against the surrender which he felt must come, and he was conscious at the instant that he hated only a little less supremely than he loved. In the end the greater passion would triumph over him, he knew; but as he lay there face downward upon the earth the last evil instincts of his revenge battled against the remorse which had driven him from Maria's presence. He saw himself clearly for what he was: he had learned at last to call his sin by its right name; and yet he felt that somewhere in the depths of his being he had not ceased to love the evil that he had done. He hated Fletcher, he told himself, as righteously as ever, but between himself and the face of his enemy a veil had fallen—the old wrong no longer stood out in a blaze of light. A woman's smile divided him like a drawn sword from his brutal past, and he had lost the reckless courage with which he once might have flung himself upon destruction.

Rising presently, he crossed the meadow and went slowly back to his work in the stables, keeping his thoughts with an effort upon his accustomed tasks. A great weariness for the endless daily round of small things was upon him, and he felt all at once that the emotion struggling within his heart must burst forth at last and pervade the visible world. He was conscious of an impulse to sing, to laugh, to talk in broken sentences to himself; and any utterance, however slight and meaningless, seemed to relieve in a measure the nervous tension of his thoughts.

In one instant there entered into him a desperate determination to play the traitor—to desert his post and strike out boldly and alone into the world. And with the next breath he saw himself living to old age as he had lived from boyhood—within reach of Maria's hand, meeting her fervent eyes, and yet separated from her by a distance greater than God or man could bridge. With the thought of her he saw again her faint smile which lingered always about her mouth, and his blood stirred at the memory of the kiss which she had neither resisted nor returned.

Cynthia, searching for him a few minutes later, found him leaning idly against the mare's stall, looking down upon a half-finished nest which a house-wren had begun to build upon his currycomb.

"It's a pity to disturb that, Tucker would say,"

he observed, motioning toward the few wisps of straw on the ledge.

"Oh, she can start it somewhere else," replied Cynthia indifferently. "They have sent for you from the store, Christopher—it's something about one of the servants, I believe. They're always getting into trouble and wanting you to pull them out." The descendants of the old Blake slaves were still spoken of by Cynthia as "the servants," though they had been free men and women for almost thirty years.

Christopher started from his abstraction and turned toward her with a gesture of annoyance.

"Well, I'll have to go down, I suppose," he said. "Has mother asked for me to-day?"

"Only for Jim again—it's always Jim now. I declare, I believe we might all move away and she'd never know the difference so long as he was left. She forgets us entirely sometimes, and fancies that father is alive again."

"It's a good thing Jim amuses her, at any rate."

An expression of anger drew Cynthia's brows together. "Oh, I dare say; but it does seem hard that she should have grown to dislike me after all I've done for her. There are times when she won't let me even come in the room—when she's not herself, you know."

Her words were swallowed in a sob, and he stood staring at her in an amazement too sudden to be mixed with pity.

"And you have given up your whole life to her," he exclaimed. appalled by the injustice of the god of sacrifice.

Cynthia put up one knotted hand and stroked back the thin hair upon her temples. "It was all I had to give," she answered, and went out into the yard.

He let her go from him without replying, and before her pathetic figure had reached the house she was blotted entirely from his thoughts, for it was a part of the tragedy of her unselfishness that she had never existed as a distinct personality even in the minds of those who knew and loved her.

When presently he passed through the yard on his way to the store, he saw her taking in the dried clothes from the old lilac-bushes and called back carelessly that he would be home to supper. Then, forgetting her lesser miseries in his own greater one, he fell into his troubled brooding as he swung rapidly along the road.

At the store the usual group of loungers welcomed him, and among them he saw to his surprise the cheerful face of Jim Weatherby, a little clouded by the important news he was evidently seeking to hold back.

"I tried to keep them from sending for you, Christopher," the young man explained. "It is no business of yours—that is what I said."

"Well, it seems that every thriftless nigger in the county thinks he's got a claim upon you, sho' enough," put in Tom Spade. "It warn't mo'n last week that I had a letter from the grandson of yo' pa's old blacksmith Buck, sayin' he was to hang in Philadelphia for somebody's murder, an' that I must tell Marse Christopher to come an' git him off. Thar's a good six hunnard of 'em, black an' yaller an' it's God A'mighty or Marse Christopher to 'em every one."

"What is it now?" asked Christopher a little wearily, taking off his hat and running his hand through his thick, fair hair. "If anybody's been stealing chickens they've got to take the consequences."

"Oh, it's not chicken stealin' this time; it's a blamed sight worse. They want you to send somebody over to Uncle Isam's—you remember his little cabin, five miles off in Morse's woods—to help him bury his children who have died of smallpox. There are four of 'em dead, it seems, an' the rest are all down with the disease. Thar's not a morsel of food in the house, an' not a livin' nigger will go nigh 'em."

"Uncle Isam!" repeated Christopher, as if trying to recall the name. "Why, I haven't laid eyes upon the man for years."

"Very likely; but he's sent you a message by a boy who was gathering pine knots at the foot of his hill. He was to tell Marse Christopher that he had had nothing to eat for two whole days an' his children were unburied. Then the boy got scared an' scampered off, an' that was all."

Christopher's laugh sounded rather brutal.

"So he used to belong to us, did he?" he inquired.

"He was yo' pa's own coachman. I recollect him plain as day," answered Tom. "I warn't mo'n a child then, an' he used to flick his whip at my bare legs whenever he passed me in the road."

"Well, what is to be done?" asked Christopher, turning suddenly upon him.

"The Lord He knows, suh. Thar's not a nigger as will go nigh him, an' I'm not blamin' 'em; not I. Jim's filled his cart with food, an' he's goin' to dump the things out at the foot of the hill; then maybe Uncle Isam can crawl down an' drag 'em back. His wife's down with it, too, they say. She was workin' here not mo'n six months ago, but she left her place of a sudden an' went back again."

Christopher glanced carelessly at the little cart waiting in the road, and then throwing off his coat tossed it on the seat.

"I'll trouble you to lend me your overalls, Tom," he said, "and you can send a boy up to the house and get mine in exchange. Put what medicines you have in the cart ; I'll take them over to the old fool."

"Good Lord !" said Tom, and mechanically got out of his blue jean clothes.

"Now don't be a downright ass, Christopher," put in Jim Weatherby. "You've got your mother on your hands, you know, and what under heaven have you to do with Uncle Isam? I knew some foolishness would most likely come of it if they sent up for you."

"Oh, he used to belong to us, you see," explained Christopher carelessly.

"And he's been an ungrateful, thriftless free negro for nearly thirty years——"

"That's just it—for not quite thirty years. Look here, if you'll drive me over in the cart and leave the things at the foot of the hill I'll be obliged to you. I'll probably have to stay out a couple of weeks—until there's no danger of my bringing back the disease—so I'll wear Tom's overalls and leave my clothes somewhere in the woods. Oh, I'll take care, of course ; I'm no fool."

"You're surer of that than I am," returned Jim, thinking of Lila. "I can't help feeling that there's some truth in father's saying that a man can't be a hero without being a bit of a fool as well. For God's sake, don't, Christopher. You have no right——"

"No, I have no right," repeated Christopher, as he got into the cart and took up the hanging reins. A sudden animation had leaped into his face and his eyes were shining. It was the old love of a "risk for the sake of the risk" which to Tucker had always seemed to lack the moral elements of true courage, and the careless gaiety with which he spoke robbed the situation of its underlying sombre horror.

Jim swung himself angrily upon the seat and touched the horse lightly with the whip. "And there's your mother sitting at home—and Cynthia—and Lila," he said.

Christopher turned on him a face in whose expression he found a mystery that he could not solve.

"I can't help it, Jim, to save my life I can't," he answered. "It isn't anything heroic; you know that as well as I. I don't care a straw for Uncle Isam and his children, but if I didn't go up there and bury those dead darkies I'd never have a moment's peace. I've been everything but a skulking coward, and I can't turn out to be that at the end. It's the way I'm made."

"Well, I dare say we're made different," responded Jim rather dryly, for it was his wedding day and he was going farther from his bride. "But for my part,

I can't help thinking of that poor blind old lady, and how helpless they all are. Yes, we're made different. I reckon that's what it means."

The cart jogged on slowly through the fading sunshine, and when at last it came to the foot of the hill where Uncle Isam lived Christopher got out and shouldered a bag of meal.

"You'll run the place, I know, and look after mother while I'm away," he said.

"Oh, I suppose I'll have to," returned Jim; and then his ill-humour vanished and he smiled and held out his hand. "Good-by, old man. God bless you," he said heartily.

Sitting there in the road, he watched Christopher pass out of sight under the green leaves, stooping slightly beneath the bag of meal and whistling a merry scrap of an old song. At the instant it came to Jim with the force of a blow that this was the first cheerful sound he had heard from him for weeks; and, still pondering, he turned the horse's head and drove slowly home to his own happiness.

CHAPTER II

THE MEASURE OF MARIA

WHEN, two weeks later, Christopher reached home again, he was met by Tucker's gentle banter and Lila's look of passionate reproach.

"Oh, dear, you might have died!" breathed the girl with a shudder.

Christopher laughed.

"So might Uncle Tucker when he went into the war," was his retort. He was a little thinner, a little graver, and the sunburn upon his face had faded to a paler shade. After the short absence his powerful figure struck them as almost gigantic; physically, he had never appeared more impressive than he did standing there in the sunlight that filled the kitchen doorway.

"But that was different," protested Lila, flushing, "and this—this—why, you hardly knew Uncle Isam when you passed him in the road."

"And half the time forgot to speak to him," added Tucker, laughing. His eyes were on the young man's figure, and they grew a little wistful, as they always did in the presence of perfect masculine strength. "Well, I'm glad your search for adventures didn't end in disaster," he added pleasantly.

To Christopher's surprise, Cynthia was the single

member of the family who showed a sympathy with his reckless knight errantry. "There was nothing else for you to do, of course," she said in a resolute voice, lifting her worn face where the lines had deepened in his absence; "he used to be father's coachman before the war."

She had gone from the kitchen as she spoke, and Christopher, following her, threw an anxious glance along the little platform to the closed door of the house.

"And mother, Cynthia?" he asked quickly.

"Her mind still wanders, but at times she seems to come back to herself for a little while, and only this morning she awoke from a nap and asked for you quite clearly. We told her you had gone hunting."

"May I see her now? Who is with her?"

"Jim. He has been so good."

The admission was wrung shortly from her rigid honesty, and there was no visible softening of her grim reserve, when, entering the house with Christopher, she found herself presently beside Jim Weatherby, who was chatting merrily in Mrs. Blake's room.

The old lady, shrivelled and faded as the dried goldenrod which filled the great jars on the hearth, lay half hidden among the pillows in her high white bed, her vacant eyes fixed upon the sunshine which fell through the little window. At Christopher's step her memory flickered back for an instant, and the change showed in the sudden animation of her glance.

"I was dreaming of your father, my son, and you have his voice."

"I am like him in other ways, I hope, mother."

"If I could only see you, Christopher—it is so hard to remember. You had golden curls and wore a white pinafore. I trimmed it with the embroidery from my last set of petticoats. And your hands were dimpled all over; you *would* suck your thumb: there was no breaking you, though I wrapped it in a rag soaked in quinine——"

"That was almost thirty years ago, mother," broke in Cynthia, catching her breath sharply. "He is a man now, and big—oh, so big—and his hair has grown a little darker."

"I know, Cynthia; I know," returned Mrs. Blake, with a peevish movement of her thin hand, "but you won't let me remember. I am trying to remember." She fell to whimpering like a hurt child, and then growing suddenly quiet, reached out until she touched Christopher's head. "You're a man, I know," she said, "older than your father was when his first child was born. There have been two crosses in my life, Christopher—my blindness and my never having heard the voices of my grandchildren playing in the house. Such a roomy old house, too, with so much space for them to fill with cheerful noise. I always liked noise, you know; it tells of life, and never disturbs me so long as it is pleasant. What I hate is the empty silence that reminds one of the grave."

She was quite herself now, and, bending over, he kissed the hand upon the counterpane.

"Oh, mother, mother, if I could only have made you happy!"

"And you couldn't, Christopher?"

"I couldn't marry, dear; I couldn't."

"There was no one, you mean—no woman whom you could have loved and who would have given you children. Surely there are still good and gentle women left in the world."

"There was none for me."

She sighed hopelessly.

"You have never—never had a low fancy, Christopher?"

"Never, mother."

"Thank God; it is one thing I could not forgive. A gentleman may have his follies, your father used to say, but he must never stoop for them. Let him keep to his own level, even in his indiscretions. Ah, your father had his faults, my son, but he never forgot for one instant in his life that he was born a gentleman. He was a good husband, too, a good husband, and I was married to him for nearly forty years. The greatest trial of my marriage was that he would throw his cigar ashes on the floor. Women think so much of little things, you know, and I've always felt that I should have been a happier woman if he had learned to use an ash-tray. But he never would—he never would, though I gave him one every Christmas for almost forty years."

Falling silent, her hands played fitfully upon the counterpane, and when next she spoke the present had slipped from her and her thoughts had gone back to her early triumphs.

She wandered aimlessly and waveringly on in a feeble vacancy, and Christopher, after watching her for an agonised moment, left the room and went out into the fresh air of the yard. He could always escape by flight from the slow death-bed;

it was Cynthia who faced hourly the final tragedy of a long and happy life.

The thought of Will had oppressed him like a nightmare for the last two weeks, and it was almost unconsciously that he turned now in the direction of the store and passed presently into the shaded lane leading to Sol Peterkin's. His mood was heavy upon him, and so deep was the abstraction in which he walked that it was only when he heard his name called softly from a little distance that he looked up to find Maria Fletcher approaching him over the pale gray shadows in the road. Her eyes were luminous, and she stretched her hand toward him in a happy gesture.

"Oh, if you only knew how wonderful I think you!" she cried impulsively.

He held her hand an instant, and then letting it fall, withdrew his gaze slowly from her exalted look. The pure heights of her fervour were beyond the reach of his more earthly level, and as he turned from her some old words of her own were respoken in his ears: "Faith and doubt are mere empty forms until we pour out the heart's blood that vivifies them." It was her heart's blood that she had put into her dreams, and it was this, he told himself, that gave her mystic visions their illusive appearance of reality. Beauty enveloped her as an atmosphere; it softened her sternest sacrifice, it coloured her barest outlook, it transformed daily the common road in which she walked, and hourly it sustained and nourished her, as it nourished poor, crippled Tucker on his old pine bench. The eye of the spirit was theirs—this Christopher had learned at last; and he had learned, also, that for him there still remained only the weak, blurred vision of the flesh.

"You make me feel the veriest hypocrite," he said at the end of the long pause.

She shook her head. "And that you are surely not."

"So you still believe in me?"

"It's not belief—I *know* in you."

"Well, don't praise me; don't admire me; don't pretend, for God's sake, that I'm anything better than the brute you see."

"I don't pretend anything better," she protested; "and when you talk like this it only makes me feel the more keenly your wonderful courage."

"I haven't any," he burst out almost angrily. "Not an atom, do you hear? Whatever I may appear on top, at bottom I am a great skulking coward, and nothing more. Why, I couldn't even stay and take my punishment the other day. I sneaked off like a hound."

"Your punishment?" she faltered, and he saw her lashes tremble.

"For the other day—for the afternoon by the poplar spring. I've been wanting to beg your pardon on my knees."

Her lashes were raised steadily, and she regarded him gravely while a slight frown gathered her dark brows. She was still humanly feminine enough to find the apology harder to forgive than the offense.

"Oh, I had forgotten," she said a little coldly. "So that was, after all, why you ran away?"

"It was not the only reason."

"**And the other?**"

He closed his eyes suddenly and drew back.

"I ran away because I knew if I stayed I should do it again within two seconds," he replied.

A little blue flower was growing in the red clay wheel-rut at her feet, and, stooping, she caressed it gently without plucking it.

"It was very foolish," she said in a quiet voice; "but I had forgotten it, and you should have let it rest. Afterward, you did such a brave, splendid thing."

"I did nothing but run from you," he persisted, losing his head. "If I hadn't gone to Uncle Isam I'd have done something equally reckless in a different way. I wanted to get away from you—to escape you, but I couldn't—I couldn't. You were with me always, night and day, in those God-forsaken woods. I never lost you for one instant, never. I tried to, but I couldn't."

"You couldn't," she repeated, and, rising, faced him calmly. Then before the look in his eyes her own wavered and fell slowly to the ground, and he saw her quiver and grow white as if a rough wind blew over her. With an effort he steadied himself and turned away.

"There is but one thing to do," he said, holding his breath in the pause; "it's a long story, but if you will listen patiently—and it is very long—I will tell you all." Following him, she crossed the carpet of pine needles and sat down upon the end of a fallen log.

"Tell me nothing that you do not care to," she answered, and sat waiting.

"It began long ago, when we were both little

children," he went on, and then going back from her into the lane he stood staring down upon the little blue flower blooming in the wheel-rut. She saw his shadow, stretching across the road, blurred into the pale dusk of the wood, uncertain, sombre, gigantic in its outline. His hat was lying on the ground at her feet, and, lifting it, she ran her fingers idly along the brim.

For a time the silence lasted; then coming back to her, he sat down on the log and dropped his clasped hands between his knees. She heard his heavy breathing, and something in the sound drew her toward him with a sympathetic movement.

"Ah, don't tell me, don't tell me," she entreated.

"You must listen patiently," he returned, without looking at her, "and not interrupt—above all, not interrupt."

She bent her head. "I will not speak a word nor move a finger until the end," she promised; and leaning a little forward, with his eyes on the ground and his hands hanging listlessly between his knees, he began his story.

The air was so still that his voice sounded strangely harsh in the silence, but presently she heard the soughing of the pine trees far up above, and while it lasted it deadened the jarring discord of the human tones. She sat quite motionless upon the log, not lifting a finger nor speaking a word, as she had promised, and her gaze was fixed steadily upon a bit of dried fern growing between the roots of a dead tree.

"It went on so for five years," he slowly finished, "and it was from beginning to end deliberate,

devilish revenge. I meant from the first to make
him what he is to-day. I meant to make him hate
his grandfather as he does—I meant to make him the
hopeless drunkard that he is. It is all my work—
every bit of it—as you see it now."

He paused, but her eyes clung to the withered
fern, and so quiet was her figure that it seemed as
if she had not drawn breath since he began. Her
faint smile was still sketched about the corners of
her mouth, and her fingers were closed upon the
brim of his harvest hat.

"For five years I was like that," he went on again.
"I did not know, I did not care—I wanted to be
a beast. Then you came and it was different."

For the first time she turned and looked at him.

"And it was different?" she repeated beneath her
breath.

"Oh, there's nothing to say that will make things
better: I know that. If you had not come I should
never have known myself nor what I had been.
It was like a thunderclap—the whole thing; it shook
me off my feet before I saw what it meant—
before I would acknowledge even to myself that——"

"That?" she questioned in a whisper, for he had
bitten back the words.

"That I love you."

As he spoke she slipped suddenly to her knees and
lay with her face hidden on the old log, while her
smothered sobs ran in long shudders through her
body. A murmur reached him presently, and it
seemed to him that she was praying softly in her
clasped hands; but when in a new horror of himself
he made a movement to rise and slip away, she

looked up and gently touched him detainingly on the arm.

"Oh, how unhappy—how unhappy you have been!" she said.

"It is not that I mind," he answered. "If I could take all the misery of it I shouldn't care, but I have made you suffer, and for the sin that is mine alone."

For a moment she was silent, breathing quickly between parted lips; then turning with an impulsive gesture, she laid her cheek upon the hand hanging at his side.

"Not yours alone," she said softly, "for it has become mine, too."

Before the wonder of her words he stared at her with dazed eyes, while their meaning shook him slowly to his senses.

"Maria!" he called out sharply in the voice of one who speaks from a distance.

She met his appeal with a swift outward movement of her arms, and, bending over, laid her hands gently upon his head.

"Mine, too, Christopher—mine, too," she repeated, "for I take the blame of it, and I will share in the atonement. My dear, my dear, is love so slight a thing that it would share the joy and leave the sorrow—that it would take the good and reject the evil? Why, it is all mine! All! All! What you have been I was also; what I am to-day you will be. I have been yours since the first instant you looked upon me."

With a sob he caught her hands and crushed them in his own.

"Then this is love, Maria?"

"It has been love—always."

"From the first—as with me?"

"As with you. Beloved, there is not a wrong on this earth that could come between us now, for there is no room in my heart where it might enter. There can be no sin against love which love does not acknowledge."

Falling apart, their hands dropped before them, and they stood looking at each other in a silence that went deeper than words. She felt his gaze enveloping her in warmth from head to foot, but he still made no movement to draw nearer, for there are moments when the touch of the flesh grows meaningless before the mute appeal of the spirit. In that one speechless instant there passed between them the pledges and the explanations of years.

Suddenly the light flamed in his face, and opening his arms, he made a single step toward her; but melting into tears, she turned from him and ran out into the road.

CHAPTER III

WILL'S RUIN

BLINDED by tears, she went swiftly back along the road into the shadows which thickened beyond the first short bend. Will must be saved at any cost, by any sacrifice, she told herself with passionate insistence. He must be saved though she gave up her whole life to the work of his redemption, though she must stand daily and hourly guard against his weakness. He must be saved, not for his own sake alone, but because it was the one way in which she might work out Christopher's salvation. As she went on, scheme after scheme beckoned and repelled her; plan after plan was caught at only to be rejected, and it was at last with a sinking heart, though still full of high resolves, that she turned from the lane into a strip of "corduroy road," and so came quickly to the barren little farm adjoining Sol Peterkin's.

Will was sitting idly on an overturned wheel-barrow beside the woodpile, and as she approached him she assumed with an effort a face of cheerful courage.

"Oh, Will, I thought you'd gone to work. You promised me!"

"Well, I haven't, and there's an end of it," he returned irritably, chewing hard on a chip he had picked up from the ground; "and what's more, I shan't go till I see the use. It's killing me by inches. I tell you I'm not strong enough to stand a life like this. Drudge, drudge, drudge; there's nothing else except the little spirit I get from drink."

"And that ruins you. Oh, don't, don't. I'll go on my knees to you; I'll work for you like a servant day and night; I'll sell my very clothes to help you, if you'll only promise me never to drink again."

"You a servant!" said Will, and laughed shortly while he looked her over with raised eyebrows. "Why, your stockings would keep me in cigarettes for a week."

A flush crossed Maria's face, and she glanced down guiltily, letting her black skirt fall above the lace upon her petticoat. "I have bought nothing since coming home," she responded presently with quiet dignity; "these belong, with my old luxuries, to a past life. There were a great many of them, and it will fortunately take me a long time to wear them out."

"Oh, I don't begrudge them," returned Will, a little ashamed of his show of temper; "fine clothes suit you, and I hope you will squeeze them out of grandpa all you can. It's as good a way for him to spend his money as any other, and it doesn't hurt me so long as he'll never let me see the colour of a cent."

"But your promise, dear? Will you promise me?"

He lifted his sullen face toward her kind eyes, then turning away, kicked listlessly at the rotting chips.

"What's the use in promising? I wouldn't keep it," he replied. "Why, there are times when but for whisky I'd go mad. It's the life, I tell you, that's killing me, not drink. If things were different I shouldn't crave it—I shouldn't miss it, even. Why, for three months after I married Molly I didn't touch a single drop, and I'd have kept it up, too, except for grandpa's devilment. It's his fault; he drove me back to it as clear as day."

His weak mouth quivered, and he sucked in his breath in the way he had inherited from Fletcher. The deep flush across his face faded slowly, and dropping his restless, bloodshot eyes, he dug his foot into the mould with spasmodic twitches of his body. His clothes appeared to have been flung upon him, and his cravat and loosened collar betrayed the lack of neatness which had always repelled Maria so strongly in her grandfather. As she watched him she wondered with a pang that she had never noticed until to-day the resemblance he bore to the old man at the Hall.

"But one must be patient, Will," she said helplessly after a moment's thought; "there's always hope of a mending—and as far as that goes, grandfather may relent to-morrow."

"Relent? Pshaw! I'd like to see him do it this side of hell. Let him die: that's all I ask of him. His room is a long sight better than his company, and you may tell him I said so."

"What good would come of that?"

"I don't want any good to come of it. Why should I? He's brought me to this pass with his own hand."

"But surely it was partly your fault. He loved you once."

"Nonsense. He wanted a dog to badger, that was all. Christopher Blake said so."

"Christopher Blake! Oh, Will, Will, if you could only understand!"

She turned hopelessly away from him and looked with despairing eyes over the ploughed fields which blushed faintly in the sunshine.

"So your spring ploughing is all done," she said at last, desisting from her attempt to soften his sullen obduracy, "and you have been working harder than I knew."

"Oh, it's not I," returned Will promptly, his face clearing for the first time. "It's all Christopher's work; he ploughed that field just before he went away. Do you see that new cover over the well? He knocked that up the last morning he was here, and made those steps before the front door at the same time. Now, he's the kind of friend worth having, and no mistake. But for him I'd have landed in the poorhouse long ago."

Maria's gaze left the field and returned to Will's face, where it lingered wistfully.

"Have you ever heard what it was all about, Will?" she asked, "the old trouble between him and grandfather?"

"Some silly property right, I believe; I can't remember. Did you ever see anybody yet with whom grandpa was on decent terms?"

"He used to be with you, Will."

"Only so long as I wore short breeches and he could whack me over the head whenever he had a mind to. I tell you I'd rather try to get along with Beelzebub himself."

"Have you ever tried peace-making in earnest,
I wonder?"

Twirling a chip between his thumb and forefinger, he flirted it angrily at a solitary hen scratching in the mould.

"Why, shortly after my marriage I went over
there and positively wiped up the floor with myself.
I offered him everything under heaven in the shape
of good behaviour, and, by Jove! I meant it, too.
I'd have stopped drinking then; I'd even have given
up Christopher Blake——"

"Did you tell him that?"

"Did I ever tell a thunderstorm I'd run indoors?
It was enough to get away with a whole skin—he
left me little more. And the day afterward, by the
way, he sent me the deeds to this rotten farm, and
warned me that he'd shoot me down if I ever set foot
at the Hall."

"And there has been no softening—no wavering
since?"

Will shook his head with a brutal laugh. "Oh,
you heard of our meeting in the road and what
came of it. I told him I was starving: he answered
that he wasn't responsible for all the worthless
paupers in the county. Then I cursed him, and he
broke his stick on my shoulders. I say, Maria,"
he wound up desperately, "do you think he'll live
forever?"

She kept her eyes upon him without answering,
fearing to tell him that by the terms of the new will
he could never come into his share of Fletcher's
wealth.

"Has he ever seen Molly?" she asked suddenly,

while an unreasonable hope shot through her heart. "Does he know about the child?"

"He may have seen her—I don't know; but she's not so much to look at now: she's gone all to pieces under this awful worry. It isn't my fault, God knows, but she expected different things when she married me. She thought we'd live somewhere in the city and that she'd have pretty clothes to wear."

"I was thinking that when the child came he might forgive you," broke in Maria almost cheerfully.

"And in the meantime we're to die like rats. Oh, there's no use talking, it's got to end one way or another. There's not a cent in the house nor a decent scrap of food, and Molly is having to see the doctor every day. I declare, it's enough to drive me clean to desperation!"

"And what good would that do Molly or yourself? Be a man, Will, and don't let a woman hear you whine. Now I'm going in to see her, and I'll stay to help her about supper."

She nodded brightly, and, opening the little door of the house, passed into the single lower room which served as kitchen and dining-room in one. Beyond the disorderly table, from which the remains of dinner had not yet been cleared away, Molly was lying on a hard wooden lounge covered with strips of faded calico. Her abundant flaxen hair hung in lusterless masses upon her shoulders, and the soiled cotton wrapper she wore was torn open at the throat as if she had clutched it in a passion of childish petulance. At Maria's entrance she started and looked up angrily from her dejected attitude.

"I can't see any visitors—I'm not fit!" she cried.

Maria drew forward a broken split-bottomed chair and sat down beside the lounge.

"I'm not a visitor, Molly," she answered; "and I've come to see if I can't make you a little easier. Won't you let me fix you comfortably? Why, you poor child, your hands are as hot as fire!"

"I'm hot all over," returned Molly peevishly; "and I'm sick—I'm as sick as I can be. Will won't believe it, but the doctor says so."

"Will does believe it, and it worries him terribly. Here, sit up and let me bathe your face and hands in cold water. Doesn't that feel better?"

"A little," admitted Molly, when Maria had found a towel and dried her hands.

"And now I'm going to comb the tangles out of your hair. What lovely hair! It is the colour of ripe corn."

A pleased flush brightened Molly's face, and she resigned herself easily to Maria's willing services. "There's a comb over there on that shelf under the mirror," she said. "Will broke half the teeth out of it the other day, and it pulls my hair out when I use it."

"Then I'll bring you one of mine. You must be careful of these curls. They're too pretty to treat roughly. Do I hurt you?"

As she spoke, a bright strand of the girl's hair twisted about one of her rings, and after hesitating an instant she drew the circle from her finger and laid it in Molly's lap.

"There. I haven't any money, so that's to buy you medicine and food," she said. "It cost a good deal once, I fancy."

"Diamonds!" gasped Molly, with a cry of rapture.

Her hand closed over the ring with a frantic clutch; then slipping it on, she lay watching the stone sparkle in the last sunbeams. A colour had bloomed suddenly in her face, and her eyes shone with a light as brilliant as that of the jewel at which she gazed.

"And you had—others?" she asked in a kind of sacred awe.

"A great many once—a necklace, and rings, and brooches, and a silly tiara that made me look a fright. I never cared for them after the novelty of owning them wore off. They are evil things, it seems to me, and should never be the gifts of love, for each one of those foolish stones stands for greed, and pride, and selfishness, and maybe crime. That was my way of looking at them, of course, and whenever I wore my necklace I used to feel like asking pardon of every beggar that I passed. 'One link in this chain might make a man of you,' was what I wanted to say— but I never did. Well, they are almost all gone now; some I sold and some I gave away. This one will buy you medicine, I hope, and then it will give me more happiness than it has ever done before."

"Oh, it is beautiful, beautiful," sighed Molly beneath her breath, and then went to the little cracked mirror in the corner and held the diamond first to her ear and then against her hair. "They suit me," she said at last, opening the bosom of her wrapper and trying it on her pretty throat; "they would make me look so splendid. Oh, if I'd only had a lover who could give me things like this!"

Maria, watching her, felt her heart contract suddenly

with a pang of remembrance. Jewels had been the one thing which Jack Wyndham had given her, for of the finer gifts of the spirit he had been beggared long before she knew him. In the first months of his infatuation he had showered her with diamonds, and she had grown presently to see a winking mockery in each bauble that he tossed her. Before the first year was ended she had felt her pride broken by the oppressiveness of the jewels that bedecked her body, like the mystic princess who was killed at last by the material weight of the golden crown upon her brow.

"They could never make you happy, Molly. How could they? Come back and lie down, and let me put the ring away. Perhaps I'd better take it to town myself." But Molly would not open her closed hand on which the diamond shone; and long after Maria had cooked supper and gone back to the Hall the girl lay motionless, holding the ring against the light. When Will came in from milking she showed it to him with a burst of joy.

"Look! Oh, look! Isn't it like the sun?"

He eyed it critically.

"By Jove! It must have cost cool hundreds! I'll take it to town to-morrow and bring back the things you need. It will get the baby clothes, too, so you won't have to bother about the sewing."

"You shan't! You shan't!" cried Molly in a passion of sobs. "It's mine. She gave it to me, and you shan't take it away. I don't want the medicine: it never does me any good; and I can make the baby clothes out of my old things. I'll never, never give it up!"

For an instant Will stared at her as if she had lost her senses.

"Well, she was a fool to let you get it," he said, as he flung himself out of the room.

CHAPTER IV

In Which Mrs. Blake's Eyes Are Opened

BEFORE the beauty of Maria's high magnanimity Christopher had felt himself thrust further into the abasement of his self-contempt. Had she met his confession with reproach, with righteous aversion, with the horror he had half expected, it is possible that his heart might have recoiled into a last expression of defiance. But there had been none of these things. In his memory her face shone moonlike from its cloud of dark hair, and he saw upon it only the look of a great and sorrowful passion. His wretchedness had drawn her closer, not put her further away, and he had felt the quiet of her tolerance not less gratefully than he had felt the fervour of her love. Her forgiveness had been of the grandeur of her own nature, and its height and breadth had appealed, even apart from her emotion, to a mind that was accustomed to dwell daily on long reaches of unbroken space. He had been bred on large things from his birth—large horizons, large stretches of field and sky, large impulses, and large powers of hating, and he found now that a woman's presence filled to overflowing the empty vastness of his moods.

Reaching the yard, he saw Tucker sitting placidly on his bench, and, crossing the long grass, he flung

471

himself down beside him with a sigh of pleasure in the beauty of the scene.

"You're right, Uncle Tucker; it's all wonderful. I never saw such a sunset in my life."

"Ah, but you haven't seen it yet," said Tucker. "I've been looking at it since it first caught that pile of clouds, and it grows more splendid every instant. I'm not an overreligious body, I reckon, and I've always held that the best compliment you can pay God Almighty is to let Him go His own gait and quit advising Him; but, I declare, as I sat here just now I couldn't help being impertinent enough to pray that I might live to see another."

"Well, it's a first-rate one; that's so. It seems to shake a body out of the muck, somehow."

"I shouldn't wonder if it did; and that's what I told two young fools who were up here just now asking me to patch up their first married quarrel. 'For heaven's sake, stop playing with mud and sit down and watch that sunset,' I said to 'em, and if you'll believe it, the girl actually dropped her jaws and replied she had to hurry back to shell her beans while the light lasted. Beans! Why, they'll make beans enough of their marriage, and so I told 'em."

Tapping his crutch gently on the ground, he paused and sat smiling broadly at the sunset.

For a time Christopher watched with him while the gold-and-crimson glory flamed beyond the twisted boughs of the old pine; then, turning his troubled face on Tucker's cheerful one, he asked deliberately:

"Do you sometimes regret that you never married, Uncle Tucker?"

"Regret?" repeated Tucker softly. "Why, no. I

haven't time for it—there's too much else to think about. Regret is a dangerous thing, my boy; you let a little one no bigger than a mustard seed into your heart, and before you know it you've hatched out a whole brood. Why, if I began to regret that, heaven knows where I should stop. I'd regret my leg and arm next, the pictures I might have painted, and the four years' war which we might have won. No, no. I'd change nothing, I tell you—not a day; not an hour; not a single sin nor a single virtue. They're all woven into the pattern of the whole, and I reckon the Lord knew the figure He had in mind."

"Well, I'd like to pull a thread or two out of it," returned Christopher moodily, squinting his eyes at the approaching form of Susan Spade, who came from the afterglow through the whitewashed gate. "Why, what's bringing her, I wonder?" he asked with evident displeasure.

To this inquiry Susan herself presently made answer as she walked with her determined tread across the little yard.

"I've a bit of news for you, Mr. Christopher, an' I reckon you'd ruther have it from my mouth than from Bill Fletcher's. His back's up agin, the Lord knows why, an' he's gone an' moved his pasture fence so as to take in yo' old field that lies beside it. He swars it's his, too, but Tom's ready to match him with a bigger oath that it's yours an' always has been."

"Of course it's mine," said Christopher coolly. "The meadow brook marks the boundary, and the field is on this side. I can prove it by Tom or Jacob Weatherby to-morrow."

"Well, he's took it " rejoined Mrs. Spade flatly.

"He won't keep it long, I reckon, ma'am," said Tucker, in his pleasant manner; "and I must say it seems to me that Bill Fletcher is straining at a gnat. Why, he has near two thousand acres, hasn't he? And what under heaven does he want with that old field the sheep have nibbled bare? There's no sense in it."

"It ain't sense, it's natur," returned Mrs. Spade, sitting squarely down on the bench from which Christopher had risen; "an' that's what I've had ag'in men folks from the start—thar's too much natur in 'em. You kin skeer it out of a woman, an' you kin beat it out of a dog, an' thar're times when you kin even spank it out of a baby, but if you oust it from a man thar ain't nothin' but skin an' bones left behind. An' natur's a ticklish thing to handle without gloves, bless yo' soul, suh. It's like a hive of bees: you give it a little poke to start it, an' the first thing you know it's swarmin' all over both yo' hands. It's a skeery thing, suh, an' Bill Fletcher's got his share of it, sho's you're born."

"It has its way with him pretty thoroughly, I think," responded Tucker, chuckling; "but if I were you, Christopher, I'd stick up for my rights in that old field. Bill Fletcher may need exercise, but there's no reason he should get it by trampling over you."

"Oh, I'll throw his fence down, never fear," answered Christopher indifferently. "He knew it, I dare say, when he put it up."

"It's a fuss he wants, suh, an' nothing else," declared Mrs. Spade, smoothing down the starched fold of her gingham apron; "an' if he doesn't git it, po' creetur, he's goin' to be laid up in bed befo' the week is out. He's bilin' hot inside, I can see that in his face, an' if the steam don't work out one way it will another. When a man ain't got a wife or child to nag at he's mighty sho' to turn right round an' begin naggin' at his neighbours, an' that's why it's the bounden duty of every decent woman to marry an' save the peace. Why, if Tom hadn't had me to worry on, I reckon he'd be the biggest blusterer in this county or the next."

Leaving her still talking, Christopher went from her into the house, where he lingered an instant with drawn breath before his mother's door. The old lady was sleeping tranquilly, and, treading softly in his heavy boots, he passed out to the friendly faces of the horses and the cool dusk of the stable.

As the days went on, drawing gradually toward summer, Mrs. Blake's life began peacefully to flicker out, like a candle that has burned into the socket. There were hours when her mind was quite clear, and at such times she would talk unceasingly in her old sprightly fashion, with her animated gestures and her arch and fascinating smile. But following these sanguine periods there would come whole days when she lay unconscious and barely taking breath, while her features grew sharp and wan under the pallid skin.

It was when she had just passed through one of these states that Lila came out on a Sunday afternoon to find Christopher at the woodpile, and told him, with a burst of tears, that she thought the end had come.

"She's quite herself and wants us all," she said, sobbing. "And she's even asked for the house servants, every one—for Phyllis, and Tobias, and so many of them who have been away for years. It's just as if she knew that she was dying and wanted to say good-by."

Throwing the axe hurriedly aside, Christopher followed her into the house, and then entering the old lady's room, stopped short beside the threshold in a grief that was not unmixed with wonder.

The sunshine fell straight through the window on the high white pillows, and among them Mrs. Blake was sitting rigidly, her blind eyes sparkling with the last fitful return of her intelligence. She was speaking, as he entered, in a natural and lively tone, which brought back to him his earliest memories of her engaging brightness.

"Are the servants all there, Cynthia? Then let them come and stand inside the door—a few at a time."

"They are here, mother," replied Cynthia, choking; and Christopher, glancing round, saw several decrepit negroes leaning against the wall—Uncle Boaz, Docia (pressing her weak heart), and blear-eyed Aunt Polly, already in her dotage.

"I wish to tell you good-by while my mind is clear," pursued the old lady in her high, sweet voice. "You have been good servants to me for a long time, and I hope you will live many years to serve my children as faithfully. Always remember, Christopher—— Is Christopher there?"

"I am here, dear mother."

"Always remember that a man's first duty is to

his wife and children, and his second to his slaves. The Lord has placed them in your hands, and you must answer to Him how you fulfill the trust. And now, Boaz—where is Boaz?"

"I'm yer, ole miss; I'm right yer."

"You may shake my hand, Boaz, for it is a long good-by. I've always promised you your freedom, and I haven't forgotten it, though you asked for it almost fifty years ago. You did something that I praised you for—I can't quite remember what it was—and when I asked you what you would like as a reward, you answered: 'Don't give me nothin' now, ole miss, but let the gift grow and set me free when you come to die.' It is a long time, Boaz, fifty years, but I give you your freedom now, as I promised, though it is very foolish of you to want it, and I'm sure you'll find it nothing but a burden and a trouble. Christopher, will you remember that Boaz is free?"

Christopher crossed the room, and, catching her hands in his own, sought to force her back upon the pillows, but with an effort that showed in every tense line of her face she pushed him from her and sat erect and unsupported.

"Let me dismiss them first," she said with her stately manner. "Good-by, Phyllis and Polly—and —and—all the rest of you. You may go now. I am a little tired, and I will lie down."

Cynthia put the weeping servants from the room, and, filling a glass with brandy, held it with a shaking hand to her mother's lips.

"Take this, dear, and lie down," she said.

Mrs. Blake sipped the brandy obediently, but as

she felt her strength revive from the strong spirit the animation reawoke in her face, and, turning toward Christopher, she stretched out her hand with an appealing gesture.

"There is so much to say and I haven't the space to say it in, my son. There is so much advice I want to give you, but the time is short."

"I understand, mother; I understand. Don't let it trouble you."

"I have had a fortunate life, my child," resumed the old lady, waving him to silence with a gesture in which there was still a feeble sprightliness, "and when one has lived happily far into the seventies one learns a great deal of wisdom, and there is much good advice that one ought to leave behind. You have been an affectionate son to me, Christopher, and I have not yet given up the hope that you may live to be a worthy husband to another woman. If you do marry—and God grant that you may— remember that the chief consideration should be family connection, and the next personal attractiveness. Wealth counts for very little beside good birth, and after this I regard a small foot and hand as most essential. They have always been a mark of our breeding, Christopher, and I should not like the family to lose through you one of its most distinguished characteristics."

"It is not likely I shall marry, mother. I was cut out for different ends."

"One never knows, my son, and at least I am only doing my duty in speaking to you thus. I am a very old woman, and I am not afraid to die, for I have never to my knowledge done anything

that was unbecoming in a lady. Remember to be
a gentleman, and you will find that that embraces
all morality and a good deal of religion."

He kissed her hand, watching anxiously the
mounting excitement in her face.

"And if you do marry, Christopher," she went on,
harping fitfully on her favourite string, "remember
that keeping in love is as much the profession for
a man as it is the art for a woman, and that love
feeds on little delicacies rather than on meat and
drink. Don't forget the little things, dear, and the
big ones will take care of themselves. I have seen
much of men and manners in my life, and they have
taught me that it is the small failings, not the big
faults, which are deadliest to love. Why, I've seen
a romantic passion survive shame, and treachery,
and even blows, and another wither out of existence
before the first touch of bad breeding. 'A man's
table manners are a part of his morality,' your
Great-grandfather Bolivar used to say."

She laughed softly while her hand played with
the white fringe on the counterpane.

"I can recall now the sympathy I felt for Matty
Gordon," she pursued, "a great belle and beauty
who ran off and married that scamp, Aleck Douglas.
He turned into a perfect rascal, they said, though
I must admit that he made a very amiable husband,
and never stinted her, even if he stole from other
people. Well, she stuck to him through good and
evil report, and was really from all appearances a
most contented woman. When he died at last,
people said that it was just in time to escape the
penitentiary, but to see Matty you would have

thought she had lost nothing short of pure perfection. Poor old Bishop Deane, who always would speak his mind, in the pulpit or out of it, went to call on her, he told me, and took occasion to reprove her for such excessive grief over so unworthy an object. 'He was not an upright man, Matty, and you know it,' he began quite boldly; 'he was a libertine, and a gambler, and an open scoffer at religion.' But Matty went on sobbing harder than ever, and at last, getting angry, he said sternly: 'And more than this, ma'am, he was, as you know, a faithless and disloyal husband!' Then the poor girl drew out a pocket handkerchief with a three-inch black border and mopped her pretty blue eyes. 'Ah, but, Bishop, I had so much to be thankful for!' she said. 'He never chewed tobacco!' Well, well, she may have been a fool, as the Bishop insisted, but he was a man, in spite of his cloth, and could never learn to understand a woman's sensibilities."

She finished, and, turning, touched him gently on the hand.

"It is the little things that count in marriage, Christopher," and after a moment she added thoughtfully: "Promise me that you will always use an ash-tray."

"Anything, dear mother; I promise anything."

With a contented sigh she closed her eyes, and, still holding his hand, fell into a broken and troubled sleep, from which she awoke presently in a gentle delirium. Her lost youth had returned to her, and with it something of her old gaiety of manner. Suddenly he felt a strange thrill pass through her, and raising herself with a last great endeavour, she sat erect, staring into the blue sky that showed through the window.

"I am engaged for this set, sir," she said in her winning voice, while a girlish smile transfigured her wan face, "but if it pleases you, you may put your name down for the next."

Rising, he bent quickly over her, but before he touched her she had fallen back upon the pillows and lay with her arch smile frozen upon her face.

CHAPTER V

CHRISTOPHER PLANTS BY MOONLIGHT

AT MIDNIGHT they left him to watch alone in her chamber, and while he sat in the shadow beside the tester bed his thoughts encircled the still form on the white counterpane. On the mantel two candles burned dimly, and the melted tallow dripped slowly down into the tall brass candlesticks. The dimity curtains of the bed fluttered softly in the breeze that blew through the open window, and in his nostrils there was the scent of the single rose standing in a glass vase upon the table. Tucker had brought her the rose that morning and she had held it for a pleased moment in her trembling fingers. Everything in the room around him was ready for her use—her nightcap lay on the bureau, and in the china tray beside it he saw her brush and comb, in which a long strand of white hair was still twisted. On her hands, folded quietly upon her breast, he caught the flash of Docia's piece of purple glass, and he remembered with a throb of pain that she had asked that her betrothal ring might be buried with her.

"Well, she knows all now," he thought in bitterness. "She knows the theft of the diamond, and the deception that lasted nearly thirty years." In the midst of his sorrow a sudden shame possessed

THE DELIVERANCE

him, and he felt all at once that his heart was pierced
by the unearthly keenness of the dead eyes. "She
knows all now," he repeated, and there was a passionate defiance in his acknowledgment. "She
knows all that I have hidden from her, as well as
much that has been hidden from me. Her blind
eyes are open, and she sees at last my failure and
my sin, and the agony that I have known. For
years I have shielded her, but she cannot shield me
now, for all her wider vision. She can avert my
fate no more than I could hold her back from hers.
We are each alone—she, and I, and Maria, and the
boy whom I have ruined—and there is no love that
can keep a man from living and dying to himself."

It seemed to him, sitting there in the shadow, that
he felt—as he had felt before in grave moments—
the revolutions of the wheel on which he was bound.
And with that strange mystic insight which comes
to those who lead brooding and isolated lives close
to Nature, he asked himself if, after all, these things
had not had their beginning in the dawn of his
existence so many million years ago. "Has it not
all happened before as it happens now—my shame
and my degradation, the kiss I placed on Maria's
lips, and the watch I keep by the deathbed of my
mother? It is all familiar to me, and when the end
comes, that will be familiar, too."

A night moth entered, wheeling in dizzy circles
about the candle, but when it went so near as to
scorch its wings he caught it gently in his hollowed
palms and released it into the darkness of the yard.
As he leaned out he saw the light shining clear in
Maria's window, and while he gazed upon it he felt

a curious kinship with the moth that had flown in from the night and hovered about the flame.

As the days went on, the emptiness in the house became to him like that of the grave, and he learned presently that the peevish and exacting old lady who had not stirred for years from her sick-bed had left a vacancy larger than all the rest of them could fill. Cynthia, who had borne most of the burden, began now to bear, in its place, the heavier share of the loss. Released from her daily sacrifice and her patient drudgery, she looked about her with dazed eyes, like one whose future has been suddenly swept away. There was nothing for her to do any longer —no risings in the gray dawn to prepare the day's stealthy work, no running on aching feet to answer unreasonable complaints, no numberless small lies to plan in secret, no stinting of herself that her mother might have her little luxuries. Her work was over, and she pined away in the first freedom of her life. The very fact that deception was no longer necessary seemed to sweep her accustomed moorings from beneath her feet. She had lied so long that lying had become at last a second nature to her, and to her surprise she found almost an indecency in the aspect of the naked truth.

"I don't know how it is, Uncle Tucker," she said one day toward the end of June, when the deadly drought which had kept back the transplanting of the tobacco had ended in three days of heavy rain—"I don't know how it is, but the thing I miss most—and I miss her every minute—is the lying I had to do. It gave me something to think about, somehow. I used to stay awake at night and plan all sorts of pleasant lies that I could tell about the house and the garden, and the way the war ended, and the Presidents of the Confederacy—I made up all their names—and the fuss with which each one was inaugurated, and the dresses their wives and daughters wore. It's all so dull when you have to stop pretending and begin to face things just as they are. I've lied for almost thirty years, and I reckon I've lost my taste for the truth."

"Well, it will come back, dear," responded Tucker reassuringly; "but I think you need a change if a woman ever did. What about that week you're to spend with the Weatherbys?"

"I'm going to-morrow," answered Cynthia shortly. "Lila is sick with a cold and wants me; but how you and Christopher will manage to get on is more than I can say."

"Oh, we'll worry along with Docia, never fear," replied Tucker, hobbling into his seat at the supper table, as Christopher came in from the woods with the heavy moisture dripping from his clothes.

"It's cleared off fine and there's to be a full moon to-night," said the young man, hanging up his hat. "If the rain had come a week later the tobacco would have been ruined. I've just been taking it up out of the plant-bed."

"You'll begin setting it out to-morrow, I reckon, then," observed Tucker, watching Cynthia as she cut up his food.

"Oh, I'm afraid to wait—the ground dries so quickly. Jacob Weatherby is going to set his out to-night, and I think I'll do the same. There's a fine moon, and I shouldn't wonder if every farmer in the county was in the fields till daybreak."

He ate his supper hurriedly, and then, taking down his hat, went out to resume his work. At the door he had left his big split basket of plants, and, slipping his arm through the handle, he crossed the yard in the direction of the field. As he turned into the little path which trailed in wet grass along the "worm" fence, Jacob Weatherby came stepping briskly through the mud in the road and stopped to ask him if he had got his ground ready for the setting out. "I've been lookin' for hands myself," added the old man in his cheery voice, "for I could find work for a dozen men to-night, but to save my life I can't scrape up more'n a nigger here an' thar. Bill Fletcher has been out ahead of me, it seems."

"Well, I'll be able to help you to-morrow, I think," answered Christopher. "I hope to get my own work done to-night." Then he asked with a trifling hesitation: "How is Lila's cold?"

A sudden light broke over old Jacob's face, and he nodded in his genial fashion.

"Ah, bless her pretty eyes, I sometimes think she's too good to put her foot down on this here common earth," he said, "an' to think that only this mornin' she was wantin' to help Sarah wipe the dishes. Why, I reckon Sarah would ruther work her fingers to the bone than have that gal take a single dish-cloth in her hand. Oh, we know how to value her, Mr. Christopher, never fear. Her word's law in our house, and always will be."

He passed on with his hearty chuckle, and Christopher followed the wet path and began planting his tobacco plants in the small holes he bored in the moist earth.

It was the most solemn hour of day, when the division between light and darkness seems less a gradation than a sudden blur. A faint yellow line still lingered across the western horizon, and against it the belt of pines rose like an advancing army. The wind, which blew toward him from the woods, filled his nostrils with a spicy tang.

Slowly the moon rose higher, flooding the hollows and the low green hills with light. In the outlying fields around the Hall he saw Fletcher's planters at work in the tobacco, each man so closely followed by his shadow that it was impossible at a little distance to distinguish the living labourer from his airy double. All the harsh irregularities of the landscape were submerged in a general softness of tone, and the shapes of hill and meadow, of road and tree, of shrub and rock, were dissolved in a magical and enchanting beauty.

Several hours had passed, and he had stopped to rest a moment from his planting, when Maria came in the moonlight along the road and paused breathlessly to lean upon the fence beneath the locust tree.

"It is the first time I've been out for two weeks," she said, panting softly. "I twisted my ankle, and the worst part was that I didn't even dare to send you word. What must you have thought?"

"No harm of you," he answered, and threw down the fence-rails that she might cross. "Come over to me, Maria."

Putting her hands in his, she passed over the lowered fence, and then stood at arm's length looking into his face, which the moonlight had softened to a beauty that brought to her mind a carving in old ivory.

"I still limp a little," she went on, smiling, "and I had to steal out like a thief and run through the shadows. To find me with you would be the death of grandfather, I believe. Something has occurred to put him in a fresh rage with you."

"It was the field by the pasture," he told her frankly. "You know it belongs to me, and pure justice made me throw down his fence; but if you wish it I will put it up again. I'll do anything you wish."

She thought for a moment with that complete detachment of judgment from emotion which is so rarely a part of a woman's intellect.

"No, no," she said; "it is right that you should take it down. I would not have you submit to any further injustice, not even a little one like that."

"And this will go on forever! Oh, Maria, how will it end?"

"We must wait and hope, dear; you see that."

"I see nothing but that I love you and am most miserable," he answered desperately.

A smile curved her lips. "Oh, blind and faithless, I see only you!"

He was still holding her hands, but, dropping them as she spoke, he threw his arms wide open and stood waiting.

"Then come to me, my dearest; come to me."

His voice rang out in command rather than entreaty, and he stood smiling gravely as, hesitating a breathless instant, she regarded him with eyes that struggled to be calm. Then slowly the radiance which was less the warmth of colour than of expression flooded her face, and she bent toward him as if impelled by some strong outside force. The next moment the storm swept her roughly from her feet and crushed back her pleading hands upon her bosom; bewildered, flushed, and trembling, she lay upon his breast while their lips clung together. "Oh, my friend, my lover," she murmured faintly.

He felt her resistance dissolve within his arms, and it was a part of the tragedy of their love that there should come to him no surprise when he found her mouth salt from her tears. The shadow of a great evil, of a secret anguish, still divided them, and it was this that gave to their embraces the sorrowful passion which he drew from her despairing kiss.

"You cannot love me, Maria. How can it be true?"

Releasing herself, she put her hand upon his lips to silence him.

"You have made your confession," she said earnestly, with the serene dignity which had impressed him in the first moment of their meeting, "and now I will make mine. You must not stop me; you must not look at me until I finish. Promise."

"I promise to keep silent," he answered, with his gaze upon her.

She drew away from him, keeping her eyes full on his, and holding him at arm's length with the tips of her fingers. He felt that she was still shaken by his embrace—that she was still in a quiver from his kisses; but to all outward seeming she had regained the noble composure of her bearing.

"No, no. Ah, listen, my friend, and do not touch me. What I must tell you is this, and you must hear me patiently to the end. I have loved you always—from the first day; since the beginning. There has never been any one else, and there has never been a moment in my life when I would not have followed you had you lifted a finger—anywhere. At first I did not know—I did not believe it. It was but a passing fancy, I thought, that you had murdered. I taught myself to believe that I was cold, inhuman, because I did not warm to other men. Oh, I did not know then that I was not stone, but ice, which would melt at the first touch of the true flame——"

"Maria!" he burst out in a cry of anguish.

"Hush! Hush! Remember your promise. It was not until afterward," she went on in the same quiet voice; "it was not until my marriage—not until my soul shuddered back from his embraces and I dreamed of you, that I began to see—to understand."

"Oh, Maria, my beloved, if I had known!"

She still held him from her with her outstretched arm.

"It was the knowledge of this that made me feel that I had wronged him—that I had defrauded him of the soul of love and given him only the poor flesh. It was this that held me to him all those wretched years—that kept me with him till the end, even through his madness. At last I buried your memory told myself that I had forgotten."

"We will let the world go, dearest," he said passionately. "Come to me."

But she shook her head, and, still smiling, held him at a distance.

"It will never go," she answered, " for it is not the world's way. But whatever comes to us, there is one thing you must remember—that you must never forget for one instant while you live. In good or evil, in life or death, there is no height so high nor any depth so low that I will not follow you."

Then waving him from her with a decisive gesture, she turned from him and went swiftly home across the moonlit fields.

CHAPTER VI

TREATS OF THE TRAGEDY WHICH WEARS A COMIC MASK

As SHE hastened on, Christopher's presence was still with her—his arm still enveloped her, his voice still spoke in her ears; and so rapt was the ecstasy in which she moved that it was with a positive shock that she found herself presently before the little area which led into the brick kitchen in the basement of the Hall. Here from the darkness her name was spoken in a stifled voice, while a hand reached out and clutched her by the shoulder.

"I say, Maria, I've been waiting hours to speak to you."

Forcing back the cry upon her lips, she opened the door and stole softly into the kitchen. Then, turning, she faced Will with a frightened gesture.

"How reckless—how very reckless!" she exclaimed in a whisper.

He closed the door that led up into the house, and coming over to the stove, where the remains of a fire still smouldered in a deep red glow, stood looking at her with nervous twitches of his reddened eyelids. There was a wildness in his face before which she fell back appalled, and his whole appearance, from the damp hair lying in streaks upon his forehead to his restless feet which he shuffled continually as he

talked, betrayed an agitation so extreme as to cause
her a renewed pang of foreboding.

"Oh, Will, you have been drinking again!" she
said, in the same frightened whisper.

"And why not?" he demanded, throwing out his
words between thick breaths. "What business is
it of yours or of anybody else's if I have been? A
pretty sister you are—aren't you?—to let a fellow
rot away on a tobacco farm while you wear diamonds
on your fingers."

She looked at him steadily for a moment, and his
shifting glance fell slowly to the floor.

"If you are in any fresh trouble you may as well
tell me at once," she said. "It is a mere waste of
time and breath to reproach me. You can't possibly
make me angry to-night, for I wear an armour of
which you do not dream, and so little a thing as
abuse does not even touch me. Besides, grandfather may hear us and come down at any moment.
So speak quickly."

Her coolness sobered him instantly, as if a splash
of ice-water had been thrown into his face, and his
tone lost its aggressiveness and sank into a whimpering complaint.

It was the same old thing, he went on, only worse
and worse. Molly had been ill again, and the doctor
ordered medicine he couldn't buy. Yes, he had
tried to take the diamond from her, but she flew into
hysterics at the mere mention of selling it. Once
he had dragged it off her finger, and had given it
back again because her wildness frightened him.
"Why on earth did you ever let her have it?" he
finished querulously.

"Well, I never imagined she would be quite so silly," returned Maria, distressed by what she heard. "But it may be that jewels are really her passion, and the bravest of us, I suppose, are those who sacrifice most for their dearest desire. I really don't see what is to be done, Will. I haven't any money, and I don't dare ask grandfather, for he makes me keep a strict account of every cent I spend. Only yesterday he told me he couldn't allow me but two postage stamps a week, and yet I believe that he is worth considerably more than half a million dollars. Sometimes I think it is nothing short of pure insanity, he grows so miserly about little things. Aunt Saidie and I have both noticed that he would rather spend a hundred dollars—though it is like drawing out an eyetooth—than keep a pound of fresh butter from the market."

"And yet he likes you?"

"Oh, he tolerates me, as far as that goes; but I don't believe he likes anything on earth except his money. It's his great passion, just as Molly's love of jewelry is hers. There is something so tremendous about it that one can't help respect it. As for me, he only bears with my presence so long as I ask him for absolutely nothing. He knows I have my little property, and we had a dreadful scene when I refused to let him keep my check-book. I gave you all the interest of the last six months, you know, and the other isn't due until November. If he finds out that it goes to you, heaven help us!"

"And there's not the faintest hope of his coming to his senses? Have you spoken of me again?"

"I've mentioned your name twice, that was all.

He rose and stamped out of the room, and didn't speak for days. Aunt Saidie and I have planned to bring the baby over when it comes. That may soften him—especially if it should be a boy."

"Oh, the bottom will drop out of things by that time," he returned savagely, tearing pieces of straw from his worn hat-brim. "If this keeps up much longer, Maria, I warn you now I'll run away. I'll go off some day on a freight train and hide my head until he dies; then I'll come back to enjoy his precious money."

She sighed, thinking hopelessly of the altered will.

"And Molly?" she questioned, for lack of a more effectual argument.

"I can't stop to think of Molly: it drives me mad. What use am I to her, anyway, I'd like to know? She'd be quite as well off without me, for we do nothing but quarrel now night and day; and yet I love her—I love her awfully," he added in a drunken whimper.

"Oh, Will, Will, be a man for her sake!"

"I can't; I can't," he protested, his voice rising in anger. "I can't stand the squalor of this life; it's killing me. Why, look at the way I was brought up, never stopping an instant to ask whether I could have a thing I wanted. He had no right to accustom me to luxuries till I couldn't do without them and then throw me out upon the world like this!"

"Hush! Hush! Your voice is too loud. It will bring him down."

"I'll be hanged if I care!" he retorted, but involuntarily he lowered his tone.

"You mustn't stay here five minutes longer,"

urged Maria. "I'll give you a diamond brooch I still have left, and you may take it to town yourself and sell it. Only promise me on your honour that you will spend the money on the things Molly needs."

"Oh, I promise," he replied roughly. "Where is it?"

"In my room. I must get it now. Be perfectly quiet until I return."

Opening the door and closing it carefully behind her, she stole noiselessly up the dark staircase, while Will, twitching nervously, paced restlessly up and down the brick floor. A pile of walnuts which Miss Saidie had been shelling for cake lay on the hearth, and, picking up the heavy old hammer she had used, he cracked a nut and ate it hurriedly. Hungry as he was—for he had not been home to supper—he found difficulty in swallowing, and, laying the hammer down upon the bricks, he rose and stood waiting beside the stove. Though the night was warm, a shiver ran suddenly through him, and, stirring the fading embers with a splinter of resinous pine, he held out his shaking hands to the blaze.

In a moment Maria entered and handed him the brooch in a little box.

"Try to keep up courage, Will," she said, pushing him into the area under the back steps; "and above all things, do not come here again. It is so unsafe."

He promised lightly that he would not, and then told her good-by with an affectionate pat upon the arm.

"Well, you are a bully good chap, after all," he added, as he stepped out into the night.

For a while Maria stood looking after him across

the moonlit fields, and then, even as she turned to enter the house, the last troubled hour was blotted from her consciousness, and she lived over again the moment of Christopher's embrace. With that peculiar power to revive and hold within the memory an instant's emotion which is possessed by ardent and imaginative women, she experienced again all the throbbing exhilaration, all the fulness of being, which had seemed to crowd the heart-beats of so many ordinary years into the single minute that was packed with life. That minute was hers now for all time; it was a possession of which no material loss, no untoward fate could defraud her; and as she felt her steps softly up the dark staircase, it seemed to her that she saw her way by the light of the lamp that was burning in her bosom.

To her surprise, as she reached the dining-room a candle was thrust out before her, and, illuminated by the trembling flame, she saw the face of Fletcher, hairy, bloated, sinister, with the shadow of evil impulses worked into the mouth and eyes. For a moment he wagged at her in silence, and in the flickering radiance she saw each swollen vein, each gloomy furrow, with exaggerated distinctness. He reminded her vaguely of some hideous gargoyle she had seen hanging from an early Gothic cathedral.

"So you've taken to gallivanting, like the rest," he observed with coarse pleasantry. "I'd thought you were a staid and sober-minded woman for your years, but it seems that you are of a bunch with all the others."

"I've been out in the moonlight," answered Maria, while a sensation of sickness stole over her.

"It is as bright as day, but I thought you were in bed long ago."

"Thar's not much sleep for me during tobacco planting, I kin tell you," rejoined Fletcher; "but as for you, I reckon thar's more beneath your words than you like to own to.   You've been over to see that young scamp, ain't you?"

"I saw him, but I did not go out for that purpose."

"It's the truth, I reckon, for I've never known you to lie, and I'll be hanged if it ain't that I like about you, after all.   You're the only person I kin spot, man or woman, who speaks the truth jest for the darn love of it."

"And yet I lived a lie for five years," returned Maria quietly.

"Maybe so, maybe so; but it set on you like the burr on a chestnut, somehow, and when it rolled off thar you were, as clean as ever.   Well, you're an honest and spunky woman, and I can't help your traipsing over thar even if I wanted to.   But thar's one thing I tell you now right flat—if that young rascal wants to keep a whole skin he'd better stay off this place.   I'd shoot him down as soon as I would a sheep-killing hound."

"Oh, he won't come here," said Maria faintly; and, going into the dining-room, she dropped into a chair and lay with her arms outstretched upon the table.   The second shock to her emotional ecstasy had been too much, and the furniture and Fletcher's face and the glare of the candle all spun before her in a sickening confusion.

After looking at her anxiously an instant, Fletcher poured out a glass of water and begged her to take

a swallow. "Thar, thar, I didn't mean to skeer
you," he said kindly. "You mustn't mind my
rough-and-ready ways, for I'm a plain man, God
knows. If you are sure you feel fainty," he added,
"I'll git you a sip of whisky, but it's a pity to waste
it unless you have a turn."

"Oh, I'm all right," answered Maria, sitting up,
and returning his inquiring gaze with a shake of
the head. "My ankle is still weak, you know, and
I felt a sudden twinge from standing on it. What
were you looking for at this hour?"

"Well, I've been out in the air sense supper, and
I feel kind of gone. I thought I'd like a bite of
something—maybe a scrap of that cold jowl we had
for dinner. But I can't find it. Do you reckon
Saidie is such a blamed fool as to throw the scraps
away?"

"There's Malindy, you know; she must eat."

"I'd like to see one nigger eat up half a jowl,"
grumbled Fletcher, rooting among the dishes in the
sideboard. "Thar was a good big hunk of it left,
for you didn't touch it. You don't seem to thrive
on our victuals," he added bluntly, turning to peer
into her face.

"I'm a small eater; it makes little difference."

"Well, we mustn't starve you," he said, as he
went back to his search; "and if it's a matter of a
pound of fresh butter, or a spring chicken, even, I
won't let it stand in your way. Why, what's this,
I wonder?"

Ripping out an oath with an angry snort, he
drew forth Miss Saidie's walnut cake and held it
squarely before the candle. "I declar, if she ain't

been making walnut cake agin, and I told her last week I wan't going to have her wasting all my eggs. Look at it, will you? If she's beat up one egg in that cake she's beat up a dozen, to say nothing of the sugar!"

"Don't scold her, grandfather. She has a sweet tooth, you know, and it's so hard for her not to make desserts."

"Pish! Tush! I don't reckon her tooth's any sweeter than mine. I've a powerful taste for trash myself, and always had since the time I overate ripe honey-shucks when I was six months old; but the taste don't make me throw away good money. I'll have no more of this, I tell you, and I've said my say. She can bake a bit of cake once a week if she'll stint herself to an egg or two, but when it comes to mixing up a dozen at a time, I'll be darned if I'll allow it."

Lifting the plate in one hand, he stood surveying the big cake with disapproving yet admiring eyes. "It would serve her right if I was to eat up every precious crumb," he remarked at last.

"Suppose you try it," suggested Maria pleasantly. "It would please Aunt Saidie."

"It ain't to please her," sourly responded Fletcher, as he drove the knife with a lunge into the yellow loaf. "She's a thriftless, no-account housekeeper, and I'll tell her so to-morrow."

Still holding the knife in his clinched fist, he sat munching the cake with a relish which brought a smile to Maria's tired eyes.

"Yes, I've a powerful sweet tooth myself," he added, as he cut another slice.

CHAPTER VII

Will Faces Desperation and Stands at Bay

Rising at daybreak next morning, Will's eyes lighted in his first glance from the window on Christopher's blue-clad figure commanding the ploughed field on the left of the house. In the distance towered the black pines, and against them the solitary worker was relieved in the slanting sunbeams which seemed to arrest and hold his majestic outline. The split basket of plants was on his arm, and he was busily engaged in "setting out" Will's neglected crop of tobacco.

Leaving Molly still asleep, Will dressed himself hurriedly, and, putting the diamond brooch in his pocket, ran out to where Christopher was standing midway of the bare field.

"So you're doing my work again," he said, not ungratefully.

"If I didn't I'd like to know who would," responded Christopher with rough kindliness, as he dropped a wilted plant into a hole. "You're up early this morning. Where are you off to?"

Will drew the brooch from his pocket and held it up with a laugh.

"Maria gave me this," he explained, "and I'm going to town to turn it into money."

"Well, I'll keep an eye on the place while you

are away," returned Christopher, without looking
at the trinket. "Go about your business, and for
heaven's sake don't stop to drink. Some men can
stand liquor: you can't. It makes a beast of you."

"And not of you, eh?"

"It never gets the chance. I know when to stop.
That's the difference between us."

"Of course that's the difference," rejoined Will
a little doggedly. "I never know when to stop
about anything, I'll be hanged if I do. It's my cursed
luck to go at a headlong gait."

"And some day you'll get your neck broken.
Well, be off now, or you'll most likely miss the stage."

He turned away to sort the young plants in his
basket, while Will started at a brisk pace for the
cross-roads.

The planting was tedious work, and it was almost
evening before Christopher reached the end of the
field and started home along the little winding lane.
He had eaten a scant dinner with Molly, who had
worried him by tearful complaints across the turnip
salad. She had never looked prettier than in her
thin white blouse, with her disordered curls shadowing her blue eyes, and he had never found her
more frankly selfish. Her shallow-rooted nature
awakened in him a feeling that was akin to
repulsion, and he saw in imagination the gallant
resolution with which Maria would have battled
against such sordid miseries. At the first touch
of her heroic spirit they would have been sordid
no longer, for into the most squalid suffering
her golden nature would have shed something of
its sunshine. Beauty would have surrounded her

in Will's cabin as surely as in Blake Hall. And with the thought there came to him the knowledge, wrung from experience, that there are souls which do not yield to events, but bend and shape them into the likeness of themselves. No favouring circumstance could have evolved Maria out of Molly, nor could any crushing one have formed Molly from Maria's substance. The two women were as far asunder as the poles, united only by a certain softness of sex he found in them both.

The sun had dropped behind the pines and a gray mist was floating slowly across the level landscape. The fields were still in daylight, while dusk already enshrouded the leafy road, and it was from out the gloom that obscured the first short bend that he saw presently emerge the figure of a man who appeared to walk unsteadily and with an effort.

For an instant Christopher stopped short in the lane; then he went forward at a single impetuous stride.

"Will!" he cried in a voice of thunder.

Will looked up with dazed eyes, and, seeing who had called him, burst into a loud and boisterous laugh.

"So you'll begin with your darn preaching," he remarked, gaping.

For reply, Christopher reached out, and, seizing him by the shoulder, shook him roughly to his senses.

"What's the meaning of this tomfoolery?" he demanded. "Do you mean to say you've made a beast of yourself, after all?"

Partly sobered by the shock, Will gazed back at

him with a dogged misery which gave his face the colour of extreme old age.

"I'm not so drunk as I look," he responded bitterly. "I wish to heaven I were! There are worse things than being drunk, though you won't believe it. I say," he added, in a sudden, hysterical exclamation, "you're the only friend I have on earth!"

"Nonsense. What have you been doing?"

"Oh, I couldn't help it—it wasn't my fault, I'll be blamed if it was! I did sell the breastpin and get the money, and wrapped it in the list of things that Molly wanted. I put them in my pocket," he finished, touching his coat, "the money and the list together."

"And where is it?"

For a moment Will did not reply, but stood shaking like a blade of grass in a high wind. Then removing his hat, he mopped feebly at the beads of sweat upon his forehead. His eyes had the dumb appeal of a frightened animal's. "I haven't had a morsel all day," he whimpered, "and the effect of the whisky has all worn off."

"Speak up, man," said Christopher kindly. "I can't eat you."

"Oh, it's not you," returned Will desperately; "it's Molly I'm afraid to go home and look Molly in the face."

"Pish! She doesn't bite."

"She does worse; she cries."

"Then, for God's sake, out with the trouble," urged Christopher, losing patience. "You've lost the money, I take it; but how?"

"There was a fair," groaned Will, his voice breaking. "I met Fred Turner and a strange man who owned horses, and they asked me to come and watch the racing. Then we had drinks and began to bet, and somehow I always lost after the first time. Before I knew it the money was all gone, every single cent, and I owed Fred Turner a hundred and fifty dollars."

Christopher's gaze travelled slowly up and down the slight figure before him and he swore softly beneath his breath.

"Well, you have made a mess of it!" he exclaimed with a laugh.

"I knew you'd say so, and you're the only friend I have on earth. As for Molly—oh, I'm afraid to go home, that's all. Do you know, I've half a mind to run away for good?"

"Pshaw! Accidents will happen, and there's nothing in all this to take the pluck out of a man. I've been through worse things myself."

"But Fred Turner!" groaned Will. "I promised him I'd pay him in two days."

"Then you'll do it. I'll undertake to see to that."

"You!" exclaimed the other, with so abject a reliance upon the spoken word that it brought a laugh from Christopher's lips. "How will you manage it?"

"Oh, somehow—mortgage the farm, I reckon. At any rate, in two days you shall be clear of your debt to Fred Turner; there's my word. All I hope is that you'll learn a lesson from the fright."

"Oh, I will, I will; and by Jove! you are a bully chap!"

"Then go home and make your peace with Molly.

Mind you, if you get in liquor again I warn you I won't lift a hand."

With a last cheery "good night" he swung on along the road, dismissing the thought of Will to invoke that of Maria, and meeting again in fancy the rich promise of her upturned lips. Body and soul she was his now, flame and clay, true brain and true heart. "I will follow you, for the lifting of a finger, anywhere," she had said, and the words reeled madly in his thoughts. Her impassioned look returned to him, and he closed his eyes as a man does in the face of an emotion which proclaims him craven.

When Christopher's footsteps had faded in the distance, Will, who had been looking wistfully after him, shook together his dissolving courage and started with a strengthened purpose to bear the bad news to Molly. A light streamed through the broken shutters of her window, and when he laid his hand upon the door it shot open and she stood before him.

"So you're back at last," she said sharply; "and late again."

"I couldn't help it," he answered with assumed indifference, entering and passing quickly under the fire of her questioning look. "I was kept."

"What kept you?"

"Oh, business."

"I'd like to know what business you have!" she retorted querulously; and a minute later: "Have you brought the medicine?"

He went over to the table and stood looking gloomily down upon the scattered remains of supper

—upon the sloppy oilcloth, the cracked earthen-
ware tea-pot, and the plate half filled with sobby
bread. "Give me something to eat. I'm almost
starved," he pleaded.

A flash shot from her blue eyes, while the anger
he had feared worked threateningly in the features
of her pretty face. There was no temperateness
about Molly; she was all storm or sunshine, he had
once said in the poetic days of courtship.

"If you've brought the things, where are they?"
she demanded, driving him squarely into a corner
from which there was no escape by subterfuge.

A sullen defiance showed in his aspect, and he
turned upon her with a muttered curse. "I haven't
them, if you want the truth," he snarled. "I meant
to buy them, but Fred Turner got me to drinking
and we bet on the races. I lost the money."

"To Fred Turner!" cried Molly. "Oh, you fool!"

He made an angry movement toward her; then
checking himself, laughed bitterly.

"You're as bad as grandfather," he said, "and
it's like jumping from the frying-pan into the fire.
I'll be hanged if I knew you were a shrew when I
married you!"

Molly's eyes fairly blazed, and as she shook her
head with an enraged gesture, her hair, tumbling
upon her shoulders, flooded her with light. Even
in the midst of his fury his ready senses responded
to the appeal of her dishevelled loveliness.

"And I'll be—anything if I knew you were a
drunkard!" she retorted, pressing her hand upon
her panting breast.

"Well, you ought to have known it," he sneered,

"for I was one. Christopher Blake could have told you so. But if I remember rightly, you weren't so precious particular at the time. You were glad enough to get anybody, as it happened!"

"How—how dare you?" wailed Molly, in the helplessness of her rage, and throwing herself upon the lounge, she beat her hands upon the wooden sides and burst into despairing sobs. "Why, oh, why did I marry you?" she moaned between choking gasps.

"Some said it was because Fred Turner threw you over," returned Will savagely, and having hurled his last envenomed dart, he seized his hat and rushed out into the night.

The scene had worked like madness on his nerves, and in the darkness of the lane, where the trees kept out the moonbeams, he still saw the flickering lights that he had left behind him in the room. He had eaten nothing all day, and his empty stomach oppressed him with a sensation of nausea. His head spun like a top, and as he walked the road rocked in long seesaws beneath his feet. Yet his one craving was for drink, drink, more drink.

Running rather than walking, he reached the store at last, and went back to the little smoky room where Tom Spade was drawing beer from the big keg in one corner.

"Give me something to eat, Tom; I'm starving," he said; "and whisky. I must have whisky or I'll die."

"It's my belief that you'll die if you do have it," responded Tom. "As for bread and meat, however, Susan will give you a bite an' welcome." Nevertheless, he poured out the whisky, and, leaving it upon one of the dirty tables, went hastily out in search of Mrs. Spade.

Lifting the glass with a shaking hand, Will drained it at a single swallow, feeling his depleted courage revive as the raw spirit burned his throat. A sudden heat invaded him; his eyes saw clearer, and the tips of his fingers were endowed with a new quality of touch. As his hands travelled slowly over his face he became aware that he was *looking* through his finger ends, and he noted distinctly his haggard features and the short growth of beard which made him appear jaded and unwashed. Then almost instantly the quickness died out of his perception, and he felt the old numbness creeping back.

"Another glass—I must have another glass," he called out irritably to the empty room. His hands hung stone dead again at his sides, and his head dropped limply forward upon his breast. He had forgotten his quarrel with Molly: he had forgotten everything except his own miserable bodily condition.

When Susan Spade came in with a plate of bread and ham, he roused himself with a nervous start and inhaled quickly the strong odour of the meat, endeavouring through the sense of smell to reawaken the pang of hunger he had felt earlier in the evening. But in place of the gnawing emptiness there had come now a deadly nausea, and after the first mouthful or two he pushed the food away and called hoarsely for more whisky. His head ached in loud, reverberating throbs, and a queer fancy possessed him that the sound must be as audible to others as to himself. With the thought, he glanced about suspiciously, but Tom Spade was stopping the keg that he had tapped, and Susan was wiping off the table with energetic sweeps of her checked apron. Relieved by their impassiveness, he braced himself with the determination to drink to the dead-line of unconsciousness and then lie down somewhere in the darkness to sleep off the effects.

"Whisky—give me more whisky," he repeated angrily.

But Mrs. Spade, true to her nature, saw fit to intervene between him and destruction.

"Not another drop, Mr. Will," she said decisively. "Not another drop shall you have in this room if it's the last mortal word I speak. An' if you'd had me by you in the beginning, I'm not afeard to say, things would have helt up a long sight sooner than this."

"Don't you see I'm in downright agony?" groaned Will, rapping the glass upon the table. "My head is splitting, I tell you, and I must have it."

"Not another drop, suh," replied Mrs. Spade with adamantine firmness of tone. "I ain't a weak woman, thank the Lord, an' as far as that goes, you might split to pieces inside and out right here befo' my eyes an' I wouldn't be a party to sendin' you a step nearer damnation. I ain't afeard of seein' folks suffer. Tom will tell you that."

"That she ain't, suh," agreed Tom with pride. "If I do say it who shouldn't, thar never was a woman who could stand mo' pain in other people than can Susan. Mo' than that, Mr. Will, she's right, though I'd be sayin' so even if she wasn't—seein' that the only rule for makin' a woman think yo' way is always to think hers. But she's right, and that's the truth. You've had too much."

"Oh, you're driving me mad between you!" cried Will in desperation. "I'm in awful trouble, and there's nothing under heaven will make me forget it except drink. One glass more—just one. That can't hurt me."

"May he have one glass, Susan?" asked Tom, appealing to his wife.

"Not another drop, suh," returned Mrs. Spade, immovable as a rock.

"Not another drop, she says," repeated the big storekeeper in a sinking voice. Then he laid his hand sympathetically on Will's shoulder. "To be sure, I know you're in trouble," he said, "an' I'll swear it's an out-an'-out shame, I don't care who hears me. Yes, I'll stand to it in the very face of Bill Fletcher himself."

"Oh, he's a devil!" cried Will, stung by the name he hated.

"I ain't sayin' you've been all you should have been," pursued Tom in his friendly tones, "but as I told Susan yestiddy, a body can't sow wild oats in one generation without havin' a volunteer crop spring up in the next. Now, yo' wild oats were sown long befo' you were born. Ain't that so, Susan?"

Mrs. Spade planted her hands squarely upon her hips and stood her ground with a solidity which was as impressive in its way as dignity.

"I've spoken my mind to Bill Fletcher," she said, "an' I'll speak it again. 'How's that boy goin' to live, suh?' That's what I asked, an' 'twas after he told me to shut my mouth, that it was. Right or wrong, that's what I told him. You've gone an' made the meanest will this county has ever seen."

"What?" cried Will, springing to his feet, while the room whirled round him.

"Thar, thar, Susan, you've talked too much," interposed Tom, a little frightened. "What she means is just some foolishness yo' grandpa's been lettin' out," he added; "but he'll live long enough yet to change his mind an' his will, too."

"What is it about? Speak louder, will you? My ears buzz so I can't hear thunder."

Tom coughed reproachfully at Susan.

"Well, he was talkin' down here last night about havin' changed his will," he said apologetically. "He's tied it up, it seems, so you can't get it, an' he's gone an' left the bulk of it to Mrs. Wyndham."

"To Maria!" repeated Will, and saw scarlet.

"That's what he says; but he'll last to change his mind yet, never fear. Anger doesn't live as long as a man—eh, Susan?"

But Will had risen and was walking quite steadily toward the door. His face was dead white, and there were deep blue circles about his eyes, which sparkled brilliantly. When he turned for a moment before going out, he sucked in his under lip with a hissing sound.

"So this was Maria's trick all along," he said hoarsely.

CHAPTER VIII

How Christopher Comes Into His Revenge

"So THIS was Maria's trick all along," he repeated, as he lurched out into the road. "This was what she had schemed for from the beginning—this was what her palavering and her protestations meant. Oh, it had been a deep game from the first, only he had been too much of a blind fool to see the truth." A hundred facts arose to drive in the discovery; a hundred trivial details now bristled with importance. Why had she been so willing—so eager, even—to give away her little property, unless she intended to divert him with the crumbs while she reached for the whole loaf? Why, again, had she shrunk so from mentioning him to his grandfather? And why, still further, had she always fearfully postponed a meeting between the two? He remembered suddenly that she had once drawn Molly behind the trees when the old man passed along the road. Poor, defrauded Molly! Forgetting his bitter quarrel with her, he was ready to fall upon her neck in maudlin sympathy.

Yes, it was all plain now—as clear as day. He saw one by one each devilish move that she had made, and he meant to pay her back for all before the night was over. He would tell her what he thought of her, freely, fully, in words that she would never forget. The names that he would use, the curses he would

utter, spun deliriously in his head, and as he went on
he found himself speaking his phrases aloud to the
darkness, trying upon the silence the effect of each
blighting sentence.

The lights of the Hall twinkled presently among
the trees, and, crossing the lawn, he crept into the
little area under the back steps. If Maria was not in
the kitchen, the servant would be, he argued, and he
would send up a peremptory summons which would
bring her down upon the instant. It was not late
enough for her to be in bed, at least, and he chuckled
over the thought of the sleepless night which she
would spend.

Pushing back the door cautiously on its old, rusty
hinges, he entered on tip-toe and glanced suspiciously
around. The room was empty, but a lamp with a
smoked chimney burned upon the table, and there
were the glimmering embers of a wood fire in the
stove. It was just as he had left it the evening
before, and this aroused in him a feeling of
surprise, so long a stretch appeared to cover the
last twenty-four hours. The same basket of chicken
feathers was in the sagging split-bottomed chair,
the same pile of black walnuts lay on the hearth,
and the rusted hammer was still lying where he had
dropped it upon the bricks. Even the smell was the
same—a mixture of baked bread and burned feathers.

Going to the door that led into the house, he
opened it and looked up the dark staircase; then a
sound reached him from the dining-room, and with
a nervous shiver he turned away and came back to
the stove. A dread paralysed him lest the meeting
with Maria should be delayed until his courage oozed

out of him, and to nerve himself for the encounter he summoned to mind all the evidence, which gathered in a cloud of witnesses, to prove her treachery. Once it occurred to him that after a few minutes of waiting he might tighten the screw upon his nerves and so pluck up the audacity, if not the resolution, to ascend the stair boldly and denounce her in the presence of his grandfather. But the memory of Fletcher's face wagged before him, and, quaking with terror, he huddled with open palms above the stove. Then, pacing slowly up and down the room, he set to work frantically to lash himself into the drunken bravado which he miscalled courage.

Of a sudden his hunger assailed him, violent, convulsive, and, going over to the tin safe, he rummaged among the cold scraps he found there, devouring greedily the food which had been set by for the hounds. A bottle of Miss Saidie's raspberry vinegar was hidden in one corner, and he tore the paper label from the cork and drank like a man who perishes from thirst. His energy, which had evaporated from fatigue and hunger, surged back in spasms of anger, and as he turned away, invigorated, from the safe, he realised as he had never done before the full measure of his rage against Maria. At the moment, had she come in upon him, he felt that he could have struck her in the face.

But she did not come, and the slow minutes fretted him in their passage. A flame shot up in the stove, and, catching a knot of resinous pine, burned steadily, licking patiently about the fading embers. The air became charged again with the odour of burned feathers, and he saw that a handful, with the dried blood of the fowl still adhering to them, had been scattered upon the ashes. As he idly noted the colours of red and black, he remembered with bitterness that he had raised game-cocks once when he was a boy at the Hall, and that Maria had smashed a nestful of his eggs in a fit of passion. The incident swelled to enormous proportions in his thoughts, and he determined that he would remind her of it in the interview that was before them.

The door into the house creaked suddenly behind him; he wheeled about nervously, and then stood with hanging jaws staring into the face of Fletcher.

"So it is you, is it?" said the old man, raising the stick he carried. "So it is you, as I suspected— you darn rascal!"

But the power of speech had departed from Will in the presence that he dreaded, and he stood clutching tightly to his harvest hat, and shaking his head as if to deny the obvious fact of his own identity.

"I thought it was you," pursued Fletcher, licking his dry lips. "I heard a noise, and I picked up my stick, thinking it was you. I'll have no thieving beggars on my place, I tell you, so the quicker you git off the better. When were you here last, I'd like to know?"

"Yesterday," answered Will, speaking the truth from sheer physical inability to frame a lie. "I came to see Maria. She's cheated me—she's cheated me all along."

"Then she lied," said Fletcher softly. "Then she lied and I didn't know it."

"She's cheated me," insisted Will hoarsely. "It's been all a scheme of hers from the very beginning.

She's cheated me about the will, grandpa; I swear she has."

"Eh? What's that?" responded the old man, shaking back his heavy eyebrows. "Say your say right now, for in five minutes you go off this place with every hound in the pack yelping at your heels. I'll not have you here—I'll not have you here!"

The words ended in a snarl, and a fleck of foam dropped on his gray beard.

"But it was all Maria's doing," urged Will passionately. "She has been against me from the first: I see that now. She's plotted to oust me from the very start."

"Well, she might have spared herself the trouble," was Fletcher's sharp rejoinder.

"Let me explain—let me explain," pleaded the other, in a desperate effort to gain time; "just a word or two—I only want a word."

But when his grandfather drew back and stood glowering upon him in silence, the speech he had wished to utter withered upon his lips, blighted by a panic terror, and he stood mumbling incoherently beneath his breath.

"Give me a word—a word is all I want," he reiterated wildly.

"Then out with your damned word and begone!" roared Fletcher.

Will's eyes travelled helplessly around the room, seeking in vain some inspiration from the objects his gaze encountered. The tin safe, the basket of feathers, the pile of walnuts on the hearth, each arrested his wandering attention for an instant, and he beheld all the details with amazing vividness.

A mouse came out into the room, gliding like a shadow along the wall to the pile of walnuts, and his eyes followed it as if drawn by an invisible thread.

"It's Maria—it's all Maria," he stuttered, and could think of nothing further. His brain seemed suddenly paralysed, and he found himself tugging hopelessly at the most commonplace word which would not come. All his swaggering bravado had scampered off at the first wag of the old man's head.

"If that's what you've got to say, you might as well begone," returned Fletcher, moving toward him. "I warn you now that the next time I find you here you won't git off so easy. Maria or no Maria, you ain't goin' to lounge about this place so long as my name is Bill Fletcher. The farther you keep yourself and your yaller-headed huzzy out of my sight the better. Thar, now, be off or you'll git a licking."

"But I tell you Maria's cheated me—she's cheated me," returned Will, his voice rising shrilly as he was goaded into revolt. "She's been scheming to get the place all along; that's her trick."

"Pish! Tush!" responded Fletcher. "Are you going or are you not?"

Will's eyes burned like coals, and an observer, noting the two men as they stood glaring at each other, would have been struck by their resemblance in attitude and expression rather than in feature. Both leaned slightly forward, with their chins thrust out and their jaws dropped, and there was a ceaseless twitching of the small muscles in both faces. The beast in each had sprung violently to the surface and recognised the likeness at which he snarled.

"You've left me to starve!" cried Will, strangling

a sob of anger. "It's not fair! You have no right. The money ought to be mine—I swear it ought!"

"Oh, it ought, ought it?" sneered the old man, with an ugly laugh.

At the sound of the laugh, Will shrank back and shivered as if from the stroke of a whip. The spirit of rage worked in his blood like the spirit of drink, and he felt his disordered nerves respond in a sudden frenzy.

"It ought to be mine, you devil, and you know it!" he cried.

"I do, do I?" retorted Fletcher, still cackling. "Well, jest grin at me a minute longer like that brazen wench your mother and I'll lay my stick across your shoulders for good and all. As for my money, it's mine, I reckon, and, living or dead, I'll look to it that not one red cent gits to you. Blast you! Stop your grinning!"

He raised the stick and made a long swerve sideways, but the other, picking up the hammer from the hearth, jerked it above his head and stood braced for the assault. In the silence of the room Will heard the thumping of his own heart, and the sound inspired him like the drums of battle. He was in a quiver from head to foot, but it was a quiver of rage, not of fear, and a glow of pride possessed him that he could lift his eyes and look Fletcher squarely in the face.

"You're a devil—a devil! a devil!" he cried shrilly, sticking out his tongue like a pert and vulgar little boy. "Christopher Blake was right—you're a devil!"

As the name struck him between the eyes the

old man lurched back against the stove; then recovering himself, he made a swift movement forward and brought his stick down with all his force on the boy's shoulder.

"Take that, you lying varmint!" he shouted, choking.

The next instant his weapon had dropped from his hand, and he reached out blindly, grappling with the air, for Will had turned upon him with the spring of a wild beast and sent the hammer crushing into his temple.

There was a muffled thud, and Fletcher went down in a hudded heap upon the floor, while the other stood over him in the weakness which had succeeded his drunken frenzy.

"I told you to let me alone. I told you I'd do it," said Will doggedly, and a moment later: "I told you I'd do it."

The hammer was still in his hand, and, lifting it, he examined it with a morbid curiosity. A red fleck stained the iron, and glancing down he saw that there was a splotch of blood on Fletcher's temple. "I told him I'd do it," he repeated, speaking this time to himself.

Then instantly the silence in the room stopped his heart-beats and set him quaking in a superstitious terror through every fibre. He heard the stir of the mouse in the pile of walnuts, the hissing of the flame above the embers, and the sudden breaking of the smoked chimney of the lamp. Then as he leaned down he heard something else—the steady ticking of the big silver watch in Fletcher's pocket.

A horror of great darkness fell over him, and, turning, he reeled like a drunken man out into the night.

CHAPTER IX

The Fulfilling of the Law

CHRISTOPHER had helped Tucker upstairs to bed and had gone into his own room to undress, when a sharp and persistent rattle upon the closed shutters brought him in alarm to his feet. Looking out, he saw a man's figure outlined in the moonlight on the walk, and, at once taking it to be Will, he ran hastily down and unbarred the door.

"Come in quietly," he said. "Uncle Tucker is asleep upstairs. What in thunder is the trouble now?"

Stepping back, he led the way into what so short a time ago had been Mrs. Blake's parlour, and then pausing in the centre of the floor, stood waiting with knitted brows for an explanation of the visit. But Will, who had shrunk dazzled from the flash of the lamp, now lingered to put up the bar with shaking hands.

"For God's sake, what is it?" questioned Christopher, and a start shook through him at sight of the other's face. "Have you had a fit?"

Closing the parlour door behind him, Will crossed the room and caught at the mantel for support. "I told you I'd do it some day—I told you I'd do it," he said incoherently, in a frantic effort to shift the burden of responsibility upon stronger shoulders.

525

"You might have known all along that I'd do it some day."

"Do what?" demanded Christopher, while he felt the current of his blood grow weak. "Out with it, now. Speak up. You're as white as a sheet."

"He struck me—he struck me first. The bruise is here," resumed Will, in the same eager attempt at self-justification. "Then I hit him on the head with a hammer and his skull gave way. I didn't hit hard. I swear it was a little blow; but he's dead. I left him stone dead in the kitchen."

"My God, man!" exclaimed Christopher, and touched him on the shoulder.

With a groan, Will put up his hands and covered his bloodshot eyes. "I didn't mean to do it—I swear I didn't," he protested. "Who'd have thought his head would crush in like that at the first little blow—just a tap with an old hammer? Why, it would hardly have cracked a walnut! And what was the hammer doing there, anyway? They have no business to leave such things lying about on the hearth. It was all their fault—they ought to have put the hammer away."

A convulsive shudder ran through him, ending in his hands and feet, which jerked wildly. His face was gray and old—so old that he might have been taken, at the first glance, for a man of eighty, and in the intervals between his words he sucked in his breath with a hissing noise. Meeting Christopher's look, he broke into a spasm of frightened sobs, whimpering like a child that has been whipped.

"I told you not to drink again," said Christopher

sharply as he struggled to collect his thoughts. "I told you liquor would make a beast of you."

"I'll never touch another drop. I swear I'll never touch another drop," groaned Will, still sobbing. "I didn't mean to kill him, I tell you. It wasn't as if I really meant to kill him; you see that. It was all the fault of that accursed hammer they left lying on the hearth. A man must have a lot of courage to murder anybody; mustn't he?" he added, with a feeble smile; "and I'm a coward—you know I've always been a coward; haven't I—haven't I?" he persisted, and Christopher nodded an agreement.

"You see, I wasn't to blame, after all; but he flew into such a rage—he always flew into a rage when he heard your name."

"So you brought my name in?" asked Christopher carelessly.

"Oh, it was that that did it; it was your name," replied Will breathlessly. "I told him you said he was a devil—you did say so, you know. 'Christopher Blake was right; he called you a devil,' that was it. Then he ran at me with his stick, and I jerked up the hammer, and—— Oh, my God, they mustn't hang me."

"Nonsense!" retorted Christopher roughly, for the other had dropped upon the floor and was grovelling in drunken hysterics at his feet. "It makes me sick to see a man act like an ass."

"Get me out of this and I'll never touch a drop," moaned Will. "Take me away from here—hide me anywhere. I'll go anywhere, I'll promise anything, only they mustn't find me. If they find me I'll go mad—I'll go mad in gaol."

"Shut up!" rejoined Christopher, listening with irritation to the sound of the other's hissing breath. "Stop your infernal racket a minute and let me think. Here, get up. Are you too drunk to stand on your feet?"

"I'm sober—I'm perfectly sober," protested Will, and, rising obediently, he stood clutching at the chimney-piece. "Get me out of this—only get me out of this," he repeated, with a desperate reliance on the other's power to avert the consequences of his deed. "I've always been a good friend to you," he went on passionately. "The quarrel first started about you, and I stood up for you to the last. I never let him say anything against you—I never did!"

"I'm much obliged to you," returned Christopher, and felt that he might as well have wasted his irony on a beaten hound. Turning away from the wild entreaty of Will's eyes, he walked slowly up and down the room, taking care to step lightly lest the boards should creak and awaken Tucker.

The parlour was just as Mrs. Blake had left it: her high-backed Elizabethan chair, filled with cushions, stood on the hearth; the dried grasses in the two tall vases shed their ashy pollen down upon the bricks. Even the yellow cat, grown old and sluggish, dozed in her favourite spot beside the embroidered ottoman.

On the whitewashed walls the old Blake portraits still presided, and he found, for the first time, an artless humour in the formality of the ancestral attitude—in the splendid pose which they had handed down like an heirloom through the centuries. Among

them he saw the comely, high-coloured features of
that gallant cynic, Bolivar, the man who had stamped
his beauty upon three generations, and his gaze
lingered with a gentle ridicule on the blithe candour
in the eyes and the characteristic touch of brutality
about the mouth. Then he passed to his father,
portly, impressive, a high liver, a generous young
blood, and then to the classic Saint-Memin profile
of Aunt Susannah, limned delicately against a
background of faded pink. And from her he went
on to his mother's portrait, painted in shimmering
brocade under rose-garlands held by smiling Loves.

He looked at them all steadily for a while, seeking
from the changeless lips of each an answer to the
question which he felt knocking at his own heart.
In every limb, in every feature, in every fibre he
was plainly born to be one of themselves, and yet
from their elegant remoteness they stared down
upon the rustic labourer who was their descendant.
Degraded, coarsened, disinherited, the last Blake
stood before them, with his poverty and ignorance
illumined only at long intervals by the flame of a
soul which, though darkened, was still unquenched.

The night dragged slowly on, while he paced the
floor with his thoughts and Will moaned and tossed,
a shivering heap, upon the sofa.

"Stop your everlasting cackle!" Christopher had
once shouted angrily, forgetting Tucker, and for the
space of a few minutes the other had lain silent,
choking back the strangling sobs. But presently
the shattered nerves revolted against restraint, and
Will burst out afresh into wild crying. The yellow
cat, grown suddenly restless, crossed the room and

jumped upon the sofa, where she stood clawing at the cover, and he clung to her with a pathetic recognition of dumb sympathy—the sympathy which he could not wring from the careless indifference of Christopher's look.

"Speak to me—say something," he pleaded at last, stretching out his hands. "If this keeps up I'll go mad before morning."

At this Christopher came toward him, and, stopping in his walk, frowned down upon the sofa.

"You deserve everything you'd get," he said angrily. "You're as big a fool as ever trod this earth, and there's no reason under heaven why I should lift my hand to help you. There's no reason —there's no reason," he repeated in furious tones.

"But you'll do it—you'll get me out of it!" cried Will, grasping the other's knees.

"And two weeks later you'd be in another scrape."

"Not a single drop—I'll never touch a drop again. Before God I swear it!"

"Pshaw! I've heard that oath before."

Strangling a scream, Will caught him by the arm, dragging himself slowly into a sitting posture. "I'll hang myself if you let them get me," he urged hysterically. "I'll hang myself in gaol rather than let them do it. I can't face it all—I can't—I can't. It isn't grandpa I mind; I'm not afraid of him. He was a devil. But it's the rest—the rest."

Roughly shaking him off, Christopher left him huddled upon the floor and resumed his steady walk up and down the room. In his ears the incoherent phrases grew presently fainter, and after a time he lost entirely their frenzied drift. "A little blow—just a little blow," ended finally in muffled sounds of weeping.

The habit of outward composure which always came to him in moments of swift experience possessed him so perfectly now that Will, lifting miserable eyes to his face, lowered them, appalled by its unfeeling gravity.

"I've been a good friend to you—a deuced good friend to you," urged the younger man in a last passionate appeal for the aid whose direction he had not yet defined.

"What is this thought which I cannot get rid of?" asked Christopher moodily of himself. "And what business is it of mine, anyway? What am I to the boy or the boy to me?" But even with the words he remembered the morning more than five years ago when he had gone out to the gate with his bird gun on his shoulder and found Will Fletcher and the spotted foxhound puppies awaiting him in the road. He saw again the boy's face, with the sunlight full upon it—eager, alert, a little petulant, full of good impulses readily turned adrift. There had been no evil upon it then—only weakness and a pathetic absence of determination. His own damnable intention was thrust back upon him, and he heard again the words of Carraway which had reëchoed in his thoughts. "The way to touch the man, then, is through the boy." So it was the way, after all! He almost laughed aloud at his prophetic insight. He had touched the man vitally enough at last, and it was through the boy. He had murdered Bill Fletcher, and he had done it through the only thing Bill Fletcher had ever loved. From this he returned again to the memory of the deliberate purpose of that day—to the ribald jests, the coarse profanities, the brutal oaths. Then to the night when he had forced the first drink down Will's throat, and so on through the five years of his revenge to the present moment. Well, his triumph had come at last, the summit was put upon his life's work, and he was—he must be—content.

Will raised his head and looked at him in reviving hope.

"You're the only friend I have on earth," he muttered between his teeth.

The first streak of dawn entered suddenly, flooding the room with a thin gray light in which the familiar objects appeared robbed of all atmospheric values. With a last feeble flicker the lamp shot up and went out, and the ashen wash of daybreak seemed the fit medium for the crude ugliness of life.

Towering almost grotesquely in the pallid dawn, Christopher came and leaned above the sofa to which Will had dragged himself again.

"You must get out of this," he said, "and quickly, for we've wasted the whole night wrangling. Have you any money?"

Will fumbled in his pocket and brought out a few cents, which he held in his open palm, while the other unlocked the drawer of the old secretary and handed him a roll of banknotes.

"Take this and buy a ticket somewhere. It's the money I scraped up to pay Fred Turner."

"To pay Fred Turner?" echoed Will, as if in that lay the significance of the remark.

"Take it and buy a ticket, and when you get where

you're going, sit still and keep your mouth shut. If
you wear a bold face you will go scot-free; remember
that; but everything depends upon your keeping a
stiff front. And now go—through the back door
and past the kitchen to the piece of woods beyond
the pasture. Cut through them to Tanner's Station
and take the train there, mind, for the North."

With a short laugh he held out his big, knotted
hand.

"Good-by," he said, "and don't be a damned fool."

"Good-by," answered Will, clinging desperately to
his outstretched arm. Then an ashen pallor over-
spread his face, and he slunk nervously toward the
kitchen, for there was the sound of footsteps on the
little porch outside, followed by a brisk rap on the
front door.

"Go!" whispered Christopher, hardly taking
breath, and he stood waiting while Will ran along
the wooden platform and past the stable toward
the pasture.

The rap came again, and he turned quickly. "Quit
your racket and let me get on my clothes!" he
shouted, and hesitated a little longer.

As he stood alone there in the centre of the room,
his eyes, traversing the walls, fell on the portrait of
Bolivar Blake, and with one of the fantastic tricks
of memory there shot into his head the dying phrase
of that gay sinner: "I may not sit with the saints,
but I shall stand among the gentlemen."

"Precious old ass!" he muttered, and unbarred
the door.

As he flung it open the first rays of sunlight splashed
across the threshold, and he was conscious, all at

once, of a strange exhilaration, as if he were breasting one of the big waves of life.

"This is a pretty way to wake up a fellow who has been planting tobacco till he's stiff," he grumbled. "Is that you, Tom?" He glanced carelessly round, nodding with a kind of friendly condescension to each man of the little group. "How are you, Matthew? Hello, Fred!"

Tom drew back, coughing, and scraped the heel of his boot on the topmost step.

"We didn't mean to git you out of bed, Mr. Christopher," he explained apologetically, "but the truth is we want Will Fletcher an' he ain't at home. The old man's murdered, suh."

"Murdered, is he?" exclaimed Christopher, with a long whistle, "and you want Will Fletcher—which shows what a very pretty sheriff you would make. Well, if you're so strong on his scent that you can't turn aside, most likely you'll find him sleeping off his drunk under my haystack. But if you're looking for the man who killed Bill Fletcher, then that's a different matter," he added, taking down his hat, "and I reckon, boys, I'm about ready to come along."

CHAPTER X

THE WHEEL OF LIFE

THROUGHOUT the trial he wore the sullen reserve which closed over him like a visor when he approached one of the crises of life. He had made his confession and he stood to it. "I killed Bill Fletcher" he gave out flatly enough. What he could not give was an explanation of his unaccountable presence at the Hall so nearly upon midnight. When the question was first put to him he sneered and shrugged his shoulders with the hereditary gesture of the Blakes. "Why was he there? Well, why wasn't he there?" That was all. And Carraway, who had stood by his side since the day of the arrest, retired at last before an attitude which he characterised as one of defiant arrogance.

It was this attitude, people said presently, rather than the murder of Bill Fletcher, which brought him the sentence he heard with so insolent an indifference.

"Five years wasn't much for killin' a man, maybe," Tom Spade observed, "but it was a good deal, when you come to think of it, for a Blake to pay jest for gettin' even with a Fletcher. Why, he might have brained Bill Fletcher an' welcome," the store-keeper added a little wistfully, "if only he hadn't put on such a nasty manner afterward."

But it was behind this impregnable reserve that

Christopher retreated as into a walled fortress. There had been no sentiment in his act, he told himself; he had not even felt the romantic fervour of the sacrifice. A certain staunch justice was all he saw in it, relieved doubtless by a share of his hereditary love of desperate hopes—of the hot-headed clinging to that last shifting foothold on which a man might still make his fight against the power of circumstance. And so, with that strange mixture of rustic crudeness and aristocratic arrogance, he turned his face from his friends and went stubbornly through the cross-questioning of the court.

From first to last he had not wavered in his refusal to see Maria, and there had been an angry vehemence in the resistance he had made to her passionate entreaty for a meeting. When by the early autumn he went from the little town gaol to serve his five years in the State prison, his most vivid memory of her was as she looked with the moonlight on her face in the open field. As the months went on, this gradually grew remote and dim in his remembrance, like a bright star over which the clouds thicken, and his thoughts declined, almost without an upward inspiration, upon the brutal level of his daily life. Mere physical disgust was his first violent recoil from what had seemed a curious deadness of his whole nature, and the awakening of the senses preceded by many months the final resurrection of the more spiritual emotions. The sources of health were still abundant in him, he admitted, if the vile air, the fetid smells, the closeness as of huddled animals, the filth, the obscenity, the insufferable bestial humanity could arouse in him a bodily nausea so nearly resembling disease. There were moments when he felt capable of any crime from sheer frenzied loathing of his surroundings—when for the sake of the clean space of the tobacco fields and the pure water of the little spring he would have murdered Bill Fletcher a dozen times. As for the old man's death in itself, it had never caused him so much as a quiver of the conscience. Bill Fletcher deserved to die, and the world was well rid of him—that was all.

But his own misery! This was with him always, and there was no escape from the moral wretchedness which seemed to follow so closely upon crime. Fresh from the open country and the keen winds that blow over level spaces, he seemed mentally and physically to wither in the change of air—to shrink slowly to the perishing root, like a plant that has been brought from a rich meadow to the aridity of the close-packed city. And with the growing of this strange form of homesickness he would be driven, at times, into an almost delirious cruelty toward those who were weaker than himself, for there were summer nights when he would brutally knock smaller men from the single window of the cell and cling, panting for breath, to the iron bars. As the year went on, his grim silence, too, became for those around him as the inevitable shadow of the prison, and he went about his daily work in a churlish loneliness which caused even the convicts among whom he lived to shrink back from his presence.

Then with the closing of the second winter his superb physical strength snapped suddenly like a cord that has stood too tight a strain, and for weeks he lingered between life and death in the hospital, into which he was carried while yet unconscious. With his returning health, when the abatement of the fever left him strangely shaken and the unearthly pallor still clung to his face and hands, he awoke for the first time to a knowledge that his illness had altered—for the period of his convalescence, at least—the vision through which he had grown to regard the world.

A change had come to him, in that mysterious borderland so near the grave, and the bare places in his soul had burst suddenly into fulfilment. Sitting one Sunday morning in the open court of the prison, with his thin white hands hanging between his knees and his head, cropped now of its thick, fair hair, raised to the sunshine, it seemed to him that, like Tucker on the old bench, he had learned at last how to be happy. The warm sun in his face, the blue sky straight overhead, the spouting fountain from which a sparrow drank, produced in him a recognition, wholly passionless, of the abundant physical beauty of the earth—of a beauty in the blue sky and in the clear sunshine falling upon the prison court.

A month ago he had wondered almost hopefully if his was to be one of those pathetic sunken graves, marked for so brief a time by wooden headboards—the graves of the men who had died within the walls—and now there pulsed through him, sitting there alone, a quiet satisfaction in the thought that he might still breathe the air and look into men's faces and see the blue sky overhead. The sky in itself! That was enough to fill one's memory to overflowing, Tucker had said.

A tall, lean convict, newly released from the

hospital, crossed the court at a stumbling pace and stood for a moment at his side.

"I reckon you're hankerin', " he remarked. "I was sent down here from the mountains, an' I hanker terrible for the sight of the old Humpback Knob."

"And I'd like to see a level sweep—hardly a hill, just a clean stretch for the wind to blow over the tobacco."

"You're from the tobaccy belt, then, ain't you? What are you here for?"

"Killing a man. And you?"

"Killin' two."

He limped off at his feeble step, and Christopher rubbed his hands in the warm sunshine and wondered how it would feel to bask on one of the old logs by the roadside.

That afternoon Jim Weatherby came to see him, bringing the news that Lila's baby had come and that she had named it Christopher. "It's the living image of you, she says," he added, smiling; "but I confess I can't quite see it. The funny part is, you know, that Cynthia is just as crazy about it as Lila is, and she looks ten years younger since the little chap came."

"And Uncle Tucker?"

"His old wounds trouble him, but he sent you word he was waiting to go till you came back again."

A blur swam before Christopher's eyes, and he saw in fancy the old soldier waiting for him on the bench beside the damask rose-bush.

"And the others—and Maria Wyndham?" he asked, swallowing the lump in his throat.

Jim reached out and laid his hand on the broad stripes across the other's shoulder.

"She was with Mr. Tucker when he said that," he replied; "they are always together now; and she added: Tell him we shall wait together till he comes."

The tears which had blinded Christopher's eyes fell down upon his clasped hands.

"My God! Let me live to go back!" he cried out in his weakness.

From this time the element of hope entered into his life, and like its shadow there came the brooding fear that he should not live to see the year of his release. With his declining health he had been given lighter work in the prison factory, but the small tasks seemed to him heavier than the large ones he remembered. There was no disease, the physician in the hospital assured him; it was only his unusual form of homesickness feeding upon his weakened frame. Let him return once more to the outdoor life and the fresh air of the tobacco fields and within six months his old physical hardihood would revive.

It was noticeable at this time that the quiet tolerance which had grown upon him in his convalescence drew to him the sympathy which he had at first repulsed. The interest awakened in the beginning by some rare force of attraction in his mere bodily presence became now, when he had fallen away to what seemed the shadow of himself, a friendly and almost affectionate curiosity concerning his earlier history. With this there grew slowly a rough companionship between him and the men among whom he lived, and he found presently to his surprise that there was hardly one of them but

had some soft spot in his character—some particular
virtue which was still alive. The knowledge of good
and evil thrust upon him in these months was not
without effect in developing a certain largeness of
outlook upon humanity—a kind of generous philosophy which remained with him afterward in the
form of a peculiar mellowness of temperament.

The autumn of his third year was already closing
when, being sent for one morning from the office of
the superintendent, he went in to find Cynthia
awaiting him with his pardon in her hand. "I've
come for you, Christopher," she said, weeping at
sight of his wasted figure. "The whole county has
been working to get you out, and you are free at
last."

"Free at last?" he repeated mechanically, and
was conscious of a disappointment in the fact that he
experienced no elation with the words. What was
this freedom, that had meant so much to him a
month ago?

"Somebody in Europe wrote back to Maria,"
she added, while her dry sobs rattled in her bosom,
"that the boy had confessed it to a priest who made
him write it home. Oh, Christopher! Christopher!
I can't understand!"

"No, you can't understand," returned Christopher,
shaking his head. They would not understand, he
knew, none of them—neither the world, nor Cynthia,
nor his mother who was dead, nor Maria who was
living. They would not understand, and even to
himself the mystery was still unsolved. He had
acted according to the law of his own nature; this
was all that was clear to him; and the destiny of

character had controlled him from the beginning. The wheel had turned and he with it, and being as blind as fate itself he could see nothing further.

Back once more in the familiar country, fresh from the strong grasp of friendly hands, and driving at sunset along the red road beneath half-bared honey-locusts, he was conscious, with a dull throb of regret, that the placid contentment he felt creeping over him failed in emotional resemblance to the happiness he had associated with his return. Had the sap really gone dry within him, and would he go on forever with this curious numbness at his heart?

"Maria wanted you to go straight to the Hall," said Cynthia, turning suddenly, "but I told her I'd better take you home and put you to bed at once. It was she who went to the Governor and got your pardon," she added after a moment, "but when I begged her to come with me to take it to you she would not do it. She would not see you until you were back in your own place, she said."

He smiled faintly, and, leaning back among the rugs Cynthia had brought, watched the white mist creeping over the ploughed fields. The thought of Maria no longer stirred his pulses, and when presently they reached the whitewashed cottage, and he sat with Tucker before the wood fire in his mother's parlour, he found himself gazing with a dull impersonal curiosity at the portraits smiling so coldly down upon the hearth. The memory of his mother left him as immovable as did the many trivial associations which thronged through his brain at sight of the room which had been hers. A little later, lying in her tester bed, the fall of the acorns on the shingled roof above sent him into a profound and untroubled sleep.

With the first sunlight he awoke, and, noiselessly slipping into his clothes, went out for a daylight view of the country which had dwelt for so long a happy vision in his thoughts. The dew was thick on the grass, and, crossing to the old bench, he sat down in the pale sunshine beside the damask rose-bush, on which a single flower blossomed out of season. Beyond the cedars in the graveyard the sunrise flamed golden upon a violet background, and across the field of life-everlasting there ran a sparkling path of fire. The air was strong with autumn scents, and as he drank it in with deep draughts it seemed to him that he began to breathe anew the spirit of life. With a single bound of the heart the sense of freedom came to him, and with it the happiness that he had missed the evening before pulsed through his veins. Much yet remained to him—the earth with its untold miracles, the sky with its infinity of space, his own soul—and Maria!

With her name he sprang to his feet in the ardour of his impatience, and it was then that, looking up, he saw her coming to him across the sunbeams.

DATE DUE	